Disclaimer: While inspired by historical events, real locations and observed cultural practices, this work is entirely fictional.

The scanning, uploading and distribution of this work without permission is a theft of the author's intellectual property. If you would like permission to use material from the book (Other than for review purposes), please contact DasherCanonLit@Gmail.com.

No artificial intelligence was used in the creation of this work. What you're about to read came from a human mind—unfiltered.

NO AI TRAINING: Without in any way limiting the author's exclusive rights under copyright, no part of this publication may be used to train, develop, or improve any artificial intelligence (AI) systems or technologies. Any such use is expressly, thoroughly and unconditionally prohibited.

Cover Design: Dasher Canon @DasherCanon
Interior Content & Illustrations: Dasher Canon @DasherCanon
Editing: Dasher Canon @DasherCanon
Book Design & Typesetting: Dasher Canon @DasherCanon

ISBN (Softcover): 979-8-9986827-0-4
ASIN (Softcover): B0DY54G17T
ISBN (Hardcover): 979-8-3109571-8-3
ISBN eBook: 979-8-3495101-3-7
ASIN: B0DXCTH5BL

Copyright © 2025 by Canon Productions
All rights reserved.

WWW.DASHERCANON.COM
Thank you for your support of the author's rights.

This story weaves four viewpoints through past and present.

Table of Contents

Chapter I
Turn Back Now

"Are we safe yet?"

"No, but we're close."

The lone Jeep trekked through Ethiopia's lifeless savannah. A dust cloud diverged from beneath the rugged tires, erupting the craquelure ground into an expanding breadth over the scattered acacia trees. The vast horizon shimmered, projecting an endlessly fleeing mirage as the shadowless vehicle raced towards the red pin icon. Distant elephants wrapped their trunks around their hobbledehoy calves, pulling them in as the foreign automobile jolted through the otherwise peaceful landscape.

Madeleine's heart lodged in her throat as Julian navigated the unusual terrain. She checked on their daughter, Leopaula, thankful she remained asleep in the hurriedly straddled car seat. Julian glanced, noticing the deep wound hiding beneath Madeleine's eyebrow. He tightened his grip over the wheel, whitening his bloodied knuckles while taking a shallow breath.

Amid the turbulence, Madeleine's hand found Julian's over the shifter. He kept his focus on the grimy windshield as she flinched a smile that didn't reach her eyes. A subtle trepidation loitered beneath, noticeable only by those who've been through a similar turmoil.

Dispersed patches of yellow grass let off a rhythmic sheer, overtaken in an instant by the passing Jeep.

Recognizing landmarks, Julian nodded, regardless of the navigation system pressuring him to return to the main road.

"Are you sure this is the way?" Madeleine asked through the roaring cabin.

"Yes," he reaffirmed, more to himself than to her. "We're almost in the clear. Francis said it's not much further."

Leopaula stirred.

"Soon, sweetheart," Madeleine said, reaching back and patting. "Any moment now."

After some time, the Jeep rumbled to a halt as the landscape shifted, revealing the winding expanse of a wide, slow-moving river.

The Omo River.

Its water sparkled beneath the high sun, leaving its surface deceptively calm. They eyed the serpentine tranquility lacing the desperately thirsty land, but the further out they followed it, the more its beauty became marred by an inexplicable sense of foreboding. The sudden silence turned deafening as the dust cloud caught up with the vehicle.

"You have arrived," the GPS gleefully chimed.

Julian turned off the ignition, lodged the shifter into first gear and pulled the parking brake.

"This," to one side, emptiness, to the other, the river, "doesn't look right."

Comparing what she saw with what Francis told them, Madeleine agreed. Besides silence, Leopaula's rattle toy clattered as it fell from her grip.

The Omo River carried on, business as usual.

"Are we early," Madeleine combed her brunette hair back, "or did you enter the coordinates wrong?"

Julian tapped his thumb against the wheel, noticing the fuel gauge's needle resting over E. He checked his Samsung. No messages, no reception. As the signal bars searched, he stepped out. His ankle-high boots crunched the graveled soil with each step towards the bank. Far east to far west, more of the same. The once peaceful gushing of the river now echoed concern for the Brit. He sucked his teeth, finding their itinerary-tight escape, roadblocked.

From the Jeep, Madeleine observed her husband run a hand through his golden blonde hair. His phone, obstructing her view, rested atop the searing dashboard. Its screen flashed, paired with a vibration. Madeleine entered their shared pin, but the prompt jiggled. The new message remained unreadable behind the passcode. Her eyebrow scab strained. The same jiggle mocked her second attempt. She looked at Julian, then the phone, making a deliberate third try, just to be sure—

Another jiggle.

She placed the device down and glared through the yellowish windshield. Julian assessed his bloodied knuckles, widening and clenching a fist. As he turned, Madeleine quickly nudged the mobile, fixing it back to how she found it.

Julian rested his arms through the window, puffing out his cheeks. He glanced at their disguises littering the Jeep's floor, then at Madeleine. She looked away. Neither spoke.

The river continued to flow, unbothered.

He grabbed the phone and sat, but not before side eyeing his wife.

"I think you got a message," she said, casually staring out the window. Through the heat, she spotted an old shed.

Julian used his fingerprint to unlock the phone.

> Francis: Bad news. My military buddy got held up, so he won't be able to meet you at the coordinates. He stowed a boat inside the nearby shed for you. Take it about two klicks south. When you dock, ask the locals for Mursi, although some call him Mun. They'll escort you to his guesthouse.

Julian considered replying, but found the reception too spotty to bother. He stepped out again, this time taking his phone.

The shed's wooden door panel croaked as Julian pushed it open. Green moss overtook majority of the walls. The rowboat leaned against the side, as prescribed. The protruding tip prided an odd marking. Julian tried to decipher whether it represented a letter or a number.

Whatever, he thought.

He returned to the Jeep, finding Madeleine breastfeeding Leopaula, shaking the rattle toy overhead.

"How's she holding up?" he asked. Madeleine shrugged. "Well, here's the deal. We haven't been caught yet, but we don't have enough fuel to go back. If someone could've gotten us, Francis would've sent them. Which leaves the boat …"

Madeleine rested her head back, cognizant enough not to unlatch Leopaula. "I was really looking forward to a shower after that whole *incognito* flight."

"I'm gonna need your help, getting the boat and grabbing an oar."

"Yeah? You're asking the petite, breastfeeding woman to help you lift? Not a chance. Besides, it would be very romantic if you'd row, like a *kiss dee girl* moment."

Although Madeleine owned a smile that made even a grunt feel as if he were home, laying on a cozy couch, Julian looked around, plain faced. He repeatedly checked his phone, but when he found nothing, he pressed the toe of his boot against a sizeable chunk of dirt, turning it to dust.

Madeleine held a weak grin. "Come on, this is nice. I mean, aren't you tired of having everything catered? A little elbow grease won't hurt."

Julian's expression didn't change. Madeleine delicately placed Leopaula back into the car seat, the way only a mother could. She snuck a translucent pink binky into her mouth and looked at the bright side.

"Juley, this is exactly why we're here. Leopaula's asleep, nobody's around. It's just us and nature. Now, come on. Come, come." She patted the seat while emphasizing her signature yellow irises.

Julian lowered his chin, fighting back his smirk. He sat beside her and rested his head against the steering wheel. She ran her fingers through his smooth, earlobe length hair. She continued to massage his scalp as he groaned. With each stroke, she exposed more of her armpit, which Julian caught a whiff of. He pulled away and gasped a recycling breath.

"Let's just, uhh, get to that guesthouse," Julian said before exiting and heading to the shed.

He stood before the boat, staring. The unusual symbol stared back. He glanced at Madeleine in the Jeep.

This is how you make up for what you've done, mate, he thought.

Once he dragged the boat towards the river, he waved. Madeleine, although small, balanced all the bags and the baby in one juggling act. She waddled over, with each step sounding Leopaula's rattle toy.

In the aftermath of a powerful kick, a wake of water lapped against the hull. The small family embarked. Madeleine gripped the edge and Leopaula. The little one cackled at the new experience, reaching over as her mother held her back.

Julian pulled his foot in, nearly falling over. Madeleine smirked. He cracked a smile. They stared at each other. Neither cared to look back at the distancing Jeep.

"*Hey.*" She extended her hand, caressing his wounded knuckles.

"*Hey, yourself.*"

A sheen of sweat shined over Julian's forehead. Every so often, they'd pass beneath a leaning tree. Its shadow glided over their kiss. Chirping birds only enriched the moment. The few nearby bees danced in the sun's rays as the calm, bristling leaves welcomed the couple.

Madeleine broke away first. "I guess my brother was right; this was all we needed."

"Yeah. There's a peaceful quiet here. Just calm—an empty calm."

The pacifying moment played differently between the two.

"What's this mean, Juley? Like … *for us?* Do we need a secret getaway every few months to keep our marriage from falling apart?"

Julian expanded and compressed his chest as he appreciated the cloudless sky. "We'll be fine—"

"Is it our lifestyle? Is it possible for people like us to be parents?"

"I said, we'll be fine."

"Juley, we're far from fine—"

"Stop." The boat's crescendoing bobs paired succinctly with the sloshing against its side. "Maddy, this isn't just a holiday; it's my wake-up call, and I've answered. Looking back's not gonna solve anything."

Rarely needing a row, the boat glided as gracefully as a swan, leaving behind ripples that shimmered like gelled silk. The water ribboned a liquid silver that bounced sunlight off the vessel. Tall grass lazily swayed alongside the banks, waving to the mellowing flow of the current. Droplets disrupted the mirror surface when fallen from the suspended oars. Shrubs lined the stream, naturally and beautifully contrasting the orange dirt they grew out of. Birds landed on the branches before flapping their wings and latching onto higher ones. All the while, their reflection did the opposite.

Julian reorganized the bags, setting up a makeshift bed between the thwarts. Once he laid down, he patted the bag beside him.

"No way—Leopaula would fall over."

"Just place her down at the bow."

Madeleine pinched her lips.

"The *front* of the boat."

"Duh," she tapped her forehead, "*I knew that, Mr. Navy.*" She turned, smiling, then stopped. "Wait, no! That's still dangerous!"

"Maddy, the gunwale is higher than my knee," he sighed, "the *edge of the boat*. She'd have to do a full pullup to get out; she can't even stand. Come on, isn't this why we're here—to spend some time together? It's a miracle we got out, let alone this far."

Uneasy, Madeleine nodded. He had a point. Leopaula, at 6-months, could barely roll, much less stand. With one arm, Madeleine spread a blanket, and with the other, eased her daughter down. She cautiously backed away. At Julian's side, she kept glancing back. The binky continued to glide in and out as the infant drifted to sleep. Madeleine lowered her shoulders.

When she laid over the bags, she turned to Julian, finding him already staring—sorrowfully focused on her eyebrow wound.

"It's been non-stop," Madeleine said, flashing him a belgard of hope, pregnant with dreams for a new beginning. "Almost like we keep trying to beat the other, instead of being partners, you know?"

Julian planted a kiss on her forehead, just above the laceration. She turned to her back and lost herself in the desolate sky.

"Remember what we used to have before all the gossip started? We would sneak out at night and sit on the hilltops, alone. Then we'd spend time with the people without all the media. You'd play football with the lads, while I watched with their mothers. You were so good with the kids."

A pressure pressed against Julian's gut. Madeleine cuddled closer, hearing his labored breathing amid his oddly beating heart. He laced his fingers behind his head, acting fine, but Madeleine knew. She tried to dry his tears, but he leaned away.

"I—I'm … sorry, Maddy." Madeleine's eyes grew soft as she heard those rare words. "Things'll go back to the way they were. I promise."

He squeezed her hand as she pressed herself closer. Each felt the other's heart. Both beat with an abnormality. Madeleine rested her mind, entering a black realm where thoughts sauntered from existence. Julian also tried resting, but with a single blink, an image flashed of a woman covered in tattoos, biting her lower lip. His eyes snapped open.

Madeleine didn't mind his flinch. She had her husband back, even if it meant traveling halfway across the world.

Sweet dreams raced past the three. The river carried them, both physically and spiritually. Deep breaths of the soothing zephyr hypnotized Madeleine to where she found deeper sleep than in the confines of her cherished bed. Leopaula resumed her faint snore that only added to the peaceful atmosphere.

—

It could've been minutes. It could've been hours. Nobody knew.

A flock of birds suddenly took flight, their wings flapping in a frenzy. A single rattle echoed between the riverbanks. The once placid boat shook. A mark appeared along the edge. Blood dripped.

"Maddy!" Julian rushed around. The gentle current morphed into a booming waterfall.

Madeleine shifted. She cozied herself deeper into the makeshift bed.

"Maddy! Wake up!"

Madeleine groggily blinked. She grabbed the side, confused why the boat wobbled so much. She nestled back towards the warmth.

"MADDY!" Julian gripped her arms, digging his fingers into her biceps and shaking. "WAKE UP, NOW!"

"Quit it—we were having a nice time."

Julian's constricted black pupils contrasted his fiendishly wide eyes.

12

"Wake up! Leopaula's gone!"

Chapter II
A Rowboat's Wake

Madeleine sat up, eyes pinched from the bright sun. She stretched as her gaze scanned around before settling at the bow. A lump hid beneath the blanket.

"No, she's right there," Madeleine said before reaching. "She just covered herself—"

The rowboat glided downstream, observing its contents and leaving behind a gentle wake. A deadly silence boarded as Madeleine's eyes grew. Her heart pounded, threatening to burst through her ribcage, each beat more painful than the last. She tossed the blanket and rushed over. The wooden planks creaked and croaked with each step. She shoved the bags out of the way, knocking some overboard.

Julian's stare remained stiff, unable to stop Madeleine's frantic search. A ringing in his ears drowned out the screams. Dark spots swarmed his vision, like ink spreading on a wet canvas. Frozen muscles kept him rooted in place, a spectator to his wife's frenzied efforts.

Splash after plunge, luggage bags plummeted into the water, their zippers clinking before submerging. Droplets of the Omo River splashed onto Julian's face, holding their place until more amassed, merging with his sweat and rolling down. A faint distant muffle, over and over, called to him. He sat unresponsive as it sharpened and intensified.

"—*something! Do something!*" she shrieked.

He only blinked.

Madeleine rushed to the edge. With flared nostrils, she called out her daughter's name, over and over. The valley swallowed her calls, responding only with mocking echoes. Her ghostlike appearance struggled to overtake her quaking urge. She shrieked, louder and louder.

Only silence responded.

Drip, slosh, splash, blip, gulp.

Nothing else.

"No, no, no, no, no," she repeated, her voice a shattered whisper. Glued between internalizing her pain of screaming out loud, she became desperate. Each creak of the rowboat usurped her gaze. Until her eyes landed on Julian.

Still unresponsive, he stared at the rippled river. Other than his few spaced blinks, he didn't move a muscle.

A chill followed Madeleine's tears as they trailed, muddying her makeup. The silence, deafening, poignant and agonizing, shredded into the fabric of her being. She reached for Julian's hand, finding a deadness had overtaken him, smudging his once crystalline-blue irises pastel-like; muted and oiled.

"No," Madeleine scoffed, "this isn't happening. Leopaula's alright. W—we ju—just—left her in the car is all. That's it. We just have to go back. We never put her in the boat. That'd be crazy. What parents would place a baby in a boat?" Smiling, she shook her head while rolling her eyes. "She's alright, she's alright …" She nodded, but Julian knitted his brows, concerned. She snapped. "TELL ME SHE'S ALRIGHT!"

"Maddy ... *no* ..."

In a knee-jerk reaction, her hand shot out, colliding her palms with Julian's chest. He waved around, unintentionally grabbing her blouse before the two fell overboard. Their feet were the last thing seen before both disappeared beneath the surface.

Julian swam to the top and slicked his hair back. He blew water off his lips before hoisting himself up. He reached down and fought through her hysteria. Through his efforts, she slapped his hand away, preferring to fall to her demise than ascend to security. She thrashed, wailed and clawed, blaming everything on the boat.

Julian wrestled through her emotions and hauled her back up to safety. Tumbling in, Madeleine rushed to the edge again, screaming words of suicide until Julian bear-hugged her.

As the nightmare unfolded, Madeleine's mind drifted back to a time when Leopaula's laughter filled their home, her infectious giggles, a balm to their souls. The stark reality of her absence became unbearable. Eight years of trying, and in an instant ... gone.

Her cries carried through the valley, racing over the distant hills, reminding all other parents to hold their children close. Julian felt her veins fighting to burst out of her skin. He tightened his clamp until her shoulders gave in. The shouts morphed into sobs and the heavy breathing simmered to pants, before the two merged into a haunting moan.

Julian held in his tears. One finger at a time, he let go when he noticed she passed out. He rested her head down and raised her feet up.

As the boat drifted deeper into Omo Valley, the land enveloped around him, swallowing him whole. The once bustling sky emptied of its inhabitants, leaving only a vast expanse of nothing, devoid of all life. The once cheerful sun hung like a malevolent eye, casting an eerie glow over the couple.

Few floating luggage bags bumped alongside the vessel. One of the budges knocked particularly loud, waking Madeleine up. The moment she smelled the odor of the river, she heaved and vomited. It amassed in the lowest part. She sat up and pulled her knees in, dragging the puke. Bobbing back and forth, she shivered as her hair dripped right where she last saw Leopaula. She covered her ears from the incessant sounds of nature and stomped her foot.

"NO!" she shrieked. Julian flinched. "NO!"

As Madeleine continued, Julian looked around. The rowboat took on water. Only one oar remained. Their belongings floating downstream. They might've passed the dock—he didn't know. He stared at the puddle beneath their feet.

"How're you so calm?"

Julian lifted his head. "I'm thinking."

"Thinking about what, exactly? These are the seconds that matter! Leopaula's missing and you're just sitting there!"

"Maddy," Julian swallowed, "I don't think she's missing." A brief silence interrupted the conversation. "There are only two places she could be, and *she's not on the boat*. We need to consider how this'll fall on us."

"*Fall on us?*" She clenched her fist. "How could you be so—so—"

She struck him. Instead of evading, he let her do it. The boat tipped, cupping in water, then returned to buoyancy. Leopaula's last spot continued to fill. Turning to Madeleine, he winced as the punch settled in.

A rage overtook Madeleine, seizing her tremors. Fury surged through her veins as she leaped over the thwart and began beating on Julian. Tightened fists plummeted down, one after the other, with Julian taking it all. Through the blows, he kept staring back, void of all emotion. Bruise after bruise, busted lip, black eye—he didn't care. Tacit, he accepted the grieving mother.

Madeleine exhausted herself, releasing her fists into limp fingers. Her sobs resumed until her once vibrant eyes dulled to a lifeless shade of gray. Julian noticed her lips moving without words being uttered. Her jaw loosened, and she fell back. After feeling the thud, he checked on her.

She hollowly stared as the flow of the Omo River took her away. "This isn't real, this can't be real."

Julian lowered his head and wept.

"Juley …"

He covered his face. Tears slipped out between his fingers.

"Juley …" She reached over to comfort him, but he slapped her away.

Through his drenched bangs, he glared. *"It's your fault."*

"You—no. You do not," her index finger pointed to the sky, "get to put this on me!"

"You went to sleep last," he lied. "What parent sleeps with an infant on a boat?!"

"No, no, no! It was your idea! Besides, she can't walk! She can't fucking stand!" Madeleine paused. Their eyes met. Their thoughts aligned. "Julian, *she can't stand* … Like you said, the edge is too high."

Julian rolled his jaw as he glanced around.

Madeleine searched around for signs of what happened. She read every inch and stopped at a small scuff along the edge's rim. A trail of blood followed it. The more she tracked it, the wider her eyes grew. Thoughts of the worst poisoned her mind, at the same rate that the red streak darkened and broadened.

"Juley," she said, still following the only colored liquid amidst the water. She repeated, this time pointing.

He found the blood trail pooling beneath his dangled arm. Droplets continued to roll off of his fingertip, painting the water.

"You're bleeding."

Julian twisted his arm up as if checking the time. A long, deep slice ran from his wrist to his elbow. Severe, but not fatal.

"Why're you bleeding?"

"Not sure. Might've been when you hit me."

"I don't think so."

He shrugged, not minding the pain. He regarded Madeleine, finding her already staring back. Neither spoke *out loud*. Madeleine's lips parted as she blinked faster than usual. Julian broke away, sniffling as he looked around. Madeleine tightened her glare. He fruitlessly checked near the crest. She narrowed her eyes. He peeked, but only for a moment. She rotated her wedding band in place as her mind screamed theories—

"Hey," he snapped his fingers, "did I lose you? We need to figure this out. Otherwise, the moment we go back home, the press will surround us for being gone this long. What're we going to say regarding our missing daughter?"

"Well, she couldn't have fallen. Could it have been an animal? One of those … what're they called? Gu—Guere—Guereza. The—the—the black and—and white monkeys!"

"I doubt that. They would've had to jump down from the trees … But then again, how would they have jumped out as we're sailing this fast?"

With his teeth, Julian tied a shirt over his wound the way Madeleine taught him, having been a nurse.

"So, what then? She couldn't have climbed over the bags or even the bench."

Julian analyzed the woodgrain pattern. "The boat might've leaned so much that she rolled out."

Madeleine tilted her head at the absurdity. "You wake up in a panic whenever I shift around in bed. You really think you'd sleep through the boat tipping over ninety degrees?"

"Well, are these planks loose? Or it's possible one of those large birds swooped in. I read something about that." The more illogical his guesses spiraled, the more Madeleine twisted her face. Julian stopped. "I mean, I don't want to say it …"

Madeleine narrowed her expression. "So *now*, of all times, you've decided not to be racist?"

"Racist?! When have I ever been racist? I'm 1/64 Cherokee—"

"No, you're not."

"Well, I'm 1/64 something."

"Everybody's 1/64 something."

"Whatever. All I'm saying is … *the locals*."

Madeleine leaned in. "Are you suggesting someone *kidnapped* our baby?"

"I mean … what other explanation is there?"

"So, you're saying an individual drifted beside us and what, *fished* our daughter out of our boat and into theirs and snuck away, like—like a raccoon?" Madeleine mocked the suggestion, but covered her mouth when she pictured it happening.

Eyebrows half way up, Julian nodded. "I mean, these people, they're—they're animals."

There it is, Madeleine thought.

"They're always dreaming of a better life. We're dying in this weather, and they have to live in it … forever! Wouldn't you do anything to get yourself out of here? Then one day you're walking along the riverbank, and wham," he slapped down the back of his hand, "you see two people *like us!* And guess what? Their innocent little baby is snoozing beside them. They damn well can't drag you or me into their vessel. But an infant … a sleeping infant … with how these drug dealers sneak around, I'm sure they could've pulled this off."

"But how would they have seen Leopaula? The sides are too high."

"Maybe they planned to take us, then when they got closer, they saw her. It's like going to steal someone's car, then finding a million-euro bill beside it. Lighter, easier to grab, more valuable …" Julian bobbed his head.

Madeleine exhaled. "I don't know … murder is a big accusation."

"*Murder?!* I never said murder! If you wanted out of this hellhole, how would murder get you what you want? Think, Maddy, think," he tapped his temple, "wouldn't you hold that baby close and safe, until you figured out how to demand a ransom?"

Ignoring her aching stomach, Madeleine slowly nodded. She tried finding anything that would validate his theory. The scuff silently stared back at her, knowing more than she did.

Did the kidnapper's boat cause the scuff? She thought. Or was it from Julian's boot when we embarked?

She couldn't stop picturing the image that Julian painted. The more she sought another explanation, the more she Julian's made sense. She exhaled, understanding the moral gravity of blaming the natives for kidnapping, especially without proof.

"What would this mean, like, politically? This accusation may spark a war; many people here would be killed. Are you okay with that, all based on a hunch?"

Julian shook his head. "The moment we suggest anything else, the kidnapper will ride that other suggestion till the end. He might even kill our daughter to cover his tracks."

He shot down anything she suggested. She lowered her head and found Leopaula's last spot flooded with water. The boat's crescendo sloshed it from side to side. She looked up to find Julian desperately nodding.

She started off with a slow nod.

"Yes—yes! It's the truth, sweetheart." He hugged her. "Now, let's find the nearest point of civilization and get the bloody hell out of here."

Madeleine clamped on his good arm. "What'd you mean by, *'Leopaula's gone?'*"

He shrugged. "She wasn't in the boat; she was gone. Why?"

She tilted her head. "Why didn't you say, 'She's missing?' 'Gone' seems like—"

"Gone, missing—what's the difference?"

Madeleine narrowed her eyes. He didn't breathe. Tension, like that back home, festered.

Suddenly, Leopaula's rattle toy clattered.

Madeleine broke eye contact and turned to find someone waving from on the riverbank. A local tribesman, dark-skinned with a piercing pair of irises, stood lightly dressed, with his chest and most of his legs exposed. At an average height, with minimal hair, he leaned against a lone tree with a flabby composure and a soft complexion, yet donning a cloak of mystery.

"Hey," he called, waving. He had a satchel slung around his chest, and Leopaula's rattle toy in his other hand.

"I know where your baby is."

Chapter III
Omo's Offshoot

24

A baby's cry boomed from the center of a dark, crammed room. Odors of sweat filled the small chamber, with streaks trailing down the walls. No talking, lethargic movements and heat. Lots and lots of heat. Floating lint swam midair, illuminated by the glow of the pre-zenith sun scorching in. As segments of the ancient ritual ended, smoke swirled within the nostrils of those in attendance.

A pale, tense baby screamed. No adult helped. No worry, no panic. Instead, cheers and laughter sounded. Smiles and celebrations overtook the cries of the helpless little one. The louder it cried, the further out the celebration carried. Eager, the crowd craned to catch a glimpse of the unfamiliar infant.

In the heart of the ritual, one woman hung her head back. The heavy iron scent emanated from her as her dull eyes observed the ceiling. She lied in agony as the cheers persisted.

After the ritual, faint wisps of smoke rose from extinguished candles. A wet towel slid off the woman's forehead, revealing a sheen of sweat. She tried to appreciate her sacrifice, but she needed medical attention as the baby continued to scream.

A sheathing sound.

A sacrament attendee gripped the blade.

The woman glanced, unfazed.

She didn't look twice. The sharp edge drew near.

—

Tribal Chief Amari gripped his wife, Zola's, hand. The blade sliced through the *umbilical cord,* severing her with the newest addition to the tribe, *baby Kamari.* 60-years-old with an unplanned child, yet Amari still smiled. The cheers silenced as he stood, impeding the sunlight. Long shadows revealed the scarification across his torso. Nearby warriors, men, women, children, even insects—all backed away. Metallic armlets depicting snakes biting their own tails hugged his arms. Because of his biceps' stony size, the bands had seized to his arm. Body builders dreamed of reaching his build, while he held no interest in what they do. Over each chiseled pectoral, ab and shoulder, lay battle scars. Plenty.

He turned to Zola. "[Spoken in Surmic] How are you doing?"

With a heavy hand, she gestured towards a jug of water.

"Rest. I'll have Imamu clean and prepare Kamari."

Amari turned to the crowd. All mouths sealed. All hands trembled. Silence, other than the newborn. "Where's my son—my successor?" Not a peep. "Why isn't the next leader of the tribe here?!"

The crowd murmured as one, unnerved member subtly shielded his face.

"You!" Amari pointed. "You're Imamu's friend, Ike. Where's my son?"

Ike rubbed the back of his head. "I might know …"

Later, Ike approached a nestled cove of trees overlooking a stream connected to the Omo River. Imamu sat alone, his silhouette surrounded by nothing but nature.

"I thought I'd find you here."

Melancholy, Imamu stared at the babbling water, not facing his friend. The sounds of the trickling river filled the air.

"Imamu?"

The stream continued, with Imamu giving it his full attention.

"Did you know that the Omo River has exactly 2,222 offshoots which branch off the main channel?"

Ike exhaled, glancing at the sky. "And why's any of that matter?"

"Did you know that this one, the one right in front of us, is unique from the other 2,221?"

"Yeah?" Ike bounced his brows. "How so?"

"Something odd started happening the last month or so. If you sit with me, you'll see."

Ike bit the inside of his cheek, forcing a hard smile. He sat and stared out at the water with his lifelong friend.

"Imamu—"

"Shh, any moment now …"

The two observed, but only one held his breath. Having the only cell phone in the village, Imamu checked the time, then darted his hawkish eyes back at the water.

"Any second now."

The insects buzzed. The birds chirped. The wind blew. But nothing happened.

Ike tightened his jaw. "Stop this, okay? This—this—infatuation with data and statistics. Ever since you got that damn phone, you've become the tribe outcast. First, you flood me with weird information about how people don't actually get possessed, but instead '[English] ha-lu-sin-ate.' [Surmic] And now this crap? How do you plan on getting married, Imamu? How are you going to have kids? Nobody likes you!"

Imamu's gray gaze remained fixed on the elusive water barreling over the rocks and pebbles.

"Dammit! At least show some emotion! Show something! For God's sake, I married Nala, your childhood sweetheart, and you didn't even lash out at me! We're adults in our twenties, Imamu! Stop acting like a child!"

Imamu's thoughts transported him to a time when he and Nala were inseparable, staring at that very stream together for hours. They shared dreams of the future, filled with laughter and smiles. However, these days, Imamu sat alone with occasional visits from Ike, consumed with sadness.

"While you're here, lost in some science project, you missed the birth of your little brother. All for what? To show me how this stream differs from other streams and spewing *did-you-knows*—"

"Did you know this offshoot runs through the mines? The same mine where Yonas is held?"

Ike inhaled the earthy scent of the river. The familiar aroma mixed with the faint metallic tang of the mines in the distance.

"Listen, Imamu. Nobody blames you for what happened to your older brother, or anybody else that's enslaved there. You know that liberating them takes careful planning and time. We're up against a superpower-country here. At least we can trade messages with our tribesmen—"

"Did you know that every day, for exactly 27 seconds, this offshoot—"

"Imamu!" Ike rubbed his forehead before adjusting his tone. "Imamu, Chief Amari sent me to give you a message. You've been banned from the village well. You're going to need to fetch your water from the river for a month. He said no brooks, streams or *offshoots*." Ike stood and dusted his bottom. "Also …" he turned his back and sighed, "he's commanding you to turn over the generational dagger so that he may appoint Kamari as the next heir; not you." Imamu remained glued to the offshoot, silent and emotionless. Ike tsked as he shook his head. "I don't know how to help you. But I think you know what the problem is. I'm always here for you, but this is something you have to realize on your own."

Ike patted his shoulder and left his friend with the desolate water, being pushed along, whether or not it wanted to be.

Soon enough, it happened.

The temperature dropped to a chill the moment the water turned a reddish hue for exactly 27 seconds. Every passing instant, the offshoot diluted until it returned to its normal transparency.

Imamu already did the math; for the water before him to sport a reddish complexion for 27 seconds meant that something red, dark, crimson red, had been poured in upstream. For the width, depth and flow of the offshoot, wed to its distance from the mines, precisely 4.5 liters of this additive would've had to be mixed in for it to turn this hue for the prescribed 27 seconds.

4.5 liters; *the quantity of blood in a human body.*

—

A few days later, Imamu woke up, and, as many phone owners do, immediately reached for his device. He scrolled through international news articles, having no benefit to himself. An article in the Times of London mentioned a citywide investigation regarding the murder of a woman from Slough, the slum-city near the famous Windsor Castle. Uninterested, he continued scrolling. Suddenly, major headlines flooded his feed, citing the disappearance of members from the Royal Family. In particular, *Prince Julian, Princess Madeleine and Princess Leopaula.*

Curious, he tapped. A portrait of the three began the article, one taken just weeks after Leopaula's birth. He pinched open the screen, zooming in on the trio. He imagined his life as the prince of the United Kingdom instead of being the prince of his tribe. A flush became visible on his cheeks as he held eye contact with Madeleine's image. However, feeling Julian's glare, he looked away.

But the stare was so sharp that hiding behind the screen didn't protect Imamu. He double-tapped to revert the image to its original size, but still felt the prince's gaze. As a shiver crept down his spine, he picked his nails—a tendency unknown among his people.

He shrugged, locked his phone and figured it best to collect his water early in the day.

With a pail in hand, he waved at the caravan delivering grain and wheat for the week. They regarded him, with only some weakly waving back. He continued until he approached the bank of the Omo River. In the distance, a rowboat sat above the water. An unusual sight, but not an uncommon one. Imamu hid behind some bushes, senses heightened. The closer he tracked the boat, the more adrenaline surged through his veins. He prayed it would just flow on, not being a rival tribe or intruder.

With a silent approach, it drew closer. Closer. Closer. Until he recognized the occupants. He covered his mouth, took a few steps back and panted.

I'm hallucinating, he thought. That's—that's what this is. This—this is what I read about.

Yet, whenever he glanced back, the rowboat continued to exist.

He jumped down to the riverbank, and with a fumbled landing, fell. His phone slid out and lodged halfway in the mud. Instead of scrambling to clean it up, he froze when he saw a muddied rattle toy lying over the wet pebbles.

Imamu kneeled down and picked it up, as the earth slowly swallowed the device. Mud smeared against his fingers as he stared at the toy, then back at the rowboat.

Imamu picked up the mud-drenched phone and wicked it. A few moments after the SAMSUNG logo appeared, he pulled up the article of the missing Royal Family again. He inspected the picture, directing his attention this time to Leopaula. In her hand, then his, he double checked, then triple.

Imamu clenched the toy. Ideas raced through his mind alongside flashes of the caravan and the couple. He looked back at his palm.

"I could use this. This is what could save me."

Upon witnessing Madeleine's assault on Julian, followed by an argument, Imamu raced downstream. He approached a tree that leaned over the water.

He readied himself.

With a single judder, he rattled the toy. Madeleine snapped her sights to him.

"[English] *Hey.*" Imamu waved.

He cracked a sinister smile, absent of any sincerity. When he pictured Kamari, a calendar of ominous events of hierarchy and inheritance riddled his view. But when he locked eyes with Madeleine, the sight of actual hope and freedom stupefied him. Her expression couldn't be faked and didn't hide behind an LCD screen. The certified, the bona fide, the uncut, the organic. She harbored unadulterated depth, which would serve as access to his aspirations. His view pinched from his grin as he shook the toy once more, this time, for the sole purpose of torturing her.

"I know where your baby is."

Chapter IV
Hostile Territory

Like a strike of lightning amid a hurricane, Madeleine heard it. Julian couldn't stop her, even if he'd handcuffed her to the hull. Imamu, smirking, rattled the toy again. Every clatter of the imprisoned beads charged him and the doting mother with optimism.

"Leopaula's alright, Leopaula's alright," Madeleine said, louder and louder.

Stepping on the edge, she tilted the boat, letting water rush in. She didn't care. The current swept their luggage away. Again, she showed no concern. Nothing could've stopped her from getting to Imamu.

She tripped over a stone lodged in the riverbed, severely spraining her ankle. That didn't slow her stampede. Step after stomp, the pain struck worse than she thought, shooting upwards. Despite falling face first into the water, she kept going. She grabbed the stones to propel herself forward. Rocks dislodged, wet dirt dispersed throughout the river, and remnants of their bags tumbled over her, but she continued to charge towards Imamu. Her baby needed her.

Julian's hand grazed her, but she kicked it away. No obstacle, not even a brick wall, was strong enough to separate her from the toy. His shouts echoed into nothingness as the rest of Madeleine's senses faded in favor of her tunneled vision. Like a shark making its move, she plunged above the surface, wasting no time.

"Where?! Where'd you find this?! Tell me!"

The shooting pain dropped her like a stone. She grabbed Imamu's hairless legs and climbed, flashing more gum than teeth. Her fingers dug into his shoulders, leaving him petrified. Her vigorous shake wobbled his head back and forth as if a bobblehead on a dashboard. His satchel flapped around, straining against his shoulder, bruising him. Again, she didn't care.

"Where?!"

Imamu broke free, but not before she grabbed his face and screamed. Splotches of her saliva landed across his grimace. He held the keys to her sanity, and she refused to quit screaming until he forfeited them. When she had to stop to breathe, he stared back, held in place, like a smashed bug. She tightened her fist, but upon raising it, Julian yanked her off.

"Easy now, easy."

As Imamu pulled himself together, the Brit gave him a waiting finger.

"What're—what're you doing?! This man knows where Leopaula is! He has her—"

"Shh!" He muddied his hand over her mouth. "Shut up!" He whisper-shouted as he glanced back at Imamu. "If he's lying, then we're walking right into a hostage situation."

"*Hostage situ*—oh, shut up! Our baby's alive and he knows where she is! What're you so scared about? Look at him—he's all pudgy and goofy looking."

They turned around in unison. Imamu returned an unsettling smile.

"I say we knock him out and hurry back to the boat before it drifts too far. We need to get the hell out of here."

Air hit the extreme radiuses of Madeleine's eyes. "Are you insane? Look around, Julian. We don't know where we are, all our things are gone and we're soaked. I can barely stand and that wound of yours needs to be cleaned. All that aside, this is Leopaula!"

After making sure the generational dagger didn't fall out of his satchel, Imamu gyrated the beads within the toy once more. "This is your baby's, no?"

In a knee jerk reaction, Madeleine shoved Julian and limped towards him.

With a slow, threatening tone, she asked, "Where did you get that?"

"You've got quite a grip, lady. I've never seen a woman beat a man up before today, but after that shake, I can see why he didn't fight back."

Julian lifted an eyebrow. "How long have you been spying on us?"

"To hell with all that! Where's my baby, and how do you have her toy?"

Imamu glanced between them, calculating his words.

"I was fetching my water for the day when I spotted something odd lying on the bank. When I approached it, I found it to be a baby. She swallowed a lot of water, so I performed some, eh, how do you say, chest 'com-presh-shuns.' Even though she spit up the water, she remained, um, 'un-con-shiss.' So, I rushed her back to my tribe and my people took her to Koka hospital."

"Great! Fantastic! Let's go!"

Imamu raised his palm. "No can do. It's an hour by car and over a week by foot. We sacrificed our only vehicle for her. Now my tribe doesn't have grain for another seven days."

"Only car, huh?" Julian asked. "Why can't they just drive back?"

She nodded.

A simple question, yet Imamu didn't respond. Madeleine noticed his mind busied finding a response as it processed millions of data points. She recognized he wasn't a nobody—he was dangerously smart.

"Our life isn't like your life, *haranchi*," Imamu said. "We only have one car for the entire region. It makes rounds. Your baby washed ashore at the same time that it made its stop to this side of the valley. She's truly lucky."

Julian didn't blink. "Is she now?"

"She is."

"Then what happened?" Madeleine asked.

"She dropped her toy when I was pumping the water out of her. The hospital should have her back here within three or four days. Until then, you two may stay as guests in the village."

Julian pulled Madeleine aside. "This isn't a good idea. And what about your foot?"

She looked down. The bruising grew far quicker than a simple sprain. Familiar with wounds of the like, she shrugged. "It'll need two, three days to heal, but I'll be fine, Juley. Come on, let's go get our daughter."

Before leading the way, Imamu stopped, sights set on the boat.

"What? What is it?" Madeleine asked.

The symbol on the boat's tip caught his eye as it drifted away, backwards and upside-down. "Where'd you get that boat?"

"Upriver, in a shed. Why?"

Imamu blinked faster than usual. He squinted to make sure he wasn't hallucinating.

"Building a boat here takes a long time because it's manually made. Meaning that when we need one, we sacrifice extra resources to fortify it enough to withstand the beasts that plague this river. So, if you're here, in a boat, *it's not a coincidence.* These aren't vehicles we spare. And based on that one's engraving, it belongs to a rival tribe. I find it hard to believe that they'd simply leave it in a shed for two haranchis."

Sensing his hesitation, Madeleine squeezed his hands. His cuticles mimed hers; picked and gnawed. That's when she spotted it. A massive burden ate away at him. One similar to what burdened her back home. The people's ridicule—a deafening stare of envy mixed with litanies of downfall. However, he couldn't flee like she did. He clawed to get out but failed to see the light.

She released her grip, wanting to help, but fearful of what a man like this would do to escape his turmoil.

She closed her eyes and saw Leopaula sliding her binky between her lips. "Please. I sense that you have a gentle heart. If you help us, we'll help you."

Imamu glanced at the sinking boat, then at Madeleine. He recognized her pain, too. His eyes shifted from Julian to her.

A small nod.

"Okay."

"Yes?!"

"Yes. Follow me."

They started walking. Imamu extended his hand.

"Imamu."

Madeleine shook. "*Imamu* to you too."

"No," he laughed, "my name is Imamu. And you are?"

"I'm Madeleine, and he's Julian. We're the Augustus's."

Imamu theatrically made a face. "A—Augustus? Does that mean … that baby … was L—Leo …"

Madeleine beamed. "Leopaula Augustus, yes! Our daughter!"

"The entire world is out looking for you three—what're you doing here?!"

Julian shoved him. "Hey, keep walking! We don't have time for this."

"But … how? And where's your entourage? Your guards?"

Julian shoved him again. "I said, keep walking!"

Imamu couldn't grasp that they were really there. Nobody could. That was the point. Since Leopaula's birth, their marriage fell apart. The media would swarm them the moment they stepped outside, flashing their cameras and clamoring over one another. Madeleine only wanted to be a mother, but became a magnet for insinuating questions and criticism.

Their stolen privacy bred additional problems—vile problems that only rot and fester when unaddressed. It reached the point that they had to take this sudden trip to save their relationship.

Julian kept pushing Imamu forward. Unlike Madeleine, he enjoyed the media. With a lean, masculine build and a kind yet commanding face, he personified leadership and with that, a love of a crowd, even a horde, armed with questions. However, here, stranded in an unknown land, after such a dramatic episode, he just wanted to return home.

He slowed his pace, distancing them from Imamu. "Psst, stop it! We don't know him, and he knows us. Remember what I said? This guy might be leading us to a bonfire for all we know. The next minute, all his tribal buddies are prancing around as we're roasted like pigs. Is that what you want?"

She rolled her eyes. "This is exactly how you were when you first met Francis, and now he's your closest friend. Please curb your theories and focus on getting Leopaula back."

She picked up the pace, but he grabbed her arm.

"Francis isn't here! It's just us! And I need to make sure we get out of here alive. No more opening up to him. It's bad enough that he keeps calling us 'haranchi,' whatever the hell that means. Hold your cards close, got it?"

"Yes, okay, fine. But let the record show that you're paranoid. This boy's helping and your presumption is rubbish. Let's just get to our baby and take some showers."

Showers? Julian thought. The boy's gathering water …

They approached a forest so dense that the other side remained a mystery. The deeper they delved, the more a secretive civilization revealed itself. It started with the animals: cattle, goats, sheep, pigs, chickens. Guarding them was a lone shepherd with a rifle slung from his shoulder, an incongruous figure in the otherwise georgic setting. He flashed an all-too-quick smile, prompting Madeleine to turn away, wide-eyed and mute. She tried to stay open-minded to the diversity, but Julian's words were seeping in.

Later, they passed a group of tribal children, barely dressed, if at all. They kicked around a deflated basketball as if it was a football. Some had odd markings over their slight bellies, while others dressed more conservatively. At the far end of the field, the younger kids played with makeshift toys, fashioned from discarded materials. They laughed and jostled while some imagined and designed new action figures. However, when they spotted the foreigners, they stopped playing and stared.

They added something to Imamu's phrase:

'*Garra*-haranchi, *garra*-haranchi …'

Madeleine noticed Julian's eyes snapping around. She didn't blame him, as her throat constricted with a sudden loss of appetite. Suddenly, loud smacks echoed from a distance, like gunshots. They both flinched, with Julian ducking lower than Madeleine.

Imamu remained calm. He pointed at a gladiator-like arena. Two men wielding long sticks battled one another as the crowd cheered them on. A line of women stood nearby.

"Donga stick fighting," Imamu said. "A tradition passed down by our ancestors that we practice every morning. It's how we pair our bachelors with our maidens."

"*Brilliant,*" Julian mumbled. The fighters proudly sported their scars, while Imamu seemed to have never hurt a fly. "So," he flatly smiled, "where's your lucky lady?"

Imamu ignored him, but couldn't hide his twitching cheek muscle. He quickened his pace.

Julian smirked.

"That was awfully rude of you," Madeleine murmured.

"Oh, shove it. I need the boy to understand that we're not friends. I won't let him cozy up to us to play little mind games."

Sighing, Madeleine pushed him away and preferred limping. "I'm only interested in finding Leopaula and leaving. Yes, this place may seem a bit creepy and unusual, but that's because we're used to luxury. No need to be unpleasant towards people who're helping us."

After crossing a demarcated tree line, like wizardry, the nestled village revealed itself. Camouflaged by the trees, it's easily overlooked by both man and beast. Hundreds of straw huts riddled the grounds, each covering the area of a typical car or two. With entrances waist high, it gave the impression that they didn't want people freely entering.

The tribespeople observed the couple. A tingle ran over Madeleine's skin as the glares converged. She glanced at Julian, finding him clenching a fist. She couldn't blame him. Although she tried being respectful, these people's image alone struck fear in the hearts of any outsider. Most of the men carried rifles, but all of them, without exception, dangled machetes from their hips—some of which were wet and red.

Then there were the women. Madeleine failed to appreciate their intricately patterned fabrics and interwoven beadwork because of a blaring abnormality. They exhibited something the couple had never before seen; gauged plates inserted into their lower lips. Some were so wide that teeth had to be knocked so that the plate would fit. When they stared, time moved at a different cadence.

Madeleine snapped her sights away, chest heaving and face ashen. Meanwhile, Julian …

"What?! What're you looking at?" he hollered. "Never seen someone who bathes before?!" Imamu stopped and stared. "Where are you taking us?! Who are you people?!"

Imamu didn't react, visibly nor viscerally.

The tribespeople whispered and pointed. Julian lost control of his breathing as his gaze bounced from one member to another.

Madeleine felt as small as him but lacked the audacity to bark. She purged out the dark thoughts and thought about Leopaula, alone, scared, hurt. She squeezed Julian's hand, but he smacked it away.

"Maddy, we're walking into a trap! Look at these freaks!"

"Th—think," Her voice, laced with anxiety, barely made it out of her mouth through the tremors. "Think of our daughter. L—Leopaula."

Imamu tilted his head and sharply exhaled. "Are you done, Prince Julian? We're not far, but if every few steps you gawk and scream, we'll never make it."

Madeleine tightened her lips until the fear played its course. "Yes. I'm sorry. This is all just new for us."

"I understand." He turned and continued.

Madeleine stole a second glance. She didn't hold any resentment against the women, but couldn't shake the feeling that they held something against her. They held their babies in makeshift slings, just as scared as her. Looks aside, they weren't much different.

"We're almost there," Imamu said.

Almost there? Madeleine thought.

She couldn't spot a single solid building in sight, no power lines above or below, no facilities whatsoever. With every step, she felt more lightheaded. Faint sunlight broke through the leaves, painting the veiled village like a cow.

She tried focusing on Imamu, but the torches lighting the path kept distracting her. They reflected off the glaring eyes. They lit half of the women's lip plates. They scattered embers and a daunting glow. They roasted the skinned animals impaled over the spits—

Madeleine's eyes rolled back as she tumbled, falling unconscious.

Chapter V
Tamed Lightning

Meanwhile, in the UK, a solemn Sir-Francis, accompanied by an entourage of guards, paced through the corridors of Windsor Castle. Dark heavy stones structured the fortress exterior, giving off an illusion of stability. Although inside, the occupants drowned in bedlam amid the Victorian perfection. Trailing Francis, the procession of footsteps muffled per transition from the marbled tile to the rich woven carpet snaking the halls. Dim sconces flickered, casting ferocious shadows juggling along the walls. The air carried a trace of artificial springtime scents, but not enough to mask the aged wood of the furniture. As the delegation passed, portraits of noble figures stared at Francis. They observed his familiar gait, predicting his joining of their ranks in the near future.

The impending thunderstorm ruptured bursts of light through the stained-glass windows, coloring the otherwise pearl-white floors. Worn books bearing tales of ruthless rulers, all of which Francis read, lined the alcove shelves. Standing eternally sentinel, showcased suits of armor interrupted the pattern at perfectly set intervals. Francis's reflection slid, expanding and shrinking, over the surface of the armors' breastplates. When the entourage turned the corner, only a muted eerie silence remained behind.

Castle officials handed Francis dossier after dossier, requesting signatures, vetoes of protocols and approvals.

Keeping the pace, he blindly signed without slowing down by a single cadence.

Those surrounding him exuded worry. Decorated guards, seasoned warriors and suited councilmen wore dark bags under their eyes. Wrinkles between their brows creased as sweat oozed out. Others in the castle worried even more. Knees jittered, nails picked and hair frazzled. The Kingdom needed Francis as a beacon of light to lift it from its recent crisis. He knew he was the only one who could rectify the situation, and he preferred it that way.

Guards shoved the visitors off the premises as Francis's party exited the castle corridors and cut through the Lower Ward. Some guests fought back, waving nonrefundable entrance passes, while others boomed into an uproar upon spotting the him.

"Where are they?! We deserve answers!"

Francis kept his glare forward. He marched over the pristine lawn until a rumble shook the ground. He glanced up, finding the clouds dark and pregnant. Silent streaks of lightning raced amid them, taunting with the readiness to strike.

He narrowed his glare.

The clouds stopped glowing.

He turned his sights back to the castle and walked at his own pace until he reached the far-end wing.

A distant murmur drifted from the media chamber towards Francis's assembly. Hordes of reporters roared as they waited for the official update regarding the missing

Royal Family. Francis stopped just shy of the door, staring at the heavy oak.

Lordes, Francis's second in command and Madeleine's Royal Guard, turned to him.

"Sir?"

"This is when our legacy begins. This is what my father died for." Francis placed his hand on the door. "It's time."

"Are you sure you want to do this? We could have the head of the Royal Communications address the public. O— or the minister of—"

"No. The peasants need a powerful figure during these troubling times. Besides, everybody else is running around as if headless chickens."

"But sir, if they're too aggressive, this'll put you in a bad light—"

"Stop. I will restore order. This is my duty to the Kingdom."

Francis pushed open the door, silencing the murmurs. Upon reaching the podium, he observed the audience.

Mere peasants, he thought.

They stared back in awe, finding a man with a multifaceted personality, booming a blend of compelling, yet striking traits. His tousled dark hair and faint facial stubble spoke of a tamed meticulousness. He imposed an air of confidence, drawing attention and prosperity. His irises shined a light brown that struck most as a charged yellow.

Reporters exchanged glances amidst the silence. Nobody wanted to speak first, although their income depended on it. Everyone knew Francis, just like they knew the king. The fact alone that he stood before them showed the grave severity.

He stepped atop the platform and gripped the podium. "It's with a heavy heart that we confirm the troubling news of the missing Prince Julian, Princess Madeleine and their daughter, Princess Leopaula. Early this morning, the three were reported absent from Windsor Castle. The search is ongoing.

"His Majesty, King Leopold, has been briefed. As we navigate this challenging time, we implore anyone with information regarding their whereabouts to come forward. Your cooperation and support are crucial.

"We'll continue to provide updates as new information becomes available. Thank you."

The reporters tilted their heads, as if in unison. Nobody spoke. Not a sound. Raw silence, except for a buzzing chandelier.

Francis scanned, expecting more of a fight.

Like the unlatching of an airplane's emergency door, the reporters boomed their questions, one over the other.

"You haven't told us anything!"

"We deserve more transparency and information!"

"This is your family! Your sister, your niece, your brother-in-law! How're you so calm?"

"Why wasn't this alarming situation made public earlier?"

"*Some timing ...*" one reporter said with a twang, glancing above his nose balanced glasses. "*Wasn't the Kingdom due for an investigation regarding the Slough murder?*" Francis shot a glance at the last reporter before averting his eyes. The journalist noticed, suddenly stricken with fear.

"*What measures are being taken in the search?*"

"*Tell us something!*"

One correspondent stood and shouted so loud that his brash voice ruptured through the clamoring disorder. "*You're Sir-Julian's Royal Guard! How dare you let this happen? How?! Tell us, dammit!*"

Francis regarded Lordes at the foot of the chamber wearing a fallen expression. A phone call pulled him away. Francis looked back at the loud reporter. His penetrating stare, so concentrated and austere, silenced the room again.

"Fate ..." he tapped pages against the podium before glancing back up, "fate only favors those with patience. Order will be restored."

He concluded his allocution, stepped down from the dais and exited. The correspondents scratched their heads.

Lordes rushed to his side, whispering, "They've landed in AMH and have boarded D'jen's rowboat."

Francis cracked a smile. "Perfect. So, everything's going according to plan."

Chapter VI
An Immovable Object

"Back off!" Julian roared, branch swatting towards the tribespeople. "What'd you do to her? When'd you poison her?!"

Laying limp over Julian's arm, Madeleine's head fell with eyes unfixed, rolling in every which direction.

"Be careful," Imamu said as the tribespeople stood on their toes, one over the other. He took out his canteen. "She's dehydrated!"

Julian stretched out his arm, but Imamu fought through and poured water over Madeleine's mouth. The more he dispensed, the closer he held her, as to not splash. He noticed something unusual as he tightened his grip.

"What's wrong with her pulse?" he asked. "Why's it racing out of rhythm?"

As Madeleine licked her lips, Julian calmed down. He sat down beside Imamu, dropped the branch and wiped the sweat over his forehead.

"She and I share a disease—"

"Arrhythmia," they said in unison.

Julian jerked his head back, surprised at Imamu's perceptiveness.

"*Irregular heartbeats.* That's very rare at her age. I wouldn't ever have imagined the two of you having it. It's tachycardia, not bradycardia. I'm assuming you have the same?"

"Yes—ehm, are you, uh, some kind of medical student or something, here on some program?"

"No."

Madeleine came to, widening her eyes before snatching the canteen and guzzling.

Imamu shushed and soothed her, patting her back. "You're okay, you're okay."

"A—alright, that's—that's enough," Julian said, prying Imamu off of his wife.

The canteen fell, glubbing out its contents. Imamu defeatedly sighed, witnessing his water for the day being absorbed by the soil.

"Here," Imamu helped them up, "let's go somewhere for you two to rest. My father is Chief Amari, *son of the Great Shaman, Haile, The Lion Tamer*. You could stay at his residence until we figure things out. It's a strong fortified clay hut resembling a bit more of what you're used to."

—

After showing them to his father's abode, Imamu stepped away, but someone suddenly slapped him upside his head.

"[Surmic] Hey!" Zola said. "Why're you snooping through my place, [English] Pillsbury Doughboy?"

"[Surmic] Mother, uh, I—"

As Kamari suckled, Zola winced from the post-labor pains. She shouldered Imamu aside and peeked into her hut. Madeleine sat with her hands over her head as Julian played with a soft spot on the floor. Zola looked back at Imamu.

"Who are they, and why're they so pretty?"

"I crossed paths with them on the river as I collected my water for the day. They lost their daughter during their trip. I found her washed up on the riverbank and gave her to the caravan."

"Was the girl dead?"

"No, but she was unconscious. The driver said he'll take her to Koka and return her once she's better."

Zola stared, tilted her head, then tightened her glare. "I can tell when my son's lying."

Imamu picked his nails, avoiding eye contact. Zola bobbed Kamari, waiting for her son to crack.

He didn't.

"Regardless," Zola glanced back inside, "it's a good thing you found them and not the Bodi, Karo or Suri. If these two were on water, then they're not trespassers, but those other tribes would've still slain them on sight. And by the tone of their skin, harming them may bring retaliation from—"

Zola found herself alone, with only Kamari. She tsked, mumbled curse words at the absent Imamu and entered the hut.

Madeleine and Julian looked around. A small flame flickered from the center of the room, dimly lighting the jagged walls, contrasting what they were used to. Instead of decorated suits of armor, portraits or sculptures, dried animal hides and weapons adorned the hut.

Lemon-pine filled the air, emanating from a small burner in the corner by heated frankincense rocks. Madeleine sat on the woven straw mat, the back of her head bobbing off the wall. A low table adorned artistically placed artifacts. On the far side, a light curtain rippled from the gentle waft. With every breeze, the fire fluttered, readjusted, then symmetrically reached up once again.

Julian swatted his neck, splatting another mosquito. He couldn't decide whether he preferred the sizzling heat of the Ethiopian sun over being eaten alive. Despite wanting to leave, he realized they were in a helpless situation. Madeleine's knocking head kept him centered as it drove her insane.

She stood and inspected the artifacts on the shelves, trying to pass the time. She found a large, bumpy stone with a unique color and texture. Although round, it didn't seem to roll. She grabbed it.

Suddenly, she shrieked. Julian caught the *skull* before it hit the floor.

"[English] Don't get comfortable, Maddy." He carelessly placed the skull on the table, sideways. "These people ... we can't trust them. Next time, let's just book a Ritz Carlton and deal with the paparazzi. Think about it. We're only breathing because to them we have no value being dead. That's the only reason they're not parading us around with spears in our backs."

"I'm not sure … Imamu seems nice. And the people don't seem to be as odd as their appearance suggests." Madeleine looked around. She jumped, jostling the table upon catching sight of Zola's silhouette framed by the doorway.

Chin up, the chieftess stood fearfully bald, while boldly fearless. Her remaining lower teeth suffered damage and misalignment, while her lip plate proudly hung past her shoulders. Kamari stopped suckling and goggled at the outsiders. With her breast exposed, Zola eyed the two. Madeleine's scabbed eyebrow stood out to her like a crack in an otherwise perfect porcelain doll. Back at Julian, she glowered, unshy and unabashed at his glance towards her chest. She stared him down, although he towered over her.

"H—hello—"

"*Git out,*" the 39-year-old new mother said in an out-of-place Jamaican accent.

Madeleine lowered her chin and hurried towards the door, but Zola held her arm out. "Not you; *him.*"

"Excuse me?"

"Ya damn well heard me."

He raised an eyebrow. "Must be that plate …"

"Come again, white-boy?" Zola cocked her head, handing Kamari to the frozen, yet rapidly blinking Madeleine.

"Listen, lady, whoever you think you are, I don't answer to you. And I'm damn well not leaving my wife here with some stranger."

Zola approached. Julian swallowed noisily, audible to all. He regarded the exit, then her. She noticed.

"I don't give a damn if ya da Jesus! If I say get out my home, you getting out!"

Julian could spot the veins in her eyes. She inhaled his scent, deflating him with every breath.

"Whatever." He gave up. "I'll be right outside, Maddy. I need some fresh air anyway." He stormed out, almost tearing down the entrance's curtain.

"Yeah," Zola nodded after him, "ya do dat."

Once alone, Zola turned to the double-brow-high Madeleine. Her fury disappeared when she saw Kamari sleeping in her embrace.

"You a good girl." She flexed a wide smile. "He don't sleep in nobody's arms but good peoples. Not even with Chief Amari."

"Who—who," Madeleine tripped over her tongue, "are you?"

"Calm down, white-girl. You ain't got nothing to be worried about."

Madeleine remained unconvinced. She'd never seen Julian put in his place, let alone so fast. She tried being cordial but could only muster a watery smile that, although forced, kept flinching back to a frown. Zola smirked.

Kamari burrowed his face against Madeleine's chest, wanting to feed. The more he searched, the stronger the ache from not breastfeeding Leopaula irritated her.

Zola exhaled. "Ya missing ya girl, huh?"

"Y—yes! You know? Have you seen her?"

Zola shook her head with closed eyes. "I can see it in ya eyes; you're longing for her … the same way you're longing for other tings." She gazed at her eyebrow.

"Are you … a fortune teller, o—or a witch?"

Zola boomed in laughter. "Do I look like a witch?" Madeleine looked away, pinching her lips. "Well, I'm not! I'm Zola, chieftess of the tribe. I know we look different, but we're just like other people. The only oddball here is ya husband … He's of the ilk that I've seen far too many times. A dickhole who thinks it's okay to lay his hands on ya. Am I warm?"

Madeleine stared dumbstruck, suddenly obsessed with Zola. Zola scoffed.

She delicately positioned the skull back on the shelf. "This belonged to the late Haile, The Lion Tamer. He taught our people honor and guidance. Since then, our men stopped acting like ya husband. So, we easily spot his kind. Whereas the rest of us, we're similar, girl. See, I even have this." Zola showed off her barely functional MP3 player. "You like reggae?" Madeleine smiled, mouthing, no. "Ah, you're missing out. Imamu gave me this gift to help."

"Help with what?"

"Years back, Amari ordered the tribe to learn English, but I wasn't having none of that. I didn't want to look up to the white-man, but my husband was strict with it. So, Imamu found a middle ground. He got me dis MP-thing, and I learned English from da reggae."

"So … everybody here speaks English?"

"Mhmm, but we don't want to. After agreements with the government didn't go down right, and we were played by the white-man, we had to. Amari said it's to stop history from repeating."

Madeleine's lips parted as she cracked a slow smile. The hut didn't feel as restrictive as before.

"It's hard being apart from your baby," Zola said. "Is dis da first time you two've been separated?"

"I don't even let my staff hold her." Madeleine's voice cracked as flashes of Leopaula raced through her mind.

"You should listen to some reggae, girl."

"That's amazing that you picked up on English through music, and honestly, a bit funny." Madeleine held a soft smile, but not for long. "Listen, I know you're trying to take my mind off Leopaula, but—"

"Just give it a go, yeah? Once you taste da reggae, ya'd see what I'm talking about."

Zola scrolled through her saved albums, knowing that other than a distraction, nothing could help Madeleine with the pain she was far too familiar with. Madeleine dropped her shoulders, flinching a grin that didn't involve her brows.

"Ya telling me dat you never heard of da Sizzla? No? Da Koffee? No? Don't tell me you of the girls that listen to Biggie or Sean de Paul and tink they part of da culture." Madeleine stayed quiet. "Ugh, you probably one of them Bob Marley fans …" She placed her hand over her forehead. "Oh, Lord …"

Once Madeleine revealed a giggle, Zola found her opening and kept providing whatever support she could to the young mother. The two swapped stories and experiences, brightening the hut with laughter. Madeleine looked up to her new friend as a mentor, as Zola discovered optimism in her guest.

Madeleine's mind wandered to Leopaula, but Zola kept snapping her back. She knew leaving her guest in silence meant Madeleine's imagination would terrorize her, so she took the role of being her emotional crutch.

"Is, ehm." Madeleine bit her lower lip. Zola glanced up. "Is someone you love also missing?"

Zola spotted Madeleine's bum ankle, happy to spot something that could change the subject. "Ya gonna be alright with dat?"

"I've seen worse. Two days, tops, and I should be able to walk on it again. By then, I should have Leopaula back, and she could meet Kamari." Madeleine smiled down at the infant.

Zola stared at the two, her face etched with a deep, somber expression.

Chapter VII
An Unstoppable Force

As Zola's slap swelled the back of Imamu's neck, he considered returning to the hut to stop her from ruining everything—

"I don't give a damn if ya da Jesus!"

Imamu froze. The neighbors muttered as they glanced, but he was used to being the village outcast.

Ike, he thought. I need to talk to Ike. This won't work without him.

Imamu made his way towards one of the Omo River's offshoots, finding his friend knee deep in the stream, fishing.

"[Surmic] Shoot!" Ike pulled out his wet spear as his prey glistened downstream. "*Another day for you, another day for me.*" He wicked his harpoon and plopped down on the bank, bested.

"Any luck today?"

Ike waved, a half wave, more of a shoo. "*Hey, Imamu.*"

"So, no dinner tonight?" Imamu mocked, smirking.

"We'll manage."

"Hmm."

"Let me guess, you're here to tell me about the tide and the fish migration patterns. That it has nothing to do with luck, or skill, right?"

Imamu struggled to hold in his smirk.

"What's up? You seem different …"

"Oh, nothing. I just found something … something quite interesting on the river today."

"Yeah? Was it a fish? Because that's all I need right now."

Imamu's restrained laughter escaped through his breathing. "No, not a fish. This was much more than even a whale!" Imamu turned to him with a grin reaching his temples. "I found the prince and princess of the UK floating down the Omo River!"

Ike shook his head, exhaling. "Listen, I'm dealing with a lot today. I can't get sidetracked by your—" Ike glanced, finding Imamu tapping on his phone, which was weird because he usually pestered him for hours, begging for his interest. But not today. Today was different.

"Huh," Imamu said. "That was easier than I thought." The British embassy's phone number spelled out before him on the screen. "+251-(0)11-617-0100," he mumbled as he tapped the digits into his mobile.

Ike stood and grabbed his spear. "Come on. How about you put that thing down and help me fish? You'll see, coming home with dinner, it'll make you feel accomplished. Your dad will be proud, too. Maybe even enough to let you keep the generational dagger. Let's go." He reached for the phone, but Imamu pulled it away with a maniacal glee.

"Oh, no, Ike. No, no, no! You want to talk about accomplishment? About fishing? Well, today, I learned that the Omo River can't be cursed. Not after what it spit out at me!"

Ike wanted to slap him, but saw Zola's effects from earlier. He sighed as he reentered the stream.

Imamu pressed call, and moments later …

"[English] Hello? Yes, uh. This is Imamu. I have your prince and princess—"

Ike splashed out of the water and snatched the phone away. With veins evident on his forehead, he froze. Imamu grinned back.

"[Surmic] You—you're not joking …"

"No. No, I'm not."

"[English] Hello?"

Ike glanced down, unsure. He hit the big red icon.

"[Surmic] Imamu, h—have you lost your mind?!"

"Believe me now?"

"Tell me, slowly, in vivid detail, what happened."

Imamu explained everything to Ike. "Then I just saw them freaking out! Don't you see?! *They think I have their baby!*"

"Dear God … you're not kidding. So, what? Are you going to tell them to pay you so you'd give them their baby back?"

"No! They're stranded here! The media's assuming they've been kidnapped, or worse, but they actually ran away! Perhaps the prince is trying to make up for something he did to her, but I don't care. They can't leave, and they have no idea that I know the truth about their daughter."

"Hey! Hey!" He shook his frazzled expression. "This is wrong! And dangerous!"

Imamu swatted the air. "I don't care. This is what I've been waiting for. This is what's needed to show everybody that I'm fit to lead. Unlike Dada, I'll be able to save Yonas, the tribe—everyone!"

"Not like this …"

"Then how?! By following *The Lion Tamer's* way? Or my dad's way? Look at where that's gotten us—stranded in this doomed valley, and always at war with the surrounding tribes! All the while, our brethren slave away in the mines! This is how it's fixed, Ike! This isn't luck, this is how we get our due! Our justice! And this is how we modernize the tribe!"

Ike slapped Imamu upside the head, right where Zola's marks were. "You're going to torture them! Don't you have a moral compass?!"

Imamu scoffed. "I didn't take their baby. I didn't harm it. Hell, I didn't *do* anything! This is all on them for fleeing here, as if we serve no purpose other than to deal with their dirty laundry."

"No, no way. I can't let this happen. I'm going to tell Chief Amari before this blows up."

Imamu held his middle and index finger up, making a V. "I'll give you two out of every ten." Ike opened his mouth, but lost all words. Imamu nodded. "Two … out of every ten." He swiped the phone back and grabbed the spear, wiggling it. "Come on, man! You'd rather go on living like this—*smelling like this?* What if you can't catch anything today? You'll feel shameful, and for what, because some trout outmaneuvered you when it had a home field advantage? Our forefathers lived this way only because they had no other option. Don't you want to spend time doing something more productive? What about Nala? Doesn't she deserve better?"

For the first time, Ike fiddled with his cuticles. He looked at the soft mud of the riverbank, biting his lower lip. The water reflected off his eyes as he gazed at its organized, yet hurried, pattern.

"If we play this right, the Kingdom will pay a lot. So, what do you say?"

Imamu wiggled the peace sign.

Ike blinked rapidly.

Imamu observed the storm of indecisiveness ravaging his friend.

Ike could tell apart the sand from the dirt. The rocks from the boulders. The twigs from the dried grass.

"What'll it be?"

Ike glared from beneath shadowed eyes. "Make it five."

Imamu planted the spear into the soil. "I figured this whole thing out; no way are you getting the same amount. I'll settle at four. Final offer."

Ike looked back at the water. After the thought of not having to do it anymore, he didn't want his dry legs getting wet again. Senioritis kicked in, and his motivation in his current role plummeted. Moving up in the tribe was his lifelong aspiration, or, at the very least, to be part of the tribe's decision-making committee. It came from an honest place. He wanted to help keep with tradition, but daily chores prevented him from ever entering Amari's inner circle. This was his chance.

"Okay."

"Okay?"

Ike nodded. "Yes, yes. Four. I'm in." In the distance, Julian shouted at a tree, alone, in the forest. Ike looked back at Imamu. "Is that him? Is he …" Ike screwed a lightbulb into his ear, "all there?"

"I'm not sure, but he's aggressive. He's not buying my lies. Blonde, yes, but he's smart, perceptive and might also know more than what I take him for. However, he might just be defensive. The good news is that with the princess around, he has to tame himself."

"What're we going to do if things unravel?"

Imamu took a deep breath. "Then … *I'll have to kill him.*"

"How will that help?"

"It'll show the UK that I'm serious. I could start by telling the embassy that I killed the baby, and that he's next if they don't comply. So, it'll be a win-win. Well … not for him. But who cares? He's a jerk."

Ike rubbed his forehead. "See! See what playing nonstop on that phone does to your brain? You don't just kill someone because they're a jerk. Besides, you've never killed anybody. Your body trembles when you merely hold a blade. Do you remember when you tried to convince everybody that the Hamar-tribe trespasser had always been part of our tribe? Or when you fainted while learning how to slaughter a chicken?" Ike picked at his nails, deeper, sharper, redder. "This is an unstable plan. Regardless, if what you're saying is true, then the prince has the royal blood. Meaning, if we're forced to send a message, it'll need to be by taking out the woman."

Imamu's face dropped. He remembered when she held his hands. "No. She's in genuine pain. I couldn't do that to her."

Ike shrugged. "Well, Mr. Morality, it'll either be her or your plan. So, decide now. I can't have you bailing when we're too deep into this."

Imamu uneasily glanced around, narrowing his eyes on Julian. "We'll figure that out later. If the haranchis are wise, and do what we demand, there'll be no need for it to go that far."

Imamu stared back out at the river. A school of fish slipped towards the depths, paused, then continued downstream. Their scales sparkled from the evening sun. They all lived freely. Free to swim wherever they wanted. Free to stop swimming. Free to stay. Free to go. If one of them lost a brother to Ike's spear, it wouldn't mourn that brother. It wouldn't feel compelled to save that brother. It wouldn't have to live with the other fish staring at it, blaming it for all the other lost brothers, sons and fathers. No, that fish would be free. Free to live without guilt, or to be a role model for a new, stupid fish that appeared out of the blue—

"Hey!" Ike snapped his fingers. "So, what's next? What's the plan?"

Imamu returned to reality, nodding as he worked his jaw. "I need something to show the embassy that I'm not joking. The entire world's out looking for these two, so," he opened the camera app, "I've got an idea."

The sun began its descent, reddening the leaves of the trees as if lighting them on fire. The pair returned to the village, leaving behind Ike's spear, with nothing caught for the day.

Chapter VIII
Football or Soccer? No, Basketball

Face red and lowered, Julian stormed out of the hut. The neighbors stared after hearing Zola's reprimand. He scoffed at them before walking around back, unzipping his pants and urinating along the hut's wall.

"Yeah," he nodded, chin raised, "you wanted a show? Well, now you've got one." He sprayed the clay surface with such gusto that he resembled a renowned artist crafting a masterpiece.

The tribespeople looked away. Feeling rejuvenated, Julian appreciated his artwork until the wetted ground beside the hut morphed inward, like a sinkhole. With a squint, he noticed the dirt softening and shaping into a funnel. He shrugged, shook himself off and zipped.

In the far distance, a hollowed-out thud echoed. Giggles and laughter trailed the sound. Julian found a group of children kicking around a deflated basketball. They didn't use goal posts or boundaries—only their imagination. But when they caught sight of him, they stopped and gazed.

"Garra-haranchi, garra-haranchi," some whispered to others.

"No, no, please, carry on," he said, but with a blank stare, they just blinked. "Alright …"

He approached the tree line, eyes darting around as he secluded himself. With the offshoot's burbles intensifying, he surveyed his surroundings once more. In the distance,

Imamu spoke with Ike as Ike fished. With the two distracted, Julian casually stood beside a large trunk and took out his phone. He wicked it a few times before powering it on.

A Samsung logo appeared. The small dose of modernity hit him like a painkiller, blushing his cheeks. As the phone booted up, he glanced at the water. Suddenly, Leopaula giggled.

Julian held his breath, finding his daughter mere steps away. She lay on her back, rattling her toy above her head as she tried to figure it out.

He rubbed his eyes.

She was still there.

"Hey …" Hope and dread enveloped him as he stumbled towards her in a hurry. "Hey! Stay there!"

Her innocent giggles resonated through the forest, haunting him. He found his footing and darted through the foliage. As she rolled behind a tree, he leaped through the air with arms extended. He bounced off the ground, sliding to a sloppy halt. Turning in pain, he couldn't find her anywhere.

"Where'd you go?!" he called into the wilderness. "Hey!"

Imamu and Ike looked over.

"*Keep looking, Joules,*" a familiar woman's voice echoed. She laughed as shivers crawled over Julian's skin.

The color drained from his face, as his palms poured sweat, syphoning away all warmth.

"No, no, no, no, no …" He stumbled back, voice scratching with dread and panic.

In his palm, the Samsung emitted a welcomed shine. However, he kept his focus on the trees. He tried to hide his fear, but his grudging swallow exposed him.

"This—this isn't real. My—my mind must be playing a trick on me. You can't be here. You're not real! You're not—"

Nobody responded.

Nobody was there.

Despite his mind's resistance, his heart desired to see her. The dichotomy nearly cleaved him in two.

Julian shut his eyes and stomped his boot. The sweat clumped his golden bangs together, draping them over his face.

"Y—you're not here!"

Out of nowhere, the mango-shaped basketball pelted Julian in the head. He found himself face-to-face with the dirt.

"Hey!" A child waved. "Give us the ball back, haranchi!"

Julian picked it up and scanned around. He rubbed the worn-out texture of the basketball, trying to grasp his loosening grip on reality. Pressing his fingers into the sphere, he created tiny vortexes over the surface.

He looked back at his phone and kept refreshing the messaging app. Nothing came through. No bars. Only a large cancel symbol sat on the banner. He typed out a text to Francis and left the phone on, hoping it would send later.

Francis will rescue us once he gets this, he thought.

He glanced back at the trees. Nobody else was there.

"Hey!" the child called again. "Some of us have chores to get back to! Hurry up!"

Julian examined the ball.   Then the boy.

He had an idea.

He punted it. The boy, unimpressed, retrieved the orange sphere and rejoined his friends. Julian joined the game, but as time passed, he noticed they weren't playing football, but more of monkey-in-the-middle, with him being the monkey.

"Is that how you want to do it? Well, alright. You asked for it …" Julian paused, narrowed his sight and leaped at the precise moment. He flipped in the air and kicked with tremendous force. The kids strained their necks, barely keeping track of the ball before it pelted a tree and obliterating the bark. They turned back and found Julian landing with eyes closed and a fist coolly tightened before his nose. "GOAL!"

The children's expressions outshined the sun.

The boy from earlier ran over. "Haranchi, haranchi! How'd you do that?!"

"You like that? Well, check this out."

Julian hustled to the ball and began juggling it between his knees. The children gasped every time he fumbled it, but he'd swoop around and save it at the last moment.

"Why don't you use your hands?" one asked.

Still juggling the ball, Julian responded, "Because it's called football, of course, not handball."

A harmonious, "Ohhhh," reverberated.

"You know the rules, don't you?" They all shrugged. "Sounds like we have a lot to learn. For starters, let's not use a basketball as a football ..." They glanced at one another. "*Never mind.*"

Julian demarcated trees for goal posts and explained the game. As the youngsters learned, some taught it to those who weren't fluent in English, triggering a glance from Julian. He listened closely, absorbing as much of the translations as he could.

As the game continued, he learned. Every goal, pass, play, his Surmic vocabulary grew. However, the one phrase they repeated, he couldn't figure out; *garra-haranchi*. And with the sun setting, he wasn't able to set up the context before they all returned home. He approached the lead boy.

"Hey, lad! My name's Julian. What's yours?"

"I'm Zelalem, but I know you Englishmen struggle with anything different, so just call me Zee."

Julian nodded at Zee's bluntness. "Pleasure to make your acquaintance, Zee. Would you do me a favor and teach me, like how I taught you the rules of the game?"

"Sure."

"I'm impressed by your English. How'd that come to be?"

"Well, after the haranchis kicked us off our land, Chief Amari required we all learn the language of our enemy so that we wouldn't get fooled again."

"*Haranchi* ... You keep saying that, but I don't know what it means. Care to explain?"

"White-man."

Julian grinned, nodded and looked around. "What's your language called? I've never heard anything like it before."

"We are the *Mun,* but outsiders call us *Mursi.* So, we speak Mursi, which is a branch of the Surmic language."

Julian recalled Francis's last text. "Y—you're *Mursi?* I thought you were Zee."

"No, I'm not Mursi. *Mursi is the name of our tribe.* Like you are haranchi."

"So, uhm," a crease formed between Julian's brows, "how do you say target? Like you're hunting for a target? A—a wild goat."

Zee scoffed. "We don't hunt goats, you crazy haranchi, we graze them. You know very little about us, huh? We heard that you're quite stupid. And the word for goat is, [Surmic] goat."

Julian exhaled as he bit the corner of his lower lip. He gave it one more shot. "[English] What is it called if that goat was defeated, killed o—or dead? What would you call that?"

Zee kicked the ball up. "Easy, that's a *garra-*[Surmic]goat." Julian froze as the child found joy in his mute fear. He juggled while observing Julian piecing it all together. "[English] I didn't think you could become any paler, ***garra-haranchi.***"

Zee cracked a sinister smile as he held full eye contact. He caught the ball and lodged it beneath his arm before leaving.

Julian stood alone on the field.

The wind blew as he stared out.

He swallowed, mouthing, 'Garra-haranchi …'

74

"… Dead white-man."

Chapter IX
Family Reunion

— Weeks After the Royal Wedding —

"It's dead," Julian said, arms crossed, looking out at Windsor Castle's courtyard. "The proposal's dead, Maddy."

The new sun brightened the manicured lawn before their morning stroll, but not enough to warm it. Madeleine stayed close, preferring Julian's arm over grabbing a light jacket. Their footsteps tapped against the centuries-old cobblestones, with guards lining each side of the pathway. Madeleine wasn't used to the media's attention, so she set their daily alone time just before the tourists arrived.

Beneath the imposing towers and turrets, the couple's bond grew deeper with every one of their walks. Although they usually bubbled with laughter and romance, this morning, the subject at hand kept them at odds.

"They're never going to approve the surplus to be spent towards more hospitals. How many ERs does Slough need, anyway?" Julian pushed his hair back as his to-do list piled up. "By nightfall, I have to figure out how to distribute the funds and pick out my Royal Guard. My father's roster is filled with his money grubbing friends, while settling on a medical sinstitution makes me look like a money grubber."

"But Slough needs it," Madeleine said, slapping her hand three times. "Or at least an expansion. During residency, the waiting rooms were a madhouse. We had to turn patients away!"

The two continued through the gardens, cutting through the perfectly postured guards. Madeleine giggled at their large, fuzzy hats, whereas Julian, having been surrounded by them his entire life, mostly overlooked them.

They approached the main gate. Julian surveyed the land as he leaned on the bricks. His hair billowed towards the courtyard. The street lights turned off, one by one, the brighter the day became.

"Hospitals?"

Madeleine rested against him. He pulled her in close.

"You'll forever be remembered as the prince who helped the people. We'd name it Julian's Sanctuary. Or—or even get one of those stone things on the foundation to venerate you."

Julian shook his head. "I don't recall any prince remembered for such a menial feat. I was gravitating more along the lines of … *conquests*," Madeleine snorted, before realizing he was serious, "like Edward III, and how he seized much of France single handedly."

Madeleine pinched a cheesy smile. "Or like *the Great*," she saluted her arm out, mocking his dream in a German-English accent, *"die Führer, Adolf Hit—"*

Julian smacked her hand. "Quit it!"

While Madeleine had fun pushing him off his high horse, it never amused him. More accustomed to political life, he understood the public tirelessly sought the chance to scrutinize them.

"Name one builder. Nobody remembers builders because anybody could do what they do. But conquerors … conquerors are marbled in history as relics etched into the eternity of time. And if one's not remembered, to what purpose was his life?"

Madeleine rolled her eyes and patted his back. "So, that settles that. Hospitals it is, *your excellence.*"

As they continued their stroll, Julian took a different approach.

"So, these hospitals … why in Slough, of all places? Why not Yorkshire, or the Midlands? *Just Slough,*" he said, as she knew where he was going. "This is politics, Maddy; we can't do whatever we please. The moment the people hear the word, 'Slough' escape our lips, they'll strip everything from us. The Kingdom's wealth isn't permissible for personal gain. Riots would ensue as the patriarchs gawk."

"Those old sags do nothing but gawk," Madeleine mumbled. Julian smiled.

Madeleine observed the castle. The sunlight hit the uppermost bricks of the towers, as shadows encompassed most of the estate.

"The more I learn about the Kingdom, the more I'm convinced it's a gigantic ruse."

Julian nodded with brows raised. "You wouldn't be entirely wrong. Nearly everything has to be done with a," he wobbled his head from side to side, "two-faced approach. You have to, or else you'll end up like my older brother, Napoleon. You know who he is, right?"

"Of course, they have whole lessons about him in uni."

"He tried to fatten his pockets at the expense of the Kingdom, but did so in a piss-poor manner. I never met him, but I learned about his antics. He acted moral and upright, but once he got lazy in keeping up the façade, he fled. When father learned about his true ambitions, he branded him a traitor to the throne. The world doesn't know where he is, or if he's even alive, but it's better that way.

"When he spouted this same *help-the-community* jargon that you're spewing, it spiked the public's curiosity, until they discovered the truth. They'll do the same with you until they find out you're simply pursuing a personal ambition with the treasury. Maddy, this is an idea that you need to scrub from your mind."

Bush after bush, fountain after fountain, the two sauntered child-free through the garden with guards flanking the path. Each one focused straight ahead, standing firm, barely blinking. Every once in a while, a guard glanced, but he'd return his sights forward before Julian would address the insubordination. However, one guard stood out from the rest. He didn't just glance. When Napoleon was mentioned, *he glared,* stopping Julian.

Madeleine unknowingly continued ahead, yapping into thin air.

"What was that?" Julian asked the guard, who stood mute.

"What was what?" Madeleine turned around.

Julian's stern side rarely appeared in public. However, when it showed, its severity was never warranted. Worried for the guard, Madeleine hurried back.

"Hey, Juley, let's just go. I'm sure it was nothing."

"Oh, so *now* you're doing your job? What is your problem, guard? Do you suppose it's permissible to give me those eyes? I recognize those eyes. They reveal your hunger for what's not yours. So, I ask you again, why'd you give the Royal Couple those eyes?"

The guard kept his composure, mouth shut, emotions in check. He didn't blink, but not out of fear. He worked too hard to get into the castle, that he refused to abandon it all over a mere argument with Julian.

Julian scoffed. "You actually think you could do better—"

The other guards peeked at the commotion. Madeleine shoved between them, facing the guard. He locked his red-rimmed eyes with hers. Her mouth poured open. "*Francis?*"

From the outside, he resembled every other guard; tall, bearskin headgear, chinstrap under the lip, red buttoned uniform, jet-black shoes. But to Madeleine, his charged, light irises gave him away.

She threw her arms around him. He remained upright, refusing to break posture. "How's this possible?! When'd you join the guard?"

Francis returned a blank expression. "Permission to speak, Lady-Madeleine?"

"Pfft, *Lady-Madeleine.* Francis, quit it! You're actually here! I haven't seen you in … I don't know! This is bonkers! How've you been?! God—it's been years since … *since you left.* How'd you get here? I didn't see your request to apply."

"Permission to speak, Lady-Madeleine?"

Head jerked back, she stood aghast.

"Granted," Julian called from behind.

"I'm here to protect the Kingdom—"

"Wait a minute," Julian said. "You're my brother-in-law? But I didn't see you at the wedding. Where were you? Everyone was in attendance."

As Madeleine's gaze bounced around, not realizing how out-of-touch she's been with her life prior to royalty, Francis turned to Julian, this time scowling directly at him.

"I had to guard the castle, Sir-Julian." His voice rasped with a restrained ferocity.

"Guard the castle? Like how you're guarding it now? You see … *Francis,* was it? I could have you disgracefully excused for what you did."

Madeleine flinched. "Julian, stop it—"

"Because I'm fairly certain you were eavesdropping, like a treacherous spy." Francis remained calm as Julian continued. "I can have you thrown into the dungeons. Or worse, back to Slough, with all the other street rats."

Francis stared forward. Unmoved. Unthreatened.

As Julian waited, a smirk stretched across his face.

"Juley, I think we should—"

"Very well, *Sir-Francis,* what's your opinion on how we should handle the surplus?"

"You want my input on how the Kingdom should distribute funds?" Francis iterated, as Julian lifted his chin, waiting to hear some tree-hugger position. The chilly wind sliced through the conversation, as if revealing Francis's inner motive. "Handouts make the weak, weaker. If the Kingdom gives Slough anything out of pity, it'll sink them deeper into despair."

Madeleine stepped back. "… Francis?"

Julian's sneer eased into a smile of intrigue. On the outside, Francis resembled the typical guard. But with a fine lens, Julian noticed the difference. This guy wasn't a pushover. His composure revered respect and authority. And nothing could deter him from his goals.

Julian unexpectedly felt an inclination towards him, unlike that of the candidates he'd interviewed. Those imaginary conquests suddenly became realizable, especially with someone like Francis by his side.

Although Francis was the one holding the rifle, Julian felt entitled enough to mess with his uniform, picking at the sash and fiddling with the epaulet. "Tell me, a man such as yourself, do you like this job?" Like a samurai before his master, Francis kept his mouth closed. Madeleine bounced her gaze between the two. "Answer the question," Julian said, flaring a bit of his harshness.

"I'd do anything that promotes the prosperity of the Kingdom. Regardless of whether or not I like it."

Julian glanced at the castle, then at Francis. *"Anything, huh?"*

Understanding the challenges of Slough, and wanting to help her brother, Madeleine had an idea. Julian posted his hand up, already on board with her proposition.

He scanned Francis from head to toe. "Sir-Francis, how'd you like to be my Royal Guard?"

Chapter X
One with the Tribe

— Current Day —

"Congratulations," Zola said, taking the sleeping Kamari from Madeleine's arms. Madeleine clasped her nursing bra, leaned back and exhaled. "You're officially a mother of the tribe now."

"*Mother of the tribe*," she whispered to herself. The weight of the title gave her the comfortable languidness of home.

But nothing around her resembled Windsor Castle. No officials burdened her with upholding formalities. No *Piers Morgans* ridiculing her every human tendency. A calm embedded into the fibers of the hut, embracing her and giving her the motherhood she'd only ever dreamed of.

She didn't shy away from the physical requirements of Omo, having grown up in poverty. It triggered a nostalgia of simpler days. However, the lack of hygiene that came with it remained unwelcomed.

Zola noticed. She fetched her a set of clean garments and handmade soap. A while later, Madeleine stood before her, head to toe, resembling the Mursi women. Zola piled on beaded necklaces, bracelets and anklets, treating Madeleine like the daughter she never had, and loving every minute of it.

"This is too much …"

Zola nodded at her masterpiece.

Madeleine gyrated her wrists, jiggling the stacked bracelets. Zola rattled her own, smiling along with her. However, when Madeleine glanced at Kamari, she lowered her hands. Then her face. Then she lowered her face into her hands.

Zola rubbed her back. "Now, now."

The grief and sadness overwhelmed her, and no matter how hard she tried to preoccupy her mind, the floodgates of emotion burst open. Memories of Leopaula's smile flooded her thoughts. The tears streamed down her cheeks, leaving a trail of sorrow in their wake. Waiting became unbearable, preventing her from finding any joy with her new friend.

"Have you ever been to Koka Hospital?" she asked in a cracked voice.

"Tsk. Almost nobody been dare. Too far for small cuts, and we'd never make it with big ones."

"Imamu said that's where they took her."

"All I know is it be northwest from here."

Suddenly, Julian rushed into the hut, as pale as a ghost. "What is that? What're you wearing? Take those off right now!"

Just then, Imamu also entered with the camera readied on his phone. Seeing Madeleine dressed up, his eyes widened as he hurried towards Zola. "[Surmic] Mama, I need to speak to you."

Zola glared at Julian, while pushing her son away. "Hold on—" Imamu pulled her outside. Once out, Julian started hollering. "Hurry, that boy's trouble and Kamari's in there! What's so important?"

"Why'd you dress her up like that? She'll be able to blend in!" He knew that a ransom photo to the embassy of Madeleine dressed as a Mursi would reveal their location and foil his plan.

Zola raised her eyebrows. *"Oh, her? You mean Madeleine?* Or do you mean [English] PRINCESS," Zola smacked Imamu upside the head, "MADELEINE," she smacked again, "OF THE," another smack, "UNITED," a final one, "KINGDOM!" Her eyes nearly popped out of their sockets. "Have you lost your mind, boy?!"

Every smack lowered Imamu, but Zola followed him down, concluding her onslaught. He said nothing, fearful to conjure another round of blows.

"You—you—you panda-shaped buffoon! This isn't some tribe you're messing with. THEY WILL END US FOR THIS!" Zola shook her head while keeping her eyes on him. "Regardless of what you did to their daughter, I won't let you hurt that girl. And you damn well aren't harming that prick boy either! I can't wait to tell your father!"

Without thinking it through, Imamu smacked his mother and held his finger up. "You say one word to that man, and I'll slit all their throats, as well as yours, tonight!"

He shamefully lowered his finger.

"This isn't about their daughter, is it? There's more. Tell me. What do you know? Where's the girl?"

Imamu looked down, panting, frowning, pinching his lips. "You and Dada have never believed in me! Nothing but Yonas-this, Yonas-that. Well, look at where that's gotten him! It's by time I save this tribe from Dada's mindless, hesitant rule!"

"Tell me," Zola spaced her words, "where   is Leopaula?"

He scoffed. "Until I see this through, no one will ever know."

Imamu barged back in and grabbed the two Royals, ignoring his brother's wails. "[English] You're coming with me."

Julian tried to break away, but Imamu's grip was ironclad. He pulled them out and stormed off. Madeleine anxiously glanced at Zola. The two helplessly locked eyes until Imamu shoved them into his hut.

"You'll be spending your days here, until I get your daughter!" he shouted, but then realized his out-of-place tone.

"But I liked the other hut, with Zola."

"It's *Chieftess* Zola to you, and no. Guests aren't permitted to stay overnight in the chieftain's residence. For the remainder of your time, you'll be here."

Julian leaned away from everything with a wrinkled nose. A chaotic assortment of mismatched electronic items scattered haphazardly around the hut, on the sleeping mat and over the earthen floor. Remnants of gadgets, guts of devices, semiconductors and integrated circuit boards clung to the walls. Wires snaked their way like tangled vines in a jungle. The tribal artifacts mixed between the electronics resembled the warring factions battling over Imamu's soul.

The juxtaposition left the Royal Couple confused. Even the air in the hut held thick with disarray. The chaos manifested in the physical space emitted a staleness. Madeleine observed the contrasted monochromatic sanctuary with a frowned lip. Imamu regretted treating her so harshly, but despite feeling vulnerable, his plan hung heavier than his concern over his appearance.

"Something wrong?" he asked defensively.

"Yes, in fact, there is—"

Madeleine stepped between the two. "Tell us about Leopaula! How'd you find her? What exactly is her condition and what's being done to get her back? How's there no update after so many hours?"

Julian spotted Imamu making small, jittery movements with his fingers.

"She was lying on the riverbank a few minutes before I found you. She was still breathing, so I took her to the caravan. They said they'll have to watch her for a few days at the hospital. Don't worry, they have formula and toys and *whatever*." He flicked his hand.

Madeleine tilted her head. "I thought you said you had to do chest compressions …"

"Yes," he said, cognizant of his misaligned stories.

He turned to exit, but she reached for his arm, rattling the bracelets. Julian stopped her, subtly shaking his head. She ignored him.

"Then, let's go to Koka. Now!"

Julian mutely observed Imamu's protruding jaw muscles.

"As I said, the hospital is more than an hour's drive from here. And considering the terrain, it's at least a five-day walk—even longer with your ankle. So, you could either trudge through the wilderness for nearly a week to find that they've already brought her here, or wait for three or four days, and she'll be returned to you, safe and sound. Which would you prefer?"

Imamu left before getting a response. Madeleine looked at Julian, speechless. He was sternly mute. Suddenly, Imamu re-entered and snapped a picture of the two. He nodded at the photo before putting the phone away. "This is for the hospital to compare you with the baby."

Julian's ears flushed red. "We're the only white people here; nobody needs a picture."

Imamu tried to leave.

"Wait," Madeleine said, grabbing his arm. "Give me your phone."

He looked at her grip, then at her eyes. Madeleine found him processing again. His rapid blinking stopped as he locked in a response.

"Why?" he scoffed. "*You want to talk to your baby?* Do you expect her to respond? Do you hear yourself?"

"No, that's not what I meant."

Imamu fixed his bag, making sure it, and his phone, weren't going anywhere.

Madeleine scowled.

He held the act.

She tightened her glare.

He stared back.

She fumed.

He breathed normally, hand tightening over the strap.

She zeroed in on the sack, ready to snatch.

In the corner, Julian felt ignored. "Where'd you find all this stuff?" he asked, fiddling with a radio's knob. "And why're you the only one around here with electronics?"

Imamu slapped Julian's hand away. "I scavenge."

"So, *you collect trash.*"

"No. I find value in things people overlook."

"Ah," Julian snapped his fingers, "I get it now; you're a bottom feeder."

Imamu tsked.

"You have no idea what I am. I'm unlike anyone you've ever met …

And that should terrify you."

Chapter XI
We were Settled …

"Is that supposed to be a threat?" Julian asked.

Madeleine's eyes ping-ponged between the two. Simmering, Imamu kept quiet. She focused on his satchel, ready to snatch it, but froze when she noticed him picking his cuticles. He had a pattern—same as hers. Claw, scrape, pick. Déjà vu hit when she looked at Julian, waiting for a response.

"Well?"

Imamu scanned his captive, from his hair to his boots. He couldn't harm him because physically, Julian would dominate. But intellectually, he towered.

He stopped picking at his nails and momentarily closed his eyes. To succeed, he had to veil his intentions.

"*I'm sorry,*" Imamu said. "This situation is stressful on me, too. I apologize if I came off as anything other than helpful."

No, Madeleine thought, leaning closer after spotting it like a wolf amid sheep. His sincerity was an act. Whatever's eating away at him, he just now burrowed it deeper.

"Yeah," Julian said, chin raised. "That's what I thought. I mean, look at yourself. Look at what you've amassed. How could someone live like this?"

"Juley, stop."

Imamu lowered his forehead.

"No, seriously. This community is composed of strong, lean men, and here before us, this guy's living in a brat's paradise. And a sloppy one at that. Look, even his iPod's busted." Julian held up the device, but Imamu swiped it from his grip.

///

I spotted what perplexed others in him. His eyes, soft and sky-blue, confused you into fearing while also admiring him.

But I'm not like others.

Those irises served as a mere tool in his arsenal. Whenever he wanted something, I suppose all he had to do was stare deep into the soul of the poor sap before him, and that fool would eventually do his bidding.

I glanced at Madeleine. Did she fall for these eyes, or has she also seen through the illusion? That wound on her face didn't appear out of thin air.

I glared back at Julian before holding up my 2003 white 3rd generation iPod with its internals gutted.

"You might see this as trash. But for me, this is invaluable—even without a screen. I repurposed the touch-sensitive scroll wheel as an attenuator for this high intensity diode—"

"What—what's an attenuator?" Madeleine asked.

"An adjuster."

Head tilted, Julian crossed his arms. "And why's any of this matter?"

I slammed the diode on the table and connected my solar charged battery pack. Time to shut him up.

Madeleine moved back. He didn't. Fool.

I rotated the attenuator. The laser shot out, striking his elbow.

Julian sarcastically clapped. "Congratulations. You've discovered light, something the rest of the world—"

I maxed out the power. The laser hit peak energy and tattooed his arm. He jerked out of the way, allowing the beam to scorch through the straw wall and race across the village. It left behind a ring of embers and my neighbor shouting at me to stop burning his hut again. With a counter-clockwise rotation on the iPod scroll-wheel, the device powered down, and the light diminished.

I blew out the small flame and shifted the reeds over the hole. Julian was speechless; just as I wanted him.

"*The rest of the world* can't comprehend my potential."

His once rebuking eyes strained when they looked around at my *trash*. He realized my ingenuity, my prowess. His blinks became few and spaced.

"I—I took—" he swallowed, "I took you as a bottom feeder, but you're just a—a run-of-the-mill, nerd—"

Face to face with him, I felt his breathing as he inhaled mine.

Scorning into his sapphire irises, I extinguished all ambiguity tied to my intention. "I see things for what they're truly worth, Prince Julian."

Madeleine placed her hand on my shoulder. "You're hurting—"

///

Imamu abruptly broke away, almost like he snapped out of a hypnosis.

"I—I'm sorry." He rushed out.

From afar, Zola followed him with her eyes. She approached the couple, this time knocking.

"Everything okay in here?"

"Zola!" Madeleine hugged her.

Julian distanced himself, muttering, "Weird kid, from a weird mom." The two looked at him, unamused. "Whatever. I'm going to lie down for a bit."

"Let's go outside," Madeleine suggested.

They sat with backs resting against a pair of trees. Few children kicked the ball around, as some young men trained for their donga fight. Madeleine found the people carrying on, without a concern or worry for Leopaula's whereabouts. She regarded the castle and how at that very moment, there must've been red and blue flashing lights swirling the walls, as the story developed. Reporters, medics, police—you name it. However, here it was just another Wednesday.

"Zola, Imamu is the last person to have seen Leopaula. I need to know if he's … is he …" Her lips moved, but she hesitated.

"*All there?*" Zola asked. Madeleine regretfully nodded.

Julian, in the hut, crossed his hands behind his head, listening in.

"He seems … different from the others."

"Yes. But wouldn't you also be a bit strange if ya found your grandfather in pieces?"

"What?"

Zola stared into the void. "I must've asked him about it a thousand times, and every time I replay it in my head, it's like I was dare."

"What happened? What do you mean by … pieces?"

Zola bounced her gaze around. A tsk escaped every few seconds as the memories resurfaced. She picked up a twig and carved two lines on the ground, followed by one more with a tremble rattling her hand. "It happened in three phases."

— Phase One —

///

At 14-years-old, we lost Imamu's grandfather, Haile. It hurt us all because he was not only our spiritual leader, but also our first chieftain. The most painful part was how he was found. We overlooked the possibility of it being a murder because of the grisly condition he was in. It couldn't be possible for anyone to be so vile. It just couldn't.

It all started when Imamu vanished. Here, when a child goes missing, it's not a big deal. Exploring is part of growing up within the tribe and the children always show up when the food's ready. Always. But not this time. Nearly a full day, and his plate remained untouched. The village rushed out, hoping to find him before sunset.

When only a glimmer of light remained, a fisherman spotted him beside one of Omo River's offshoots.

He told us he found Imamu in a trance, his only movement coming from his spaced apart blinks, fixed towards Haile's body blocking the flow of the river. Since that day, I haven't seen my boy as he once was. He stopped talking to everybody, even that sweet Nala girl he daydreamed about. He'd distance himself, spending long hours, at times, days, just staring out at the water.

I tried snapping him out of it, but the most I could pry out were the words 'dark red, red, pink, clear.' Then silence, before he'd reenter his trance, fearing that one day his insides would scatter, like Haile's.

We had Imamu join his older brother, Yonas, on hunts and expeditions, hoping he'd snap out of it. But after the first attempt, Yonas insisted we should let him grieve and find his own way. That's who Yonas was. The calm, easy going leader. He recognized his little brother's pain, but didn't think forcing him to move past it would work.

Instead, Yonas found that orange ball there and started a small sports field for the children. He figured it would be an easy alternative to the donga stick fighting ceremony most youngsters were being primed for, while also fueling their competitive side. The youth magnetized towards it, all except Imamu. So, Yonas decided to simply let time heal his younger brother, and to cheer him up however he could.

He had this annoying habit during dinner. Whenever Amari and I were in the middle of a tense conversation, Yonas would flash a goofy face at his little brother to lift his spirits. Imamu would laugh, sometimes spitting up food, while it effectively pissed me off.

This behavior couldn't go on forever. Eventually, Imamu reached the age where he had to start pitching into the community. First on every parent's mind is to enroll their child into hunting. But because of his phobia, Yonas recommended we assign him another role. He didn't have a knack for building huts or farming. So, we tasked him with collecting firewood. It made him contribute while remaining in his comfort zone.

One day, during his rounds, Imamu crossed a wild animal. Usually, he'd stand absolutely still whenever he'd encounter a predator, but in this case, he was out in the open. So, he took refuge in a nearby cave until the threat passed. With a peek, he found the predator nearing, before stopping, stepping back from the entrance and fleeing.

Imamu tipped his head back as he caught his breath and waited for the footsteps to saunter away. However, a gentle hum emanated from the deep crevices of the cave. He turned to find the grotto leading into an inky black darkness, as if a black-hole, pulling in the sparkles which glimmered off the rocks lodged in the side.

The whirring sound continued, pulling more than his attention. He stepped deeper into the cavern, using the wall as a guide, noticing the silvery-white surface wasn't rough, but more so, like smooth polished steel. It funneled him in as if a calm flowing stream gelling his soul. He described the sensation as an unreal energy entering his body that gave him hope, extracting him from his depression.

If it meant no more sulking around, I didn't mind him talking about the cave. He'd constantly revisit and stay long stretches of time like a monk, sometimes spending the night there. However, when the tribe began complaining about the lack of firewood, he had to improvise. He chipped off a piece of the cavern's wall and carried it with him wherever he went. He kept it in that stupid bag he always has slung across his shoulder. To me, it looked no different from an oddly colored lump of coal, but who am I to tell him what'll make him feel better?

A few days passed, followed by a few weeks. Amari chose Yonas to be his successor and therefore received the tribe's generational dagger. Yonas let Imamu play out his imagination with it, hoping it would make him comfortable handling a blade.

It didn't.

If anything, it made Imamu more lost in his fantasy world. Yonas later pushed him into the sports field as a last attempt to curb his social anxiety. Most players received cheers from their fathers, but Amari had to oversee the donga ceremony, so only Yonas stood on the side, rooting for his brother.

During one particular match, Imamu tripped and the stone fell out of his bag. He abandoned the game and hurried after it, but a spectator occluded it with his foot. The man raised it towards the sky, squinting.

"[Surmic] Excuse me, sir. May I have that back?" Imamu asked, reaching before flinching. "L—Lieutenant D'jen, I'm sorry. I didn't know that was you."

Yonas hustled over, picking up his pace with each stride, as he was fully aware of Amari's second-in-command, D'jen, and his short temper.

"Boy," D'jen said. "Where'd you find this?"

Chapter XII
… Then the British Came

— Phase Two —

"Hey, give my brother his stone back!"

D'jen lowered his eyes. He refocused on Imamu. "And can you show me this *special* cave?"

"Sure. It's magnificent, with the walls shining and—"

"Give," Yonas said, stepping between the two. "It back."

D'jen locked horns with the young contemporary, enveloping him in his shadow. "Listen, boy. You might've been named Amari's successor, but you'll always remain beneath me—"

"Now!"

D'jen scoffed, impressed, yet irritated. He threw the stone, turned and left. As Imamu scrambled to pick it up, Yonas spoke to him, while his gaze planted on D'jen's back.

"Don't talk to that man. I have a bad feeling about him."

"But he said that if I showed him the cave, it'd help a lot of people. Apparently, this stone is called 'lithium,' and the world needs it because there are so many that are hurting, like me."

Yonas helped Imamu up. "Lithium, huh? Dada used to say that word a lot when I was younger. Regardless, everything from D'jen's mouth always sounds enticing, when in reality, it's toxic. Do not trust that man."

Imamu later told me that the lithium's effects were too magical to keep for himself, that doing so gave him the guilt of a millionaire's greed. So, being the kind soul that he was, he took D'jen's offer, hoping it to help others suffering the same pain. However, mere hours after he showed D'jen the cave, government officials swarmed our village.

It's important to know that the tribes and the Ethiopian government always harbored animosity. Decades ago, they pushed us all off our land. Are you curious why? Perhaps for building schools, hospitals, or maybe even roads.

No. They established a national park.

Imagine if someone forced you from your home because they believed your land was aesthetically pleasing to others. After giving us nothing, they did the same thing to the Dizi, the Nyangatom, the Me'en and the Suri. Worst of all, they installed a hydroelectric dam that messed up the flow of the Omo River, causing most of our livestock to perish.

These interactions with the government started the rivalries between the tribes of Omo, causing nonstop friction. So, understand Amari's hesitation when D'jen brought those same officials to our land.

However, this time, they came with new, unusual people. People, bright like you, with colored hair and eyes. They were paler, *yet darker*, than anybody we've ever met.

Yonas labeled them 'haranchis.' He morphed two words in Surmic, meaning *puffed up chest* and *vomit*.

After a lot of convincing, Amari joined the meetings. They made deals and signed contracts. D'jen played the role of interpreter and translator between the three parties. Back then, he was the only one who spoke English—something that, as time would tell, became our downfall.

Imamu, worried about the cave, spied from the bushes, motionless. No different from how he concealed himself from a predator.

He saw everything. Day in and day out. The handshakes, the translations, the signatures. Let me tell you, ethical agreements shouldn't take weeks. Moral contracts don't include shifty eyes. Fair trade doesn't involve whispers. But what stood out most to Imamu were D'jen's winks.

He said one time, D'jen spotted him. He looked him right in the eye and flexed a disconcerting smile, just enough to show off that golden tooth of his. After that day, the meetings ceased. No more haranchis. No more government officials.

What replaced them were lines, bright and red, painted on the ground. Us on one side, engineers and workers on the other. Some wore suits, like the men from our government, while others sported construction hats, wielding pickaxes and machinery. After demarcating work zones, they posted signs, lots and lots of signs. They knew we couldn't read them. *They knew.*

Then they brought in the guards who stopped anybody from crossing their precious red lines. They flanked the border, rifles at the ready, reviving the same problem as before because our livestock and access to the river remained on the forbidden side.

Déjà vu? No. Someone instructed them.

Amari objected, claiming that this wasn't part of the agreement. But the haranchis just shrugged, rolled their eyes and pointed at the signs.

We restored some of our dried-up wells, but they weren't enough to sustain us. Amari demanded D'jen to undo everything.

D'jen left that day and without a translator, the haranchis made it very clear with their hands: cross this line—bullet between the eyes.

And so, we grew hungry.

If you haven't ever heard the cries of starving children, you'll never truly understand Yonas's response.

The haranchis unfolded seats and ate their packaged food in plain view. They watched us diminish for entertainment and killed our cattle for play. That's when we realized it—we were being ethnically cleansed.

Every day, Amari waited at the border for D'jen. First, it hit the children. Then, the old. Soon after, the hunger reached everyone. Only Yonas's voice sounded throughout the village. We all remember him, standing in the center, provoking resistance.

"We can't idly sit by as they starve us to death!"

Those who wanted to help could barely raise their sight to him. Hollows burrowed beneath the eyes, casting a shadow over their cheekbones. Ribs showed. Shoulders slumped. We looked like a colony of lethargic bees, helplessly staring at the intruder to the hive.

Only Amari held onto hope. That hope, for the first time, brought arguments into our marriage. I refused to attribute existence to our occupiers, while he commanded everybody to learn their language. Our shouting matches reached such severity that Imamu couldn't sleep.

As he approached Yonas's hut, he noticed that the border guards were missing.

He stopped before the red line, keeping himself hidden.

Did they take the night off? He spotted the haranchis turning out their trailer lights, echoing off their last few laughs as they tossed beer bottles at their trash pile.

Imamu had an idea.

He remained absolutely still until, one by one, the lights turned out, and one after the other, the snores began. He took a deep breath and stepped over the red line.

Nothing happened.

He brought his second foot along.

Again, nothing.

He told me that his thrashing heart nearly cracked his ribcage. But he agreed with Yonas; we couldn't just let them starve us.

Imamu slinked into their camps. Litter lined their trailers, scattered aside the worn-out construction equipment. The air hung heavy with the scent of machinery and earth, mingled together in a violent clash. Even the grass crept out from beneath their campers, doing whatever it could to push out the intruders.

These people … they came, made themselves at home, harbored no shame. No dignity. No respect.

A helicopter parked in the distance, with the cockpit door flung open, and no sign of the pilot. Welded to the landing skid were heavy duty ankle-shackle hooks, with a heavier duty net cinched and laid beside it, half filled with bulky lithium ores.

The ores calmed Imamu down. He might've not had the same valor or bravery as Yonas, but that cave was his equivalence of home. Not only were the haranchis invading, they were literally taking it.

When he approached the trailers, he told me it didn't differ from tiptoeing past a pride of sleeping lions. At first, he only wanted to tamper with the haranchi's belongings, to irritate them or slow their progress. He hoped it would've been enough to make them leave. But when his eyes caught a glance of the gadgets and electronics, it gave him the same calmness as the stones.

He had another idea.

He grabbed anything that fit into his satchel. Then he went back and took more. And more. And more. That's how he got that phone, and how I got the MP3 player. But soon enough, the devices ran out of juice, so he snatched solar chargers and battery packs. As everybody tried to survive, Imamu's eyes scrolled, swiped and bulged as he saw how the rest of humanity lived. He told me the device had some special chip inside that lets him see and talk to anybody around the world, from anywhere.

I didn't care because none of it mattered. The workers just replenished their missing items while their border remained guarded. However, the next thing he found did matter.

Their guns.

— Phase Three —

Imamu told me that their rifles were no closer to him than you are to me. That moment became his most replayed memory. Not finding Haile, or the cave, or even involving D'jen. No. His regret comes from not grabbing those weapons and slaughtering every last one of those invaders.

In their clothes, they slept, blackout drunk over the couches and sprawled across the floor while living in squalor.

He considered killing just one, to cause them panic, thinking there's a murderer in their midst. However, he feared the sound would awaken the others, including those in nearby trailers. He then contemplated killing them all. Because if one survived, he'd be like a parasite, growing and spreading into more.

He nodded and reached for the rifle.

His hand froze. He'd seen adults use them a hundred times, but as his arm hung midway towards the barrel, he told me he couldn't stop picturing Haile. The thought of blood spraying, dismembered limbs, revealed organs … it was too much.

His hand fell.

It wasn't him.

He always said, 'Mama, they might've invaded our land, but I won't let them invade my soul and turn me into something I'm not.'

He turned to leave, but then spotted a small, brass pointed tube. Holding it towards the moonlight, he thought of a different approach.

Later, Imamu poured out thousands of bullets before his older brother.

"Are—are you sure you got them all?" Yonas's eyes darted as he asked, struggling to count the bronze casings.

Imamu nodded. Yonas sprung for the generational dagger, but Imamu swiped it first. "No!"

"You've done enough, little brother! And you've done well, but with one call, they'll restock. We need to strike, and it needs to be now!"

Yonas stood, but Imamu gripped his arm.

"Please!" Tears connected his eyes to his mouth and chin. "I've brought all of this upon us! Don't make it worse!"

Yonas grabbed his shoulder. "None of this is your fault, and it's not your responsibility to fix it. D'jen abandoned us, and Dada's too delusional to see that. This is my tribe, and I will protect it!" He rushed out.

///

Zola's lip trembled, magnified by her plate. She covered her face with a single palm, as the other held onto her restless knee. Madeleine hesitated to pat her back. Julian glanced outside, then at a gleaming dagger hidden beneath the electronics. Zola wiped her tears away, but the redness remained in her eyes. In a cracked voice, she continued.

///

They held Yonas up like a trophy.

Bloodied and bruised, his head hung as we all looked on, helpless. A bullet lodged in his side, which they didn't rush to dress. He needed help, but they had other intentions for him.

Yonas's squad littered the ground as the haranchis reloaded their weapons. The sight that caused the most anguish wasn't that of Yonas toeing the line of death, but rather Imamu, screaming and reaching out as Amari dragged him to safety.

I can still hear his cries now. His glazed eyes, tongue pulled back, jaw extended, strained cheeks. Meanwhile, Yonas attempted making that goofy face, but the swelling was too severe. Even today, the image haunts us all.

They flooded our huts. They seized those who couldn't flee and forced them to mine the lithium. All the while, the other haranchis pointed—taunting, laughing, mocking.

I'll say it again—*they knew*. In fact, they planned it. You don't hold up your side of a deal by bringing a military-quantity of ammunition to an excavation site. Unfair agreements would prompt us to resist. Starvation wasn't their weapon; it was their catalyst. Because once they opened their locked reserves, we learned they brought more munition than food. What Imamu swiped was merely a blade of grass from their vast countryside.

My boy you see today was once as promising as Kamari. His smile used to radiate such brightness that it became infectious. But now …

I tried many things to raise his spirit, but nothing sticks. He's become the only 22-year-old in the village that doesn't contribute, and I can't help but be strict with him.

However, I still fear whenever I see him go off alone towards the river. Because when carrying guilt like that … *harm becomes the only way to feel anything.*

Chapter XIII
The Omo Effect

///

Madeleine rested her head back as a congested sigh escaped. Her jaw muscles tensed. The wind slowed, settling the heat onto the village. Beads of sweat glistened her forehead. She pulled her fingers in, raking deep scarring lines into the dirt, as she made a fist.

I can't trust him, she thought.

Everything Zola shared supported what Madeleine noticed the moment she grabbed Imamu's hands on the riverbank.

"[English] Ya never told me," Zola said. "Why are you here? We don't get many visitors, especially someone like you." Madeleine's foot wobbled as she kept quiet. "You're making this harder on yaself."

"Well, how am I supposed to react when my daughter's missing, and the last person who saw her is an angry lad that's in pain? You want to know why I'm here? Yeah? Because my marriage was hanging on by a thin thread. This was the only place we could go without the bloody paparazzi and reporters bombarding us at every corner. Same goes for those *fans* who believe my life is some sort of fairy tale. We couldn't walk outside the castle gates except to have microphones shoved in our faces. We had to lie and hide to get out, so I can't imagine what Imamu would do to flee from his turmoil. Coming here was our final effort to repair our family, but it just made everything worse."

Zola situated Kamari as she held her gaze on Madeleine. "This valley … I, too, used to tink it was cursed. That was before I seen its effect. As consistent as the river flows, I real-eyesed dat it only does one thing; it reveals the truth."

"Truth? What truth?"

"Well, for starters, we assumed Yonas would be our next chieftain. But this valley revealed we weren't worthy of his lead. We viewed Imamu with promise, but his true character is now apparent. We thought D'jen was a loyal lieutenant, but yet again, this place showed us just how loyal he was. As for you … who knows? Perhaps something in your life is dishonest and Omo brought you here to show you the reality. Not some," she flicked her hand, "marital problem."

"No," Madeleine, with heavy eyes drained of energy, shook her head, "I'm here because of my stupid brother. Regardless, it's nice. Especially how you don't stare at me as if I were an artifact. Yes, some of your people glanced as we entered, but nothing like back home."

"What do you mean?"

"We got married eight years ago. I was just some nurse from Slough, a downtrodden city beside the castle, while he was the prince. It took everybody by surprise because there's an unwritten rule: Nobody leaves Slough. If you're born there, you die there. So, for me to have not only gotten out but also moved into the castle … well, that didn't come without some backbiting and glares.

"I was only eighteen at the time, while Julian was 27. That was a bit of a talking point, but not too unusual. What they loved to balk about was how, for the last eight years, I couldn't conceive. They had fully blown talk shows, chit chatting for hours on end about nothing other than how my tainted Slough-body wasn't *biologically suited* to house royal sperm. This rubbish went on for nearly a decade.

"The rumors eventually won me over, especially because of the miscarriages. The media never learned about them, but it made me buy into their gossip. It was as if my body rejected any of our efforts. Like *I* was the problem.

"I hoped Leopaula's birth would shut them up, but boy, was I wrong. What sort of society criticizes a baby? Saying things like her body's disproportionate, or that she's too dark—she's a baby!" The memories strained Madeleine's mind as she tried to flush them out. "But here, there's none of that." She inhaled Omo's lack of pollution. "It's nice."

Some tribal women chiseled, shaped and decorated lip plates for their daughters. They dabbed white spots along the circumference, keeping each impression equally spaced from the former. A few men worked on constructing a hut, calling to one another as they held support beams. Others grazed their animals in the distance. The scent of crackling wood carried through the village as the families prepared supper. The woodchips popped and hissed beneath the pots.

"I'm sorry about what happened to you," Madeleine said. "I wouldn't wish that on anybody. But I need to know. Did Imamu tell you anything else about Leopaula—anything at all? I can't help but feel like he's not being honest with me."

Zola scoffed. "Nobody here knows what's really going on inside that boy's head. Although people in pain usually scream the truth, Imamu's silence means his agony is far beyond our imagination. Yonas meant the world to him. So, until he's back, we won't ever understand Imamu.

"You might've lost a daughter, but that day, I lost Yonas, my son and my husband. Ammi, now, is nothing but a shell of his former self. He's broken, desperate and dangerous. First stabbed in the back by his best friend, then losing everything for his people … Yonas was his firstborn. So, you should understand his burden."

Madeleine tilted her head. "Isn't Yonas also your first born? Wait … how old is Yonas?"

"Yonas is the son of Amari's late wife. I'm his step-mother and he's older than me by one year; 40. Like you, I also married into *royalty* young, but I'm glad I did. Amari was the man of my dreams, regardless of our age gap. After everything, Mad-girl, *the main thing I want back is my husband*. Because our territorial, fearful chieftain today … that's not the man I married.

"So, I understand what you're going through, girl. I really do, but you don't understand us. Every single person here has lost *a Leopaula*. But unlike you, we know where they are, but, girl, we'd rather not. We communicate through some letters here and there, with the help of some sympathetic guards. Although they're alive, they're in hell. But the haranchis couldn't care less.

"If one dies, the haranchi just come in the middle of the night and snatch another. Our government doesn't help, because they've labeled our people as animals, barbaric terrorists—the typical slurs of anybody resisting. Meanwhile, humanity stopped helping after the haranchi spread the lie that we're, '*The World's Most Dangerous Tribe.*' So, we recognize how hurtful slander is and how it stabs you from every angle, rotting out any joy in your life.

"The people you're surrounded by are suffering the same way as you. That's why we don't glare. You're one of us."

Madeleine looked around, realizing Zola was right. Pain gripped everybody's soul, relentlessly squeezing without mercy. She could tell that all their hearts were stuck in their throats.

"What could we do to fix this, Zola?"

"I'm not sure." Brows furrowed, Zola exhaled. "Everybody has a different approach to that question. Imamu swears our salvation lives in modernizing the tribe. That we should use more technology and become 'more civilized,' and only then the haranchis would treat us as humans. Others, like that friend of his, Ike, prefer to stick to our tribal ways—that The Lion Tamer knew best.

"Sometimes I agree with Ike. Why should we change? Haile never imposed his teachings on anybody, nor harmed others by living this way. We should have the freedom to live how we want on our land. Nobody's looking to expand. We just desire to continue our tradition and beliefs.

"But at other times, I side with Imamu, especially when he shows me what's possible. His peers used to mock him for being unable to start a fire, but then he goes and makes that laser-thing, which can torch an entire village in a blink of an eye. He also shows me amazing things on his phone, like moving pictures—" Zola slapped her knee, flinching Madeleine. "That's how I recognize you! On the phone! Your wedding! Imamu showed it to me!"

"You saw my wedding?"

"Yes! With—the—the—things, and the other things!" Zola circled her hands in the air as she tried to say chapel and wreaths, but it wasn't in her vocabulary. "It was so pretty!"

Madeleine chuckled in disbelief. "You really did see it!"

"Oh, girl, I remember wanting to jump on the Imamu-wagon and demand Amari modernize us! It was by far the most beautiful thing I ever saw. I'd die for a day like that."

"It was livestreamed, so I guess you did." Madeleine's smile fluttered, stumbled and drooped. "You watched it … *while you were starving.*"

A coldness pierced her soul as her face fell. The guilt rummaged over her like an avalanche, roaring and getting louder by the second. She noticed Imamu from afar, disappearing into the darkness of the forest. She looked at the tribe, trying to rebuild what they've lost.

Flashes of the wedding raced through her mind. Sunshine glittered the dresses. Dimples pierced the cheeks of the beaming guests. Flower petals scattered in the air, as photographers snapped

> *Kodak moments. Cheers,*
> *clanking glasses, laughter.*

Her throat tightened as she lost her ability to smile.

"So, while I was living the best day of my life, you were experiencing … your worst."

Zola stood and patted her lower garment. Specks of dust filtered over the ossified Madeleine. "Welcome to Omo."

Chapter XIV
We're the Oppressors

As the sun kissed the horizon, Madeleine returned to Julian inside Imamu's hut.

"She's lying," he said, from the cot, one knee raised. "About the whole thing. Father told me about the local tribes' atrocities when this event occurred. It was just as the tabloids reported; they're blood thirsty lunatics."

Madeleine observed Imamu's mess once more. The chaos now made sense. She began tidying up. "Then tell me about the lithium contracts. Lordes would mention it in passing to Francis, but it never interested me. However, considering our alibi for being here is to smooth out the recent developments, I need to know."

"Well, they started with my father. Followed by my brother, Napoleon, muddying the waters by trying to suggest some misdoings and trade disagreements. Turns out that he was only attempting to alter the contract to pocket more for himself. That's what led to his whole," Julian windmilled his hand, "drama. Whatever that necromancer out there told you, it isn't true. We're captives here and she wants to gain your sympathy."

Madeleine carried on with dusting and organizing, overly blinking without facing Julian. "No," she muttered.

"No?"

"Juley … we might be the bad-guys here. These people, they're the oppressed, and *we're the oppressors.*"

Julian rolled his eyes as his exhale reverberated off the walls. "This is the real world, Maddy. There aren't any good-guys or bad-guys. Only winners and losers. And these forest dwellers, they're the losers. So, they'll do and say anything to get out of their self-imposed rut. They signed the dotted line and didn't live up to their end. How's that make us *bad?*"

Madeleine stopped cleaning and picked at her nails. "From what Zola said, Chief Amari signed those contracts when he didn't speak a lick of English, let alone read it. I'm fearing that this was done intentionally, possibly by Napoleon. Regardless, if we've upheld that agreement after-the-fact, then we're in the wrong—"

"Listen. I only care about one thing right now, and that's getting us out alive."

"I don't think we're in danger—"

"Maddy! These people beat each other with sticks as part of their marriage ceremony! They slice their lips and stick plates in them. Look at how they even paint their bodies! How're you not seeing this? They're savages, and we've seen what savages do to civilized, decent folk, like us. Especially when we give them any sympathy."

Madeleine recognized this type of rhetoric. Every genocide started with similar words; the separation between the pure and the filthy, children of light versus children of darkness, and so on. She stared at Julian.

"What? What's that look for?"

"Our people pierce their bodies all the time. And when they tattoo themselves, they go up to and into the eyelids.

We're not that different from these tribespeople. But by the way you talk about them—"

"They're feral animals! Approaching one puts you in danger. Think, Maddy, think," he tapped his temple as she flinched a frown, "we're a gold mine for them. You'll see. This whole *peaceful host* they're posing as," Julian scoffed as he shook his head, "it's a ploy before they show their true colors. So, before you or I roast over their spits, I plan to save us." Madeleine softly shook her head. "Hey, you heard what he said—that we should be terrified of him. That's a threat."

"He's hurt, Julian. They're all hurting because of us."

"No! We're *garra-haranchis* to them! Don't you assume anything else!"

Madeleine realized they were at odds and feared the people outside would hear them. She took a deep breath and sat, staring frankly at Julian. "You should know better than taking a child's words over that of a chieftess."

He sat beside her. She noticed his frazzled hair and his five-o'clock shadow coming in.

"Children are honest, Maddy."

"I know, I know. But every time I picture what you're saying, I can't understand how Imamu got Leopaula's rattle toy. Because either she fell overboard with her toy, or he grabbed it while snatching her. But would a kidnapper really only take a child's toy and nothing else? He could've instead taken her binky to keep her quiet." Madeleine rubbed her forehead as Julian pinched the bridge of his nose. "We know she couldn't have climbed, and she's also not strong enough to throw her toy over the boat's edge. So, to assume Imamu took her, then the rest doesn't add up. Like, where's her blanket, and where's the boat he used? Besides Kamari, we haven't heard another baby crying. Moreover, Koka hospital exists and Zola confirmed the caravan was just here."

Julian noticed a single knot in one of the tangled wires. It pulled him in as he drifted in thought. The more he recalled his daughter, the more the knot seemed to tighten. He remembered her plump cheeks and her cackles whenever she saw him. A small smile flashed as the memories continued.

"*That toy* ..." Madeleine said. "Although it's giving me hope, it's the only thing that doesn't make sense."

"That's usually how lies work. He knows something that we don't, and without that, the toy will consistently throw a wrench into our understanding. But Maddy," he caressed her hand, "we need to worry about ourselves. Our escape window shrinks the longer we don't do anything. We have to run."

"But how? We can't go anywhere with my ankle like this. And even if we found a way back to the Jeep, it's out of fuel. Also, I won't ever abandon our baby."

Julian gave an honest nod. "I understand you're a mother, but I'm not only a father, I'm the head of this household. That means I have to protect my entire family. I haven't forgotten about our little girl, but if getting her back equates to both of us dying, then that's not a route I'm willing to take."

—

Imamu met with Ike near the river.

"[Surmic] This is bad."

Ike looked over. "What happened?"

"My mother," Imamu drew a deep breath before releasing it in a huff, "she dressed the princess up before I got a picture of them!"

"So?"

"*So?* Ike, if I send this image to the embassy, they'll see that we're the Mun. Which means they'll be able to figure out where we are. Then their troops would storm in and we wouldn't stand a chance! This is all ruined because of my stupid mother!"

"Hey, hey, calm down." Ike held his hands up. "You snapped the photo, right? Okay, then, this is actually a good thing." Imamu shook his head, shrugged and waited for an explanation. "Our village is well hidden. We Mun hold the most territory in Omo Valley, so they're going to have a lot of trouble figuring out exactly where *we* are. Also, the government knows how dangerous we are to outsiders, especially trespassers. In fact, tell them you're The Lion Tamer's son. It'll sow fear in their hearts."

"You're right …"

"Now, let's see if you'll actually go through with this."

Imamu dialed the number. He looked at Ike. Ike nodded once. The phone trilled. Someone answered.

"[English] Hello? Uh, yes." Imamu deepened his voice. Ike bit into his fist. "This is Imamu, son of Chief Amari, son of the Great Shaman, Haile, The Lion Tamer." Ike nodded as he went on. "I have your jewels. If you ever want to see them again, you'll do as I say."

A sigh emanated from the speaker. "First, it's that Nigerian prince, and now this … Stop calling!"

"Wait! Please, hold on!" Imamu's voice squealed like a seagull. Ike rolled his eyes. "I have proof!"

The receptionist paused. The two leaned in.

"*Proof?*"

"Y—yes. A picture!"

Imamu opened his gallery before tapping the share icon.

"I swear to God, if this is another dick-pic …" Nobody said anything. The friends exchanged glances, wondering if she'd take the bait. "Whatever." Imamu pumped his fist. "Send it to this email." After a few minutes of the receptionist ranting about how much she hated her job, Imamu received the gasp he sought. "It—it's really them …"

Imamu's grin stretch. "Yes. I have them all. And if you don't do exactly as I say, I'll start by killing the baby."

"W—wait! Just wait! Okay? I—I have to get my supervisor—"

The phone toppled off the desk, knocked against the creeping chair and dangled back and forth.

"Hello?" Imamu asked into the void line before looking at Ike. "[Surmic] Did she leave? Should we call back?"

"Don't look at me. This is your plan. I have no idea how that thing even operates."

As the landscape swallowed the last portion of the sun, Imamu's gut stomped with the pangs of doubt.

"[English] Hello?" Imamu asked again.

Nobody responded.

"[Surmic] What if she tripped on her way to her supervisor, and has been unconscious ever since," Ike said.

Imamu's expression fumed nonsense. "And how likely is that?"

"… As likely as finding a prince and a princess defenseless on a rowboat."

Imamu defeatedly sighed.

Suddenly, a burly man picked up. "[English] Who's there?!"

"H—Hello? Hi!" He nearly dropped the phone. "Yes—yes! This is Imamu, son of Chief Amari, son of the Great Shaman, Haile, The Lion—"

"I'm not looking for your bloody family history, you twat! What's the location of the Royals? WHERE ARE THEY? TELL ME NOW!"

Imamu imagined bits of the man's spit making it through the phone.

"Not only do I know where they are, they're my captives! And if you don't tone it down, I'll be sending them back, piece by piece."

"YOU LISTEN TO ME, YOU MOTHERF—"

Someone snatched the phone from the brash man.

"Hello? Is this Imamu? Son of Chief Amari, son of the Great Shaman, Haile, The Lion Tamer?" The new voice embodied a calmer, more inviting aura.

Imamu glanced at Ike, who gestured to him to respond.

"Uh, yes. And who's this?"

"You're speaking with the British Minister of Foreign Affairs; Mr. Butts, Harry Butts."

Ike instantly developed a serious case of the giggles. Imamu tried to shut him up, but Ike couldn't restrain himself and it echoed through the phone. He rushed to the edge of the river, letting out a burst of laughter that nearly toppled him into the water.

He lost the ability to breathe. "[Surmic] Why—would his parents—ever—"

Imamu shrugged. "[English] Maybe they're dumb or something."

"I'm sorry. Did you call me dumb?" Mr. Butts asked. "Our experts have analyzed your picture and confirmed it's not a fabrication. Do you truly have the Royal Family or not? This is not a laughing matter!"

"Yes! Yes. And no, it's not—"

"What?!" Mr. Butts hollered. "Which is it?!"

Imamu cleared his throat and straightened his back. He re-deepened his voice and angled his eyebrows.

"*Mr. Tushie,* your people have displaced us, abused us and imprisoned us. Under Article 51 and 84 of the United Nations Charter, we have the right to respond. So, we've displaced your jewels, abused them and imprisoned them in retaliation, and to deter further escalation and aggression from your Kingdom."

"I don't need a lesson in jurisprudence, son of The Lion Tamer. I'm here to discuss a diplomatic solution to our situation. So, what'll it be?"

Raging obscenities, the other man filled the background noise.

"What will what be?" Imamu blinked, confused.

"What do you want?"

"*What do I want?*" He openly stared out at the water, suddenly forgetting how to talk.

Ike bounced his gaze between the river and his friend. "[Surmic] Psst. Say something!"

Imamu stood dazed. Nobody ever asked him that question. The current continued, pulling his attention away with it.

"[English] Imamu, did I lose you?"

"I want … uhm …"

"[Surmic] You can do this," Ike said. Imamu looked him in the eye and nodded, slowly, then more.

"[English] I want no harm to reach the Royals. But that's going to depend on you. Is that understood?"

"Yes, Imamu, but I'm not seeing Princess Leopaula in the picture. What's her condition?"

"She's safe, *for now*. But if my demands aren't met by midnight, my time, she'll be the first to go. And every day you delay, you'll be collecting more and more pieces of the Royal Couple as my asking price climbs. Got it?"

"Yes, I understand," Mr. Butts said as Imamu imagined the sweat rolling over his face, as if caught in a sudden downpour. "So, what're your demands?"

"Number one, all the earnings from the mined lithium are to be transferred to me. Not to my tribe, not to my father. Number two, the release of all the prisoners in the Northern Omo Mine. All of them, including the corpses. Thirdly, not a single Mun is to be harmed in this process. And finally, the withdrawal of all UK forces from our land. Do I make myself clear?" Imamu mimicked what he'd seen on TV and in movies. Flashes of Walter White, Bane, Negan and even Dr. House raced through his mind as he concluded his exhortation.

"Mr. Imamu ... I doubt I can get all of that done, especially by midnight."

"Is that really how you want to respond—by revealing what you *can't* do? Unacceptable! I've seen what you haranchis are capable of. Bombs here, bullets there. But now that you're forced to negotiate, you suddenly act like you can't do anything."

"It's just, the logistics, approvals and—and—"

"Ah, yes, your beautiful red tape. Are they similar to those red lines that you love to paint on our land? Well, the time has come for you to cross them if you ever want to see little Leopaula again."

Imamu hung up.

Ike glued his eyes to the phone flashing the call time. "[Surmic] If this doesn't work, we're dead."

Chapter XV
Nothing Like Them

— Twenty-Nine Years Earlier —

"[English] She's dead," Francis's father said as men dressed in jet black suits carried his mother's casket.

Everyone lowered their heads. Everyone, except for the six-year-old Francis. His father pulled him in.

"We'll be alright; we've suffered losses before and we've weathered those. That's why we're the Mayweathers."

Swollen clouds loomed. The cool wind seeded irritation throughout the procession. However, nobody showed any sign of discomfort, out of respect for Francis's father.

Francis followed the descending casket as bits of dirt dribbled in. He stared intently, just as he witnessed her death.

"Wallis, our condolences," some said as they passed by the widowed father and orphaned son.

A young girl with dark hair and steely blue eyes gently hugged Francis. "I'm sorry about your mum, Franny."

Francis's arms hung slack as he supported her weight.

Wallis kneeled down. "Son, hug your friend back." He didn't, not with his attention usurped by his disappearing mother. Wallis turned to the girl. "I'm sorry, Scarlett, was it? Let's give him some time."

The lass regarded Wallis and left with her family, looking back every few steps with glossy eyes.

More departed towards the parking lot, some patting Wallis's shoulder, while others nodded once. When the proceedings concluded, only Wallis and Francis stayed behind as the workers began filling in the grave.

The shovel thrusts made Francis flinch as every hollow echo of earth thudding onto the casket deepened his frown. Soon after, the ground flattened, as if his mother never was.

The surrounding green grass mocked the leveled patch of dirt.

"So, that's it?" Francis asked.

"What's it?"

"Life. We eat and talk until the day that we just stop moving. Then, we're placed into a box and lowered into the ground."

Pelting rain drops splattered over the father and son, as the reality of death dawned upon the child. Wallis sighed as he looked out at the other tombstones combing the cemetery.

"Only if you're lucky," he said as the rain picked up. He found refuge under a tree and gestured for Francis to join. But the boy stayed put, consumed by the brown rectangle.

"Lucky?"

"That's right. Most can't afford a casket. These days, many wrap the bodies up, toss em into a furnace and well ..." Wallis wiggled his fingers upwards, imitating the flames of a cremator. "Know that this fate is inescapable. That," he pointed to the patch, "is everybody's conclusion.

Never has one, nor will one ever, find a different destination. That's exactly where your story and my story ends."

The dirt muddied as it absorbed the raindrops, sheening over like a sloppy mirror.

"But we're one of the poorest families in Slough; how were you able to afford this?"

Wallis disregarded the question. "Decades from now, that coffin will decompose, leaving your mother's body exposed. It'll eventually be eaten by the earth. Then in the future, when land is limited in this cemetery, the descendants of those same gravediggers are going to shovel into the dirt in which your mother had become, to make room for more corpses. And that's it. That's all there is, son."

"No!" The rainwater wicked from his hair. "There must be more—"

"There isn't. That's how it'll always be." Wallis rested his head against the bark.

"No! I—I feel it in my heart!" Francis tightened a fist. "I'm not here to breathe, eat and simply die! There's something inside me that's different! It's scorching and refuses to be put out in a—in a—hole!" He stood alone before the headstone, unable to make sense of the anger grappling with his grief.

Wallis observed the storm rage onto, and inside, his son. "Come, please." Francis dragged his feet as his soaked hair slithered towards his jawline like snakes. "There's—" Wallis's lips and chin fidgeted. "There's a reason you feel this way …" He turned, cursing under his breath, knowing it would be futile to hide the truth.

I was naïve to think he wouldn't have inherited it, Wallis thought.

"That's because …" he exhaled and gazed out at the sea of headstones, "your peers—you're nothing like them."

— A Few Months After the Funeral —

Familiar faces waved as they entered Cranbourne Park for Wallis's wedding reception. Francis didn't bother waving back. His suit sagged, as his tie slung. His frowning, soon-to-be step-mother fixed his messy hair and tidied him up. All the while, she wished he would go mope somewhere other than the entrance.

After making sure Wallis wasn't around, she grumbled, "Listen here, you little brat. Your mother is rot now, and I took her place. Either get with the program or go sulk behind the loo, but quit depressing my guests."

She glowered with a wrinkled nose, hating that he was part of the package. But when another guest passed by, she'd flash a grin before showing them in. Moments later, her glare returned.

Francis moved his hair out of his eyes and tucked it behind his ear. He locked his electric gaze on his make-up plastered adversary, unbothered.

She knew nothing, he thought.

"I don't care for you, nor this day." He stood and shuffled his restricted shoulders, then loosened his tie while holding eye contact. "I have other, more meaningful matters riddling my mind." He left.

She scoffed, muttering, "Big words from a small brat." She shrugged, just glad that he no longer spoiled her special day.

As Francis strolled through the park, he spotted his father, who smiled back. He approached.

"Having fun, France?"

Before Francis responded, Wallis's new wife yanked him towards the festivities.

As the park filled with attendees, Francis distanced himself from the celebration. Scarlett noticed and followed him. He passed winding lines for the rattly carousel rides, damaged porta-potties and garbage cans needing to be changed. Every passing face reminded him of his father's words at the funeral.

They're all … so oblivious, Francis thought. Mindless, ignorant peasants. Shallow and dead, as they'll soon become dirt.

"But not me—"

"Hey!" Scarlett called. "Come dance with me. Or at least buy me an ice cream cone."

A flower bloomed above her temple, as her dress glittered from the setting sunlight. She owned a smile that she constantly posted for sale. But the only buyer she wanted was the one boy who never gave her a second glance.

"Go away," Francis said from his back.

With every step, he felt her looming presence. The squirrels crossing his path didn't irritate him, nor did the cyclists whizzing by. But Scarlett …

"I said, leave!"

She picked up her pace, as did he. The further they migrated, the less the scent of the food trucks reached. The music's echoes morphed into background noise as their breaths intensified. Their steps turned into strides and their strides turned into sprints.

Tie long gone, first button plucked and suit jacket torn at the seams, Francis gave up. Scarlett kneeled beside him, smirk stretched as she panted.

"I just want to be alone!"

"You always want to be alone."

"And?!"

She kneeled lower, hoping her smile would brighten his day. However, when Francis glanced, all he kept picturing was what he saw whenever he faced anybody; a dirt patch. Brown, wet and dead.

They reached the park's northeastern periphery. In the distance, what was visible of Windsor Castle's walls illuminated through the trees. Young Francis mounted atop the stone barrier and dangled his feet, waiting for his sweat to dry. As the horizon swallowed the sun, he kept his eyes planted on the Kingdom's coruscating icon.

Scarlett sat beside him and gleefully hung her feet, too. She'd sway them around, trying to have her shoe laces touch his.

"Come on, Franny, cheer up. So, what? Your dad found himself another squeeze, is all. It's not a jab towards your mum, it's just sex. Everybody does it and everybody needs it. At least he's going about it morally, yeah? That's rare these days."

"I said go away."

Scarlett smirked. "Hey now, we're kids and it's a wedding. No need to act like you've been dumped."

Francis regarded the castle, appreciating the silence of the decorative arches.

"You don't understand. How could you? You're just one of them." He tipped his head back at the reception.

"Why're you here? Tell me. I hate seeing you like this." She followed his line of sight until she too noticed the castle. "Oh, Franny. Don't torture yourself by ogling at that thing. We're Slough scum. We'll never, and I mean ever, get to stand on any of those balconies."

Francis stayed mute. The faint tunes continued. Scarlett tried to downplay the situation, but realized her crush was genuinely going through something.

"Let it out." Her calm blue eyes grew, reflecting the stray light of the castle walls.

"May I confide something in you?" His voice revealed a hint of his pain.

"Probably not." She leered honestly. Francis exhaled. "*I'm kidding, I'm kidding.* Of course you can. I want to help you. It's like you've changed since your mum passed."

"It's not that."

"Then what?"

A chilled breeze floated by.

"My father told me something that day. But if I tell you, you must vow to never speak a word of this to anybody. Understand?"

She gripped his hand. "I promise."

"I'm going to stand on that balcony one day ..."

He harbored something she'd never seen in any other person in Slough. He wasn't sharing his dream; he was sharing his plan.

She rested her ear on his shoulder, smashing her flower. He leaned his head over hers.

"You know what, I believe you."

Their fingers intertwined.

Scarlett glanced down, noticing black and blue blotches on Francis's wrist. With strained brows, she looked at him. He pulled his sleeve down, eyes steadied on the castle.

Chapter XVI
If You Want It Done Right

— Current Day —

With Omo Valley bathed in moonlight, Madeleine quietly pulled the sheets off. She scooted until she rested against the wall, staring at Julian's shoulder blades as he remained asleep. He breathed fine, with a snore now and again. Nothing out of the ordinary.

Every few minutes, clouds overtook the moon, throwing the valley into pockets of abyss-like darkness. This was one of those moments. Blink after blink, eyes opened or closed, it made no difference. Julian disappeared, along with all visuals. Sounds, which typically went unnoticed, amplified. The crickets chirped. The trees swayed. A waft swept through the village. Another occasional snore.

Moonlight.

Julian's chest expanded before falling. Inhale in, exhale out. Madeleine wondered how much he knew regarding the lithium contracts, and how little he told her. She grazed her eyebrow. The scab sealed over, leaving behind a rough shell, seemingly reaching down to the rim of her eye-socket. Julian continued to breathe.

Darkness.

"Imamu's hiding something from me," she whispered. "But so are you."

Moonlight.

"Until you're honest with me, I'm going out on my own to find our daughter."

Madeleine stood and snaked through the landmines of wires and sharp gadgets. She glanced once more.

"*Stop!*" Julian shouted. Madeleine held her ground with tightened fists. "*No!*"

Darkness.

She stared into the inky black, frozen in fear.

"*You're not real!*" Julian groped the cot, tearing along the seam. "*Go away!*"

Madeleine saw nothing but heard everything. With a racing pulse, she stepped back, frailly holding her posture.

Moonlight.

Julian's groans suddenly simmered to a mumble as he released his grip. With his fingers falling limp, the blanket relaxed back over the cot as his drooling resumed.

Madeleine hesitated to move another muscle.

"Here, take dis."

Madeleine flinched around, finding a donga staff shoved into her hands. "Z—Zola! What—what're you doing up?"

She tilted her head, dangling her earrings against her neck and shoulder. "I'm a mother, too."

Madeleine grabbed the staff and found it to serve as a suitable crutch.

"I don't know where Koka is, but it's far. So, I prepared this for you." She wrapped a sack over her neck. "It won't be enough, but it's all I can spare."

Madeleine looked through the bag. It contained dried food, a canister of water and ointment. "I … I don't know what to say."

"I'd stop you if I could, but there's nothing anybody can do to restrict a mother from her child. So, all I could do is warn you of three things. First, the savannah. It'll consume you by high-noon, so remain in the tree line. Second, white marks on trees. That's the border we share with our rival. And third, long leafy stalks. Those are dangerous plants that'll give you confusing visions."

Madeleine looked at her hands, then back at Zola, not knowing how to express her gratitude. "Thank you."

Darkness.

They hugged, but just then, grunts emanated from within the shadows of the hut.

"No! Stop! Go away!"

Far too familiar with buried demons, Zola's stomach knotted, knowing there's worse to come. However, Julian's groans differed from what she'd heard after the displacement. With eyes blindly fixated on the cot, a bead of sweat formed over her forehead. The stifled shouts continued.

Zola harshly swallowed. "Something deep-seated is gnawing away at that boy …"

Moonlight.

"I don't care. I need to save Leopaula, not worry about a grown man's mental state."

Zola nodded before pointing at the North Star and wishing Madeleine luck.

—

"[Surmic] Get up!" Ike barked at the sleeping Imamu, who spent the night in his hut. "Get up, now!"

Imamu snapped his eyes open and reached for his phone. Noon. He pounced up. "Did the embassy call?"

"No! Your boy—the prince, he's causing a commotion!"

Imamu jolted out. The two rushed to the donga stick fighting arena, finding Julian brandishing a staff towards the surrounding tribespeople. With each swing, a whooshing sound sliced through the air.

"[English] Where is she?" The people leaned back, avoiding the swat. "What'd you do with my wife?!"

Like a cornered animal, Julian's gaze darted around. The tribesmen considered ambushing him, but whenever someone neared, Julian whacked. His unpredictability forced everybody to stay on the defensive.

Ike approached with extended hands. "You're Julian, no?"

"Who are you and where is she?!"

Imamu pushed Ike aside. "Julian! Stop this! Where's Madeleine?"

The moment Julian spotted him, he launched, tackling him to the ground and ramming the pole against his neck with murderous intent.

"WHERE—IS—SHE?!" he grunted with demonic eyes.

Abruptly powerless, Imamu watched Julian's strength manifest. In an instant, a brigade of fear seized his nerve endings. Every word became a prisoner, caged behind his pinched throat. Every movement turned lethargic and minimal. Every plan, futile.

As a blackness clouded his view, the mere seconds stretched to eternity.

Ike wasted no time. He took Julian's back, interlacing his limbs over his body. He squeezed, restraining Julian, while simultaneously choking him. With surgical precision, he clasped until the Brit's arms fell, motionless.

Imamu tumbled away, gasping for air. His eyes bulged as his lungs refilled themselves. He hesitated a glance at Julian as Ike patiently waited for the inevitable.

"Are you done, Prince? Ready to talk?"

Julian, mute, only frowned.

Imamu called from a distance, "Are you saying Madeleine's missing?" Julian's resistance toned down as he sensed the honesty in Imamu's voice. Ike let go. "I left her with you in my hut." He looked around. "Did anybody see anything? [Surmic] Anything at all?"

Imamu feared the plan falling apart.

Julian dusted himself. "[English] What is it with you people?! My family came here to relax, and this is how you welcome us? Each day, you snatch another? Is this a game for you?"

Imamu glared. "What'd you just say?" He clenched a fist, digging his nails into his palms. "You dare accuse us of what you haranchis do?!"

Julian tossed his gaze around for anything to use as a weapon, but he was too slow as Imamu already charged forward. Ike couldn't decide which side to quell first.

"Stop," Zola said, casually approaching with Kamari in hand.

The people made way for their chieftess, lowering their heads.

"*You*," Julian muttered.

"Your wife did what any mother would do; she left for Koka to find ya daw-ta."

"Which way?! Tell me, now!"

Zola smirked, observing his desperation disguised as authority. Every passing moment tortured him, so she prolonged the pause.

'*Please,*' he mouthed.

Zola nudged her chin. "Northwest." Julian immediately sprinted away. Narrowing her eyes, she stared at him distancing—consciously holding back the fatal warnings she gave Madeleine.

Chapter XVII
The Others

Ike grabbed Imamu's arm. "[Surmic] No, stop."

"NO, IF WE—" Imamu glanced around and lowered his tone to a whisper, "*if we* lose him too, we'll have nothing for the embassy!"

Ike pulled him away from the crowd, lips sealed. He dragged him towards the offshoot and made sure nobody followed.

"He's hot right now. Let him cool off. He won't get far. This is our chance to send the embassy a message letting them know we're serious."

Imamu inhaled sharply as logic overtook his emotions. "You're right, you're right. He just—he caught me off guard." He wrung his neck, feeling it swell. Ike noticed.

"No. There'll be more outbursts like that because we're meddling with a man and his family. But right now, we need to focus. The lack of a response from the embassy is a red flag. They're stalling, possibly planning to pull a fast one on us." Imamu checked his phone. No new messages. "Do you still have the toy?"

Imamu nodded. Ike held his hand out. The moment it touched his fingers, he dropped it and stomped, scattering the beads over the riverbed's pebbles like sprinkles over a sundae.

"What're you doing?!"

"Send a picture of that to the embassy. Say that you bludgeoned the infant to death."

"But—the Royals!" Imamu's palms echoed off his bald head. "They'll ask about it!"

"Doesn't matter. This entire ordeal should be wrapped up within another day, at most. The longer we sit on our hands, waiting, the worse. So, don't call and don't play their game. Just send that picture with a message saying," Ike swept his hand, captioning the sky, *"one down, two remain."*

—

Julian halted just before the savannah fields. He shielded his eyes from the blazing brightness as the desolate expanse stretched before him. It was a never-ending abyss, swallowing all hope in its vastness. He considered challenging it, but doubts crept in as it invincibly returned a glare. Vulnerable and panting, he leaned against a tree. No Jeep, no reception, no boat, no help.

The blistering wind howled, kicking up swirls of hot sand and swaying the few scattered trees who were bold enough to grow in that climate. Even from the shade, the savannah extracted Julian's sweat, boasting its hunger for another soul.

Enter, only those foolish enough.

"[English] Oh, Maddy …"

Julian resembled a lost child, staring out at an ocean, armed with nothing but an undersized duck-shaped floatie. The shimmering air hazily distorted the horizon. The sweat broke and raced towards his chin. He placed one foot into the sunlight—

"Nope," he jerked it back into the shade, shaking his head, "No way. No."

The savannah remained impenetrable by nothing but its existence.

"Why, Maddy? For all I know, you're already dead out there, getting cooked. Stop trying, and just let me help you! I could fix all of this!" He tapped his fist against his forehead. "Dammit!"

The savannah seemed to expand the more he tried to gage its size. Not a single blade of grass resembled greenery, nor a single animal dared stand in the sunlight.

The weight of his failing marriage crushed him as he realized that words alone couldn't mend what he broke. Glimpses of Madeleine's smile from the day they met riddled his thoughts as he evaluated his options. There used to be no responsibilities, no stress. Only love. He wanted that again, but with every passing second, the sunlight crawled closer. It salivated at the scent of another mortal, audacious enough to face Ethiopia's silent might. It inched over his boots, sizzling the leather.

She's worth it, he thought. She's worth it.

He looked down, nodding to himself. Just then, he spotted an odd, perfectly round hole in the ground. Another. And another. He squinted, observing their spacing and the footprints beside it.

"She's using the donga staff as a crutch …"

The pattern snaked through the trees, remaining in the shade. He chuckled before flipping the bird at the sunny emptiness.

As Julian trailed the tracks, an unusual stillness eerily flooded the area. He stopped, only moving his eyes.

Silence.

No birds, no insects. The only constant was the babbling Omo River. His skin rippled as he listened closely.

Someone was watching him.

Julian spun around, but nobody was there.

A whisper.

He snapped his head the other way. Nothing, just trees.

Again, a murmur—so delicate and faint that he questioned whether he heard it or simply thought it. He resumed blinking, but not without shuddering breaths. With a subtle headshake, he continued.

Julian refocused on the prints, glancing around every few strides.

He heard it again.

"Who's there?!"

Only a haunting hush.

He doubted the sounds of his steps as being his own. His boots crunched the fallen foliage, but every so often, a snapping twig or croaking tree trunk sounded off-step, breaking the rhythm.

"Maddy?"

The river purled over the smooth stones and pebbles. Julian didn't want to stare at it too long, fearful he might miss his pursuer. He reached down to grab a thick branch for defense, but stopped midway to look around.

Still, nobody.

He exhaled slowly, eyes darting as he continued to kneel. The moment he grazed the branch, he swung it around.

He landed a solid blow *against the air,* slicing the emptiness while overextending his shoulder.

Snap out of it, he thought. You're fine, you're fine. Find Maddy, and get home.

Julian dropped the branch but not before spotting an odd marking on a tree. White and thick, it resembled what lumberjacks used. He leaned in, finding it to be like chalk, but thicker. He couldn't decipher whether they represented a letter or a number.

As he narrowed focused on the jagged surface, the mmaarrkkiinngg ddoouubbllleedd. He pulled his hand in, opening and closing his palms, but it didn't stop. Suddenly, an agonizing headache struck him, stabbing at his temples with merciless force.

He collapsed, fingers through his hair. Rivulets of sweat slid down his side, drenching his skin in a cold, clammy sheen. He hugged the tree for dear life.

"These—these tremors! They're—"

As he searched for help, he spotted a person lying face down in the dirt.

"Maddy!"

Julian wobbled to his feet and stumbled with faltering steps. His body whisked him from side to side, but he refused to give up. One foot after the other, he kept his sights locked on her as he barreled through the forest. His eyes rolled back as he tripped, tumbling beside her like a dropped dozen of eggs. Before the blackness settled in, he caught a glimpse of a small rod sticking out of her neck.

—

"[Surmic] We have to hurry," Ike said, kneeling beside Julian and sitting him up. "[English] Prince, wake up."

Imamu focused on Madeleine, noticing a red ring surrounding a tiny hole in her neck. He ran his finger over the wound before promptly reaching into his bag and uncapping a canister of schnapps.

"Prince, hey, wake up," Ike repeated. Julian's eyes remained closed as his head freely tilted and leaned. "[Surmic] He doesn't seem well ..." Ike looked over. "What're you doing?"

Imamu poured the liqueur over Madeleine's wound, wearing a concerned look. "She's been hit!"

As the alcohol trickled over the sore, Julian's nose flinched, like a dog latching onto a scent.

"[English] Prince?" Ike asked, snapping his fingers in his face.

Julian's eyes popped wide open as he lunged for the canister like a frog extending its tongue. The liquid splashed across the ground before he eclipsed the opening with his mouth. He chugged. Imamu reached back for it, but Julian pulled away, holding guard.

Imamu found no alternative besides biting Madeleine's neck like a vampire and sucking. Julian stared with lips glued to the flask, bothered, but not enough to stop drinking.

Imamu spit to the side. "[Surmic] That's poison! That's definitely poison!" He wiped his mouth and scrubbed his tongue, spitting out more. "I think I got most of it."

He scanned the area, unsure if they were being stalked.

Following the last drop, Julian licked around the opening. He slurped as he inhaled like a vacuum cleaner, reaching for the far crevices of a couch.

Now empty, Julian chucked the container at Imamu. "[English] The hell're you doing love-biting my wife?!"

"Calm down, Prince," Ike said, patting Julian's torso.

Julian swatted, but with great fatigue. "Don't tell me what to do while your buddy here tries to cuck me."

"What's wrong with you?" Imamu asked. "Why're you moving like that?"

"I'm fine," Julian said, angling away while dropping his chin to his chest.

"No, you're not." Ike smirked. "[Surmic] We just got a peek at what the Royal Family does behind closed doors."

"[English] Whatever, I'll get over it. It's not the first time I've had to detox. What're you boys doing with alcohol way out here, anyway?"

"Well, like you haranchis, we, too, drink. Maybe not as much. But, on long journeys, we bring some along for first aid. Imamu was pouring it over your wife's wound to disinfect it. Tell us, what'd you last see?"

"Nothing. I just found her here, passed out, right before I collapsed."

"This isn't good," Ike said. "[Surmic] We need to go, now!"

"No, she needs to be treated! If there's any poison left, it'll kill her!"

Ike grabbed his friend's face. "Listen! None of this matters if we're caught here! Either we abandon the plan, or we all die. What sounds better to you?"

Imamu ignored him and rummaged through the sack that Zola gave Madeleine, finding a small pouch of activated charcoal. He tilted Madeleine's ear towards her shoulder and sprinkled the powder onto her wound.

"I read about this; it should help. Mama must've known this could've happened."

Ike shot his gaze around as he picked at his nails. "Imamu, we might be under surveillance right now. Whoever hit her with the poisoned dart must've fled when he saw Julian. And when Julian passed out, the assailant most likely retrieved his projectile from the princess's neck. This means he's alone out here and his ammunition is low. In other words, we're dealing with one of the *Karo*."

Imamu kept working, understanding the threat, but too concerned for Madeleine to pause. Zola packed enough for Madeleine, but he couldn't figure everything out without labels. Ike waved his hand in front of his face, but Imamu kept focus.

"Hey, if we flee now, we'll catch a break, because the scout probably didn't see us; only two random haranchi. So, the Karo will never know that we violated the treaty. But if we get caught—" Furrowing his brow, Imamu persisted as he ignored the threat. He pressed the powder deep into the opening, until each grain was thoroughly embedded. "Are you even listening?!"

Julian winced. "[English] Would you fill me in on what you're saying, mate?"

"No," Ike said, looking at Imamu. "*We're leaving.*"

"[Surmic] Fine. But don't tell them about the poison. If you do, word will spread to Mama, then to Dada. If Dada knows we've crossed, he'll preemptively strike, inciting a war and rendering our plan useless."

Julian shook his head. "[English] Again with this gibberish?"

"[Surmic] Deal. Now, let's get out of here!"

"[English] Hello?!"

Ike tightened his fists, muttering under his breath, "[Surmic] Loud ass! [English] We're going, we're going, but keep your voice down. We're not safe—" Imamu widened his eyes at him, "from, uh, *predators* and such."

"Alright," Julian said. "You two carry her, and I'll follow. But give me a moment."

"[Surmic] Let's just go before this idiot gets us all killed," Ike said. "We only need one captive for the embassy, anyway."

"[English] Do you know your way back?" Imamu asked, holding a scowl. Julian nodded. "Alright then. Be careful."

Julian half-rolled his eyes. They left. He stood and dusted himself before leaning on a tree and taking a few deep breaths. He pushed off to leave.

A whisper.

Julian turned around, suddenly and accidentally spotting a distant, lone, disguised man. "Uh—oh, h—hello …"

Camouflaged, the individual remained absolutely still. His cloaked dark skin imitated the vegetation, with even similar white markings as those on the trees.

"How—how long have you been there?" His breathing inadvertently paused. "W—were you the one watch—watching me earlier?"

The man wasn't from the village. His aura alone set him apart from the others. Julian braced himself, but the lurking figure emotionlessly stowed his blowgun and took a step back, melting into the darkness of the forest.

Chapter XVIII
A Knight's Scars

— Twenty-Five Years Earlier —

Buried in the darkness of his closet, ten-year-old Francis grimaced so tightly that his teeth nearly cracked. He opened his mouth to scream, but knew the repercussions that would bring. The shouting continued from the kitchen as he muffled his ears with his fists.

"… And don't think that makes you part of this family! You're a leech that drove your father to his grave!"

Francis ignored his gaping ulcer, piercing a burning hole in his stomach lining. Flashes of a violent fantasy raced through his mind. It was the only vision in the blackness of his hiding spot. *He grabbed the largest knife from the depths of the messy sink and ran it deep into her gut, finally shutting her up.* The imagination alone slowed his pounding heart. He lowered his shoulders and threw his head back, despising this routine.

Francis usually woke up first, then open his room's door but stop just before the creak of no return. With bated breaths, he'd snake his way across the creaking floor as if it were a minefield. He skillfully maneuvered through a sea of discarded syringes and rubber bands, scattered haphazardly on the shag carpet, which hadn't seen a vacuum in ages. He would then pick up the torn stuffed animal and re-plug the broken window, blocking the waft of pot smoke from entering.

But this morning, baby-Madeleine heard the fridge door shut and woke up the *breadwinner*—a title his stepmother made sure he would never forget. His only option was no different from a band aid which wouldn't stick; hiding in his closet and wait for her to tire herself out. There was also the benefit of delaying the beating for a couple of seconds as she searched for him after barging into the room.

Her words still reached him though, playing their effect like decaffeinated coffee for an addict. He couldn't grieve his father while trying to survive his step-mother. But that's all he wanted. He wanted Wallis back. He wanted silence with his sister. He wanted anything, anything but this.

"You don't belong here! Madeleine wakes up like this because she recognizes that you're a stranger to this family!"

Francis glared through the shadows, imagining Madeleine wailing in her arms, struggling to go back to sleep as the screams went on.

"She's not your sister, and Lord help her if she was, because everybody in your family is cursed. Your slut mum and your dad both croaked to get away from you, Francis. And I won't let you do the same to her. I'm going to raise this girl to be a fighter, while protecting her from the likes of you—a leech with nothing to live for."

Recalling his father, Francis squeezed his eyes. He relaxed his fist and waited for the barrage of insults to cease. As Madeleine quieted down, so did his step-mother. But that wasn't enough. He didn't budge until the nursery door latched, indicating that the coast was clear.

He crept out of his room, backpack over his shoulder. Without the opportunity to make himself lunch, he peeked into her purse. A large stack of banded bills stared back at him. It bulged fatter and tighter than any amount of money he'd ever seen. Surveying the flat, he concluded it would be better off in his hands.

With his window closing, he reached in, grabbed the pound of pound sterlings and raced off to school.

—

"So, what's the approximate decimal equivalent for this fraction?" the teacher asked, tapping her chalk for the dot in the equation's question mark. With half-shut eyelids, Francis stared at the board stretching before the front of the classroom.

$$6/56 = ?$$

0.11, he thought, before slouching into his seat and sighing, as his peers scribbled long division and scratched their heads.

The teacher's computer was black. It wasn't in standby mode; it was off. That's because it didn't work. It never worked. However, it remained and Francis noticed it every day. Something with boundless potential, just wasting away.

"Uhh," another student said. "Is it 0.17?"

"That's incorrect," the teacher replied, carrying a drone in her voice.

"No, it's right," he shot back.

Francis exhaled. This child's biggest problem was rudimentary math, while he had to figure out the best way to pay the rent without his step-mother figuring out he swiped her drug money.

The teacher lowered her forehead, staring above the rim of her glasses. "No. It's not."

"Yes, it is! I did the work, look!" The boy raised up his notebook, as if the teacher could check his scribbles from her end.

Rubbing his temples, Francis heard the children in the adjacent class laughing at something their teacher said. Some of his peers zipped their backpacks, preparing for the bell to ring. Meanwhile, he imagined his landlord's face as he, a ten-year-old, handed him a wad of cash.

Would he even take it? Francis thought. Of course he would; it's money. People kill for this crap.

The student battled with conviction that 0.17 was the answer, whereas the teacher stood her ground. A few classmates shot their glances back and forth, excited by the showdown. Others gave up and crumbled their paper. Francis considered splitting some of the money; some for food, some for rent. But last time he tried that, the landlord acted like he didn't receive the payment when his step-mother went to pay the rest. His knee jumped as he tapped his fist against his forehead, eyes closed.

"No," the teacher said.

He realized they also needed baby food for Madeleine, which cost more.

If only I found some privacy, he thought, I could figure out how to split the money. But rationing it might be pointless.

He knew about the eviction-warning that his step-mother acted as if it didn't exist. He bit his lower lip as the numbers jumbled his brain. Meanwhile, some students whacked close their textbook, knowing this battle of student v. teacher would consume the remaining minutes of class.

"Yes! Yes! Yes! If you divide the—"

Francis slammed the desk, bouncing his pencil out of its ridge and over the edge. "No, you imbecile, it's not! You skipped a decimal!"

Everybody stopped. Francis scowled at the boy, fuming like a bull. The teacher wasn't sure if she should reprimand the future Royal Guard or thank him.

Nobody said anything.

Francis sighed, glancing at the clock above the door. Suddenly, he spotted his step-mother storming through the hall. He ducked in his seat, holding completely still.

Scarlett noticed. Everyone thought embarrassment paralyzed him, but she knew his fleeting breaths stemmed from the bull outside marching, sniffing out his scent. Francis tried to time it right, ready to slink by with the horde of students once the bell rings.

"Young man, that's not how we speak to others in this class—"

"May I use the restroom?!" he asked, frog in throat, eyes on door.

"The period is almost over; try to hold it."

Scarlett raised her hand, flailing around her now bleached platinum blonde hair. "May I?"

The teacher glowered. "No."

As she turned towards the board, Scarlett reached into her lunchbox and grabbed her fruit punch juice box. She punctured the straw hole and poured it over her uniform's crotch. The redness spread through the fabric, some creeping up her white button up. She raised her hand again, this time, thumb extended.

"I, eh, *really* need to go …"

"Miss Scarlett—"

Scarlett subtly spread her legs open, glancing down at the faux blood.

"*I—I see* …" The teacher jittered a nod. "Go now, hurry on, dear."

Scarlett grabbed her things and left, but not before winking at Francis.

In the hall, she hastened towards his step-mother. "You're Francis's mum, yeah?"

Veins bulging from her thin arms, she grabbed Scarlett's shoulders like a vending machine that stole her money. "No, but where is that petty thief? He's going to get us all killed!"

Scarlett noticed the track marks dotting beneath her biceps, as if a gang of mosquitos ambushed her and tried to burrow through to the elbow. They looked just like her father's arms.

"Well?" Her teeth stained yellow as her skin became a battleground between tattoos, freckles, wrinkles and sores.

"He's—he's—" Scarlett froze, conditioned not to speak when her father addressed her in the same way. With the same yellow eyes. And the same cracked lips. "He's in gym, yeah. It's second period, innit? Th—then, he's—he's in the gymnasium. That's at the other end of the school."

She hurried away the moment the bell chimed. The students flooded the halls. Scarlett found Francis hurrying in the opposite direction with shadowed eyes, shoving through the crowd.

The fire door slammed shut behind him as he rushed beneath the first flight of steps. He hugged his knees as he thought of a way out—hiding, just as he was in the morning.

The door suddenly unlatched, echoing through the stairwell. He flinched, anticipating the inevitable.

Students poured in, pitter pattering up the steps as he tucked himself deeper into the shadows.

"It's alright," Scarlett said, subtly parting from the horde and joining him. "It's me. She won't find you here."

He kept his red-rimmed eyes hidden between his legs. His uniform sleeves strained back as he held in the discomfort of his stomach. The shooting pains revealed themselves as micro grunts that he couldn't conceal.

Scarlett rubbed his back, but gasped when she spotted the lines beneath his wrist. Thin, yet embossed. Faint, yet plenty.

"Oh, Franny ..."

She raised his face, running her thumb over his cheek.

"What do I do, Scarlett? I'm stuck; suspended in failure. My purpose, what my father told me, I can't just ignore it. But how can I ever fulfill it? And Madeleine … if I figure this out, it'll undoubtedly put her in danger. It's like she was dropped into an acidic cesspool and expected to float. She's everything that Slough isn't, and it's not fair that he left her with that witch. I don't know how to help her. I'm stuck, Scarlett. Stuck and alone, without him."

Scarlett reached for her sleeve, but stopped. She glanced once more at Francis before rolling it up and revealing, beneath the dim, flickering light bulb, the lines underneath her forearm.

"You're—you're not alone," she said. Francis's gaze snapped up and down, at her face, then at her arm. He never saw them on anybody else. They were similar, but hers were a lot more severe, thinner and longer. Some were completely healed, while others were still red, no older than a day. She rolled her sleeves back down and buttoned them, angling away from him as she felt more exposed than being naked. "It only drowns out the pain for a few seconds, but it's something."

"I'm sorry, Scarlett. I didn't know." Francis rested his head against the underside of either the fourth or fifth step, too exhausted to do the math. "I really hate this town."

The students continued stomping over their heads.

"It's our parents," Scarlett said. "They don't get us."

"My father did. He was the only one who understood me, and now he's gone."

Scarlett pulled out a pack of cigarettes from her bag. It had a lighter in the void spot of past smokes. The ten-year-old whacked it against her palm like a seasoned addict. She slid one out and offered it.

"No, thanks. Besides, it'll trip the alarm."

Scarlett smirked, flicking the lighter. "That's the plan," she murmured, with the cigarette pinched between her lips.

As other students paused and sniffed, fire-sprinklers erupted in a cascade of showers. Screams blared alongside the alarm, with the faculty repeating that it's not a drill.

Scarlett flicked the ash, pulling a drag while eyeing Francis. The water trickled beneath the flight, soaking their clothes. She dabbed the lit end in the puddle, hissing out the ember. She stepped out into the rain and threw her head back. The droplets washed over her face, drenching her bright, splattered bangs. She smiled and spun.

Francis joined her, and for the first time since his mother's funeral, also smiled. She slid his hair to the side. They sunk into each other's eyes, his charged, hers conductive.

They kissed.

Her tongue tasted like takeout and smoke, but he didn't care. Unsure of what to do with her hands, she hung them lifelessly at her sides.

He pulled away first and looked down. Both panted the humid air as the emotions confused them.

"What's wrong?"

"Nothing in my life is normal! I can't promise you anything. Even your safety."

"Normal is boring—I don't care for it," Scarlett stole his hands and squeezed, planting a kiss on his knuckles, "all I care for is you."

Chapter XIX
When Nothing Else Works

— Current Day —

The village torches, once a symbol of fear, became a sight for sore eyes. Julian glanced back, making sure the mysterious man didn't follow him. He leaned against the last of the parameter's trees, recalibrating his thoughts and observing Imamu from afar, unsure.

If he wanted us dead, Julian thought, we'd be dead. Yet …

He carefully placed Madeleine down and tended to her wound. None of his actions supported his lie.

But he might only need one of us alive, Julian thought.

He pushed his hair back and approached.

"Everything alright?" Ike asked. "You look as like you've seen a ghost."

Julian kneeled towards Madeleine, who rested her head on Zola's lap.

"I'm homesick, is all."

Ike regarded Julian's emotions. He handed him a stalk, no bigger than a pencil. "Here, you must be hungry. It's sugarcane. Just bite into it."

Julian compared it to his daily five course meals at the castle. He sighed before chomping the end. The sweetness coursed through his mouth, prompting him to take a second and third bite.

The three stared at him, rejuvenating his energy. He didn't want to admit it, but it tasted better and more natural than any dessert, any meal or any appetizer he'd ever eaten.

"[Surmic] Where'd you find her?" Zola asked.

Julian glanced, trying to dress the conversation with the Surmic words he learned.

"She made it to the border, but passed out before the markings," Imamu said.

He lied just now, Julian thought.

"I gave her enough to last her a day or two; I don't understand how she'd pass out."

Imamu casually shrugged. "Maybe she overexerted herself." Julian recognized the tone shift again.

Zola spotted the activated charcoal powder on her neck. "Why'd she use the antidote?"

"Eh ..." Imamu picked at his nails, "no, that was me. She got hurt when she collapsed and couldn't find anything else."

"Boy, this isn't for minor cuts. This is for—"

"[English] Zola?" Madeleine said, fluttering back to consciousness. "Where am I? What happened?" Madeleine tried to sit up.

Zola shushed her, patting her chest. "You tell us."

"Well ... last I remember, I was traveling northwest when I spotted those white marks you mentioned. I kept my distance, but then," she began shaking, "I heard these—these—*whispers*." Julian glanced from the corner of his eye. "At first, I thought I was imagining things, but they became louder, and louder." Zola felt her pulse race. "They were talking to me, but I didn't understand a word. The tone alone was so haunting that I just had to get away from it, so I ran. Barely a few steps on my bum ankle and suddenly something poked my neck, like a syringe. I'm not sure if that threw me over the border." Madeleine touched below her ear, grazing the powder. "What is this?"

Imamu nonchalantly looked at his mother, finding her already glaring at him.

"[Surmic] Boy, be honest with me!"

"Mama—"

"Those whispers—that's how they disorient you! Don't you bullshit me!"

"Mama, you know that if a Karo spotted her, she'd be **slain** by now."

Zola held her scowl, freezing time. Imamu stood his ground, but barely.

Julian noticed the word, '**garra**.' He grabbed Madeleine off Zola, eyes glued to the other two. "[English] Maddy—"

"Oh, shut up! What'd you expect me to do? How could I sleep through the night, knowing Leopaula is all alone out there?"

Julian stroked her arm. "I know, I know. But we— we— need to—"

"Oh, can it. Don't act like you care now." She shoved herself off him, but winced from the soreness in her neck. "Can someone please tell me what the hell this is?!"

"You must've hurt yourself when you collapsed," Zola said, still staring at her son and his friend.

Julian recalled the small rod before he, too, passed out.

She's in on it, Julian thought. *Everybody here is in on it!*

"Come on, Maddy." Julian lifted her up. His shuddered breaths burst in and out. "Come on, let's go!"

"Go where?!" Madeleine asked.

"Somewhere—anywhere else!"

Imamu's fingers fidgeted, but Julian wasn't going to let him take another step.

"Let's just," Zola patted the air, seeing the situation densify, "try to calm down—"

"Madeleine, Lady-Madeleine? Is—is that really you?" someone asked using British pronunciation.

The ears of the Royals perked up. The accent rang home. They turned to the figure clumsily emerging from the tree line. He was a Caucasian man wearing business casual clothes.

"It's really you!"

He tripped over himself in excitement, picking up his pace with his sight strained on the couple. The terrain wasn't easy on his polished black dress shoes, nor his tight silk necktie.

Madeleine replied, wearing a slack expression, "Y— yes. And you are?"

For Julian, the man's attire plastered a grin across his face. Madeleine looked around as others noted the newcomer. Upon spotting his car parked in the distance, her heart galloped.

"I'm a messenger from the embassy; Mr. Butts's office!"

Struck with fear, Imamu and Ike looked at each other, swallowing harshly. Julian noticed, but didn't care— freedom was in sight.

"Lady-Madeleine, Sir-Julian, I was sent to confirm—"

Imamu whispered to Ike, "[Surmic] We can't have Dada—"

Just then, a deep voice boomed. "[English] Where is your guide?!" Chief Amari emerged before a masquerade of tribesmen. They instantly surrounded the lone messenger.

The Brit halted. "Chief—Chief Amari, I—I—"

Amari unsheathed a massive machete as long as a baseball bat, muting the scene. The messenger, sight stuck on the blade, stumbled back. He crab-walked in a flurry, but bumped against more surrounding men. Like a magnet, he attracted more and more of the tribesmen the longer he stood in the spotlight. They held more than their glares towards him—they pointed their weapons, too.

The tribal mailman rushed over, dropping his mailbag as he lunged for the nearest spear. Letters fluttered about, scattering across the ground. One drifted in the wind, lodging right between Ike's toes. Imamu was too stunned to notice. Ike reached down and read the letter. Following a gasp, he concealed it.

"I said, where's your guide?!" Amari repeated, pointing the machete like a baton.

"I'm—I'm with the embassy, sent to—"

"There wasn't a request for any visitors today! Yet, here you are, without an invitation, and without a host."

"N—no, I'm from—from the government office of—"

Amari scoffed. "No guide, no invitation *and* you're with the government?!"

As Madeleine darted her gaze, Julian extended his arm in front of her.

Amari swung the machete to the side, swishing the air. "We have a protocol." The blade reflected the sunlight, gleaming its edge in a slather of thirst.

On the ground, disheveled and dusty, the messenger couldn't stop his trembling chin.

"Ch—Ch—Chief Amari, p—p—please. The circumstances—"

After a sudden shatter, the tires of the messenger's car blew out, and all the windows shattered.

"No!" Madeleine shrieked, but Julian pulled her back. Her chest heaved as her means of getting to Koka hospital demolished before her eyes.

Akilu, Amari's second in command, approached the vehicle with a lit torch, tossing it through the rear passenger window. Within moments, the car burst into flames, reflecting off Madeleine's bulging eyes.

The messenger, sweating and hyperventilating looked direly at Amari. "Chieftain, in your midst," Imamu tensed up, "you have—"

Amari swiftly planted the machete square into the man's skull, stopping just shy of the bridge of his nose. The blade stayed in its position on its own.

The messenger stopped talking.

He stopped blinking.

As did Madeleine.

Her scream echoed across the village as the image seared into her memory. The man's white button up loomed red with every long, lingering second.

Amari grunted as he removed the blade, then dropped it once more, harder this time. With every strike, a squelch and crunch. Only the tie kept the messenger's head from sliding apart until Amari severed that, too. He continued to slam down the steel as if a butcher, struggling with a stubborn tendon.

Eventually, he sliced all the way through. The cleaved halves balanced against each other, until one side gave in, dropping the innards like a viscous smoothie pouring out of a blender.

Unaffected and indifferent, Imamu stared as the rest of the tribe cringed.

No one said a word.

Not the adults.

Not the children.

Not Julian.

And not Madeleine. Her flight-response kicked in, but she had nowhere to flee to. Her heart, oddly beating, lodged in her throat. With a harried, wild appearance, she cried into the silent village, arm straining towards the scene, with the other cupping her mouth.

Julian dragged her back. He wanted to keep Ike and Imamu in his line of sight, but couldn't pull away from the horrific scene.

Amari wicked the machete, painting the dirt. "[Surmic] They never learn." He focused on the Royals, with a bead of blood rolling down the bridge of his nose.

"[English] Julian!" Madeleine screamed. "Julian, he's looking at us! Julian!" Pale and blank, the prince stared ahead. "Julian! Do something!"

A woman's laugh echoed throughout the village, for none to hear but him.

"No, no, no, no, no," Julian muttered under his breath.

"Julian!" Madeleine shook him, but his head remained locked in place, staring at an image, which nobody else saw. "Julian! Julian, he's coming!"

"Oh, Joules ..."

She stood behind the messenger's remains, nude and covered in blood. Her platinum blonde hair clumped together, forming thick locks which dripped the excess gore. Tattoos of vines, roses and petals snaked from her wrists, up towards her neck and down her cleavage, as she cupped Leopaula in her arms, flashing a sincere smile.

"Julian!" Madeleine jostled him as Amari approached.

Julian's lip jittered ...

168

"S—Scarlett ..."

Chapter XX
Whispers Beneath the Chimes of Wedding Bells

— The Royal Wedding, Eight Years Earlier —

Amid the murmuring audience, the 27-year-old Scarlett sported a punk pixie style haircut. The longer bang covered half her face, leaving only one dark brow above one steely blue eye exposed.

During the wait, everybody held small conversations. Some giggled, some nodded, some cheered. However, Scarlett, well, Scarlett sat mute, with only her Monroe piercing escaping her lips. Her smooth, curved back, forbidden yet visible through her airy mesh diamond dress, revealed the extent of her tattoos. With her shoulders also bare, the artwork screamed at any bystander. Nevertheless, she remained silent. Waiting. Focused on the altar.

That day, if someone sought a friend, it only took a keen eye, and they'd be able to spot them in fancy clothing. The men and boys wore jet black suits, while the women and girls varied in their outfits. Some sported large, solid color fascinators, while others displayed what looked like bouquets of assorted flowers and jewels sparkling in the sunlight. A little girl stole the show as she donned a sunhat wider than her entire body. Her comical expressions gave the photographers a heyday.

Families stood side-by-side, their faces shining with anticipation, holding wine glasses as they awaited the bride and groom. The air filled with the intoxicating scent of freshly bloomed roses, their fragrance mingling with the aroma of champagne. Young adults flirted with their childhood crushes, finding it to be the perfect opportunity to hint at the idea of a happily ever after together.

Joy filled the chapel. Smiles in every corner. All were present and accounted for.

All ... *but a single guard.*

Throughout the morning, attendees continued to trickle in. Laughter and chatter toned the air, blending with the melodic notes of the orchestra. An aura of joy flooded the fields of the Royal Chapel of All Saints at Royal Lodge for Prince Julian and Madeleine's wedding ceremony. Even the birds celebrated as they gleefully played a game of aerial tag. Photographers fixed their cameras on the route, anticipating the brigade of luxury vehicles carrying the soon-to-be newlyweds. Everybody waited, including Scarlett.

The High St. shops along the route closed for the event, leaving Slough a ghost-town. Rats roamed undisturbed through the alleys and rooftops. Orphans kicked cans across the street as the echoes from the wedding reverberated between the desolate intersections. A child lay flat on his back in a usually busy boulevard, knowing that no cars would pass by and that he'd never get another chance to do that. Some elderly folk smiled at the sight, as loved ones attending the reception abandoned them.

Church bells chimed as a vintage Aston Martin arrived at the chapel's front gate. The surrounding crowd clapped as the Naval-decorated Prince Julian stepped out, leading the cavalcade. All watched as the heir to the throne ascended the staircase, entering the chapel with utmost dignity and poise. Upon spotting him, the conductor began composing a lively symphony, flavoring the moment with sophistication and awe, forever etching it into the memory of the masses.

Through the cheers, Scarlett held her position, gazing from a single eye over her shoulder. Julian caught her mien, regal and radiant, like a full moon illuminating the night sky. With a dropping jaw, his head remained static as his feet continued. He missed a step and stumbled, falling midway to the altar. Ignoring those rushing to his aid, he took the opportunity to satisfy his eyes once more. The once-regal prince faded away, replaced by a weary traveler, his face etched with lines of exhaustion. He kneeled before her as she emanated an air of forbidden allure: an oasis in the dry desert, a mirage, off-limits and barred.

Scarlett slowly blinked, slightly smiled, then turned. The tattoo petals triggered Julian's heart rate, pulsing faster the more he followed the chaotic vines racing down her lower back. Their madness made sense to him, peaking his urge beyond any thriller movie or novel. He wanted to know where they went. He wanted to see her face again. He wanted to—

Just then, roars resonated from outside. The cheers and ovations overtook the symphonies. The guests, save Scarlett, turned towards the gleaming doorway, anticipating His Majesty. They hurried Julian towards the podium, but he kept looking back. The conductor paused, too eager to hold the tempo. Lost in timing, the orchestra members shrugged at each other.

The bulletproof Bently gently rolled to a halt. The youth raised their cell phones as the adults leaned in. King Leopold eased out of the vehicle with the help of one of his bishops, sparking a fresh surge of cheers. With great frailty, he held up his hand, insisting to walk on his own towards his son's big day. One step after another, the widowered king ascended the stone staircase. Every few strides, he'd stop, turn to the people and wave. The outdoor guests burst into tears of joy that only a citizen of the Kingdom could understand.

The King continued into the chapel, stopping before his son and meeting his gaze.

Julian lowered his head, but not before stealing another glance at Scarlett. "[English] Father."

King Leopold placed his hand on Julian's shoulder, grazing the epaulet. "My son, you've outshined Napoleon on this day, filling my heart with pride." He patted Julian's arm, and for the first time, gave him an approving nod. "May your union safeguard the Kingdom, and allow you to discover strength in your progeny, as I have."

The reporters' camera shutters drowned out the symphonies. However, when the most extravagant and elegant of cars approached the doorway, silence prevailed. In the stillness, the conductor raised his hands so high that his suit's coattail cracked the air, before he vehemently snapped them down, grimacing to his face's extent. The orchestra boomed *Mendelssohn's Wedding March.*

Faces glimmered.

Excitement lingered.

But behind the passenger door of the Porsche, Madeleine blushed through a veil.

"Come, dear! It's time!" an official instructed her from the open door. But Madeleine froze, never imagining so many people anticipating her presence. "Come, dear! Come, now!"

Security rammed reporters away from the automobile as Madeleine blew air in and out through her rounded mouth. The prime example of rags-to-riches couldn't move until the official gently reached in.

"You'll be fine, sweetheart. But you need to come along now!" The phobia and anxiety glued her to the backseat. "Come now!"

Madeleine hesitantly stepped out. The moment she placed her crystal slipper onto the pavement, the crowd lost it. With red cheeks and hand over her chest, her odd heartbeat fluttered her fingertips. She tried to recall everything reviewed during the rehearsal, but no way was that possible. Her wide grin caused her neck arteries to flex out further than her glimmering earlobes.

She confiscated all gazes upon entering the chapel, without exception. Those outside watched the livestream as those inside despised the requirement to blink. The up-and-coming church children held up her dress, as others sprinkled her with white and pink petals. A giggle escaped, challenging her attempt to keep with formalities as she continued over the red carpet.

Madeleine stood before Julian, coy, shining, a little fearful but happy. She stared down and reddened. He raised her veil.

"You ready?" he whispered.

She nodded, but noticed him sneak a glance at the crowd. "Are you?"

He dropped all expressions. Scarlett's magnetism tugged at his eyes, but with Madeleine staring directly at him and in her wedding dress—

Julian snapped his eyes shut just before he glanced once more, saving himself. He concentrated on the memory as Madeleine watched him grimace. He exhaled. "I am."

Julian nodded at the archbishop, with his bride suspiciously side eyeing him.

Among the silent thousands, Scarlett clasped her matching pocketbook shut. It clapped, echoing between the pews, but nobody cared, save Julian. She knew he had eyes on the back of his head for her. His mind flashed him her radiant minidress with slitted sides, revealing all but her buttocks as she crossed one leg over the other.

Look at me, Scarlett thought. Look at me, now!

Julian heard her thoughts, but alongside Madeleine, during their wedding, he fought the temptation. He glanced up at the architecture, the stained-glass windows, the wreaths, the decorated pillars, the pews, the people—

Again, Scarlett.

Their gazes fastened to one another, torqued and seized beyond the hope of any power tool. She flashed him one more seductive smile, biting her lower lip. He broke away and turned before anybody noticed. Scarlett narrowed her eyes at his slick, groomed, golden hair. He sensed her mentally undressing him as his mind insisted that he do the same. Fidgetingly patting around, he reached for Madeleine's fingers before tightly intertwining them.

Feeling his shaky grip, Madeleine glanced. Before she could ask if he was alright, the officiant raised his chin, innocently grinning.

"Dearly beloved ..."

—

With fiercely open eyes, Francis, absent from the celebration, stood alone in Windsor Castle's shadowy and rarely visited documentation cellar. Liquid trickled through the waste-plumbing pipes running behind the underground walls. Streams of moisture painted the partitions of the basement. Ahead of him, page after page of records, all flickered by candlelight, each more significant than the last. As the sound of the distant wedding bells resonated above, a deathly silence lingered in the fireproofed dungeon. A few loyal guards, who, in later years, would help the newlyweds flee with Leopaula, kept watch.

Francis read all the documents, absorbing everything; the reality, the proof, but most painfully, the betrayal.

"He was telling the truth," Francis muttered.

A supporter descended into the cellar and tapped the corner of a folded note against Francis's arm. "Here, from Napoleon."

Francis took the letter and read, wrinkling the edges of the paper following each scanned line. Before making it to the end, he hid his reddened eyes, breathing the stale cellar air.

The supporter patted him on the shoulder. "I know you'll do the right thing."

Francis folded the note and stowed it away before he returned to the time critical task at hand.

Lordes sounded two bellowing knocks from above. "Scarlett sent the signal; the ceremony is concluding. We must hurry."

Francis sifted through more evidence of the real criminals at the heart of the nearly 30-year scandal, which was all but forgotten. With a stern expression, he rifled through more drawers, pulling out transactional archives, communication records and incriminating photographs. Individually, they were insignificant, but collectively they unveiled the truth behind the late Wallis's words.

"This Kingdom," Francis muttered. "It's built on nothing but an ocean of lies."

Another knock. "They're on their way; we must go, now!"

Francis clenched his teeth as he learned the truth about everybody—those who've lied to his face, and those who didn't even know they were lying. His nails dug into his palms as he tightened his fist in contempt of the entire establishment.

Lordes leaped down. "Come now, we have to grab whatever's most damning before it's too late."

"No!" Francis swatted his hand away. "If we play by their rules, they'll do to us what they did to *him*. We'll be called terrorists—a mere footnote in history. We're on the side of truth! Whereas the abomination going on right now," he pointed upward, "is the product of their corruption. It's their sin being forced upon them! And our obligation is to cleanse the Kingdom of such vermin!"

Another member of the cause warned of the visibly approaching wedding party, and a phone call for Julian from someone named D'jen.

"I'll take the call," Francis said before storming towards the ladder. Now equipped with the unambiguous veracity to fuel his once misunderstood childhood ambition, he grasped the first rung. He stopped and glowered back at Lordes. "Assign everybody a target as I handle Julian myself. It's time we kill them all!"

—

Separating their lips, Julian and Madeleine beamed after having shared their first kiss as a married couple.

Chapter XXI
The World's Most Dangerous Tribe

— Current Day —

"Julian!" Madeleine shook him, but it was as if his body didn't house a soul. "Julian!" Amari drew near. The blood slid. The machete gleamed. "Snap out of it!"

The people converged on the Royals. Madeleine pelted sweat from every pore as she sought an escape. Her grip on the dazed Julian cut off his circulation. But Scarlett's presence kept him paralyzed, eyeing him the same way she did during the wedding. Her eyes hypnotized him as his body begged him to flee. The fear clashed with his sexual drive, both warring over his heart. All other sounds muted for him, save her laugh—her laugh, and Madeleine's scream.

Thick black smoke billowed from the flames engulfing the messenger's car. It loomed over the village as a doomsday cloud, overtaking everything in its path, like an army of slathering ghouls, led by Amari at the helm.

Drop after drop, the blood dyed the dirt as if a trail of breadcrumbs stalking his footsteps.

"Julian, please! Please!"

Amari raised the blade towards the couple. Madeleine hid behind her husband, clenching his shirt and burying her face.

Julian, skin ashen, stared through the Chieftain. Scarlett stopped laughing when the smoke swallowed her.

"Was that your man?" Amari asked. Julian's eyes refocused on the leader before him. His head shuddered right to left. "Then how'd he know you, and where is your guide?" His deep voice demanded answers. Nothing else.

Zola stepped in. "Imamu's their guide, and I'm hosting them."

Amari observed the three. "[Surmic] What's the meaning of this? Who are these two, and why's this boy look familiar?" He leaned in, squinting.

Colorless, Julian faced him.

Zola stood. "They're—"

Imamu rushed into the scene. "They're in my care!"

Amari pushed his son aside, attention welded to Julian. "[English] Are you ... *Napoleon's brother?*"

"How—how do you know my—my b—brother?"

Amari turned to Imamu and Zola. "[Surmic] What's going on? Why's the prince of the United Kingdom here?"

Ike pursed his lips, shielded his face and crept away.

Through a faint whisper, Madeleine's prayer resonated. She tried ignoring the amassing red puddle beside Amari's foot.

"Nothing?" Amari rhetorically asked. "[English] Perhaps you could tell me what you're doing on Mun land."

Madeleine paused. With eyes unblinking, she pivoted. "*Mun?* Did you say, Mun? You're, Mun?"

"Yes."

She stood, patting her husband's chest as if playing whack-a-mole. "Julian, this is Mun! Francis's friend, Mursi! Remember? From his text! This is him!"

Amari held up his free hand. "No, Mun is the name of our tribe. Mursi is what outsiders call us. Now, why're you here?"

Imamu re-entered the conversation. "[Surmic] They came here for more lithium. They want to negotiate."

Julian noticed the tone shift again. He pulled Madeleine back.

Amari squeezed the machete's handle, oozing out the embedded sweat. "Not interested!"

"[English] Stop! No, everybody, stop! Tell me, is Mun a person or are you all, Mun, or—or Mursi?"

It was common sense for all but Madeleine. Zola nodded.

"No," she said with a delusional smile. "No, no, no, no … NO!" The people flinched. "Julian, give me your phone!"

He slapped her hand away. "Quit it!"

"What?" Madeleine asked.

"That's right. You're not calling the shots, got it? Last time you did, we ended up face down in the woods."

She growled through gritted teeth as the tribespeople watched. "*Francis*, my brother, *the great goddamn Francis*, doesn't have a military buddy here! This tribe is Mun! This was never about helping us! I—I don't know what this is! But it's definitely not a gesture of good-faith!"

Madeleine turned to Amari. "You! Did you kill Leopaula?!"

He raised an eyebrow. "And who is this *Leopaula?*"

"[Surmic] They're here to negotiate for the lithium," Imamu said. "But upon their arrival, they lost their daughter, Leopaula."

Rippling his grip over the hilt, Amari asked, "So, they came unannounced?"

Imamu stood before his father, chin raised. "No, I've been communicating with them through this." He wobbled his cell phone before the traditional leader's face. "This is how we save our people; through diplomatic means, not through blind brutality." He glanced at the cleaved body.

Zola recalled his story, and Madeleine's recount of everything. He never mentioned anything about talking to them on the phone.

"I'm working on it," Imamu said. "Now please, stop frightening my guests. This whole … *display* of strength of yours is unnecessary."

Amari scoffed into Imamu's face before addressing Madeleine. "[English] No. I didn't kill your daughter. But if it was me that spotted her, I would've. So, if you and little Napoleon aren't off my land by sunrise, you'll be seeing this blade again, but a lot closer and cross-eyed."

"Hey!" Julian barked.

Imamu slid between them before they locked horns. "[Surmic] No threats. No fear. We aren't only negotiating the lithium—we're also discussing the release of the prisoners." The entire tribe's ears, without exception, perked. "Don't you want Yonas back?"

Amari shoved the blade beside Imamu's foot, fixing into the ground like a flagpole. Imamu didn't flinch. "Are you lying to me, boy?!"

"They're here, are they not? This is their gesture; they've sent their prince to our prince. That should show you how serious they are. They now have machinery that doesn't require workers to excavate." Breaths deep and forceful, Amari eyed the royals. "But with the development of their missing daughter, we're at a standstill."

"Where is the girl?" Amari asked.

"I found her beside the river, alive, but unconscious. I gave her to the caravan, who've since taken her to the hospital."

"Which hospital?"

"Kibish."

Zola tightened her glare, but didn't say a word. Julian noticed it, too, as Amari only sensed it.

"All deals go through me," he said. "Understood?"

Imamu growled, "I wanted to *actually* make a deal, *unlike last time.*"

Amari clenched his fist, but suddenly saw Yonas in Imamu. The memory shackled him. He relaxed his hand as his mouth poured open.

"The girl should be back within two, three days, max," Imamu said. "The hospital confirmed." Amari, exposed and weak, glanced at Zola. She nodded. "Until then, we can't have them running off in fear. So, please …" Imamu gestured towards the crimson machete, still stained with grime and gore.

Amari regarded the couple. Madeleine trembled as Julian prepared himself to defend. He hated them, but not more than his love for Yonas.

"Keep me informed." He wicked, twirled and sheathed the machete into its scabbard. "This valley won't be turned into a resort. If our people aren't free in three days," he flashed his fingers at Julian, "then they'll be staying *indefinitely*." Before leaving, he side eyed Imamu. "And don't think I forgot about the generational dagger. It's Kamari's. He's our next leader, not you. Now, go fetch." He smirked a frown before he turned and left.

Imamu wanted to race home, grab the dagger and run it through his father's spine. But he remained in his place and exhaled as he dropped his shoulders.

"[English] Hey," Madeleine said. "Where's Leopaula?! Did that man kill her?!"

Zola was too busy observing her son, giving Madeleine a waiting finger.

"[Surmic] What?" Imamu asked.

"Why'd you lie? You said the girl was at Koka, and now you're saying Kibish."

"Koka told me yesterday that she had to be transferred."

Zola slapped her thigh, just missing Kamari. "You're lying!"

"Believe what you will. I'm the only one helping this tribe, while you and your simpleminded husband chase rituals and chosen daggers." He snapped his fingers before Julian's face. "[English] You. We need to talk." He grabbed his arm, leading him away.

Madeleine grabbed Zola. "Hey! Why's everybody okay with what just happened? And where's my daughter?!"

Zola wriggled her shoulders free. "You're surprised? Mad-girl, dis is what we do to trespassers! This is why they call us *The World's Most Dangerous Tribe!* After everything we went true, Amari commanded it. And guess what? None of us are against it! We don't play their lip-smacking games. This is the only way that has kept them off our land for the last eight years. And we're going to keep doing it, because it's the only thing that turns you haranchis even paler. Just as we like ya."

Madeleine needed a door to storm through and slam shut, or at least someone to understand how insane it all was. Zola, her only friend, now seemed like a wolf in sheep's clothing. "You're monsters—you're all monsters!"

"Monsters? And you tink wearing a suit and tie makes one human? To us, dat attire ain't no different from the grim-reaper. Tsk, monsters …" Zola shook her head, name-calling under her breath and looking out at the scene. The flames of the car balled as it wrestled with the air, reaching for the sky. The asphyxiating smoke grew into an overlord who ruled the hidden settlement. "Monsters," Zola repeated in disbelief. "And what would you do if someone kidnapped or killed Leopaula and just walked into your home, dressed and groomed like he was going ta church?"

"I'd—" Madeleine immediately opened her mouth, but found herself at a loss for words. "I'd …" She slowed down, finding herself in their shoes. Her disgust and resentment simmered as the smoke seemed to comfort her. Brutal justice, when put in that perspective, suddenly made sense to her.

"I'm not sure where Leopaula is, but I'm trying to find out for you. I'm really trying. There's a lot on the line, and rushing to learn the truth will make matters worse."

"… *Worse?*" Madeleine found two Mursi men carrying the halves of the messenger's body towards the car. The blood soaked the dirt like a garden hose leaking out what's left after the faucet squeaked shut. As if yesterday's trash, they tossed the corpse into the inferno. "There is no worse. This is hell."

"Princess, this is what we, Mun, are known for."

The lifeless body roasted with every passing blink. Its skin shriveled and charred before it couldn't get any darker. Absent of hair. Absent of color. It no longer held any characteristics. Just black.

Madeleine couldn't tear away. "And this is exactly where my brother wanted us."

Chapter XXII
I Know You Know

"[Surmic] We can't hurt them," Akilu said.

He followed Amari to a small nestled pond, hidden past a winding trail and fed by one of Omo's offshoots. The secluded pool provided the chieftain a distant view of the mountains of Mago National Park, while the opposing horizon hazed a glimmer of the Kenyan border.

Amari dipped his feet. The chill contrasted his fuming demeanor. He glided the machete through the pond. The blade shined again, as the water tinted pink for a brief moment. The steel clanked as he placed it beside him.

"And why not?" Amari asked. "A haranchi is a haranchi. I don't care how else the world views them."

"The Kingdom would retaliate."

Amari looked at his reflection in the pond. The messenger's blood dried along the creases of his forehead.

"We never wanted any of this madness, but they keep bringing it into our lives." He turned to Akilu. "If we don't hold our ground and stick to what's worked, they're going to continue. No exceptions."

Akilu sat on the opposite side of the pool. He didn't submerge his feet out of respect.

"We cannot harm them, whatsoever. These two, *they get an exception*. Last time, Yonas only killed a few of their labor force, a bandit of nobodies. Whereas, these … these are Royalty. The Kingdom's jewels."

The aquatic rippling caustics decorated the sheltering boulders, pacifying the longtime friends. Amari reached in and splashed some water over his face. The droplets echoed and undulated through the pool, reaching Akilu's side.

"What should we do?" Amari asked.

"We need to retrieve their daughter, Leopaula. Until then, we shouldn't have them venturing off on their own. Their situation leaves them with nowhere to go, and it's possible they're unaware of this. If they leave, they'll either cross into Karo land, where D'jen will be another problem, or they will attempt to hike the savannah on foot, which'll result in their demise. Your son's right, we can't scare them."

Amari exhaled as he turned towards the heavens.

"Akilu, we're a forgotten people, forced to make do with what little we have. And what we have here is a divine opportunity that can finally liberate us. We won't just hand them the girl back. No," Amari tsked, "when we find her, we use her to free us, and our brothers in those mines. That girl is our only way of escaping this hell."

"They don't negotiate." Akilu stared with utmost sternness.

"But this time, they'll have to. We must capitalize on this. So, until we could think of something else, we hold them until our demands are met. Let's give them the impression that we're hosting them. It'll keep them calm, as you wanted, while the Kingdom panics. And in their panic, they'll mess up." Unbeknownst to him, he mirrored Imamu's plan.

"No, when the Kingdom panics, it lashes out. Regardless, we can't count on a mistake."

Amari withdrew his feet and laid flat on his back. The leaves shuddered the sunlight, slicing it with every passing zephyr. He noticed Akilu's silence. "What is it?"

"I don't think the girl is missing, or harmed," Akilu said. "If she were, the Kingdom would've sent their entire military to find her, and wouldn't depend on Omo's poor hospital sector. Yet, they're here. No armed forces. No hysteria. Almost like the Kingdom isn't aware of where they are, or their status."

"So, where could their daughter be?"

"I'm not sure. But if she's dead, we're ruined. The mother's reacting as though she were missing, while the father," Akilu took a deep breath, "something's off about him. His demeanor's no different from those who've seen a spirit, demon or something of the like. Because as prince of the UK, I'd expect him to be more callous to the sight of blood."

Amari recalled Julian's tremors. "He's an alcoholic, probably having withdrawals."

"Perhaps."

Amari widely blinked at the sky. "Something isn't lining up. If he was here to negotiate, and an alcoholic, where're his rations? In fact," he sat up, "where are his clothes, his supplies or guards?"

"Chieftess Zola told me their things fell out of their boat when it flipped over."

"Boat ... where in this valley could they have gotten a boat? What is this? When do you ever see the prince and princess of the United Kingdom unguarded in a place like this? Even tourists don't come here without protection from the Ethiopian military. Either the spirits are blessing me beyond my imagination, or someone's behind this."

Akilu tapped his fingers along the edge of the pond's rocks. "What do you want to do?"

Amari's guttural growl visibly vibrated through the serene pond. The shading leaves overlapped, blotting shadows over his scowl. "As long as we have them, I won't pass up the chance of freeing Yonas ... or taking vengeance."

———

Back in the village, Imamu pulled Julian along as they met with Ike.

"Good thing Chief Amari believed you," Ike said. "But now, time is against us."

Julian shot his gaze at the two, trying to pick up as much Surmic as possible from what Zee taught him.

"Yes," Imamu said. "Now that Dada's involved, I can't follow up on my bluff to the embassy."

"Let's tie him up," Ike glanced at Julian, "somewhere far. That way, if the Kingdom doesn't pay up, or if they send someone else, they'll only find the princess and we'll still have him as a hostage."

"Wait, I have an idea," Imamu said, before turning to Julian. "[English] You're going to need another drink soon, aren't you?"

Julian didn't regard Imamu. He instead glared at Ike. "What'd you drug me with? What was in that stick you gave me?"

"The stick? You mean the sorghum?" He pulled out another stem. "It's just a boost of energy; sugar."

"It was drugged—don't play dumb with me!" Julian knew it wasn't possible for Scarlett to be there.

"You've never heard of sorghum?" Imamu asked.

"No! Because I don't feed off the land like an—an animal!"

"Prince," Ike said. "You're in shock. We get it. But we didn't poison you, nor would we want to. See?" He chomped off a piece of the stalk and chewed. "Harmless."

"You're probably hungry," Imamu said.

"Just bring me more of that schnapps. No more of your food."

"We're low on liquor, but I know where we could get some, and food you'd be more familiar with."

"Where would that be? We're in the middle of a Godforsaken wasteland."

"The mines."

"You want me to go to the mines? The lithium mines?"

"Yes. They'll have more schnapps than you can swim in, and food you're acquainted with."

"What's in it for you?"

"My father, you see how he is. If you come with us there, I'm sure, upon hearing it from you, the haranchi guards will free some of our people. My father would be grateful and he doesn't harm those whom he owes favors to. They'll also have vehicles to return you home. Win-win."

Julian understood it was a trap. To him, Imamu's tone shift was like a piercing whistle during an opera. However, his grumbling stomach found the logic to be airtight. "What about Madeleine?"

Imamu was quick to respond. "With her ankle the way it is?"

Julian studied him. He picked at his nails. He also held his expression for a long time. An uncomfortably long time.

Smirking, Julian asked, "You look before you leap, don't you?"

Imamu tilted his head. "Would that be a problem?" Even his pulse remained leveled.

"Give me your phone." Julian reached out. "I could call the guards." He envisioned it. A single dial, and paratroopers, commandos and rangers would flood the village. All the Mursi would have their hands up, begging and groveling for their lives. A tic overtook his cheek, jittering a grin across his face. He curled his four fingers, leaving his thumb stationary as his palm faced the cloudless sky. "Give it here. I'll ring the guards and they'll pick me up, bringing along with them your buddies."

Imamu's memory reeled with episodes of the expulsion. The burning huts, the children's screams, Yonas's face. Before him, Julian pompously grinned, mirroring the haranchis from then. Handing him the phone would be no different from when Amari signed the documents. He wasn't going to let it happen again.

"There's no reception here," Imamu said.

"Is that right—"

"That's right."

"Not even beside the river?"

"Zero."

"So, all those things you've learned—the arrhythmia, the lasers, science, all of it, you're saying all of that happened while you were outside of the village? Because from the talk of the town, you're generally huddled away in your hut, riding daddy's coattail."

Suddenly, Imamu wished he hadn't stepped in earlier and just let his father do the deed. His imagination flashed images of the would-be blood trickling down Julian's face, dripping from lip to lip as his smirk disappeared into nothingness.

"That's correct. The reception comes and goes, and right now, it goes. The best spot is near the excavation site. Besides, those guards of yours, they're not too bright. Mere brutes with guns. If you called them, they wouldn't believe it to be you. And if I approached alone, they'd throw me in with the rest."

Both wanted the same, while neither believed the other.

Ike bounced his gaze between them.

Neither spoke.

Neither blinked.

Ike stepped back.

"Very well," Julian said. "Let's go." Alone, out in the wild, with a defenseless Imamu—he found it to be the perfect opportunity.

"Good. We'll have to leave at daybreak. Otherwise, it'll get dark before we make it."

Imamu reached his hand out. Julian regarded it, looked him in the eye once more, then shook …

194

Neither mentioned Leopaula.

Chapter XXIII
In the Shadow of the Crown

— 14 Months Earlier —

"Where is she?" the apothecary asked.

Julian, panting, leaning and sweating, found the doctor atop Windsor Castle's tallest tower; the Round Tower. A stethoscope slung around his neck, resting over his chest as he leaned against one of the sixteen cannons, which haven't seen action in over two hundred years.

Julian told Francis to guard the stairwell as he approached the oncologist, catching his breath with every step. The wind fought him back, billowing his hair out of his line of sight. The closer he drew to the doctor, the more the scenery revealed itself.

"It's just us," Julian said. "Madeleine's not coming. She has to take care of something." He looked around. "Doctor, this is truly a lousy place to hold a private conversation. We're on an 800-year-old tower that hovers dominant over every other building. All eyes are drawn upon this point."

The doctor held a smug grin as he observed Julian's fatigue cripple him. "You should really invest more time towards your cardio, sir." The afternoon sun broke past the tower's battlements, casting stretched, daunting shadows, as the draft whistled through the cannon's bore. "You've just accomplished the 'Conquer the Tower' tour, and now you're awarded this spectacular view. Look," he pointed over the southern edge, "there's The Long Walk, and its end is actually visible from up here."

"Doc," Julian leaned over his knees, "I couldn't give a damn about that right now. This is my castle, and I didn't climb all the way up here to sightsee. What's this about? Why'd you want to meet with me like this?"

The doctor's smile reeked of beans he was ready to spill. "Technically, you're right; this is your castle. But is it *really?*"

"What do you mean?"

"Sir-Julian, you've found yourself in quite an anomalous situation." The doctor regarded the flag, which waved and flapped above all else. Julian noticed it was the Union Flag, not the Royal Standard. He raised an eyebrow.

"Is father not in the residence?" Julian asked. Francis stole a glance from the corner of his eye. The doctor's grin spread, slimy and knowing. "Is he going to make it?"

"The call is mine," the doctor bit his lip as he mentally tallied his gains, "but I want something in return …"

Later, he left, beginning the long descent back to ground level.

"What was that about?" Francis asked.

"My father …" Julian observed the view of the castle, then met Francis's gaze, "his time is up …"

A strong wind blew. Stoic, Francis parted his lips as his mind assembled the puzzle pieces. However, Julian … well, Julian adopted the doctor's expression.

He dialed Madeleine to give her the news, excitedly placing the call on speakerphone.

"Juley?"

"Maddy, you're never going to believe this—"

"Neither are you—"

"My father—wait. What?"

"You go first," Madeleine said. "I promise my news is bigger!"

"Alright, well, get this. My father—they're admitting him into hospice within the next two to three years! I just spoke with the oncologist!" Madeleine gasped as Julian's face didn't fit the news. "He'll issue a public statement declaring His Majesty unable to uphold his duties and recommend he abdicates the throne. Abdicate, Maddy! Abdication, not regency!"

Francis tightened his fist as his view of Julian's joy reddened. Julian was too eager to notice.

"What's this mean?" Madeleine asked. "You know I'm horrible with all this Royal terminology rubbish."

Julian rolled his eyes. "Regency is when the king withdraws from his duties, but still holds onto his title. But abdication is when he steps down entirely, meaning—"

"Are you saying you're going to be crowned king of the United Kingdom?"

"Yes, Maddy, yes! From duke to prince, and now from prince to king!"

Francis's sudden instinct told him to shove Julian. He pictured it. *He'd topple over the cannon's barrel after stumbling back. The entire time, his eyes would align with Francis's right before he rolled over, arms flailing as he plummeted towards the ground like a failed bird attempting its first flight.*

He snapped back to reality, realizing that if Julian became king, he'd no longer have a single Royal Guard. He'd have a full team; The King's Life Guard—ten troopers, two non-commissioned officers, one officer, one corporal major and one trumpeter … making it impossible for Julian to even go to the restroom without constant protection. Let alone Omo Valley.

"Well, I have some news for you, too," Madeleine said. "Check your phone. I sent you something …"

Julian couldn't imagine anything that could drag him down, nor better. But when he opened the picture message, his heart dropped.

(+)

"Well?" Madeleine asked, anticipating his response.

The rollercoaster plunged. Julian said nothing. No scream or thrill sounded as the tourists below laughed at something unrelated.

"*Hello?*" Madeleine's faint voice sounded from the phone dangling beside Julian's hip.

Francis spotted the picture of the positive pregnancy test. He no longer had to shove Julian over the edge. The prince was already falling.

His smile faded. His joy muted. His understanding of life as he knew it meant nothing.

"What is this?" Julian asked.

"It's finally happened! Juley, I'm pregnant!"

The sun suddenly felt too warm, the breeze too cold. Vertigo struck, collapsing Julian to where he had to grab hold of Francis, who didn't help him up. Like an expired star, he imploded before him, ceasing from existence.

"Juley?" Madeleine asked.

Francis picked up the Samsung. "Your husband isn't responding the way you would've wanted him to."

"France?"

"Yes, I'm here. I'm—I'm happy for you," he lied. "But are you sure? You don't want news like this getting out too early. The media will have their way with you if this turns out to be another miscarriage."

"Well, I'm late, and we've been trying—w—would you put Julian back on the phone?"

"As you wish, but I advise you to keep this matter private until the second trimester. This news rarely holds water for you."

"*I see you've also bought into the rumors.* Just give me back my husband."

Francis forced Julian to his feet with little care. He handed him the phone and returned to the stairwell, making a phone call of his own.

"Umm," Julian said.

"Wow. Well, okay. I figured you'd be more …"

"What?"

"*Excited.* This is what we've always wanted. You're going to be a father—we're about to be parents!"

"Are you, eh—are you sure it's mine?"

An awkward pause lingered.

"The bloody hell, Julian? What's wrong with you? You prance around at the news that your father's dying, and fall into a gloom when you hear about your baby on the way. What an arsehole!" She hung up.

Francis rejoined the prince. Neither spoke. Murmurs of the tourists continued below. Some laughed, some observed the castle. Julian looked over the edge, holding the bricks for stability. The opposing sun painted his face orange. He turned and slumped, helplessly staring at his hands.

"Yes, yes; we've been trying, but after seven years, Francis, I never thought it would happen, and I began to like the idea of no kids. But now … I'll never be able to be with another woman. This seals it for me."

"No, marrying my sister should've sealed that."

Julian swatted the air, turning his head towards the mighty cannon, which never gets used to its potential.

"There's always the option of divorce, but a father will forever be tied to the mother," Julian said.

Suddenly, Francis found the opportunity he'd been seeking. It widened his eyes as he reminded himself to appear sympathetic.

"Is there another woman you'd rather be with?" Francis asked.

Julian regarded the pebbles between his legs, dirtying the otherwise maintained castle tower.

"It's awkward talking to you about it, considering you're my brother-in-law."

Francis sat beside him, placing his arm over his shoulders.

"For this conversation, consider me a friend. We're men, after all. It's normal to notice other women. I won't hold it against you."

Julian blushed as he reminisced. "I can't get her out of my head." He appreciated the auburn atmosphere. "This one little bird." He pinched his legs to conceal his body's accustomed reaction to the memory. Francis noticed. "She attended the wedding."

"*Your wedding?* So, some random woman from seven years ago is ringing your bell?!"

"You don't understand. I can't unsee her, Francis. She's everything I've ever wanted."

"Sir-Julian, you're the prince of the UK who's set to take the throne. What could you possibly ever want and not have?"

Julian scoffed. He absently toyed with the few pebbles, running his fingertips over them, back and forth, causing a grudging noise that soothed his ache. "By now, you know this royal life of mine. The telly is the only place I've ever seen teen-rebellion. I'm forbidden from everything, Francis. I've never gotten drunk at a pub, or attended a house party while the parents were out. Hell, I've never broken the speed limit or shouted at the top of my lungs towards the night sky. I can't even make a bloody prank call. I'm just this—this—perfect specimen, who's now going to become the king of a people that I don't resemble at all."

Francis welded his eyes on Julian, never before seeing this side of him.

"How's this tie in with your fantasy girl from the Royal Wedding?"

A weighted sigh escaped as Julian threw his head back. "This woman, Francis, she had *depth*. The same quality you had, which prompted me to take you as my Royal Guard. It's worn only by those who've actually lived life. She embodies the freedom I've always wanted. The people call this place a castle, but all I see is a prison. Even if I abdicated my position, I have no skills that'll support me in the outside world. And I know your sister doesn't truly love me; she's only with me for this title."

"That's not true—"

"You think someone like me has no wants? No desires?" Julian shook his head. "Francis, I want to be free."

Francis suddenly recalled Wallis as he looked at his brother-in-law. The words he shared at the funeral were similar.

"This woman," Julian said. "She was free. Free from all this nonsense. This mock civility and bullshit order. We're just liars, Francis. For God's sake, we call this The Round Tower, and it's not even round! I'm a man who's been to war and returned home unscathed. Yet, this one lady, her memory alone, brings me to my knees. Her radiating dress, her back, her ink, her hair. Oh, her hair … it caught me like a fish."

Francis narrowed his vision.

No way, he thought. It's not possible.

He needed to be sure. "What—what color was her hair?"

"Blonde."

Francis leaned in closer, unable to believe the chances. "What shade?"

"Bright. Like, *really bright.* But it contrasted her dark eyebrows in such a sexual way."

"Bleached blonde?"

"No, no," Julian closed his eyes, shaking his head as he saw her perfectly in his mind. "I think it's called *platinum blonde.*"

Francis's grin stretched. It kept stretching. More and more.

"I tell ya, ever since I saw her, she's lived in my head, absolutely rent-free. She thrills me in ways beyond my imagination. And yet—" He stopped talking, realizing how open he was becoming.

"Go on, you can confide in me," Francis said as Julian turned away with burning cheeks. "Hey, there's no judgment here. I'm a friend."

"Well, sometimes … when Maddy doesn't put out, or excite me, I … I have to think about this mystery woman in order to …" Julian covered his face. "God, I'm such an idiot."

"… To climax?" Francis finished the confession.

"Yes." Julian rested his head against the bricks. "If Madeleine discovered how much time I spent searching for that woman in the wedding footage, she'd stab me through the throat."

"Did you ever find her?"

"Mhmm. Want to see?"

"Sure."

Moments later, Francis stared at the bookmarked YouTube video on Julian's phone. His mouth poured open as the image of Scarlett, sitting on the pew, shined into his retinas. He was speechless.

"I know," Julian said.

Francis looked at Scarlett's image. Then at Julian. Then back at Scarlett. Then finally, back at Julian.

He smiled. A slight smile. One that didn't involve the movement of the eyebrows.

Julian put the phone away, but not before peeking at Scarlett's freeze-frame once more.

"Sounds like you've gotten yourself into the age-old dilemma," Francis said.

"What's there to do? This woman, as long as her memory exists, will prevent me from ever being able to give Madeleine the attention she deserves. Let alone our child."

"Well, that's easy."

"Easy? Francis, I'm going mad here."

"Only love can conquer love, Sir-Julian. If you love someone that's forbidden, all you need to do is pivot that love towards something else." Francis could tell that he wasn't getting it. "If someone loves drugs, then finds God, he'll sober up quicker than undergoing any rehab. Because his love for God will be greater. Or, let's say someone falls in love with a married woman. All the lad has to do is find someone else, and that new love shall dominate. Get it? So, if you love this mystery woman, then let's pivot your love towards something else. Perhaps I could show you some of those experiences you've missed out on. It'll get your mind off her."

"Like what?"

"You have nearly every supercar in the world, Sir-Julian. Let's go out and break the speed limit tonight. Let's get drunk and party. I know some people who wouldn't mind the prince in their midst, nor would they blab to the public. It'll be fun and make you forget all about that fantasy girl."

"You'd do that for me?"

"You need this, so let me help. Let's grab a bottle and celebrate you." Francis firmly poked Julian's chest. "It'll be your last chance at fun and freedom before the little one enters the picture."

His heart fluttered as the spirit refilled his body. Francis reached down and hauled him up.

"I'll take care of you, Sir-Julian."

"Then just make sure to grab that black-label whiskey. That's my favorite."

Francis patted his shoulder. "I'll bring two."

—

Moments later, Julian's Porsche revved on as the garage door ascended. The vehicle prowled off the driveway before grumbling and roaring towards the sparsely occupied highway. The cabin carried the scent of his cologne as it mixed with the dying cigarette dangling between his lips. He swerved in and between small batches of traffic, slicing each car with his sharp HID projector headlights. Francis bobbed up and down in the passenger bucket seat as Julian pushed on the accelerator.

"More," the knight muttered, eyes on the road. The prince firmed his grip over the wheel, slamming the pedal to the floor. The exhaust boomed through the otherwise quiet evening. "More!"

Julian shifted, before flicking the butt out of the window and glaring at the road ahead. He woo'd at the top of his lungs as the cigarette raced along the pavement, scattering embers into the air. Sparse flames burst from the exhaust as the night swallowed the minimizing tail lights.

A smile crept across Francis's face.

Chapter XXIV
Suddenly, Parenthood

— Three Months After Leopaula's Birth —

The hazy memory looped in Julian's mind. The single moment that would forever change his life.

> *Disheveled, Madeleine pinched a weak smile as she lay over the delivery room bed. "I know you always wanted a son."*
>
> *"It doesn't matter," Julian said, cradling his new, wrinkly daughter. "I love her."*
>
> *"Instead of Leopold, how about we name her Leopaula?"*
>
> *"Leopaula ..." he softly repeated. "It's perfect."*
>
> *The newborn wrapped her tiny fingers around his thumb.*

Within the time span of a single blink, he'd fallen into the pool of the previous generation. Her smile, her warmth, her breaths—she entered existence. And with that alone came parenthood.

—

Midday, Francis made his rounds. He passed most guards, but to some, he'd inch a nod and they'd subtly return the gesture. Upon reaching the Horseshoe Cloister, a group of tourists argued with their guides. Francis approached the simmering scene. "What's the problem here?"

The guide shielded his mouth with a brochure. "He's here. *Again ...*"

Francis glanced through the entryway. His forehead vein ticked as he understood the implications which lingered at the other end.

"Get these people away. We can't have anybody see him."

The murmurs of the outsiders sauntered as Francis paced towards the bushes beside the walkway's awning. In the thick of it, he spotted the passed-out Julian with Lordes standing guard. Empty bottles of the black label whiskey scattered beside him.

"He's been like this all week, sir," Lordes said, restraining his grin.

"I'll handle it."

"Why? We should just let them in and he'll be his own catalyst—"

"I said, I'll handle it. You know it has to happen in Omo. So, shut it before he hears. Everything we've worked for would vanish if someone simply tilts their head. Now, go!"

"Yes, sir." Lordes saluted and left.

Few birds sat along the chimneys and chatted with one another as the clouds took their turns shading the vicinity.

Insects buzzed and chirped as the scent of freshly mowed lawn swirled around the curved architecture. Julian's snore ravaged through the peace.

"Hey." Francis nudged his leg, then surveyed his environment before punching his arm, leaving a bruise. The snores momentarily amplified. "Hey!"

Julian peeked through his gluey eyelids, finding that he wasn't in the delivery room anymore. "Sup?"

"You're on the verge of becoming the Royal Family's laughingstock."

As Julian sat up, Francis kept him from tipping over. The prince gazed his shadowed eyes through his sweat-soaked bangs. "I can't sleep. Leopaula—she—she cries all the time!"

"Yeah, well, that's parenthood. Now, come," Francis placed Julian's arm over his back and hoisted him to his feet, "we must clean you up before your meeting with the Ethiopian ambassadors. They want to renegotiate the lithium contract. The miners are riling up some trouble—"

"Stop!" Julian fought himself off, poorly imitating karate. "Just—please! Let me get some fun back into my life!" He held in a belch. "Okay?! It's always meeting-this, and meeting-that, contract-this and contract-that! After which, I return to my bedroom and it's Leopaula-this, Leopaula-that. What happened to me? What happened to us, Francis? Remember when we used to own the night? Remember?! We controlled our destiny!" He squeezed his guard's cheeks, puckering his lips, but Francis didn't find it amusing. "Why'd we stop?"

"You became a father."

Julian tossed his head up and groaned. "Well, it's not as special as everyone makes it out to be."

The children among the tourists wailed and moaned as their parents argued. Their cries carried through the roundabout renovations. The prince and his guard glanced at each other. Julian raised his eyebrows, making his point.

"How's my sister doing?"

"Who knows? All she ever talks about is Leopaula—"

"As a mother should—"

"I'm invisible when we're alone, and nothing but an attention magnet when I walk outside. This," Julian shook the bottle, sloshing its contents, "this is my only reminder of what life should be."

Francis appeared bothered, but that was part of the act.

"That *fun* of ours was only meant to take your mind off of the blonde woman, but you've simply replaced your toxic infatuation of her, with love towards the bottle. So, which do you think is worse, or do you just like circling the drain?"

"Both. They're both worse. Because I want both. I refuse to act all buttoned up and civilized anymore. I'm meant for action, for conquests, for feats, not—not— *changing diapers.*"

After the renovations, the Horseshoe Cloister had become an integral extension of the castle, transforming its once debilitated and uninhabitable condition. Although others lived there, Julian would shoo them out as he used the area to drink himself to sleep. He'd imagine the place before it underwent its reconstruction, finding its new image uglier than the original—a forced plaster over its true nature. The idea of renewing something made him sick, and getting drunk and urinating there comforted him.

"Here we go again with your grandiose plans," Francis said. "How about you first worry about cleaning yourself up before trying to reorient the sun's orbit about you?"

Julian kicked the bush. He did little damage, save for a few twigs snapping. He kicked it again and slapped, over and over, as if fighting a baby brother for not sharing his toys. The leaves scattered around, but in the end, Julian's efforts amounted to nothing. The bush stared back. It had defeated him.

"Because if the world saw who I really am, that's what would make me a laughingstock," Julian said. "I need to keep up this façade and I can't do that while being commanded by a baby."

"You don't have to do any of this. In a few weeks, your father is expected to abdicate. You can always do the same."

Julian covered his veiny eyes as his hangover reached its peak. "If I step down, I'll no longer have my get-out-of-jail-free card. They'll see the real me—a rich brat without talents for the real world. No, I'm going to be crowned king, and have to hold up this manufactured civility for the rest of my miserable life."

"Oh, boo-hoo for you." Francis pulled Julian away from the bushes. "If only you could've grown up poor, then everything would've been fine."

"Wait, wait! I have an idea!" Julian flung his finger like a flagpole. "Let's blow it off—this meeting, just this once! What's the worst that could happen? The ambassadors will have to come back!" His grin shook hands with his imagination. "Others take sick days. Why can't I?"

Eyebrows flat, Francis responded, "Because you're not sick."

Julian sucked his teeth before taking a different approach. "Where'd you go? Who are you? Where's the Francis I went out with? I could see it in your eyes; you need this too! You've introduced me to a world that I've only ever dreamt of, and I'm only asking for one more night. Just one. I'll purge it all out of my system. Then, tomorrow we'll meet with the Africans and throw some more money their way. Deal?"

Francis didn't blink, flinch or entertain the thought. Although he appeared conflicted, this was exactly what he wanted. If Julian met with the Omo representatives like this, it would've sped up his plan, but he had a better opportunity to get everything to align. He forced a sigh and looked around. He glanced from the corner of his eye. "One?"

"That's it! That's all I'm asking for!"

Amid the long, manufactured pause, Julian held his breath.

"Very well," Francis said. Julian pumped his fist. "I'll reschedule with the ambassadors. But listen," he held up a stern finger, "last time."

"I love you!" Julian went in for a kiss, but Francis pushed back, returning him to the bushes. "I don't even care—I'm too happy!"

Francis turned and exited the cloister. Walking through the breezy entryway, his footsteps echoed one after the other. Lordes waited at the far end of the Lower Ward, anticipating the news. He passed without a step out of tempo, speaking from his back.

"Inform Scarlett. It's happening tonight."

Chapter XXV
When Memory and Intellect Fail

Julian, under the cloak of night, stealthily approached the door of the Royal Bedroom. He depended on the illumination of Leopaula's plastic-nightlight as he inched closer to the edge of the plush carpet. With every dragging second, he reached for the doorknob. Lightly gripping it, he took multiple silent breaths before twisting. Fully aware of the door's squeaky point, he thrusted it open, stopping just past the angle-of-blown-cover. A miniscule creek sounded.

Leopaula's baby snores paused.

Julian froze, petrified like a gargoyle, with even his heartbeat waiting. He closed his eyes as his hand gripped the twisted knob, his feet shoulder length apart and his lips pinched.

As Leopaula resumed snoring, he peeked out of one eye before exhaling.

"*This again?*" Madeleine called out at full volume after witnessing the entire ordeal.

Her stoic face, flaring nostrils and narrowed eyes pierced his soul. He hadn't acclimated to the darkness, but he saw them all. After muttering profanity, he dropped the covert act and widely opened the door. The creek bellowed out into the hall.

"I thought that was just a phase," Madeleine said. "A *last hoorah* before entering fatherhood. But Julian, you *are* a father now."

"We've been over this; I'm working on things that have no time to get done during the day. I didn't want to wake you."

"Mmm."

"Don't give me that—*that look!*"

Madeleine remained mute, lowering the temperature of the room with her glare as he continued lying about details regarding the lithium deal.

"What?!"

"I'm not stupid, Julian."

"I never—ugh!"

She sat up, wedging the pillow as a backrest, but not wanting to argue. She just wanted to let him know she knew he was lying. "So, you're going to work dressed like that?" Leopaula woke up, crying. Madeleine latched her without breaking her scowl. "In clothes that only one type of person wears at this hour."

Julian sarcastically nodded. "Oh, okay, and what *type of person* is that?" She said nothing, letting Leopaula's screams express her torment. "You better watch it with these accusations, or—or else …"

"Julian," Madeleine spoke slowly, damningly and directly. "You better pray I never find out, because even a bribed jury wouldn't blame me for what I'd do."

Julian scoffed before storming out and slamming the door. The light seeped into the room until a hallway guard switched it off. Madeleine glanced down at their daughter.

"We're going to be okay," she said, petting Leopaula's hair. "Everything will be alright."

—

Julian met Francis in the wine cellar, both dressed to the nines. With a resounding thud, the slammed door echoed through the dim underground room. The guard paused and scanned him up and down. He sported a jet-black button up, hidden beneath a tailored blazer which emphasized his shoulders while barely revealing the faint ticking of his Rolex Explorer II.

Francis fixed the jacket. He made sure it draped neatly over the slim fit trousers, which lined perfectly over the polished leather shoes. He unbuttoned Julian's top two clasps.

"Last time, remember? These actions aren't befitting of the future king." He patted the prince twice on the shoulder, but noticed Julian didn't bolster the excitement he had while in the cloister. "Everything alright?"

"Let's just go."

"What's the rush?" Francis held his palm up. "You seem on edge."

Julian leaned against a rack of bottles, clanking them together. "Your bloody sister; she's onto me." Francis observed, interested. "If she catches wind … she seems like one who'd run to the tabloids with this, or worse …" Francis turned around. He grabbed two glasses and poured a bit of the black-label whiskey into both. "Aye, did you hear me? You'll fall for this too!"

Francis scoffed before slipping something into Julian's glass. Julian yanked him around, but was met with his favorite drink.

"Everything'll be fine, Sir-Julian," he raised the spiked whiskey just beneath his nose, knowing exactly what the scent does to him, "order will be restored."

Julian took a few deep breaths as he stared at the amber-brown liquid swaying from rim to rim. The aroma rose into his nostrils, placating him.

"You're right; you're always right." He shot the glass back, grimacing as he let the alcohol do its job.

"I'll never allow wrong to befall the Royal Family. You have my word."

Julian opened his eyes and hugged him. "You mean the world to me, Francis. I can't tell you … how much … I v … value y … your …"

Francis pulled him off and stepped back, not blinking once, nor hinting a single emotion. It was a sight he'd been waiting for, for years. The skyscraper rumbled and leaned before the collapse. Knees buckled as confusion filled the air.

Francis just stared.

Julian wobbled with a slight stumble. "W—what's—in—"

His view of the arrayed bottles panned, shifted and blurred on his way down. Francis waited, making sure all movements ceased before he approached. Julian's glass shattered across the stone tiles, with a single shard reflecting Francis's blank expression.

— The Following Morning —

One eye wincing from the pain of a pounding headache, Julian woke up to a morning talk show host with an annoying twang in her voice. He rubbed his face as the harsh sunlight poured in through the floor-to-ceiling windows. Post groan, he pushed his hair back as the AC kicked on. Memories of laughter and bass echoed with every blink, worsening the migraine. The television continued, with the audience laughing at sanitized jokes and useless nothings. Instances from the night prior fragmented Julian's mind, hazed by his cocktail of intoxicants still lingering in his system.

He pawed for his go-to ibuprofen, but his fingers swatted at thin air. He turned. Not only was his nightstand missing, *everything was missing*. The Victorian Art, the furniture, the lights—they were all different.

He sat upright, hyperventilating. The bedding wasn't what he was used to, both in texture and color. Off to the side, his clothes were sloppily tossed over the heated marble tiles. His eyes darted around wildly.

"Where—where am I?" He pulled back, fearing someone had kidnapped him.

The furnishings were bright, modern and sleek. All the shelves exhibited smooth, tempered glass. Stainless steel accents melded with the dark stone cabinets lining the walls, sporting a cool glow of LED strips around the edges. A massive aquatic tank, encasing exotic fish, acted as a partition between the suite's rooms. Another wall housed a wide, linear electric fireplace, glistening the shiny rocks beneath the flames. Julian felt the dichotomy between the elements, as he couldn't settle his gaze.

Remote controls for the curtains and the television rested on the carpet. As Julian lunged for them, he fell over, pulling the comforter with him. It became his life's mission to turn off the talk show. He smashed the buttons until he hit the red one and drowned the hotel suite in silence.

Only his panting sounded.

To the left was a bathroom, but the Royal Bedroom didn't have a bathroom there. He shook his head just before noticing … he wasn't alone.

On the bed, a woman lay face down.

As Julian stumbled back. The sheets dragged off with him, revealing the woman's bare buttocks.

"M—Maddy?"

No response.

Trembling, he inched towards the woman's shoulder. His fingers twitched, as if grasping at some semblance of stability. Once he touched her skin, his digits curled back upon seeing the tattoos.

"No, no, no, no, no," he muttered, before clapping his palm over his mouth.

He turned the woman around until she settled flat on her back. Her breasts juggled from one side to the other as she re-comforted herself into the bed's warmth. Her platinum blonde strands scattered, disheveled over the pillow, mingling over the contours of the sheets. The woman's vine-styled ink, depicting petals, with roses and dandelions on either side, ran across her neck and continued down her cleavage. Adorning her shoulder, a skull and crossbones mocked him as her arm hid a third tattoo, spelling out a couplet from a poem which he had no interest in reading.

Anxiety etched into his forehead as he frantically searched for any evidence of his presence in the room. Time stretched, with each passing second, a torturous reminder of his sin. Upon spotting the splayed, filled condom, a whirlwind of shame and regret slammed him against the wall. It leaked between her and where he slept. His chin quivered, but he grabbed his stubble, forcing it to stop. His heavy breathing ran across his knuckles. Panic rapped his chest, as his irregular heartbeats threw his exhales off-rhythm. The cold reality of his betrayal bled into his bones as his sweaty palms smeared against his mouth, void of his wedding band.

I can't be here, Julian thought as he retracted.

He reached for his clothes, but bumped the floor-lamp, knocking it over. He froze.

"Leaving?" Her voice, soft and welcoming, echoed warmly into his ears. Crouched over, he focused on the two walls joining before him to make a corner. He imagined that analyzing it would turn him invisible. "Julian?"

He slowly stood, but shamefully bowed his head. "You—you know me?"

"*Do I know the prince of the UK?*" she scoffed. "Joules, all my dreams are about you."

Blinking several times, Julian looked up. They gazed at each other, completely naked. He couldn't believe his own sight. Her hair was longer now. As she rested against the headboard, her bright blonde waves hypnotized him as if he had fallen into a vast ocean. Her hair's twists and twirls were the last bit of light he saw as his heart plunged deep into the murky depths.

Scarlett tilted her head, pushing her hair aside, as she seductively glanced up.

"It's—it's you," Julian said. "It's really you."

Chapter XXVI
Fantasies Should Remain Fantasies

"No," Julian scoffed. "This—this isn't—no." Weakly smiling, he shook his head.

Scarlett clasped her intricately woven bra. The pink flowers and petals in the fabric rivaled those of her tattoos, erotically contrasting her tanned skin. "This isn't what?"

"This isn't real." Julian flinched a smile riddled with delusion. "Y—you're my fantasy. There's no way."

She took her time rolling her gaze up, patiently usurping his complete and utter attention, caging him in a realm where he couldn't decipher the difference between hallucination and reality. Every blink drew him in, as each long, stretching second of witnessing her beauty left him in thrall, prepared to obey her every wish.

"Your fantasy?" she asked softly. "So, you've been thinking about me, too?"

"You're all I think about, ever since—"

"*The wedding,*" they said in unison before a mute fell over the suite.

Now sober, their hearts raced faster than they did throughout the night.

"What is this?" Julian asked. "Fantasy never meets reality. And if it somehow does, it's never as good as the imagination. But this …"

"This is fate, Julian. We're meant to be. Last night," she fell back into the pillow, poofing it before sinking, "was amazing."

"But how? How'd we even find each other? I've been searching for you for these last—I—I don't," Julian shrugged as his head jittered, "decade! And now that you're here, in front of me, exactly as perfect as I imagined you. But … I can't remember a hint of yesterday."

Scarlett giggled, pinching together her taut, light pink lips. "You're a lightweight. Whereas, I remember everything that happened."

Julian got back onto the bed, grabbing her hands and staring deep into her calm, icy blue eyes. "Tell me everything."

"Well," Scarlett glanced around the hotel, appreciating the chaos of the abstract art, "I missed my flight last night, so I stopped by the pub. There, I found you, with that stern guard of yours. What's his name?" She winced as she repeatedly snapped her fingers.

"Francis?"

"Yes, him!" She pointed. "I couldn't understand why he'd allow the prince of the UK to get drunk in public."

"Wait, you're saying Francis actually took me to a pub?"

Scarlett flashed her pearly white teeth. "No, not at all. From the look of it, you dragged him there. You were saying something about a childhood dream. He kept the people away from you, as you raged like a frat boy in the States at his first party. It was quite the scene."

Julian blinked blankly. "None of this sounds even vaguely familiar."

Scarlett tittered. "Oh, it gets worse. You bolted out and tried to steal someone's car! Sir-Francis attempted to stop you, but you started throwing a barrage of girly punches at him. The owner came out with his friends and before long, it turned into a full-blown mob fight." Julian leaned in, like a child listening to a mythical tale. "The bartender charged out, face red with fury, shouting that the pigs were on their way. The people scattered like rats when the red and blue lights neared, and that's when you and I found ourselves alone in the alley."

"Then what?"

"It started raining, so I took you back to this hotel until the heat died down, and well, one thing led to another …" Scarlett lightly bit her lower lip as her eyes grew and glistened the way a toddler seeks pity.

She placed her hand on his cheek, and inches closer, their lips met.

—

In the Royal Bedroom, Madeleine opened her eyes.

It was quiet. Unusually quiet.

Her alarm didn't blare, nor did Leopaula cry. She checked the gigantic grandfather clock, which told her she should be sleeping for a few more minutes. She found her daughter, dressed in her onesie, towered her tiny butt as she damped the bassinet with her drool.

"Julian." No response. "Julian?" She pawed beside her. Nobody. Nothing. Just bedding.

She blinked at the vacant spot. No crumples in the sheets, no phone charging on the nightstand, no sign he was ever there.

*Kid-Madeleine ran into
Francis's room.
His bedsheets,
uncrumpled, his phone,
missing.
He was gone.*

It was happening again.

With a trembled headshake, her mouth formed an O as her breathing raced away. She strained the sheets, needing anything to remind her she existed. As Leopaula stirred, Madeleine blindly grabbed her, clutching her close and flexing her biceps, bobbing back and forth. The tears formed and splattered over Leopaula's hair.

"We're okay," she muttered. "We're okay."

—

Julian inspected his body. Nothing supported Scarlett's story. When he looked back to question her, he'd fall silent upon realizing the woman of his dreams sat naked, in bed, before him.

"I have to—I have to check on Francis—"

"Or …" Scarlett dropped one of her bra straps, "we could spend some more time together. You know, before life hits play again."

*Leopaula cackled as
Madeleine held her,*

*smiling. Julian poked her
plump tummy, igniting
another series of giggles.*

"I'm sorry." Julian stood and stumbled away. "This—this was a mistake. Fantasy or not, we can't be together."

Scarlett lowered her head, swallowing harshly. A frog lodged in her throat as she nodded. "No, I get it. Girls like me," she sniffled, reddening the domed tip of her nose, "we're just used."

"Hey, hey, hey," Julian returned, "it's not you, I swear. It's them; the media. They'll never let this go."

"Yeah." She smudged her tears against her cheek. No makeup smeared because she didn't need any. "That's why I just wanted these last few moments before never seeing you again. Just … just to make me feel … *not so worthless.*"

Julian checked his phone. No messages. He had less than an hour before the meeting with the Ethiopian ambassador. He glanced back at Scarlett. Following a smirk, he set the device to do-not-disturb.

"No, you're not worthless. You understand me … yet, I don't even know your name. I still can't believe it's you."

Scarlett tilted her head. "How do you think I feel? I travel the world for work, and here I am, in bed with the bloody prince."

"When're you coming back?" Julian hesitantly, yet eagerly, asked. She waited for the next part. "May—maybe this doesn't have to be it."

"So, you want me to be your mistress? Your once-a-week lover?"

"No!" He grabbed both her hands. "I could … I could …" He imagined Madeleine, but closed his eyes until all he saw was black. Madeleine's smile faded as the darkness swallowed her. "I could leave her!"

Scarlett felt the weight of his decision, although this was precisely what she wanted. But she needed him cemented. "Oh, Joules, don't make me carry that burden. I should go—this was a bad idea. I have to catch my flight."

Julian grabbed her arm. She froze. He froze. They once again stared, hypnotized.

"I'm a man who gets whatever he wants, and right now, all I want is …"

Scarlett showed him exactly what she revealed during the wedding, before gently pulling her arm back.

"Seeing you get married … that was the worst day of my life. You left me waiting for something I knew would never happen. Don't put me through that again."

"I won't! I'm going to break things off with Madeleine and come back for you. I promise. Just give me a few weeks, please. *Please,*" he begged. She loved it when they begged. She sloppily gathered her things, got dressed and reached for the knob. He planted his hand, forcing the door shut. "At least tell me your name!"

His cologne's remnants were faint enough to ignore, yet it still swirled into her deep sigh. She leaned in slowly, reeling him into a final kiss. Parting first, she playfully dragged his lower lip with her teeth. She witnessed his heart beating through his chest hair. With glee, she pulled out a pen from her purse and scribbled her number onto his palm before closing his fingers over it.

"Meet me here next week, and I'll tell you."

She exited, leaving Julian alone and dumb in the luxury suite. As he celebrated like a giddy teenager, she placed his wedding band into her pocket and pulled out her phone. She found a new text message.

Francis: Well?

Her stilettos resonated with every step towards the elevator. She tapped on her iPhone, echoing off a rapid series of ticking sounds before she hit send. The doors opened just before the signature woooop noise sounded.

—

A vibration. Francis glanced at his phone.

Scarlett: Like a fiddle.

He smirked.

—

With the small crowd surrounding Scarlett, the doors slid shut.

She, too, smirked.

Chapter XXVII
The Vacillating Heart

— Current Day —

"Stop dat," Zola said.

"Stop what?"

"That." She pointed at Madeleine's face, accidentally poking her eyebrow scab. "You're judging us."

The fireball, just meters away, held Madeleine's attention.

"Ya still don't get it."

"I think I do—"

"We're brutal, yes. We're territorial, yes. But you seem to forget that we're occupied. We have the right to retaliate. There's no clean way to do this; freedom is married to blood."

Madeleine arced her neck, looking towards the heavens for guidance, but the smoldering vehicle distracted all prayers. The crackling, the heat, the growls of the blaze. It was all so horrid, yet honest. Raw. Unapologetic. Candid.

"Why'd Chief Amari have to go so far?" Madeleine asked.

"To send a message."

"But we could've used the car!"

"No," Zola shook her head, "we're not scavengers. If we take their things, we're suddenly dependent. That isn't what this is about. This struggle is for our freedom—our families. Not some trifling wealth. The moment we swipe even a single garment from our victim, we'll be trumpeted as petty thieves."

The smoke billowed from the wreckage, morphing from black, to gray, to white. Madeleine wondered how the people resumed their day, unbothered, as if pushing play on a remote. The mailman picked up his sack, chasing after the scattered letters. The children returned to their schools as some restarted their games. Men and women lined the donga arena.

In the distance, Madeleine spotted Amari and Akilu heading towards the secluded pond. She couldn't help but glare at his silhouette.

As Kamari clawed and cooed for milk, Zola noticed Madeleine's disgust. "Have ya ever killed anybody?"

"… No."

"Have you ever killed anything?"

Madeleine thought back. "A bug, here or there."

"How'd you feel after killing that bug?"

Madeleine sighed. "Look, I know where you're going with this—"

"Did it writhe? Or did you just smash it, completely obliterating it?" No response. "Imagine it was a cat. Or a dog. Or a horse. Is it as easy to kill that *irritating* thing anymore?" Madeleine dazed at the flames, popping and sizzling. "What if that pesty annoying bug was a person? Someone with burdens, duties, dreams. Something with a soul."

The smoke morphed from black to a thick pale cloud, tainting the highest of the luscious green leaves. Madeleine contemplated the transformation. The branches still swayed, the trees still stood. Everything was the same, yet they were different because of what happened out of their control.

"It takes a toll on you. Even when your life is what's weighed against theirs, or your family versus that one person. It's easier, but that doesn't mean it's easy. That individual, that vile, disgusting aggressor, still has potential, dreams, duties, burdens. Killing … it hardens the heart."

Madeleine couldn't see Amari anymore, but he seized her thoughts. Every person resembled him; their sweat appeared thick and red while their steps left a trail of destruction in their path.

"I told ya before; that's not the Amari I married. But we need him and we're grateful for what he does. He's sacrificing his heart to keep this tribe safe."

Madeleine lay back, unknowingly staring at the same sky as Amari, discussing the same thing. "I need Leopaula. I just need Leopaula." The smoke wafted, tinting the clear blue atmosphere. "This madness is yours, but don't get me wrong—I am sympathetic towards your people's plight."

As Julian approached, Zola stood to leave. "Try not to judge us, dear. My people and you … we want the same thing." Madeleine flinched a wan smile. Zola regarded Julian before leaving.

He joined Madeleine, who faced the celestial emptiness. "We need to talk about Francis and why he sent us here. We also need to eat."

"Don't pin any of this chaos on your brother. Since becoming my guard, he's been a Godsend. This isn't his fault. These monsters, they're the ones responsible for this mayhem."

Madeleine sat up, the smoke scratching and clawing at her throat. "After what we just learned, you still believe Francis is trying to help? Really? By sending us to a people who kill trespassers? You only know him as your Royal Guard, but I knew him from before. Ever since he abandoned his family as a lad, he's been ..." Madeleine glanced back at the trail entering the secluded pool, "he hasn't been himself."

As the fumes rushed by Julian, he slapped his tongue around before spitting. "You'll never convince me out of trusting Francis. He has done everything possible to keep me safe. You should be more thankful. He saved our marriage by sending us here. Consider what that takes. He's even handling the public's outcry on our status.

"No, this isn't some scheme by Francis. It's our fault we lost our daughter, our fault we trusted Imamu and our fault we're in this mess. Not him."

The smoke crept between them, turning the day to night and darkening Julian's face. For a brief moment, he resembled Francis.

In the crescent hours of the night, teenage Francis ran his thumb over young Madeleine's cheek as she drooled. Stroke after stroke, she fluttered awake, finding her brother kneeling by her bedside.

Madeleine rubbed her eyes. Through the darkness, she noticed his red, wet face. The moonlight pierced through the Slough flat's misaligned window and the towel being used as a curtain. It illuminated Francis's wrist and cast short shadows off his scars.

"Where you going?" she asked with her limited vocabulary.

A small bag slung over his shoulder, holding only a few necessities.

"Oh, Mads," he said through a silent weep. "You're the one stopping me. Not her."

He turned towards the slightly ajar door.

"Come back," Madeleine called.

He pushed the door.

"France, come back!"

"I have to go. Father's waiting."

Following the latching clunk, the young girl plummeted into an isolated darkness.

"Come back!"

Madeleine returned to reality as both her and Julian's stomach rumbled in unison.

"I'll see what Zola can get us," she said. "It's impossible to think straight when hungry."

"No, we need to leave. The longer we stay, the higher the likelihood we end up like that charred chap."

The flames died down, just as the two became accustomed to them.

"Honest question," Madeleine said. "What would you do if you were in their shoes?"

Julian audibly breathed through his nose. "Now's not the time for what-if's, Maddy! Get your head on straight—"

"Did you ever kill someone?"

"What?!" Julian wanted to dismiss the conversation, but he had no other place to go and no one else to sit with.

"Did you," Madeleine said, taking her time with every word. "Ever kill anyone?"

"Yes, a few, when deployed in Iraq. Why? Why's that matter, right now, in this instant?"

The flames might've swelled over, but the smoke hadn't.

"Was it hard?" Madeleine asked.

"No."

"No?"

"That's right, it's easy. I pushed a button and they exploded. I barely saw the aftereffects. But even if I did, I wouldn't care. Those Arabs … they're animals. Just like these freaks."

He couldn't peel his frown away as others glanced at him.

"Julian, the entire world condemns that war. Those Arabs, those Iraqis, they were people, and they were innocent of everything they were accused of. The whole conflict was based on blatant lies to feed greed. Yet, you're unbothered by taking part?"

He bit the inside of his lip. "I don't care about any of that. It's simple. I killed them because they were trying to kill me—"

Madeleine turned to him as if he entered the women's restroom. "Because you invaded them!"

"Why're we even discussing this? Do you want me to have sympathy for these barbarians after what we just saw? I won't, Maddy! I'm going to get us out of here before we're also tossed into a makeshift hell."

"How hard is your heart, Julian?"

He backed away, twisting his face. "Don't you get all Stockholm on me—"

"Do you hear yourself? Don't you see why they despise people like us?"

"We're done talking about this." He stood. "I'm going to find some food. Then, we'll contact the Kingdom and finally get out of here. Eat nothing and go nowhere. Understand?"

His shouts passed right through her. With a set jaw, she waited for him to leave. He marched away from the crackles of the blackened automobile, distancing himself from her as she suffocated him more than the smoke. Upon reaching the tree line, he glanced back to make sure he wasn't followed. Imamu wasn't in sight. Neither was Ike, Amari or Akilu.

With his gaze back at the trees, he readied himself. First, he searched behind the trunks, then beside the shrubs. He even peered up at the branches.

He couldn't find *her*.

"Scarlett?" he softly called.

With one more glance back, he made sure Madeleine wouldn't notice him. He took out his phone.

Messages > New message > Recipient

"S C A R," he softly muttered as he typed.

He tapped her name. Their past conversation shoveled a smile across his face. He composed a message and, after hitting send, peeked back again. Madeleine remained captive in thought, pensive and alone.

Before putting his phone away, he noticed the messaging app's banner:

Scarlett is responding ...

Chapter XXVIII
The Ghoul is Within Sight

Scarlett is typing ...

Julian felt a lightness in his chest as his grin grew. With the sun setting, the illumination of the cell phone gleamed over his arched, pink cheeks. He couldn't stop wondering what she was going to say.

Suddenly, the banner text changed to a boring: *Message Read.*

"No," Julian muttered under his breath. "No, no, no, don't be like that. Talk to me, please!"

"How long do you want to keep doing this?" Scarlett said, approaching from the trees.

Julian stumbled back, fumbling his phone. He blinked repeatedly, making sure he wasn't seeing things. But with every step, the downed leaves crunched, footprints engraved in the soil, and Scarlett's scent filled the air.

He closed his eyes and intoxicated himself. Nude, she came closer, cradling Leopaula in her arms. Her tattoos twisted and curled towards her wrist, outlining the sleeping infant. She stopped.

Julian stayed still, only blinking when necessary. "It's really you."

She owned a smile that would melt the sternest of men. Her hair, long, wavy, messy and exotic, flowed the same way he last saw her. Strands obscured her face, but she peered through playfully as if they were threads of a beaded curtain. Her eyebrows, eyelashes, lips, ears—everything. Everything about her gleamed perfection, toppling him to his knees like a homeless person at the doors of a church.

"I miss you," she said.

"Me, too—every day. I can't stop thinking of you."

Leopaula cooed, as Scarlett rocked her back to sleep. "We need you to return home. Didn't your mother ever teach you it's rude to keep a lady waiting? And Joules, I really, really, hate waiting." She emphasized her toned body by squeezing Leopaula close.

"I'm stuck, and can't get out. I've been messaging you."

"No. I need you. The actual you. You promised me you'd leave her, but I know the truth. You used me, then ran away with her towards the sunset. That was supposed to be me, Joules, me!"

"I'm trying!"

"Don't keep me waiting, Prince Julian. The temptation is so," she bit her lower lip, closed her eyes and trailed a finger down her cleavage, "torturous …"

Julian's gaze explored every bit of her figure. He looked down to re-grasp reality, but found Scarlett grabbing onto his belt, with her index finger between his pelvis and the waistline fabric. He heard nothing but his heavy gasps, but upon raising his eyes, she was gone.

Behind him, Scarlett whispered into his ear, "You don't look so well. You should really eat."

Julian turned to find her plenty of meters away. He looked back out at the vast swath of nature, suddenly feeling Scarlett sitting beside his feet, head resting against his leg. "I'm afraid they're going to poison me."

Scarlett laid on her back and erotically moaned, leaving Leopaula beside her on the ground. Julian shook his head and found her sitting before him on a pew, in a glittering minidress, one leg crossed over the other, her lower buttocks slightly revealed.

"Eat some of those plants. Those, beside you." She shrugged. "Vegans do it." Julian suddenly spotted Scarlett overhead, sitting on a branch. She rested her back against the trunk, with one knee up while the other leg dangled. Like a hippie, she stared out at the blood-red sun. "And they're … sort of fine. I guess."

"You're right. You're always right."

Hypnotized by the majestic beauty, Julian reached down and grabbed whatever greenery he touched. He didn't care about their color or texture, as long as his stomach was filled. The taste was far from sapid, but it did the job.

Above the horizon, a rapid ticking echoed as tiny gnats glided around like birds. Julian squinted and strained, but couldn't make out what they were. He leaned closer, but backed away upon sensing a roller coaster drop. He grabbed onto a tree as the flies vanished, but with another blink, they reappeared.

Julian glanced down at his hand, finding it morphing, doubling and shifting. Some digits disappeared while new ones grew.

Jumping back, he shook his hand.

"I need a drink. I need another drink …" The ticking rang out again. He spotted a fleet of helicopters sweeping the savannah. "That's them. They're coming to save me." He cracked a sinister smile. "Time to kill them all."

"I wouldn't be so sure," Scarlett said, reappearing, drenched in so much gore that her tattoos were no longer visible. Only her eyes contrasted with the red. "They might be too late."

"They're Francis's commandos; if anybody could do it, it's them."

"Hmm." She nonchalantly placed a finger against her chin. Blood dripped off her hair like leftover water after a shower.

"*Hmm,* what?"

"If I were you, I'd check on Ike's hut. I'm pretty sure those two are talking about you in there."

"What're they saying?"

She shrugged. "Probably planning out how to kill you tomorrow, during your," she rolled her eyes, "*trip to the mines.*"

Before his eyes, she disintegrated like sand scattering in a passing breeze.

—

Ike gazed at Nala, sleeping between them. "[Surmic] Anything from the embassy?"

"No." Imamu's tone held a dismal absence of hope. "I'm going to call them."

"Now?"

Imamu nodded. "Everybody's asleep. And the longer we hold off on delivering on our threat, the higher the likelihood they won't take us seriously. I'm doing it."

An answering machine.

"Just hang up," Ike said, but Imamu kept his focus, waiting for the tone.

Beep.

"[English] This is Imamu, son of Chief Amari, son of Haile, The Lion Tamer. Your messenger's dead. Another attempt like that and the Royals will join him. Do not test me, Mr. Butts." He hung up and exhaled. "[Surmic] Something is going on at the mines and we need to hurry."

"H—how'd you know?"

"The offshoot, remember, every 27 seconds? Blood is being poured into it. A lot."

"It's worse than you think …" Ike handed Imamu the letter he'd intercepted while the trespasser distracted everybody.

"What's this?"

"Read for yourself …"

> [Written in Surmic]
>
> Chief Amari,
>
> This is an emergency!
>
> Damage on the route for the supply shipments has prevented food from arriving at the excavation site. The haranchi guards are rationing what's left of the remaining inventory. After hitting our limits, they

began a sadistic practice of executing the least productive Mursi of the day. They hang the corpse over Omo's southern offshoot until it's drained.

They've been doing this for about a month. From the 1,500 of us, I don't think they'll be slowing down soon.

It's crucial for you to surprise attack them so that it'll give us the opportunity to flee. Details are critical, so inform us of the time of your strike and we'll be ready.

Please, hurry!

Imamu covered his mouth as he read the letter over and over. He waved the note around. "This is what I wanted to show you! This is why the offshoot's color changes! That's the blood of our people, Ike! Yonas!"

"I know. You were right, Imamu, and I'm sorry I didn't believe you. But let's be grateful that this news hadn't reached Chief Amari—"

"Grateful?!" He slammed down the wrinkled note. "Grateful?!"

"I'm so sorry, Imamu."

Tears streamed as he struggled to comprehend the emotions. "Stop saying that! It's not your fault, it's his!" He pointed outside, ignorantly pointing at the eavesdropping Julian through the wall. "He needs to die! To hell with the plan, the embassy, all of it. This is our only chance to get vengeance!"

"You're right; he deserves to die." Ike patted his lifelong friend's shoulder. "But you know we can't kill him."

"No!" Imamu smacked his hand off. "I have to! Even if it's the last thing I do!"

"Hey," Ike softly patted the air, "let's calm down and not forget who we're dealing with here. This is the United Kingdom, the genesis of the Western world, not some rebellious tribe. So, for everybody's sake, not only can we not harm him, we have to keep him alive."

Still hot, Imamu slammed his fist against the note. "They do this, and we host him?!"

"Yes. We stay on track. After the embassy pays up, we give them the Royals. It's that simple. We'll be able to start a new life here, Imamu! Everybody will finally have a chance of being free. The type of wealth you demanded, it's what's needed to brighten this dark episode of our history."

With a red face and crimson eyes, Imamu refused. "Don't you get it? They won't stop! We're not human to them! They'll come back whenever they want to use us again!"

"Then ..." Ike tilted his head. "What's the point of getting all this money to *modernize the tribe?*" He started piecing it together. "Unless ..." he paused, realizing his friend hadn't been truthful with him either, "that wasn't ever part of the plan." His eyes scanned back and forth until they pierced Imamu. "You're ... you're—"

"What I do with my share is none of your business!" Feeling exposed, Imamu stole a shameful glance.

"*You're trying to run away.* That's what this is all about …"

"I can't take it anymore! They do this, over and over, and, what, we're just supposed to accept it? It's not fair, Ike!"

"No, it isn't, but neither is what you're doing."

"A—and it's not just us either. He's hurting Madeleine, too! She's like us—beaten and tortured by the Kingdom. While this is all a big game for him! He's toying with us and agonizing her in the process. How else do you think she got that wound on her eyebrow? He has to go! You know he does!"

Ike tapped a fist against his forehead as he thought through the various scenarios. "We need him. There's no other way for this to end cleanly. He's the only one that can stop this cycle from repeating."

Imamu turned away, looking outside, with Julian below. "Whether or not the embassy fulfills their end. I swear, I'll be the one who kills him!"

That's it, Julian thought. I've understood enough. I have to—

Just then, someone abruptly grabbed Julian, muffled his mouth and forced a bag over his head.

Chapter XXIX
Fooling in Love

— One Week After Meeting Scarlett —

Francis glanced at Julian, who remained glued to his phone during the summit with the Ethiopians.

The ambassador cleared his throat in Julian's direction. "[English] Your Royal Highness …" Julian tapped on his phone, sending emojis, GIFs and pictures. "Prince Julian," he said in a deeper tone, "I receive this behavior back home from my teenager. This is unacceptable—"

Julian looked up. "What?!" The room stared at him. "We all know why you're here; you want more money. Fine. It's yours. Francis, facilitate the transfer already and get this meeting over with."

Francis forced a hard smile at the other officials. "Excuse us." He grabbed Julian's arm and pulled him outside. "Hey, what the hell's gotten into you this past week?"

Julian swept his bangs away, sighing. "You should thank me for saving you from that snore-fest. I gave them what they wanted and saved us all the back and forth—"

Francis scowled. "You just dipped the Kingdom into a nonprofitable agreement. Get your head on straight before we go back in there and show them some respect and poise. Hopefully, they're still willing to negotiate. We need this to stabilize our economy. Do you understand, or are you too busy behaving like a child?"

"No."

"No?"

"That's right; no. I don't care about any of this, Francis. If you do, you go in there and handle it." He pointed with his chin. "I have better things to do."

Francis spoke slowly and pensively, staring at him as if eyeing a needle. "In just under four months, you're to be crowned. Be an example, Sir-Julian. A king cares about this, about the economy—his people." "But all you care about is your pathetic freedom and night escapades." He flicked the cell phone right when it chimed.

"Jesus, what's your deal?" Another text chimed. As Julian went to check, Francis grabbed his wrist. "Let go of me."

A chime.

"Most of the Kingdom will suffer if you fail to get back into that room—"

A fourth chime. Followed by a fifth and a sixth.

"How could you be so blind, Francis? I don't give a flying fuck about the Kingdom. It's been nothing but a burden on me since father announced his plan to abdicate. I finally have all I want, and it was no thanks to the peasants, the press or even you. Now, take your hand off me, and let me get back to my life." Finger by finger, Francis let go. Struggling to maintain the act, he couldn't believe how well everything was falling into place. Julian yanked his arm back. "We're done here."

—

Julian gripped the hotel room's doorknob, feeling as though he reached for his liberation from the confines of the castle. For the last week, every interaction with Madeleine and Leopaula had been soul crushing. Now criticized by Francis, he found his only solace behind the hotel's door.

"There you are," Scarlett said, lying in bed, dressed in a light laced, black lingerie, revealing just enough to stupefy him. "I was starting to worry."

—

Beneath the makeshift pillow-fort, they gazed deep into each other's eyes, sliding their breaths over their bare skin.

"This is too good to be true," Julian whispered.

"I think this is love."

"No." His calendar app didn't ring. Francis wasn't pointing and directing. Madeleine wasn't badgering. Leopaula wasn't crying. It was warm. Everything was warm. "It's …" he softly swiped a strand of her hair away from her face, "it's more than that."

As the television blared to mask their earlier noises, they took comfort in each other's body heat as the sun sunk into the land.

"I almost gave up," Scarlett said. "Every day this week, I nearly hopped on the soonest flight back, just to see you again."

"Is that possible with your job? Could we meet sooner? What do you even do for work?"

"I own my own business. It's doing well, but I have to travel to meet with investors and clients, so my life becomes a bit hectic."

As she spoke, her eyebrows animated her vocabulary, drawing Julian into the mystery behind who this woman was.

"Do you live out of hotels? I mean," he toppled the pillows over, looking around the luxury suite, "this is a nice place, but it doesn't seem like *you*."

"I live in Slough. These hotels are brief escapes from my reality—"

Julian jerked his head back.

"Slough, like *Slough, Slough?* Like right beside Windsor?" he asked.

"Mhmm."

"So, all these years, you've lived a few blocks away?"

As the skyline became silhouetted by the hellish red horizon, the skyscrapers' logos and offices illuminated like stars.

"That's right. Every once in a while, I'd glance at the castle, wondering how you were doing. Whenever you appeared on the telly, you always seemed sad."

"I am," Julian admitted, something he never told Madeleine. "I want nothing I have. Do you have any idea how suffocating that is?"

"Oh, Joules, plenty would kill to be in your shoes for a day."

"Would you ever move into the castle?" he asked.

Scarlett shook her head. She got off the bed and sat on the armchair overlooking the city. After slumping to her comfort, she widened her legs and flashed her vagina to the world. Amused by the vulgarity, Julian joined her and did the same.

"Never," she said. "The castle is too … *buttoned up* for my liking." She repeated all the rehearsed words. "Same goes for these hotels—they're just my little getaways. Because this isn't me. Slough is home. That's where I don't mind the mess—where I'm free."

"So, you wouldn't be able to handle moving into the castle, huh?"

"Would you be able to handle moving into Slough?" she bargained. Julian laughed. He then considered it.

The celestial bodies revealed themselves as the moon hid elsewhere. With the city growing dark, people poured into the streets in droves. High above, the prince was invisible to them. He held Scarlett's hand, feeling that she was his ticket to freedom from the castle.

"Before we talk about moving in together, I need to know your name," Julian said.

She locked her gaze on him as she reached for her phone and texted.

He checked his message. "Scarlett," he read before glancing back at her. Her dimples appeared charmingly deep and defined. "*Scarlett,*" he said again, just as he did upon hearing Leopaula's name for the first time.

She lifted her wineglass from the center table and raised it towards the city. "Look at all those drones down there,

Julian. They're all trapped in their jobs and tasks, slaving away and missing out on life. Bollocks to you all, every last one of yous."

Julian raised his tall, stilted glass, doing the same. "Bollocks, indeed."

They clinked the glasses together before taking a drink.

"I have to go." Julian rose first and began getting dressed.

"I'll be counting the days, lover boy."

"Miss Scarlett, I promise it'll only be a few more weeks. I'm getting everything in line to prevent a media circus when I reveal the news of the divorce."

"Until then," Scarlett threw her head back over the armchair, observing Julian upside-down as he shoved his foot into his shoe, "I'll stay on this rollercoaster."

He blew her a kiss before heading out. She held a playful smile, which vanished the moment the latch sounded.

> Scarlett: He's hesitating. Should I speed things up?

> Francis: Yes, but not too fast that we blow it. We need this done before the coronation.

— Three Months Later —

During the morning hours, Madeleine and Julian took their daily walk through Windsor Castle's courtyard, pushing Leopaula in the stroller. These days, neither talked. Stride after stride, their footsteps pitter-pattered, but other than that, an uncomfortable silence hung in the air. The guards held their places as the tourists waited beside the entry gates.

From time to time, Julian's phone would chime. Madeleine glanced from the corner of her eye, finding him smirking before each reply. "So," she said, but was met with a waiting finger from Julian as he continued to give his phone all his attention. "Hey …"

Nothing. He chuckled, tapping on his device. Madeleine swiped it out of his hands, holding it far away as if an archer drawing an arrow.

"What're you doing?" Julian asked.

"Could we please get a few minutes together? These last few weeks, you've been obsessed with your phone, like a little kid with a new toy."

All she had to do was glance up to see Scarlett's name. Julian lunged forward, reaching for the device while hurting Madeleine. He clamped her arm before snatching the phone back and hiding it in his pocket.

Madeleine suddenly regretted opting out of all those marriage classes growing up. Her husband wasn't living up to the basic expectations of the title and she stood at a loss as her wrist throbbed. "A—are you at least going to tell me where you've been? You disappear, then come back all chipper."

He turned with a reddened expression, darkening with every volcanic word, erupting her way. "What more do you want from me? You wanted these walks, we walk. You wanted the castle, you live here. You wanted to marry me, you're the princess. You get everything you want, yet you keep nagging for more. Just like the bloody Ethiopians—demanding more and more per meeting!"

The guards glanced.

"Hey, don't talk to me like that—I'm your wife."

"Yes, and I'm the next king. Which means I have more to answer for than your pesky wishes."

A guard approached, notifying them that the tourists were about to enter.

"Return to your post, foot soldier!" Julian pointed until the guard fled from sight.

Madeleine waited until they were alone. "So, that's where you were yesterday? *Meeting with the ambassador?*"

Julian turned away, shaking his head. "Let me guess, you don't believe me."

A chime.

> Scarlett: We need to talk.

"I checked the registrar, Julian. Nobody visited the castle on official business yesterday. Or last week, or the week before. In fact, Francis told me you offered them everything but the kitchen sink during the first meeting, giving the Kingdom the lower hand."

"Wonderful." Julian widely nodded. "We have ourselves a bloody spy."

Another chime.

> Scarlett: Please. Call now.
> It's important.

Julian stared at the phone for a prolonged moment.

"You're welcome to some privacy," Madeleine said. "But if you're not hiding anything from me, why's your phone always by your side? Why do you tilt your screen away," she pointed, "like that? And why don't you ever wear your wedding band anymore?"

Julian slipped the phone into his pocket. "You know what? Maybe we should stop taking these damn walks. You've changed, Maddy! Don't act like this—this—*friction* between us is my fault!"

He stormed off, leaving the bothered Leopaula alone with Madeleine. She wanted to just grab him and shake the truth out. She helplessly stared at his distancing back as he marched towards the vacant Albert's Memorial Chapel.

Julian slammed the door and rested his back against it until the echoes ceased. Godliness surrounded him, but he didn't care for any of that. All he cared about was changing his pin before she found anything damning. However, upon unlocking the phone, a picture message from Scarlett flashed open:

(+)

Chapter XXX
Abort! Abort!

With shallow breaths, Julian stared at the picture message. His trembling hand shook the screen, making the positive sign resemble a short segment of train tracks. The more pluses he saw, the more his heart palpitations thrashed around his chest. He dropped the phone as the vertigo kicked in. Sweat rolled over his forehead as he tried to recompose himself. But the memory of the image alone disoriented him. The morning light pierced through the stained-glass windows, searing his skin. He tightened his muscles and gasped. The bright chapel surrounding him made him feel like Satan pleading for clemency, but only to have God turn a blind eye.

People approached the chapel. He got up and sloppily fixed his hair before texting her back.

Julian: Can't talk now.

Moments later, he sprinted across the Lower Ward towards the castle archives cellar. He ordered everybody out, even stopping a guard from locking out his computer. He locked the door and hopped on the PC, searching for Scarlett's address. However, without a last name, he gazed at over 300,000 results. He narrowed it down to Slough residents, yielding about 1,400. After slamming the keyboard, he found himself at a dead end.

Julian clamped his eyes shut. He needed Francis, but being his brother-in-law, couldn't involve him. His knee jittered as he darted his gaze around the room.

With another glance at the monitor, he discovered a search-by-phone-number option. He punched in her digits.

Addresses found: Zero

"She's—she's using a burner …"

Taming his throbbing heart, he called an old friend in the MI-5, the UK's domestic security service.

"Well, well, well. To what do I owe the pleasure?"

"Archie, I need an address!"

"How come you only reach out when you need something?"

"Hey! Not now!"

"Alright," Archie started filling out a form, "what's this for?"

"I'm the fucking prince. Just do as I say!" Julian took a moment as Archie held his breath. "Please. I need this."

"Alright, alright. What's the name?"

"No name, just a number. Ready?"

Julian proceeded with Scarlett's digits, tapping his fingers along the desk as he waited.

"Got it. Looks like that phone is currently in Slough—"

"Address! I need an exact address!"

—

Later, Julian threw on a leather jacket before exiting the castle grounds, donning a generic cap which shadowed his eyes. Heading north, he approached Windsor Eton Bridge. A soft drizzle sprinkled the bridge's stone tiles, glazing the surface and polishing the light over the ground like an oil painting. A couple flirted against the anchorage at the start of the arched walkway. The woman's back was against the cement footing as the man planted his palm beside her ear while playing with her hair. They giggled useless nothings until Julian passed. The man asked him to photograph them, but the covert prince proceeded to the dim street lamps on the other end. After flipping the bird, the man returned to his lover.

The drizzle muffled Julian's footsteps over the wet tiles. Near the crest, a homeless man slept on a bench as his fallen blanket soaked up the rain. Discomforted, the bum tried re-situating himself mid-slumber. Julian glanced, but didn't stop to help.

Once over, the prince solely used the back roads of Eton. He popped his collar and tucked his chin as he turned down the alleyways snaking between the weathered buildings. The closer he approached Slough, the more tourists lessened and denizens crawled out. Julian felt an out of place nostalgia. The lack of guards, uniforms and civility— he was a lost hyena that finally found his pack.

In the far distance, the repetitive blinking lights of the power plant's gigantic cooling towers flashed, flooding the slums with a dreary red ambiance. To an outsider, it mimicked stepping into a horror film. Exactly every other second, the whites of people's eyes, teeth and skin would glow a hellish hue. As stated in the ICAO Annex 14

Volume 1, this is an international standard for aviation safety, yet for the residents of Slough, this is home.

Snaking through the impoverished buildings, Julian continued. Unfamiliar faces followed the outsider, while no one could identify him. Beside the walkway, stacks of water-stained crates lined the sides of the shops, as bags of trash delicately balanced over one another. The sound of dogs rummaging through the garbage was white noise for the tenants. The stench of cigarette smoke drifted through the air, merging with the occasional waft of vomit from a nearby drunkard leaning against a graffitied brick wall.

Julian noticed a rugged child sitting on the curb with his high, unconscious and unwed parents beside him. The boy fiercely glared.

"This is nice," Julian said, nodding around. "Proper dodgy, innit?" The child tightened his scowl. The prince smirked, tipped his hat and continued.

Further down the alley, he stood before the door of a rundown flat. He checked his palm and nodded when he found the same street number before him. The rusty hinges complemented the loose knob. Mouse-chewed insulation spewed out from cracks in the wall. Spliced wires for the doorway light twisted and tangled out of the wall like a bad haircut. As the raindrops picked up, a bridge of electricity flashed between the exposed copper. The street continued flashing red.

Julian raised his fist to knock, only to find the door already ajar. He cautiously stepped in, finding Scarlett lying on the couch in nothing but her underwear, no bra, watching a live studio audience sitcom.

"Hey, Franny," she muttered without turning away from the TV. "There's some takeout left if you're hungry."

She raised the remote with a bent wrist, endlessly cycling through the channels.

Flashes from the altering scenes of the sitcom reflected off the walls. The rotten carpet emitted an aura that paired agreeably with the musty cushions and torn couch pillows. Julian watched the screen for a moment, amused by the show. It almost distracted him from the crack smoke drifting in from the large hole in the wall, exposing the neighbor's living room.

During a commercial break, Scarlett saw Julian's reflection on the screen. He stood behind her, glowing dark red for a full second. Her laziness vanished as her eyes bulged. She sat up, fumbling the remote as she grabbed a couch pillow to cover herself.

"Woah, Julian. What—what're you doing here?!"

"We need to talk."

"You—you could've called." With strained tendons along her neck, Scarlett snapped her sight around.

"Show me the test."

"The—the test? The pregnancy test? I—I tossed it. How'd you even find me?"

Julian observed the living room, finding it to suit Scarlett more than those high-end hotels. Her tattoos finally made sense. He could tell that she didn't have a coddled upbringing, nor did she have connections with some fat-pocketed CEO. This was her, unmasked, raw and true. But that's not why she stuttered. Things were quickly spiraling off-script.

"*You threw it out?*" he asked.

Scarlett, out of the controlled confines of Francis's plan, sported strained eyes and an uncontrolled tremor. She nodded.

"It's—it's not some—something you keep."

"Madeleine kept it until the ultrasounds."

"Well. That's—that's good for her."

Julian leaned against the dining room table, head lowered with eyes menacingly raising towards her. "This can't happen."

Scarlett took a deep breath. She reached for a glass of lukewarm water resting on the coffee table, attempting to restrain her quaking. She tilted the cup and a gulp later, she found herself back in the driver's seat. With a gaze that explores and suggests, she approached, twirling his slick hair over his ear.

"No, baby. You need to leave her, now—"

Julian slapped her hand away, flinching her back. "Stop telling me what I need to do! I get enough of that in the castle. I'm only here for one reason." He glared at her abdomen.

Scarlett inadvertently placed both hands over her belly. "Julian … I'm not a murderer."

He slammed his fist against the table, leaving cracks in the surface. "I don't care about any of that! You were my escape from all these noises in my head! You were my getaway from being Royalty, but most of all, you were my freedom from parenthood! How's this going to work if you're dropping another child on me? Especially as a whore!"

Scarlett's mouth theatrically fell open. "Really? You have the audacity to slut-shame me after you beg to fuck me every chance you get? These last three months meant something to me! How dare you throw that all away?!"

Julian pounded his boot down, quaking the floor so much that the TV nudged.

"None of it matters if it means I'm going back to being a father! So, are you going to abort that thing or force me to do it?"

"Force? No, Julian, that's not how this works." Scarlett stood straight, puffing up her inked chest. "You better break things off with Madeleine. Otherwise, everybody will know what we've been up to when a little, Royalty-blooded child, that's the spitting image of you, slips out of me in less than nine months after you leave her."

Julian scoffed as he shook his head. "You're just like Francis—thinking that I care about the public's opinion. I don't! I'm not going to have another kid because we're heading to the clinic this instant!" He firmly pointed down at the cheap hardwood slats as the red light flooded the room, demonizing his eyes.

Scarlett knew relinquishing authority would result in him learning the truth. "I'm not going anywhere. And if you love me, you'll leave her today and quit making me wait."

A short chuckle escaped Julian. Out of place, it grew. His chest heaved as the maniacal laugh expanded.

Scarlett stepped back. "Joules … you're scaring me."

A pulse of red flashed through Slough again. Julian laughed harder, ignoring the fact that the neighbor heard everything.

"Love you? I don't even know your full name!"

Scarlett pointed away as her noisy breaths torched out of her nostrils. "Then, leave. Now!"

He stepped closer. She backed away. He took another step. She glanced at the coffee table, finding her phone halfway over the edge, just beside the Chinese food takeout container. Scarlett peered at him before leaping for it like a fleeting frog. He intersected her face with his fist, like a sniper striking a moving target. She splayed over the floor, knocking down the corner lamp. As she crawled away, she slipped and panted, knocking over more furniture.

She frantically looked around. However, the collapsed bookshelves and skewed paintings finally caught up with her.

"Get out!" she shouted, as she had nothing left in her arsenal.

Julian observed his reddened knuckles. They trembled without his consent, as Scarlett, the woman who had once ignited the peak of his passions, now shivered before him with a beauty marred by a bleeding, broken nose.

She covered her face as the pain settled in. "Get out!" Her voice muffled through her palm.

One boot at a time, he stepped back, avoiding the carpet ripples and the uneven slats. He turned away, hearing the laughter of the sitcom blaring as the crimson light swirled by again.

Before him stood the door. He understood how his life would change forever if he walked through it.

Scarlett spotted the wedding band gleaming from beneath the couch. As her only lifeline, she snappily swallowed it. She checked to see if he saw, but he was gone. However, the door never opened. A red wave passed.

Julian's silhouette suddenly contrasted the kitchen's entryway, holding the longest, sharpest knife.

Scarlett's face dropped. "Woah, woah, woah! Slow down!"

Julian approached, red, then normal.

"Hey, hey, you do this, and there's no coming back! You won't get away with it!"

He directed the blade at her belly. "We're either leaving for the clinic, or I'm going to do it myself!" Scarlett gauged every bit of the room, but his shouting pulled her attention back. "And where's my wedding band?!" Mute, her eyes flinched. "That, right there," he shoved his index finger against the gap between her brows, "you know where it is! You really thought that I wouldn't notice it gone after the day we met? I went against my instincts with you, Scar; I wanted you to be different. But you're just like any other whore; always preparing a backdoor."

As the smooth edges of the ring slid down her esophagus, Scarlett pleaded, "Julian, I swear, I don't—"

"Bullshit! Tell me where it is!"

Black spots peppered Scarlett's view, occasionally being enveloped by red. With each step closer, the claustrophobia clutched her heart tighter in her throat. The redness glowing over her skin bounced least off of her sweat-soaked panties. Her tremors were impossible to hide, especially with the tattoos giving Julian a point of reference.

He stepped closer, shoving the coffee table aside. The phone thudded, promptly followed by the ashtray which scattered a plume of grayish white dust over the rug. Scarlett flipped the table in an attempt to flee, but he stomped his boot into her gut like a sledgehammer. The dogs outside barked as the red light drowned the scene. She kicked and flailed to get out, but only smeared the splattered takeout deeper into the rug's fibers. The television spewed waves of laughter.

Julian towered over her, her body convulsing just from his presence. "Clinic, or no clinic?" Regardless, he intended to achieve the same result.

Although she had no other options, she incessantly shook her head, with her tattoos tugging like the strings of a puppet. She couldn't imagine what he'd do after the clinic told him the truth—that she wasn't pregnant.

The floor creaked with each approaching step, only stopping as he kneeled. He pressed his knee against her collarbone. Literally cornered, she sought her phone, with her last hope residing in calling Francis.

"After everything," Julian said. "It turns out that you're just another stubborn nail that wants to tell me how to live my life. No, you need to be beaten down." In a desperate attempt, she stretched towards the phone, but not before he punched her square in the nose. Her facial expression dropped as she blinked a few times. "Hammered, again and again!" Countless blows rained down.

Faint thuds echoed from behind the wall as the high, motionless neighbor gazed at the ceiling. Bags drooped beneath his eyes, with a dark brown bellied glass pipe tipped beside him. The dull pounding continued.

Bloodied, naked and deprived, Scarlett quivered. Her Monroe lip piercing pressed through and lodged into her gums between her now contorted teeth. She panted, with eyes misaligned, yet one helplessly staring at the red prince.

In her final attempt, she screamed for help, but he gripped her throat and squeezed beyond the limit, as if wringing a rag. Following a sheathing sound, he raised the blade. It hovered in the air as a recurrence of the red light whirled by, glinting the sharp, crimson edge.

Chapter XXXI
History Never Fails

— Current Day —

Minutes before nighttime, Zee found Julian wandering into the village. A smile stretched across his face as he juggled the basketball between his knees, hoping to attract Julian's attention. But when left ignored, he caught the ball and waved. "Hey, garra-haran—" Zee lowered his hand when Julian strolled by, completely ignoring him.

Julian's drool spilled aimlessly as he stumbled between the huts. He flinched a sudden twitch every few seconds, randomly stopping and severely itching his forearms. He chomped his teeth at nothing and whispered into thin air.

Zee hid behind some trees, taming his bursting breaths before racing towards Chief Amari's hut. He bumped into Akilu standing guard.

"[Surmic] Easy there, little one. What's the problem?"

"Uncle Akilu, Uncle Akilu, the—the haranchi. He's acting weird."

"What do you mean?"

Zee pointed. "Look."

Upon witnessing Julian eavesdropping beneath Ike's hut, Akilu drew the boy behind him. "Go home, Zelalem. And don't come out, even if you hear shouting."

"Yes, sir."

Moments later, Akilu, under the stealth of the night, muffled Julian's mouth before shoving a sack over his head.

—

In the hut, Ike wrapped his arm over his friend. "Are you going to tell your father about the mines?"

Imamu leaned forward, resigning his forehead into his hands. "How? He'd kill me before I finish the sentence. And besides, he'll just ask about the generational dagger."

Ike sat beside him, observing Nala sleeping. "You don't want to hand it down to Kamari, do you?"

"If I do, that'd be submitting to Dada's rule," Imamu said. "But if I pull this off, then there's nobody more worthy of owning that dagger than me. This needs to work, but every added complication pushes the goal post further away."

Ike reviewed the obstacles, as one main thing irked him. "Why'd you lie about Koka and Kibish?"

"Really? Ike, that's easy. Both Dada and Lieutenant Akilu know that Koka is in ruins. They could also send some Mursi, who'd return before this damn embassy ever responds. Whereas Kibish is suitable to handle an infant in distress, and it's too far for them to check. It'll take them at least a week to learn the truth. That should give us enough time to—"

"Shh!" Ike abruptly stood.

"What?"

He approached the window. "I heard something."

The two friends raced outside, finding Julian bagged and disoriented. Akilu hauled him off the ground, panting. "You two, come with me."

—

Madeleine stepped outside upon hearing a solid thud. A dust cloud welcomed her as Akilu stood over a grunting prisoner—head covered, limbs bound. Akilu snatched the bag off, revealing Julian with a gag in his mouth. The Royal writhed in place as Imamu, Ike and a crowd converged on the scene.

"[English] What is this?" Madeleine asked with an obvious fear strangling her tone.

Julian grunted and nudged towards her for help. Akilu placed his foot on him, as if to prevent a ball from rolling away.

"Last night, I caught your husband eavesdropping beside Ike's residence. This action is not acceptable among our people, regardless of their status—"

Julian spit out the muffle. "Maddy! Help! They tied me up for hours, interrogating me non-stop!"

Madeleine looked at Akilu. His expression bled honesty.

"It was for a few minutes, max," Akilu said. "We can't allow this type of behavior, but I also understand your delicate situation. Therefore, I didn't want Chief Amari to act in haste. I'm giving your husband one last opportunity to tell us what he was doing, otherwise I'll have to include the Chieftain."

Madeleine's eye twitched. Dried mud chipped off Julian's chest as he slowed his struggle.

"I wasn't spying!"

"Then tell him what you were doing," Madeleine said.

Julian snapped back and forth. "Who—who's side are you on here?"

She waited. As did everybody else.

"Maddy—"

"Tell him," Madeleine commanded. "Tell us all. Why's my husband snooping around at night?"

"Mad—"

"You know, these questions, back home, you could just run away from them. But here, where you have to be honest, you can't. So, out with it. What were you doing?"

"Alright," he mumbled as he glanced at how outnumbered he was. "Sure."

Julian nudged Madeleine to come closer, but Akilu held his arm out. "You stole something private. Your only redemption is in saying it out loud, publicly."

Julian looked around. "I, uhh …" The crowd leaned in, as if orchestrated. "I was, ehm …" Madeleine's flat eyebrows lowered further. "You're really going to make me say it?" Madeleine waited. "I was … eh … *beating the bishop.*"

She blinked repeatedly. "Y—you …" some people covered their mouths, while Akilu struggled to restrain his smirk, "you—you were wanking it to these women, after all you've said?"

Julian turned his face towards the dirt, waiting for the moment to pass.

Limp after limp, Madeleine charged forward and pelted countless kicks into his gut. One after the other, he tried to shield himself from the blows, but the onslaught was too severe.

"You manky, knob slapping, son of a—I should rip off your bollocks!"

Before she gave him internal bleeding, Akilu pulled her off. Her arms flailed as she screamed, but Akilu couldn't allow the hurdled situation to get any worse. He dragged her away as the crowd laughed at the coughing Julian.

"Lady-Madeleine, a word."

"Give me five minutes before untying him! Just five!"

Akilu clutched her shoulders, looked her in the eye and inhaled until his chest maxed out. She unintentionally did the same. He repeated the exercise. With every exhale, Madeleine's redness lessened until she felt a wave of embarrassment.

"I'm—I'm sorry," she said. "I don't know what got over me."

"It's alright, but he might not be fully to blame." Akilu glanced at Julian spitting faint blood. "His eyes. Notice how yellow they are? He must've eaten some of that no-good khat."

Madeleine momentarily froze. "*My husband ate a cat?*"

"No," Akilu chuckled for an instant before resuming his stern demeanor, "*khat*. It's a plant that intoxicates. It'll give you visions and rile you up. Expect him to have incoherent speech or fantastical stories. I wouldn't believe much of what he's about to say. Persuade him to eat some real food and rest. He should sober up by sunrise."

"I understand. Thank you, Akilu. I'm sorry for all of this."

"Stay safe, Princess," he said, turning to leave. "We're working hard to find your daughter."

Later, the Royals entered Imamu's hut as the people dispersed. Julian rummaged through the electronics, seeking a cable to charge his phone. Madeleine glared from across the room.

"No," Julian said to himself as he checked a cable's end. "No, no, no." None of the cables fit his phone's port, until he found one that did. "What is this?" He held the cable up. "Why's this the only charger frayed?! Imamu did this! See?!"

"Don't look at me, you—you—you knacker hugger!"

"Not now, Madeleine! I need to tell you what I heard! And no, I wasn't being a peeping Tom—I just needed them to leave! Imamu *is* holding us for ransom! They were talking about it all night; they called the embassy and left a message and everything!"

Madeleine's chin quivered, simmering before a boil. "You know … I'm really trying here."

He approached her and tried to touch her face. She flinched. "Maddy, they hung me upside-down and beat me for at least six hours. You can't believe them!"

Tears balled at the corner of her eyes. "Juley, you left to get food only an hour ago …"

"No! That's—that's not right!" He stomped, deforming the floor and knocking a lithium ore off a shelf. "Quit it with these games!" The yellow overtook the whites of his eyes, resembling a reptile. "Why don't you ever believe me? Isn't it obvious how much I'm striving to mend our relationship? And what're you doing trusting these people over your own husband—the same people who just shamelessly slaughtered a man earlier today?!"

"Julian," she said softly, yet directly. "You're high. Nobody's trying to harm us."

Hyperventilating, he looked around the hut for any semblance of sanity. "We're garra-haranchi! Zee said we're garra-haranchi! Doesn't that mean anything to you?"

She jerked her palms up. "Julian, stop it. You're scaring me."

"*I'm* scaring you? *Me?* We're surrounded by murderous freaks, and I'm the one scaring you?"

Madeleine gazed as if staring at a rabid dog, with a bead of cold sweat sliding down her lower back.

Julian waited for her to say something, but as they stared at each other, he spotted a set of black lines scribbling marks across her neck. They started crawling over her skin, leaving behind petals, vines and bones. Soon enough, they raced over her body, inking her shoulders and cleavage, in a race down towards her wrists.

Saliva formed at the crevice between his lips. As he followed the pattern scatter through her arm hair and near her elbows, the drool stretched, splattering onto his boot.

"We need these people, Julian. Nobody else is going to help us find Leopaula. We can't do it ourselves, the Kingdom isn't coming and Francis—"

"*Don't you dare say a word about Francis.*" He tilted his head, curious how far the tattoo traveled beneath her clothes.

"We need them all," Madeleine said. "Only they can—" she stepped back. "Why—why're you looking at me like that?"

"*What's it say?*" Julian blurted, bubbling the slobber.

"What's … what's what say?"

He wiped his chin, smearing the spit. "*The poem,*" he mumbled, observing her side. "*I never got to read it.*" Madeleine looked over her torso, clueless. "And no, we don't need any of them. The commandos are here. They're close by."

"Commandos—you saw the commandos?! Julian, they're only deployed when it's a shoot-first-ask-questions-later situation! They'll kill everybody here and leave Leopaula!"

Julian suddenly, hastily and aggressively, reached for his belt buckle, observing Madeleine's side.

"What're you looking for?!" She tried pushing him away. He yanked his jeans down, dropping them to his ankles before forcing Madeleine over and tearing off her top, searching for the words of the couplet. "Stop it!"

He didn't. When she resisted, he slammed her head down, bashing her eyebrow against a sharp edge of an old-fashioned steel radio. As a random Ethiopian folksong crackled through the speakers, her blood surged down her cheek, branching off into multiple streams, connecting her eye, mouth and nose.

A spasmodic twitch jittered his forehead. "TELL ME WHAT IT SAYS!"

Imamu and Ike turned in unison towards the hut.

Madeleine shrieked, "Help—"

Julian grabbed her neck. He squeezed, harder and harder, pinching off her air in an instant. She kicked around, worsening her already bad ankle and bashing off the radio. Wisps of grunts reverberated within the walls as the electronics bore witness.

Envisioning himself as one of the tattoos, he wrapped his fingers tighter. He continued clenching through her barrage of strikes. Each whack fueled him, reminding him of Scarlett. A hellish hue flared from behind his sweat-fused locks.

Madeleine's teeth clanked and jittered as she struggled. She wanted to argue; she wanted to snap him out of it. But she couldn't do anything besides spring a series of diminishing flinches.

"Shut up!" But she was silent. "Just shut up!"

As she attempted to smuggle in any air, her eyes rolled back. Her weakening efforts personified in her limbs falling to her side, as her reopened scab continued to stream blood down his arm.

Silence.

A whistle sounded from outside.

"Everything alright in there?" Ike asked.

Julian let go, dropping Madeleine like a stack of books among the tangled wires. Scrambling to her knees, she feebly stumbled away, gasping for air. She didn't look up or respond, only interested in widening the distance.

"We're fine!"

"Are you sure?" Imamu asked. "It sounded like a crash."

Muttering hoarse profanities, Julian boomed once more, "I said we're fine!"

When they left, he turned to Madeleine. Her chin shined red, painting the cot, along with everything beneath it.

"Again?" She shuddered over the weighty silence. The red droplets continued, dying everything they splattered over. "*Again?!*" Jaw tightened, he glared through the huffs, casting his flaxen, red-ringed eyes. "Get out!"

He stepped closer, towering over her like a wide, skeletal tree, its haunting branches a toxic representation of nature.

She lifted a random dissected gadget, dangling its motherboard and panels while cocking it back. "Get out, now!"

His phone chimed, signaling that his battery fell below 10%. He looked at it, before opening the messaging app and seeing Scarlett still responding.

Clouds swallowed the moon, blackening the hut. The electronics in Madeleine's grip rattled as she could only smell him, but couldn't see a thing. Her heart's pounding deafened her until the moon broke free, revealing that she was now alone. The device fell, clattering over the other gadgets before she covered her face and sobbed.

Chapter XXXII
Broken Stanza

Static crackled from the blood covered vintage radio. Madeleine lowered her fidgeting hands, spotting the smeared red trails following the crease pattern of her palm. With footsteps outside, she snapped her fists up and faced the entrance.

"Go away!"

The static continued as the murmuring from the other huts reached her ears. She couldn't tell if they were talking about her or Julian. But focused on the opening, she didn't care. She patted around until her nail chipped on the lithium ore's surface. She raised the rock up, ready to defend herself.

A flock of ravens burst forth from the tree line, dipping into the village, bellowing an eerie gurgling croak which gripped the spine. Their disorienting flutter scattered few of their feathers over the silent huts.

Tensed, Madeleine held ready on the entrance as the hut's straw rattled around her, with the ravens passing overhead.

"Go away, now!"

When nothing happened, and Julian didn't return, she dropped the ore and collapsed. She pinched the bridge of her nose until her breath caught up with her. The scent of iron and sweat floated from one wall to the other. She turned off the radio and switched on a lamp, illuminating the aftermath. Between the rust lines of the electronics, red droplets and scuff marks painted the surroundings. Amid it all, the lithium stone gleamed a dark crimson.

Madeleine picked it up and spit-shined it, knowing its value to Imamu. She placed it on a table and began tidying the mess. Starting from the furthest corner of the hut, she organized his clothes and stacked some booklets. The thick ones were technical manuals, but she wasn't sure of the thin ones.

Page after page, it read poems written by Imamu.

"Again today, a remnant of yours crossed my sight," Madeleine softly whispered as she read the couplet. *"To forget requires my blindness. But what's life without light?"*

She flipped through the journal, finding more. He wrote in different languages, dialects and styles. A slight buzz emanated from the small light as it dimmed with every passing minute.

"I saw her," Madeleine gasped upon reading the least wrinkled of the pages. *"Alone, defeated. Is she free, or is she me—"*

The light's battery ran out, making it too dark to read. Madeleine neared the window and, using the moonlight, found the next page blank.

"What is this?" She flipped and flipped. Nothing. "He's still writing this one ..."

Closing the journal and placing it atop the other books, she resumed cleaning. But with every device she organized, she kept glancing back at the diary. Its presence beckoned her, urging her to open its pages once more. The curiosity grew, distracting her from distracting herself.

Unable to resist any longer, she pushed aside the electronics and reached for the notepad. She flipped back through previous pages, seeking whatever she could regarding Leopaula's mention. The one line kept nagging her.

"*Is she free, or is she me?*" she read, over and over. "What does he mean?"

—

After some time, Madeleine wondered about Julian. She peeked outside but couldn't spot him. A few fireflies glittered as some flames illuminated various huts, but the people were mostly indoors.

The crickets stridulated under the moonlight, filling the quiet night with their gentle song. Madeleine glanced at Ike's hut, finding Imamu sitting outside, somberly looking towards her with the letter from the mines dangling from his hand.

She waved.

He waved back.

Madeleine walked over, using only the glow of the moonlight to guide her.

"Did Julian come here?" she asked as she sat beside him.

"No," he said. Sitting beside each other, the pair stared out at the village. "Are you two alright?"

Madeleine stayed mute. A gentle breeze swirled between them. Imamu glanced at her.

"You're bleeding." He leaned her head to the side, looking closer. "Did—did he do this to you?!" Madeleine pulled away, still silent. "Princess Mad—"

"I don't want to talk about it. I want to talk to you about something else."

The crickets chirped as the distant trees swayed and ruffled. Some fires crackled, as others extinguished, carrying an asphyxiating current of smoke towards the two.

"Sure," Imamu said. "But let's step inside."

Nala slept in the hut's corner, as Ike sharpened his spears over a diminishing candle. "Princess," he said, nodding once.

She regarded him, but only that.

Imamu took a seat. "Can I get you anything?"

"I just want you to be transparent," Madeleine said.

"Uhm, okay, I'll try."

Ike glanced between the two.

"How'd you feel the last time you saw Leopaula?"

The honing stopped, dropping the hut into a momentary silence.

"How'd I *feel?*"

Madeleine nodded. Imamu suddenly didn't know what to do with his hands.

"I—" A weakness plummeted his shoulders as his mind had seemed to teleport elsewhere. "I—"

Ike mutely observed. Imamu's fingers fell slack as he stared down, neck arching.

"She was … she was—"

Wet. The water, the river, Omo—it was a barrier between Imamu and the remedy to his turmoil. Leopaula's weakness and frailty before him posed as a searing hot spear, stabbing through his heart.

But he froze. This was the last dose. After which, the pain will cease.

"She—"

Leopaula's cry, the brief scream—he heard it. The echo transcribed into text which was etched into his stone heart, forever to reread.

Her fingers wiggled as her lungs struggled before him.

"I'm sorry," he whispered to her. "I'm sorry."

Imamu blinked a few times, finding Madeleine with welling eyes.

"I've seen worse, but I've never felt worse," he said.

"Was she cold? O—or—" As Imamu's stomach gripped him in place, he dipped his chin. "How about her h—hands, her face? Or—or her feet? Tell me. Anything, please."

Imamu juggled his sight between two of Ike's floor mats, trying to recall the details.

"Her feet weren't blue if—if that's what you mean. She was alive."

Madeleine's sniffles slowed. "Her feet?" Imamu nodded as a tear hurried over his cheek. "Like her feet, *feet,* or …?"

"Yes, her toes and all."

"You—you saw her toes …" Madeleine's tears ceased entirely as she straightened her back, "*through her onesie?*"

Imamu's lips joined as he stopped blinking. Ike remained quiet. Madeleine reached, but Imamu flinched. She continued until she placed her thumb on his face and wiped his tear.

"You're lying," she said. Imamu swallowed, but she smiled. "And I know why." As Imamu shamefully looked down, Madeleine swiftly swiped the mine-letter without their knowledge. "I don't blame you," the ravens returned to the trees surrounding the village, "but I need you, Imamu. I really do."

Imamu's hitching breaths rooted him as his focus drifted over every inch of the floor.

Ike noticed the crack in the dam. He had to prevent the leak. "Tomorrow, we're going to the mines with the prince to facilitate the freedom of our people. They'll have access to vehicles and communication with the Kingdom. After we return, they could take you straight to the hospital."

Madeleine ignored him completely and continued to stare at Imamu until his tears stopped moistening the fibers beneath. She stood. "Let's make sure Julian's around first."

Ike nodded. "Give him a few minutes to cool off from whatever you two were arguing about. But if he doesn't return soon, we should inform Chief Amari."

"You know where to find me," Madeleine said before leaving.

Once alone, Ike patted Imamu's shoulder. "[Surmic] Hey, what the hell was that?"

"This isn't right. I—I can't go through with this. I have to tell her the truth."

"Woah, woah, woah, we're in too deep now. Someone's dead because of us."

Imamu shook his head. "She's hurting—she's not like the rest of them!" He raised his face, radiating his raw emotions.

"What is this? Are you trying to save yourself, or her?" Ike rubbed his temples. "How is it that I'm now pushing for the plan, and you're the one backing out?"

"I've never seen our pain in a haranchi. We were wrong to think they're all savages. This isn't right!"

Ike grabbed Imamu's shoulders and dug his fingers into them, staring deep into his dark, wet pupils. "Hey, hey, listen to me. Everything's going to work out, but we need to keep her at arm's length. Once we cash out, then you could tell her where Leopaula is."

Imamu, struggling to calm down, shoved his friend off and ran outside. With the village vacant, he turned towards the isolated moon with a hole in his chest. The celestial orb hung lonely in the vast, empty sky. It didn't have a place to go or stay as the scattered stars kept their distance from it. The clouds passed before it, as if it had no existence. The sun would routinely defeat it, giving it no option but to retreat month after month.

It was lost.

It was alone.

Chapter XXXIII
The Phantom of Freedom — Part 1

Storming out of the village, Julian's stomps disturbed a batch of roosting ravens. After fluttering in pandemonium, they found their bearings and sought refuge in trees far from the wide-eyed prince.

"[English] Where ya going?" Scarlett asked, dangling upside down from a branch.

"Away!" Julian barked as he passed beneath her. "Far, far away from these animals! I'll walk home if I have to."

"Oh, baby, that'll be so romantic of you!" She appeared before him, cupping her breasts as if juggling. "These'll be waiting for you when you arrive."

He passed without a glance.

"Oh, you're serious," Scarlett said. "But, how? Walking across that no-man's-land is certain doom."

"I'll use the rowboat, the one we came in!"

Dressed as a castle guard, with a tall fuzzy hat, Scarlett scratched her chin while raising a brow. "To where? The Jeep's outta gas, remember?"

Following a guttural roar, Julian frazzled his hair.

"I'll—I'll take it upstream, even if I have to use my arms as paddles. Then I'll—I don't know—I'll build a motor or something. Just let me do this!"

Scarlett appeared to his side, leaning back on a chase-couch, one leg exposed with half her head shaved.

"Well, I won't stand in your way, *your highness,*" she said, mockingly throwing her hands up.

Julian stopped. He glanced at her. She held a faint smirk, looking the opposite direction.

"What is it? What do you want to tell me?"

Nude, with styled hair reaching her elbows, she gave him her full attention, flashing her vagina his way.

"I gotta better idea."

She winked.

—

"[Surmic] Stop," D'jen said to his men from their cover. "What is this?"

D'jen narrowed his sights on Julian talking into thin air. As he argued with Scarlett, D'jen concealed himself behind the tree trunks.

He whispered back, "Everybody, stand down."

A Karo hunter approached.

"Chief D'jen, why? This is our chance to take out The Lion Tamer's son for the Mursi trespassing. That man there is one of the four we spotted yesterday."

D'jen kept his eyes trained on Julian.

"An opportunity, far more valuable than revenge, has presented itself," he said, trying to understand Julian's state-of-mind. "Stay back, but not too far. I need to lure him away from the village so that we could get a clear shot at the princess and the baby. Otherwise, they'll huddle around those two, preventing us from fulfilling Francis's mission."

"Yes, sir," the hunter said before disappearing into the night.

—

Julian waited for a response. Scarlett stood before him, dressed as a professor with plenty of cleavage visible for the males to fail over. Glasses clung onto the balled tip of her nose. She whacked her wooden pointer on a boring green floating chalkboard with bulleted items.

"[English] Number 1. Take Imamu's phone during your trip to the mines. Number 2. Insert his sim card into your phone. Number 3—"

"Woah, hold on," Julian said. "How am I supposed to snatch his phone? He keeps that thing glued to his hip. And his buddy will most likely be tagging along."

With a punk-do and spiked leather bracelets and chokers, Scarlett shrugged.

"Just kill them, like you killed me," she said nonchalantly.

Julian furrowed his brows as he puckered his lips and nodded.

"I could do that."

"Duh, you could," Scarlett said, normal again. "Killing the problem is always the answer. Otherwise, it'll grow again, only to pop up at the worst possible moment. Look at how slaying me shut me up from ruining your image and giving you a second child."

"Well ... are you sure his sim card would work in my phone?"

Scarlett slapped his forehead the moment a fallen leaf did the same.

"*Would it work?* Joules, of course it'll work. You're the one that mandated all the engineers the Kingdom sends overseas be equipped with those special sim cards. Remember? The ones that'll give them reception even in the middle of the ocean. That's what Imamu stole—that's what he has!"

"That's right," Julian said, nodding blankly.

"And once you pop that thing in, then you could call Francis. You'll be able to come back to me, where you'll be free. And where I'll be able to hear your voice again, no more of these puny texts."

"Yeah, yeah!"

"Don't you remember how much fun we had—how happy you were? How about that magic you felt during your wedding? That flutter in your heart didn't come from Madeleine, it came from me. And you so, so need that again. *I* need that again. We both deserve it, especially after all you've had to endure."

Julian smiled at the torrent of memories flooding his mind.

"And all you have to do is get that nigger's phone!"

"You're right," Julian said. "You're always right."

—

"[Surmic] The boy's gone mad …" D'jen said, observing the entire episode from a distance. A wide grin grew beneath his nose. "*Even better.*"

Chapter XXXIV
The Phantom of Freedom — Part 2

"[English] Then where are we going to stay tonight? Maddy's not—"

Scarlett slapped her hand over Julian's mouth.

"Shh. Someone's watching us."

Through the daunting depths of the forest, a lone man stepped forward. He entered part of his face into the moonlight as few fallen leaves scattered by him. His frame rivaled that of Amari's, even bolstering similar armlets of snakes vying for control over his biceps. Beneath his throat, a sharp, curved hyena tooth dangled against his chest, nudging from side to side as he approached. An endangered Abyssinian black lion's mane draped his shoulders, while he wore a short, dark loincloth rolled at the hip like a towel as his lower garment. A pouched belt, holding bullets, darts and poison, kept everything in place as the stranger revealed himself.

"Who goes there?" Julian asked, balanced between ready to defend himself and ready to flee.

"Boy," D'jen whispered. "You need to come with me now."

Julian eyed him while murmuring, "Scarlett, who's that?"

Scarlett shrugged as D'jen glanced between Julian and the lack of anybody else there.

I see, D'jen thought.

"Francis sent me to save you and …" D'jen gazed at the tree beside Julian, *"and Scarlett."*

Before his adrenaline tingled his body, Scarlett stood before Julian.

"Ask him if he's with the commandos," she whispered.

"Are you?" Julian asked.

"Am I what?" D'jen asked back, before piecing it together. "I … *I couldn't hear her.*"

"Are you with the commandos?"

D'jen held a sidelong glance at the few Mursi searching from hut to hut. Knowing that time pressed against him, he refocused back on Julian.

"No, I'm D'jen."

"D'jen? The same D'jen who screwed over kid Imamu?" Julian asked.

"He fits the description," Scarlett said.

"I'm not sure. From the way Zola made it sound, this mate wouldn't ever approach the village without being strapped to the teeth."

"Everything they say about me is a lie. Only I know the truth and only I could save you," D'jen said, reaching his hand out. "Isn't this what you want? To get out of here, to be free again?"

Julian looked towards the empty forest beside him. "You think he's lying?"

D'jen snapped his fingers to pull Julian's attention back.

"If I'm lying, how would I know you were sent here on a Turkish Airlines flight with a layover in Stockholm? Then you boarded an Ethiopian Airlines flight to AMH?"

Scarlett whispered something to Julian.

"That's right; anybody could have Googled that."

D'jen dropped his eyebrows. "You wore a fake mustache."

Julian quickly raised his finger, before slowly lowering it, realizing only someone in on the getaway plan would've known that detail. He checked with Scarlett.

"It still might be a trap," she said. "You can't trust any of these people."

"Prince Julian—"

"Tell me what you did to Imamu and the lithium and all that stuff," Julian said, still sporting half-lidded yellow eyes. "I've lived among both parties from that transaction, so I'll know if you're lying."

As more Mursi exited their huts, D'jen shifted his sights back and forth.

"Are you sure? They're looking for you."

Julian shrugged a single shoulder. "They can't outright harm me. Whereas, I don't trust you."

With slicing eyes, D'jen tapped his fingers against his thigh.

"Alright, alright, I'll summarize. Decades back, when Amari and I led beneath The Lion Tamer, we and the Ethiopian government had a pact with the Kingdom: Lithium from us, cash from them. Your kingdom was suffering a brutal economic recession, with lithium being their only glimmer of hope. All was good, until your brother, Napoleon, interrupted the transaction. He claimed wild allegations regarding human-rights violations, crimes-against-humanity and what have you. We later learned he was trying to take a cut for himself. Does this sound familiar?"

Julian created a Venn diagram in his mind with what he learned as a child. He compared what Zola said to Madeleine with what D'jen shared.

"King Leopold sentenced Napoleon to death for being a traitor to the throne. However, with the accusations out there, nobody wanted to get into a deal with Ethiopia. That was until about eight years ago when little Imamu found a sea of lithium quarries beside Omo River. He thought it was just a small hollow, but the mines and caves ran deep within the valley, like an underground world.

"The tribes had their own financial struggles, preceding fatal consequences. I didn't want a repeat of last time because my people are valuable to me, Prince Julian. The government wants to keep taking our land as we watch from the sidelines, hungry and debased—exactly like when they set up boundaries for Omo National Park and the Gibe hydroelectric dam. So, I went behind my government's back because this lithium belongs to the tribes, not them. I reached out to you during your wedding, to congratulate you and attempt to strike a new deal. But Francis answered and through him, we made a fair contract that promised our safety and prosperity. But one man stood in my way."

"Who?" Julian asked.

"The Great Shaman, Haile, The Lion Tamer. He was the inside man who worked on the backdoor deal with Napoleon—willing to sacrifice his own people just for a share of the profits. We could've improved our standard of living and modernized the tribe, but no. Amari's father developed this whole spiritual persona around himself, so that nobody would question him.

"I tried stopping him, but before I did what had to be done, Haile informed the Ethiopian government, and within days, they cut the tribes out of the deal. Amari, now in charge, didn't want to face the humiliation that his father went through the first time. He blamed it all on me, banishing me from the tribe, as if I was attempting to imitate Napoleon's crimes."

Scarlett scratched her head. "Something isn't lining up. Zola said that The Lion Tamer was killed before Imamu discovered the lithium."

Julian ignored her, finding more of what he'd been taught in line with D'jen story.

"Trapped in my own land, I had nowhere to go, Prince Julian. Those who learned the truth behind Amari's accusations joined me and we started the Karo tribe. When Francis heard about this backstabbing, he began a series of negotiations in order to share the profits with the tribes.

"Although everybody agreed, Amari refused. He'd rather the Mursi starve and struggle than to admit he wrongly accused me. Sacrificing his people for his ego— just like his father. This is why he's so territorial. He's ruling by instilling fear-of-the-others into the Mursi.

Because without that dread, Amari will lose all authority. You must've witnessed his brutal ways by now."

Julian nodded, eyes bulging. "I did!"

Scarlett nudged him. "Something he's saying isn't right."

"Shut up," Julian muttered. "This guy's the real deal. He sees these Mursi freaks for who they really are. No mind games or tricks like what Imamu and Zola have been feeding us. What he's saying about Napoleon and Francis and the Kingdom, it's what I know to be true."

"But his narrative isn't adding up—"

"Scarlett, earlier today, Amari cleaved through a Brit coming to save us! Are you telling me to go back to him instead of trusting D'jen, who's been nothing but a straight shooter?"

D'jen mutely let Julian and his imaginary friend work out the kinks. Unsure how much Julian learned, he knew nothing held water with him other than what lined up with the Kingdom's narrative.

"After Francis sent you here," D'jen said. "He asked me to keep an eye on you and assure your safety. But when you crossed into Mursi land, my hands were tied, until now. I see your struggle, Julian, from the torment by what you've been through and what's to come. I'm here, risking my life near these barbarians, just to help Francis, as he's helped me in the past."

D'jen extended his palm, while glancing at the rapidly nearing Mursi carrying torches.

"Come, come now, Prince Julian. Let me free you."

Julian regarded Scarlett, who remained hemmed and hawed with a restless knee.

"I'm going," Julian said to her, walking towards D'jen's hand, peering from the dark array of trees.

D'jen's cheeks grew a faint shade of pink as he thought, *just a few more steps.*

Chapter XXXV
Not Part of this Family

— Three Days Earlier —

Just a few steps from the King Henry VIII gate, Francis checked his phone once more. *Nothing from Scarlett*. Visitors flocked through the arched entrance, enchanted by the castle. All the while, Francis tried ignoring the quiver in his stomach. He glanced at the phone again. His messages were going through, but they weren't being read. He knew calling her could blow the entire operation.

With a frown soldered onto his face, Francis sliced through the crowd of what he called pathetic minions. He rested his back against the gate's bricks, glancing out at the Queen Victoria statue.

"Sir, could you help me find—" Francis looked through the tourist, fingers galloping over his phone. "Sir?"

A vibration. Francis quickly checked. No new message, only an event reminder: Changing the Guard Ceremony. "Dammit."

"Excuse me, Sir—"

Like a demon preparing for a possession, Francis flared at the tourist. "WHAT?!"

She flinched, dropping her pamphlets and purse. As she scrambled to pick her things up, Francis typed out yet another message to Scarlett.

> Francis: Any response from him? He's not

answering his phone, and I can't find him on the castle grounds. Call me ASAP.

Message sent. Message received. *Message unread.*

Something's wrong, Francis thought. I have to go to her flat.

As the tourist hurried away, a peculiar man observed the entire scene from afar. Francis simultaneously noticed him. He wasn't a normal visitor. He donned a short-brimmed hat with a briefcase slung over his chest. Regardless of where Francis glanced, the man wouldn't take his eyes off him. A tingling sensation ran down Francis's spine as the man approached.

Every step closer, the man's simper stretched, becoming more and more evident. Francis checked his phone for the millionth time, but the man kept cutting through the people, laser-focused on the Royal Guard. Still unread, the man still approached.

Francis tried to disappear into the gates, aswarm with onlookers. Occasionally looking back, he saw the man hustling. His attire blared that he carried bad news, like a grim reaper, locked onto his victim. Francis pushed his way through the crowd, even knocking some elderly visitors down. People cleared and chattered as the man desperately reached, grazing Francis's armlet.

"Oh, Sir-Francis," the man called.

Just then, Francis's phone rang. Francis answered, while pointing at the phone and regarding the man. "Sorry, I must take this." He rushed towards the base of the Salisbury Tower.

The man scoffed before taking out a notepad and writing, all while monitoring Francis.

—

"Scarlett!" Francis's voice echoed into the hollow structure.

"H—hi, uhm, no. Is this Sir-Francis, of the Royal Guard?" an Asian sounding ditsy lady on the other end asked.

Past a forced exhale, Francis responded, "Speaking."

"Yes, sir. Uhm, there's a situation here at Thy Spa that you should be aware of."

"I only handle Royal Family affairs. Call the authorities—"

"Well, this has to do with Lady-Madeleine. Please come, and fast."

The line disconnected.

Francis jerked his head back before glancing out of the windows. The man was gone. Catching his breath, he checked his messages again.

Scarlett still hadn't read the message.

He sucked his teeth before marching out of the tower and towards the spa.

—

From the sidewalk, floor-to-ceiling glass panes of Thy Spa welcomed the customers. However, today, blinds stood guard. The ajar door housed a slanted closed sign. Francis entered, dinging a bell. In an empty lobby, Leopaula wailed, strapped in her car seat. The frazzled worker kept getting pulled in every direction.

"Were you the one who called?" Francis asked.

The young Thai woman nodded amid the surrounding chaos. Artificial sounds of nature filled the background, but Leopaula's screams took center stage. The phone rang off the hook as the teakettle's power cord sparked. Every few seconds, the door's ding malfunctioned, repeating over and over as the fish tank leaked into a bunched pile of paper towels.

The worker looked at Francis, face sagged and hairs astray. "Please help! We have repeat customers booked. They'll be here soon!"

"How long do I have?"

"Few minutes! I can't shield the princess forever! I don't want the people outside to see; they'd be so mean to her!"

Francis nodded.

Upon picking up Leopaula, he noticed her weight. With skin smooth and soft, plush yet taut, she clenched her fists while kicking her small feet around. Her nose, domed and normal sized, looked tiny compared to her gigantic cheeks. They were so plump that her marbled tears found residence atop them, before racing down and sprinkling over Francis's uniform. He buried her in his chest. Her cries mellowed to a whimper.

"Now, now."

Between her shuddering breaths, she'd sniffle. Baby snot sunk into Francis's attire, smearing between his medals and pins. He peered down at the mess. He didn't mind.

"Now, now," he repeated, this time with a cracked voice.

He stroked her back, tracing her vertebra as if playing a piano. Soon after, her pudgy lips parted and a stream of drool warmed his torso. He sunk into the sofa chair as the frantic worker tidied up.

"Thank you, thank you!" she whispered, bowing multiple times.

Francis flashed a smile that faded once the worker turned away. He remained in the seat, cherishing the faint thump of Leopaula's heart against his. Fighting through the tightness in his chest, he glanced down at her parted hair held in place by a tiny clip. He bit his inner lip with his canines, holding back tears.

"*I'm trying, sweetheart,*" he whispered. "Everything is so close. I just need her to leave him, for both your sakes." Leopaula's snores deepened as she warmed his chest. "I'm really trying. Just a bit longer."

The worker glanced mid-mop.

"Where's my sister?" Francis asked.

"Down the hall, to the right," she held her arm out, "sir."

A few knocks later and a masseuse answered. She jumped at the sight of the Royal Guard, bowed and left. Madeleine remained face down on the table, staring at the wooden slats, staggered across the floor.

With a voice muffled and crackled, she cried, "I paid for this," her breaths were loud and full, "I should be able to get what I paid for!"

Tear drops sprinkled the boards beneath her.

The blissful sounds reverberated off the calming walls. Madeleine's figure shaped the sheet covering her body. Francis approached the face cradle, obstructing her view with his shiny jet black shoes.

"Your family needs you, Lady-Madeleine."

She sat up, pulling the sheet around her breasts as a wave of shame showered her. He placed his hand over her trembling chin, lifting it.

"My God," his brows knitted, "you look just like *him* ..."

Madeleine pulled away.

"Well, he had it easy, didn't he?" She stood off the massage table and began getting dressed. "Dying and leaving our poor mum to raise us on her own. Seems like a coward to me! For the love of God, Francis," she clasped her bra and turned around, "I can't even get a bloody hour to myself! Every time I cross paths with my deadbeat husband, he's reeking of booze. Meanwhile, this little one—"

Leopaula innocently slept in Francis's arms. A crease centered between Madeleine's brows. The waterworks started.

"Oh God, I'm a monster! What kind of mother leaves her baby like that? That poor worker ... I ordered her around as if I owned her." She covered her face. "I needed a break, but with Julian always gone, how else—when—just—why—can't—but—"

She vanished into her sobs, gripping the sheet of the bed.

"I remember you saying you didn't want to be seen as one of those stuck-up women who hire a nanny to do their job. But you're entitled to a break, Lady-Madeleine."

She raised her face, now glowing with anger. "Just—just—shut it! Stop it with the whole *Lady*-Madeleine! I'm your sister, for God's sake! And why are you here? Where's Julian?!"

Francis handed her Leopaula before taking a deep breath and crossing his arms. "I don't know where he is—"

"*Don't know where he is?* That's your job—your only job!"

"No. Right now, it's more important for me to be here, with you."

"You think I need you now, *as a grown woman?*" Madeleine balked, nearly forgetting she held an infant. "No, I needed you when I was six and you abandoned me."

Albeit the nature sounds attempted to soothe the scene, Madeleine heated the room like a slow bolstering wave of lava, consuming anything in its path. Francis lowered his head, hitching his long-stretched breaths. Madeleine yanked her top over her head, all while glaring at her brother.

"We all have a purpose, Lady-Madeleine. If that purpose isn't fulfilled, then everything we've experienced and strived for amounts to a single, rectangular patch of dirt." Francis bit his lower lip as memories of his mother's burial threatened to consume his thoughts. "My potential ... I wouldn't be able to fulfill my purpose by staying. I hope you understand."

He glanced at Madeleine, who already shot daggers at him.

"I don't."

Francis pinched his lips as he didn't fill her in.

"And there you go again," Madeleine said. "Being all quiet and weird. Where are you, Francis? Where's my brother who used to sneak into the nursery just to make me laugh, or smuggle me sweets after bedtime?"

"The plan always involved coming back for you, but after seeing you on the news, dating Sir-Julian, I realized you'd be fine. That wouldn't have been the case if I stayed."

Madeleine wiggled her hips as she pulled up her tight pants. After getting dressed, she locked onto him like an agent throughout an interrogation.

"That's it? You're not even going to tell me where you stayed?"

"I was with a friend," Francis said, before checking his phone again. All messages remained unread.

Madeleine picked Leopaula up from the table, snappishly resting her atop her shoulder.

"Tell me who," Madeleine said.

"I'm not here to reminisce about the past. I'm here to help you with what's happening now."

Madeleine shook her head, flaunting a fake smile. "You're saying what everybody else says—"

"You need to leave Julian."

The room fell silent. A waterfall trickled in the corner as Madeleine blinked throughout her pause.

"Leave Julian?"

"He's the source of all your pain. Nobody's telling you this because nobody wants to criticize the Royal Couple. But I'm your brother—I have to say something."

She resigned her shoulders at the tone of authenticity. She tilted her head.

"I can't. Thank you, but I can't."

"Why not?!" His voice carried to the lobby, poking the attention of the workers. "He's horrible to you! The world can't see it, but I can! He's out all the time. He ignores you, he abandons you—like you said, where is he now?!"

"There's no going back to Slough … Even if I witnessed him cheating, I can't go back. You don't know how bad it got before I married him. And with the media the way it is … if I left him, I'll be forever shamed in public. How could I put Leopaula through that?" They stared at each other, expressing their hell, while the blissful environment mocked them. "I can't just run away like you, Francis."

"Then live with me. Please, Madeleine, I can take care of you both. Let me help you!"

"Then what? Hide indoors for the rest of my life? It's a gracious gesture, but—"

"This isn't a gesture—"

She slammed the bed. "Francis, stop!" They heard each other's breathing. "I don't know who you are anymore. And to be honest," her harsh swallow echoed into his ear, "*you scare me.*"

Francis stepped back, mouth agape.

"*I* scare you?" he asked.

"Where do you live? Who are the people in your life? You don't resemble my older brother that I loved. Ever since I saw you in the courtyard so long ago, I've been talking to someone else that just looks like you. For God's sake, this is the first actual conversation we've had in over two decades! And you want us to move in with you?"

Francis darted his gaze around, trying to think of something, anything else—

"Francis … I don't know you. You're mad to think you could take care of Leopaula and me when …" her lips moved as she looked for the best way to say, "*you're not part of this family.*"

Francis stumbled back as flashes of his step-mother shuttered before him. He bumped into a side table, knocking over the incense as he grabbed his forehead. The memories continued, crippling him.

"You don't belong here," Madeleine said. "Everybody around you keeps getting hurt, and I'm thinking it's you. That's what scares me."

"Wha—what?"

Darkness surrounded him as the shouts boomed from the kitchen. The syringes stood in his way every time he tiptoed to the nursery.

Madeleine sighed. "I'm sorry to be so crass, but I'm trying to be honest with you. You're a leech, Francis. You leeched off Mum when you were with us, and now you're leeching off the castle. How could I trust someone like that to support me?"

Grabbing the toppled table for support, Francis heaved in as much air as his lungs allowed.

"A leech?"

"Come on, now. Don't take it like that," she said.

"You just called me a leech …" Francis tilted his head at her, suddenly seeing his step-mother before him, holding baby Madeleine.

"France …" With a bent posture, she looked back, regretful for being so transparent.

Francis faltered up, gasping. "No, it can't be."

His step-mother glared back, cigarette dangling between her lips, with the fumes drifting into baby Madeleine's nose. The track marks on her arm raced from the wrist to the elbow, blotching the skin yellow and purple. A wart, the size of a marble, grew over one of her eyebrows as she stared him down.

He stumbled, falling over the side table again.

Madeleine gripped Leopaula, stepping back.

"No," he muttered. "No, no, no. I killed you. I already killed you." His breathing became a hurricane, burrowing through the shrinking room. A vein on his forehead throbbed and engorged as he bared his teeth. "You're not here!"

"Francis, you're scaring me," Madeleine said.

"Give her to me!" He reached for baby Madeleine.

Madeleine tilted Leopaula away, waking her up in a distressing cry.

"Give me my sister!"

"Francis, stop it! She's not your sister! What is this? You're scaring her—you're scaring me! Get away from us. You're not part of this family!"

Francis rushed forward to grab baby Madeleine, but Madeleine shoved the tabled into his gut with her foot. She pushed the table over, entangling him in the foam mattress and sheets. His uniform's sleeve pulled up as he panted beneath the wreckage. His scars bled into his sight as he heard Madeleine race out of the spa. Every horizontal mark, a reminder of what he'd been through.

Only Scarlett understood. Only Scarlett mattered.

Nobody else.

Chapter XXXVI
Messages: Read

Francis limped towards Windsor Castle, fighting through the crowd of onlookers and clenching his bruised arm. Amid the cheers for the Change of the Guard ceremony, he searched for Lordes but found only trumpets and trombones. However, Francis only heard his forced breathing. His phone vibrated as he reached Lancaster Tower's base. He checked.

"Dammit!"

It was an email. A general email. One that didn't concern him, yet he was cc'd on.

He planted a hand on the tower, lowering his gaze as he cleared his head of what happened at the spa. "Snap out of it. She's gone. She can't hurt me anymore."

He checked his messages to Scarlett again.

All unread.

> Francis: Please respond. Say something!

He tapped send. Suddenly, Scarlett's message tone chimed from behind him. Francis's heart fluttered as he spun around.

The odd man from before stood mere feet away, holding Scarlett's phone up with a wry expression. "Sir-Francis, a word?"

"Who—who are you?" Francis asked, as his gaze shot between the phone and the man.

He casually sauntered closer, with a leer plastered between his cheeks.

"You're a tough man to get a hold of," the man said. "I feel like if it were only you and I here, without all these," he looked at the people enjoying the ceremony, "*nobody's* around, I'd still have trouble getting a moment with you."

"*Who*," Francis's glare shifted from the phone to the man as his gasps turned turbulent, "*are you? And why do you have that?"

"Me? I'm detective—"

He stopped talking, but it sounded as if he hadn't finished his sentence.

"… Detective … Detective who?" Francis asked.

The man sneered.

"Just *detective*. That's all." He spoke in a giddy tone, like a cheerful office secretary on a gloomy Monday morning. "And instead of chasing after you all day, like a little mouse scattering around the castle cellars, to just put out a bit of cheese and," he tapped the button on Scarlett's phone, sounding a lock tone, "staple you in place. Funny how that works, innit?"

The man stopped before Francis, chin raised, goofy smile flashed, and a scent, that although faint, flooded Francis's senses. Another step closer and they'd be kissing. He wore large, black, round framed glasses, which didn't house lenses. His disheveled, light brown hair peered out beneath his short-brimmed fedora.

Based on his chipper, dumb face, Francis thought, he's Finnish and forcing a British accent.

The bag strained over his shoulder as his shirt, shoes, tie, watch—even his ears were all out of place. The overflow of peculiarities, paired with the encounter with Madeleine and the silence from Scarlett all threw Francis off. He tried to get his mind into the proper persona, but the detective's butt chin made it impossible.

"How may I help you, *detective?*"

The detective pulled his notepad out. With each flipped page, he'd eye Francis, studying his every emotional tell. "By now, you must've heard of the murder, no?"

"Murder?"

The detective froze with a page mid-flip.

"You're the Royal Guard, in charge of this here castle, yet you're unaware of a murder that occurred just outside these walls? The one in Slough."

Francis's lips parted. His throat constricted as genuine worry knotted his gut.

"In—in Slough?"

"Mhmm," the detective held the same silly smile as before while Francis's eyes welled. "And in case you still insist on playing the fool, the woman found was butchered every which way. I mean, it was a proper bloodbath; quite the spectacle."

As the ceremony continued, the instruments sounded, but to Francis, absolute deafening silence filled the air. The ulcer sliced and clawed at his stomach lining. Despite being mid-summer, Francis felt a chill racing down his chest.

"Anywho, I'm here to officially request an interview with thee Sir-Julian Augustus, The Prince of Wales."

"W—why?"

The shadow of the hat's brim suddenly swallowed the detective's eyes. "Oh, you already know."

A staring contest ensued. Neither said a word … with their mouths. Francis blinked first.

"Because I found this." A chime sounded as the detective flicked Julian's wedding band in the air like a coin, catching it before Francis's face. He held it against his eye, as if a magnifying glass. "It floated within the stomach contents of the victim. Shame really, she sure was a pretty little thing. Wouldn't you agree?"

The detective glanced at Francis, but Francis looked through him as the chilly wind fluttered his hair back.

"So, mind telling me what the prince's wedding band was doing inside the belly of a dead druggie?"

Francis clenched a fist. The detective noticed. Francis tightened his jaw. The detective noticed. Francis fought the shooting pain in his abdomen. *The detective noticed.*

"You see, after doing some digging, I found that you and our late, little miss Scarlett Atlanta Pitman, had somewhat of a fling going on."

Francis returned a distant, empty stare.

"Are you even curious as to why your lover was slaughtered—"

"I don't know who you're talking about," Francis responded in an unintended broken tone.

The detective glared through his hollowed glasses. He wasn't just good at his job; he was the best. His goofy character threw his suspects off guard, but Francis was a tough cookie to crack. So, he came prepared.

"No? You're saying that a finely built, successful, young man, such as yourself" he patted Francis's chest, "35-years-young, is single? Nah, I don't buy it." He nudged his glasses downward—not that it made a difference. "And you're certainly not gay. I could tell. I have a pretty good gaydar, being a detective and all. No, not only were you acquainted with her, but you've been sending message after message since her passing." He wiggled Scarlett's phone beside his face. "Remember?"

Francis stood motionless, as if trapped in an alternate reality. The emotions wreaked havoc on him, while the cheers and claps carried on nearby.

> *Scarlett's smoke-laced breath mingled beneath the stairwell.*
>
> *Her fingers interlocked with his as they stared out at the castle.*
>
> *She waited outside for him as he left his little sister sobbing in the dark.*
>
> *She was always there for him—*

"Yoo-hoo," the detective snapped his fingers, "did I lose ya?"

Francis blinked back to reality. "I never met this *Scarlett,*" he said.

"Then show me your phone." The detective licked his lips, reaching for Francis's hand holding the device. Francis shoved him back. The detective giggled as if he was a child caught sneaking a candy bar. "Very well then, we'll go about this the mundane way. As I said, I have evidence linking both you and Prince Julian to this murder, and not a guard, nor the king himself, can stand in my way."

Francis swallowed before nodding. With dull eyes, he responded, "I can set something up one week from—"

"Today will do—"

"Tomorrow evening is the best—"

"Tomorrow morn—"

"Tomorrow afternoon, take it or leave it," Francis said, spearing the detective with his charged irises.

The detective flexed a wide smile. "I'll take it, but keep in mind that I could easily demand one sooner."

Francis couldn't hold back his flaring nostrils. "Get the fuck off the property."

The detective smiled, tipped his hat and left, jovially swaying his hand with the procession's tempo.

Francis tightened his fist, feeling the pulse in his heated palm. His canines nearly punctured through as his jaw tensed, bulging the stubble beneath his ears. He scowled at the distancing detective although he had someone else on his mind.

"Julian."

Chapter XXXVII
Standing on the Royal Balcony

The Royal Bedroom's ceiling, intricately painted with regal motifs, stared back at the dazed Julian laying over the bed. His mouth fell open. Not a single word. Thoughts congested his mind. Not a single emotion. His blinks missed their queue. Not a care in the world.

The art depicted celestial scenes from Genesis, portraying bursts of light between magnificent bodies blown away by a tremendous event, a moment of grandiose and awe. But the room remained mute. The staring contest stalled. Neither won. Neither lost.

Nothing mattered.

With a drooping blink, he saw Scarlett smile. With another, he saw her bloodied, lifeless body splayed across the floor.

Her hair, everywhere, trailed the pillows, like a scenic road winding over a hilly landscape. Suddenly, locks of the platinum blonde strands soaked red as they slapped across her face, pulled into her agape mouth as she choked.

The painted light on the ceiling brightened. Julian kept gazing, ignoring the intensity, as if gawping at the scorching sun.

Lines of her tattoos scribbled over the ceiling art. They were the same lines he saw on his wedding day. The same ones he saw yesterday, creating avenues for the blood to race down.

Although the light burned his retinas, he didn't blink. His blood covered boot fell off the bed, snapping him out of it. He sat up, finding Scarlett's gore sprinkled over his pants. He smeared a bit with his finger, then sniffed it, hoping to smell her again. However, all he received was a faint iron scent.

He approached the door, needing a breath of fresh air. Just as he reached for the knob, Madeleine swung it open, bashing the oak against his nose.

"Julian! Francis just—"

He winced as blood trickled out of one of his nostrils, sliding over his shirt, pants and boots. Madeleine rushed him towards the bed.

"Oh God, are you alright?" Madeleine asked, but he didn't respond. She looked him up and down. "What—what happened to you?"

She couldn't distinguish Scarlett's blood from his own. Madeleine gripped his hand, feeling his arrhythmia sync with hers.

"Julian …?"

They locked eyes. Madeleine wanted something, but he wanted something else. Their eyes couldn't tell the difference.

He yanked her in, leaving a trail of fiery kisses along her neck. She tilted her chin up, witnessing the painting and giving him consent.

She left Leopaula asleep in the stroller.

She ignored how hurt she was.

She ignored what happened at the spa.

She needed this.

—

Francis bolted through the castle halls, shoving everybody out of his way. Lordes grabbed his arm and pulled him into a vacant room. The door slammed shut as Francis panted, dripping sweat over his long-time supporter.

"Get your hands off me!" Francis said.

"Easy, now, easy—"

"He killed her!"

Lordes pulled back, eyebrows low and drawn together. "Who killed who?"

"Julian! The cheating, incestuous bastard killed Scarlett!"

Lordes paused. "What's this mean? This'll ruin everything—"

"I'm going to kill him!"

"Woah, woah, woah, easy now. If it were that simple, we'd have done it long ago. Get your head on straight. We've been far too patient for you to blow this all up at a hiccup like this."

Francis struck Lordes square on the nose, snapping his head back.

"She wasn't a hiccup!"

Lordes held himself over his knees as the pain ran its course.

"I know what she meant to you, so I'll give you that one. But no more. This is bigger than one person, and she knew what she signed up for. Her death will mean nothing if you go into that room and kill him."

Francis, caged in his emotions, clenched his fists as spit sputtered from his bared teeth. A guttural roar emanated as he found only one option.

"Then we send them both to Omo!"

Lordes's eyes grew. "But Lady-Madeleine's innocent of all of this!"

Francis slammed one of the million-euro paintings, shattering the glass. He banged it again. And again.

"She's not us! She chose him, so she'll fall with him!"

—

Julian tore open Madeleine's blouse, searching for tattoos. Her bra strap snagged in the act, mimicking a vine. He kissed that shoulder, blindly pulling off the other strap. She reached down, tugging at his belt as she arched her back.

Madeleine closed her eyes towards the holy depiction, focusing on the intensifying sensation. The two rummaged over the sheets, nearly falling off the mattress. Julian's foot knocked over the ibuprofen bottle on the nightstand. The rattle stirred Leopaula. Madeleine froze as Julian continued to fondle.

"Shh, stop, she—she's waking up!"

Julian didn't care. He kept ripping her clothes off. His breaths picked up, becoming ones of frustration rather than passion. Madeleine tried pushing him away, but he pulled her closer, flexing his biceps as he gripped her skinny belt. His yank was so severe that her buckle gave in and her back cracked.

"Stop!" Madeleine shouted.

He didn't.

"Julian, stop it!"

He grabbed her neck and squeezed. She tried and tried, but not a sound, not a wisp, nothing. She convulsed, direly seeking reason, but only savageness glared back. He squeezed harder, envisioning the tattoos wrapping around her neck, arms and what her dangling bra partially concealed. Her only movement came from his flexed muscles, jittering.

Leopaula woke up. As Madeleine's eyes showed the signs of passing out, Julian kept trying to picture her as Scarlett, dead or alive. However, his daughter's cries kept interjecting his fantasy.

She screamed, as her mother internally did the same.

Francis kicked open the Royal Bedroom's door, crashing it so hard against the doorstop that it broke. He shouldered Julian off his sister and rammed him back, shattering framed portraits of the small family over the floor.

Madeleine thumped her head against the bedpost. A sudden flash followed a distancing whistle. Momentarily lost in a void, she blinked aimlessly. Blood instantly flooded her eyebrow and traced her jawline. She didn't care. She just wanted air back into her lungs.

Francis's forearm chafed against Julian's stubbed chin as he pinned him against the wall. Julian shot a vain stare back, as if he were the victim.

The carpet fibers beneath Madeleine's fingers morphed from a light tan to a dark, menacing red, growing, and growing.

Julian shoved Francis off as the room echoed nothing but pants and cries. When the guards rushed over, Francis slammed the door and locked it before anybody saw.

"What is this?" Francis asked.

Neither said a word.

Francis hurried to Madeleine's aid. His fingers felt her warm blood before her skin. His eyes jittered at the scene, while hers glared back.

"I'm not," she muttered between the gasps. "Going back to Slough."

Francis shuddered at the sight of her eyebrow wound pouring blood over her resolve-set trembling chin.

"I won't."

She meant it.

Behind her, a light sheering curtain drew over floor-to-ceiling French doors. They guarded a concrete slab that arched out towards the horizon, facing Cranbourne Park's northeastern border. Only a few steps away, and Francis's feet would step on the one spot that he promised Scarlett he'd one day stand. The curtain swayed from the room's thermostat triggering the AC, welcoming Francis's imagination.

He slowly let go of his sister. As Leopaula's wails pierced the eardrums, the couple stared at Francis, hypnotized, approaching the set of glass doors. With a gentle swipe, he moved the curtain out of the way, placing his hand on the smooth surface, painting it with Madeleine's blood. A light fog built around his fingers, turning the glass translucent.

"I'm going to stand on that balcony one day."

Scarlett rested her head against his shoulder.

"You know what," Scarlett said. "I believe you."

Windsor Castle shined off the surface of their eyes as they sat in silence, warming each other.

Francis picked Leopaula up and rocked her, simmering the disorder.

"You two need to get out of here," Francis said. "Get a change of scenery."

Julian wiped his face. "That won't solve this—"

"It will," Francis said. "All of your problems started the day you became parents. Nobody helped you. The media made you out to be this epitome of marriage and family, but you're still human. And like anybody else, you need a holiday together to rekindle what you had."

"Anywhere outside of this bedroom and the media swarms us," Madeleine said.

Francis gazed down at Leopaula. Her lips puckered out when she slept. A half-hearted smile drew between his ears as he spotted the first bit of saliva peer out, just like he'd seen baby Madeleine do hundreds of times.

"Omo Valley, Ethiopia," he said.

Madeleine twisted her face. "Ethiopia? Why there? Their ambassadors hate us."

With eyes dull and dead, Francis regarded Julian. "It's a quiet place, far from any civilization. No media. No reporters. Just nature. I have a military friend there. He has a luxury yurt, with plumbing, electricity, and whatever else. Nobody would find you, and it'd give you time to soothe out your troubles. Nobody will know. I can have Lordes prepare the getaway for you, by early morning. So, getting caught will be highly unlikely. And if that happens, Sir-Julian will use the alibi of going to meet with the Ethiopians, as a sign of good-faith, to reconcile without the public's interference."

Madeleine never considered it before. She's been so caught up in trying to fight, shame or guilt Julian, that she never considered an alternative.

Madeleine's blood gripped Julian. It was the same shade as Scarlett's, but when dripping from his wife, it hit him differently. If Madeleine showed her face in public, the people would piece it all together. He needed an out.

This trip would provide enough time for her wound to heal, he thought. Then she'd have nothing.

"Will this yurt be able to accommodate Leopaula too?" Madeleine asked.

Francis pulled the infant back, squeezing her.

"No," he rapidly said. "She'll stay with me until you're back. I'll take care of her."

Madeleine tipped her head, flashing the same expression she had from behind the massage table. "I'm not leaving my baby."

"Besides," Julian said, needing this plan to go through. "We'd return to a whirlwind of accusations for abandoning our daughter in favor of political gain."

Madeleine pinched her lips, tasting some of the blood. "Oh, you're one to speak of abandonment—"

"Just wait," Francis interrupted. He wanted to say something—anything, to stop them from taking Leopaula. "You could—" The blood soaked. "You could—" The motif waited. "You cou—"

The curtain rippled, revealing a brief glimpse of the balcony as Leopaula's warmth radiated into his fingertips.

"You—"

He felt the two waiting. It was the first time he didn't have a backup plan.

The innocent infant didn't deserve what he plotted for the parents, but the entirety of all he'd worked towards relied on this final attritional test on his soul.

With every snore, Leopaula's slight wheeze eviscerated him.

"Francis," Madeleine said, grabbing the bedpost for support as she stood. "Leopaula needs this too."

She pulled his niece from his arms, through his attempt to keep her for himself. But nothing could prevent a mother from her child. Maintaining a vacant look, as if staring into space, he trailed Leopaula being stolen from his hands. His posture broke as his arms fell.

"Don't worry," Madeleine said. "I'll make sure she's safe."

A bird landed on the balcony railing, whistling at Francis before tilting its head in a robotic fashion.

I can't save you either, Francis thought. Forgive me.

Madeleine approached Julian, who turned away.

"If you promise me that this," she pointed at her eyebrow, "will never happen again. I'll go."

Julian observed his boots, finding Scarlett's blood dressing the left one. Madeleine lifted his chin until he took a long, hard look at what he'd done.

"Promise me."

He lowered his head again, draping his down-turned mouth behind his golden locks. His shoulders followed suit.

"I promise—"

Francis curtly gripped the prince's arm, just above the elbow. "Sir-Julian, a word." He dragged him outside.

He dismissed the nearby guards and waited for the door to latch behind him. The moment it shut, he socked Julian, loosening a molar. Before slugging him more, he noticed

Lordes at the end of the hall. Francis strained his fist in midair, ready to launch it. But instead, he planted Julian against the decorative molding of the wall and blew in his face, like an enraged bull.

"You killed her!"

Frozen, Julian's mouth cracked open. "How … how'd you know?"

"I'm your bloody guard; you can't hide anything from me!"

"I can't get her out of my mind, Francis."

He smacked his ear, knocking his head for a third time. "Well, get her out!"

Julian pushed Francis away and punched the wall, like a teenager lashing out for losing in gym class. His four knuckles immediately bled, as if synchronized.

"I never wanted any of this!"

Francis scoffed at how pathetic Julian sounded.

"Doesn't matter what you want anymore. The detective has your ring! He's going to storm this castle tomorrow with warrants and what have you. So, you need to turn around and pack, now! Because the only way I could save you is by getting you out of here. Or else they'll hang you by sunrise."

—

Early the next morning, the Royal Family stood in the rain, loading the cover car with their disguises in the back, beside the baby seat.

Julian embraced Francis.

"Thank you," he whispered.

Francis's arms remained by his side, with Julian ignorant of his cemented glare.

The three began their journey towards Omo Valley.

Chapter XXXVIII
The Approaching Precipice

— Current Day —

"[Surmic] What do you mean he's missing?!" Amari boomed.

Ike shielded his face for a moment, as Imamu stood firm.

"We mean," Imamu repeated. "That he and the princess got into an argument and she kicked him out. It's been a few hours."

Akilu slapped his palm against his forehead as he exhaled, eyes clenched.

"And in those *few hours,* neither of you thought of informing us?"

"Sir," Ike said, facing the floor. "Don't get mad at Imamu. We figured the prince just needed to cool off."

Akilu twisted his mouth as if a sour candy hit his tongue. "You think this is about getting in trouble? This is an existential threat to the tribe—"

"Akilu," Amari said, silencing the room. "Don't waste your time with these two. This is exactly why they're not in the ruling committee, and instead fiddling with gadgets and toys."

Ike noiselessly sucked his teeth, wishing he had never affiliated himself with Imamu.

"Grab the princess before she runs off, too. I don't care if she struggles; you bring her here and place two men outside to guard the entrance. This is the only fortified hut in the village."

"Easy now," Zola said from the corner of the room. "Instead of manhandling her, tell her I'm here."

Akilu nodded before bolting out.

"You two," Amari pointed at Imamu and Ike, "come with me. We have to wake everybody up and start looking. We can't have the boy getting killed here."

—

"[English] What is this?" Madeleine asked amid the shove into Amari's hut.

Two Mursi men stood behind Akilu, holding spears.

"This is for your safety," he said. "We're looking for your husband."

"My husband? No, ehm," Madeleine bit her lower lip, "he's not snooping around, that was just—"

"This has nothing to do with that. He might be in danger. To be gone that long, at this hour, could mean countless things. We need to be sure he's safe."

"What do you mean countless—"

Akilu hurried out, leaving Zola with the princess.

"We don't have a border patrol," Zola said, with Kamari coiled asleep in her makeshift sling. "Most Mursi men are too busy providing that none can stand guard. We depend on our peace treaties. But dat doesn't leave us safe from a surprise attack."

"Why would anybody want to surprise attack you?" Madeleine asked.

The guards outside rested the butt of their spears down and scanned for Julian. The others hurried out of their huts, lighting torches and passing them around. Imamu rushed to his hut, seeking his dagger and lamp, but couldn't spot the blade while finding the lamp's battery dead.

Zola returned a dark scowl.

"There are a thousand and one reasons, but right now, it's the boy. The other tribes are in a tougher situation than we are. If one of them caught a whiff of the Kingdom's prince here, they'd pounce on the opportunity. They're not as many as us, nor as diplomatic."

D'jen curled his fingers, waiting for Julian to approach.

"So, if they grab hold of Julian …"

Julian noticed the moonlight hitting all around the forest, seemingly avoiding D'jen's hand—as if he was a darkness that refused even the faintest of illumination.

"It'd be the end of us all," Zola said.

"How so?" Madeleine asked.

"They'd either take it as an opportunity to carry out vengeance, a ticket to reignite a past conflict or worse."

Candlelight illuminated the chieftain's hut, scattering shadows across the walls. Every so often, a Mursi would pass with a torch, brightening the hut as if a lighthouse were making its round. Madeleine placed down the books she was reading. She bit the skin beside her nails, revealing her tremors to Zola.

"Wat's dat?" Zola asked. "And whatcha doin?"

"These are some books I found in Imamu's hut; his writings. We shouldn't be worried about another tribe getting to Julian." Her tremors grew to shudders. "I think we should worry about what Julian might be plotting."

The Mursi patrolmen signaled across the village that they cleared another portion. When a torch bearer passed, the inside of Amari's hut flashed brightly again. Zola noticed the reopened eyebrow wound.

"When'd that happen?" she asked.

"Zola," Madeleine, sat still and limp, "I don't want to talk about it."

"Ya gonna have to. If a man does that, then he really has no limits to what he'd do to get his way."

"It's not just that." Madeleine's eyes grew wary and strained. "There might be men coming—terrible men. Before we got into our fight, Julian told me he saw the Kingdom's commandos. But I'm not sure if it was a hallucination from the khat he ate."

"Who are dese commandos?"

"The Kingdom sends them for HRHV missions." She noticed Zola's raised brow. *High-risk-high-value.* The Kingdom can't send in troops, because that'll put the captives in danger—in this case, Julian and me. Instead, these commandos are sent. They travel by shadow and are given free rein to complete their objective. They slaughter anybody who stands in their way—civilian, elderly or child. All that matters to them is to rescue the subjects."

Zola glanced at the guards.

"We'll be safe in here though—"

"Zola … no. What you told me of the day you were displaced … that'll be a fairytale compared to what these commandos would do. Our only hope is that what Julian saw was a vision, and nothing more."

"Those visions," Zola said. "They show you what you really want. And knowing that boy for only a day, you could tell that he doesn't take too kindly to people of our complexion."

"Maybe there's another way."

"What's that?"

"Imamu's phone," Madeleine said. "He uses a sim card in it that gets him reception anywhere. If I could use it, I can contact my Royal Guard, Sir-Lordes, and have him call off the commandos. I'll explain the situation; that we're waiting for Leopaula, and that Julian and I are safe."

"Then let's do dat."

Zola approached the hut's doorway and tapped on one of the guard's shoulders. He immediately pointed the spear's tip at her face, causing her to jump back.

"[Surmic] Chieftess Zola, get inside now!"

Her gaze bounced between the blade and the guard. "Have you lost your mind, pointing that thing at me?! Need I remind you who I am?"

"Orders from above, Chief Amari. Neither of you are to leave. This is for your safety."

"My safety?" Zola asked. "Pointing a spear at my face, while I carry a baby in my arms, is for my safety?"

The guard reaffirmed his grip over the spear's handle. "Yes, ma'am."

The other guard glanced. "Chieftess, please stay inside."

Zola slowly stepped back. Behind them, the torches swarmed around like giant fireflies without a home.

"[English] Getting dat phone's not an option at the moment," Zola said to Madeleine.

"That's not the only thing." Madeleine pulled the crumpled letter out from the journal. "I found this with Imamu. I can't read it, but I think he might plan to hurt Julian."

"Why do you think that?"

Madeleine handed her the letter from the mines. Zola's eyes slid across the page as Madeleine continued.

"If the commandos aren't on their way and Imamu does something to Julian, that'll certainly give the Kingdom a reason to send the commandos. So, either we do nothing or—"

"Oh, no!" Zola covered her mouth so fast that the candle fluttered. "You're right!"

"What? What's it say?"

Zola lowered the note, eyes wide. "Imamu's going to kill him!"

Chapter XXXIX
What Follows Ignored Protests

Meanwhile, in Windsor Castle's meeting hall, the lead council member surveyed the gray faces, each focused on the charrette. Stern stares reflected from the Foreign Secretary, the Prime Minister, the Secretary of State and all else in the Privy Council. Nobody opposed, as the field report was too damning.

"Then it's unanimous; the Royal Couple and their daughter are declared deceased—"

"Wait! Wait! Just wait! What about the ransom demand? Why're we dismissing that?"

"We've been over this," the lead said. "We don't negotiate with terrorists, pirates, fanatics or captors. These animals only understand pain. After what they did to the ambassador, deploying Francis's commandos was our only remaining option. And they've confirmed," Francis folded in his lips, "the Royal Family ... is no more."

All heads lowered in respect. All but Francis, whose steely eyes swept across the room, observing what he saw as pathetic, worthless puppets.

"Retribution!" The Foreign Secretary slammed his fist against the table, breaking the order and cracking the surface. "Is this how the Ethiopians respond because we don't bow down to their absurd demands?!"

The council leader let the rage play its course, then continued, "Yes, in due time. First, we need to retrieve their bodies, after which we'll reconvene to discuss a war plan. But for now, we have a more pressing matter. Hierarchy must prevail before chaos floods the streets. We'll break news to the public at dawn, then follow it up with the appointment of Sir-Oliver as heir to the throne."

"*Sir-Oliver?* But," the Secretary of State scoffed, looking around the room for reason, "he's a child; barely seven years of age. You can't be serious." Nobody opposed. His expression dropped. "You are …"

Following a deep sigh, the council leader responded, "He's the next in line—"

"But His Majesty is 85-years-old! He's barely able to sit up; we need someone to rule, and now!"

The council leader wore a pained expression as he waddled a pen between two fingers, occasionally tapping it against the tabletop. Francis stared at the pen, predicting every time it would make contact.

They're here, Francis thought. *They're all here. Every one of them, and the Royal Standard flag is up. Tonight's the night. Nearly 30 years and it's finally here. After this little chat, it's happening. It's finally—*

"Sir-Francis!" The leader waved his hand. "Are you with us?" Francis slid his eyes upward. "What's the update on this detective friend of yours? He's awfully persistent. Even amid this turmoil, he's demanding a full round of interviews today, especially with you."

"I'll handle him. You just worry about the hierarchy."

"Please do. That man is annoyingly tenacious at his job, making it impossible to—"

"Are we done here?" Francis asked.

"Yes, but—"

Francis's seat groaned as he suddenly stood. Everybody looked as he ignored the leader and left. He cut through Windsor's courtyard, pacing towards one of the castle's dimly lit towers. In the distance, the Royal Standard flag fluttered in the nighttime sky.

"Everything is in place," Francis muttered as he smirked. "Everything is finally in place, father."

Upon facing the pair of the tower's metal bunker doors, faint murmurs emanated from the other side. Francis slid on black tactical gloves before grabbing the handle. Only a single black crow, resting atop the highest castle wall, witnessed. After a final glance over his shoulders, he pulled.

Francis descended the rusted ladder into the control cellar. He turned to find perfectly lined brigade of masked men waiting with straightened backs. He studied them. All wore gloves. All held weapons. All glared back.

Francis placed his own mask on and paced back and forth ahead of the militia. An array of monitors glowed behind him, revealing full surveillance of the castle grounds. Each member harbored a fire in their eyes that trailed Francis's gait.

Francis approached one. "Where's Lordes?"

"Unknown, sir."

Francis glanced at his phone—no messages, no missed calls. He tapped his fingertips over the phone's back.

"This moment will not be delayed any longer." He raised his voice, addressing the others. "Tonight's the night. Is everybody ready?"

They nodded in unison.

"This is it. Tonight, we take back the Kingdom!"

"Yes, sir!"

"We will be silent, we will be invisible, and we will restore order!" Francis clenched his fist as the band of partisans did the same. "Tonight, you'll see how black corrupt blood is!"

"SIR!"

"Ready yourselves, men. This night beholds justice."

Francis turned to the control board. He gripped the red emergency lever, closing his eyes and taking a long, concentrated, measured breath.

"Father," he whispered.

He tugged the lever down, cutting all power to Windsor Castle.

Gasps.

Huhs.

Then, silence.

A haunting silence.

340

"NOW!"

The militia scattered like spiders from a hive, unnoticed by even the closest bystander. They dispersed into the darkness, reaching every corner of the property without leaving a trace of their presence. Francis held one back.

"Find me Lordes."

—

One with the shadows, each follower positioned himself to a strategic advantage.

Some pointed snipers on sleeping adults.

Others jimmied the locks, including that of the king's chamber.

The most hardhearted of them towered in the doorway of the sleeping children.

They waited.

—

King Leopold awoke to find a lone assailant at the foot of his bed, silenced pistol in hand.

"So," King Leopold grumbled. "Napoleon finally returns."

—

With news on Lordes taking too long, Francis cracked his knuckles, holstered his pistol and darted out.

—

King Leopold sat up.

"Not another word." The assailant advanced, pistol leading the way. "Not another inch."

The king scoffed, then had to clear his throat.

"Son, I haven't obeyed another man for the last 45 years."

———

'Where's the signal?' an assailant signed to a cohort. His partner responded with a shrug. *'Something's wrong. Should we proceed?'*

'We won't have another chance.'

The two nodded, focused down their respective scopes, slowly exhaled and pulled their index fingers simultaneously.

Instantly and concurrently, two Royal family members slammed against the far end of their respective rooms. Seemingly orchestrated, they held their place before each slid to the floor. A red smear disturbed the wallpaper's neatly intertwined patterns.

The assailants packed their rifles and fled.

Moments later, screams carried throughout the castle. Pandemonium spread from one corner to the other, following the discovery of the bloodied bodies. Before their opportunity slipped away, the other assailants took out their targets. Some stabbed the elders in their sleep, while the grunts cinched plastic bags over the heads of King Leopold's grandnieces and nephews. None remained— save the king.

———

Shoved towards the tower's window, King Leopold's forehead knocked against the glass as the assailant trained the pistol beneath his ear. He forced the old man to witness the total annihilation of his family. Tears slipped between the smooth surface and his cheek.

"You're killing children," he cried through his fragile tremors. "You're nothing save honorless thugs!"

"No."

—

Francis hurried through the disorder, face darkened, eyes charged. He spotted the king being held in his bedroom, just as instructed.

Dashing up the tower, Francis leaped over slain guards scattering the stairwell. Gore and broken furniture riddled the corridors as a small fire began spreading from the antechamber furthest down the hall.

"Finally," Francis grunted.

Stride after stride, his breaths grew heavy. The flames latched from one wall to another, from one curtain to another, from one rug to another. Francis drew his firearm as he neared the king's chamber door, silhouetting the roaring flames.

"Finally."

Chapter XL
The Phantom's Promise

"We have to stop him!" Zola said, placing down the letter from the mine. Her pained gaze was contagious. Even Kamari adopted it.

"What could we do?" Madeleine asked. "Those guards won't let us out!"

Zola's knee bounced as she looked around. The Mursi swarmed alongside the hut, as Amari's men had their spears forming an X at the entrance. Zola turned towards the soft spot on the floor along the south side wall. She handed Kamari to Madeleine and shoved a table aside. A clay jar tipped, juggled back and forth, then shattered. The guards, busy protecting, didn't budge.

"This way," Zola said, pointing down.

Madeleine blankly blinked. "What am I looking at?"

"Amari had this built during the construction of the hut."

"Had what built?"

Zola removed her lip plate and shoved it into the floor, hauling a pile of dirt aside. Again and again, she dug deeper.

Madeleine approached, shielding Kamari from the bits scattering. From outside, the spot which Julian urinated on the day earlier began sinking deeper and deeper with each of Zola's shovels.

"It's a tunnel—a way out. Amari had it built in case we were ever cornered," Zola said.

"A back door!"

"Dat's right! Now grab something and help!"

With Kamari dabbing the dirt pile, both women scooped batch after batch, one after the other, like two sides of a zipper, getting the job done. Not long after, the light from the search committee's torches shined through.

"Let's go," Zola said, ready to dive in, but Madeleine held her back.

"You have to stay!"

"Notta chance! I'm Imamu's mother—"

"You're also Kamari's mother."

Zola paused, suddenly realizing her lapse. She turned to find Kamari, looking as if he had eaten chocolate spaghetti.

"I understand Imamu's pain," Madeleine said. "I can get through to him."

Zola's head snapped around.

"What about your ankle? And what about you? We can't have you getting hurt, either."

Madeleine rotated it. "I'll manage. And we don't have another option. Just keep Kamari safe."

Zola pulled Madeleine in and squeezed. Madeleine hugged back. They felt the warmth of each other's skin.

"Be careful, girl."

Zola ran her fingers through Madeleine's hair, hoping that there'd be another way.

"I will," Madeleine said.

"Remember, Imamu won't be able to kill Julian in front of the others, so he's probably hiding out in the woods, waiting for the opportunity," Zola said before letting go.

"I'll find him, don't worry. Just keep the guards fooled, or else Imamu will be spooked and disappear."

Zola nodded before helping Madeleine through the makeshift tunnel.

Quietly, Madeleine emerged from the other side, staying out of the moonlight. She planted her back against a hut as patrolmen continued their search for Julian. Through the chatter and the torches, she tried spotting Imamu among them.

He's not here, she thought.

She glanced out at the trees and squinted, seeing two people talking.

"Must be Ike," she muttered.

Moments later, she sidestepped behind the tree trunks. None of the Mursi spotted her, but the closer she got to the two talking, the more she realized they weren't Imamu nor Ike. Crouched, she crept incrementally, bit by bit.

As the crickets masked her sounds, she reached a point where Julian's skin became evident.

> "*… before I did what had to be done, Haile informed the Ethiopian government.*"

Haile? Madeleine thought.

She inched closer, as if zooming in with a camera.

Haile … Haile … Where'd I hear that name before? She thought.

"Scarlett, earlier today, Amari cleaved through a Brit coming to save us! Are you telling me to go back to him instead of trusting D'jen, who's been nothing but a straight shooter?"

Scarlett? D'jen? Madeleine thought, furrowing her brows.

A gasp escaped just before Madeleine snapped her hand over her mouth. She realized this was the same man Zola mentioned.

The Karo, riddling the trees, orchestrally converged their sights on the princess. Whispers began floating between the rustling leaves, sending shivers down the spine of any soul they reached.

"What's that sound?" Julian asked D'jen.

The haunting chatter merged the screams of crying infants and adults arguing. Far, yet near, deep yet soft, loud yet silent, the whispers continued, perplexing the senses. Julian didn't know where to look, who could help or how to even stand properly. Scarlett's image shifted like a Picasso painting as Julian's knees buckled. She glitched and morphed before his eyes, eventually disintegrating into particles that sprinkled off with the wind.

D'jen lowered his hand and searched the surroundings.

"Quiet," he said. "Someone's snooping."

D'jen readied himself, despite being unarmed. As he prepared for the worst, he never let Julian out of his sight.

"No, no! You don't get it," Julian said. "I heard these whispers before!"

"I said, quiet!" D'jen glared from the village to the tree line, unable to spot a single Mursi. The patrolmen were still near the huts. "My men spotted someone. This is how we disorient our enemies."

Madeleine covered her ears, but the murmurs still found their way in. It reminded her of darker days when her mother would chastise her, while also ridiculing her for not breastfeeding her wailing daughter. Her breasts ached as the milk filled. Her scars seemed to ignite, recalling all the abuse. She pushed harder against her head, but the whispers only amplified.

"STOP!" she screamed.

D'jen, Julian, the Karo, Imamu, Ike, Akilu, the Mursi—everybody snapped their sights at her.

Princess Madeleine, D'jen thought. This just keeps getting better and better …

When the Mursi arrived, their torches illuminated the scene, revealing countless Karo hidden amid the trees. The stage was set.

"Make it stop!" Madeleine stomped her foot.

Once Imamu's sight locked with Julian's, Julian reached behind his back and unveiled the generational dagger, pointing it straight out.

The glint of the tribal blade shined the moonlight onto D'jen's growing grin.

This is just too good, D'jen thought.

He couldn't contain his relaxed smile elongating across his face.

"Stand back!" Julian stabbed the air, little jabs at everybody approaching. "Not another step!"

Seeing his own dagger being wielded at him, Imamu flexed his fists as a vein pulsed over his temple.

"Everybody back up!"

The Mursi retreated, save Imamu.

"*That's my dagger.*" Fangs exposed and eyes set, the image seared into Imamu's mind. "You stole my land, my brother, and now my dagger?"

Akilu placed his hand on Imamu's shoulder, keeping his tone low.

"[Surmic] As long as he's holding onto it, we have a chance—" Akilu noticed his words didn't have any effect on him. "*Imamu ...*"

"[English] Give it back!" Imamu shouted through his forceful breaths.

The yellow in Julian's eyes dissipated as his heart pumped sober blood through his veins. The moment overcame the khat, putting all on edge, like watching airplanes doomed to collide. Julian pointed the dagger through the breeze, square at Imamu's forehead. A few meters away, Imamu remained unfazed.

"I've had enough of your lies!" Julian said. "I'm leaving! No more waiting, no more playing this little game! If you follow me, I swear to God I'll run this blade through your skull until it comes out the other end!"

"*That's,*" Imamu's knuckles cracked from how tight his fist strained, "*my,*" spittle fled with each word, "*blade.*"

"Julian, stop!" Madeleine screamed. The dagger pivoted towards her. "What—what're you doing?"

"You, too! Stop right there! You fell in love with these animals, so you could stay with them, but I'm going!"

D'jen's smirk held as he shot his glance at the couple.

"This," Madeleine pulled back, a crease forming between her brows, "*this is who you are* ... What about Leopaula? Do you even care about her?"

Behind Madeleine, Scarlett eased her chin over her shoulder, reflecting D'jen's slanted smile. She faced the ·princess's cheek, softly planting a long, intimate kiss, leaving an imprint of lipstick on her face before casually retreating. Leopaula comfortably suckled on Scarlett's tattooed breast. Scarlett glanced at Julian, biting her lower lip whilst beaming nonchalantly.

"Tell her what you see, baby," Scarlett said.

"*Do I care*—Maddy! She's fine; she's right there!" He pointed to Scarlett, drawing the attention of every single person, except for one.

With lightning legerity, D'jen snatched the generational dagger from Julian's grip and, in one swift motion, wrapped his arm over Julian's head.

"No!" Akilu reached out, muscles tensed.

D'jen butted the edge of the dagger against Julian's jugular, drawing blood and freezing Akilu in place. The more Julian flailed, the deeper the blade sliced.

"D'jen," Julian stammered, scuttling futilely, his heels scraping against the dirt, fallen leaves, and downed branches, "what is this?!"

It started with a mute chuckle, but soon after, D'jen erupted in maniacal laughter. "[Surmic] Ahh, Akilu, *my replacement.* How's it feel, seeing that the blade finally chose me? After everything you and your precious ilk have said regarding big, bad D'jen. Well, feast your eyes. The dagger has decided. The right decision! Not Haile's decision and certainly not that imbecile, Amari's decision."

Julian couldn't translate in his state of panic. He only had one thing on his mind, and it rested beneath his jaw.

"D'jen," Akilu said, panting. "You kill that boy, and you've killed us all!"

"That was always the plan!" His laughs continued as everybody leaned on edge. Every giggle and the steel covered more real-estate. "Haven't you pieced it together yet, you moron? You really believe that the Royal Family of the United Kingdom would just stroll into Ethiopia, without guards or protection?"

His sweat didn't affect his grip, neither over Julian's head, nor the dagger's hilt. Akilu wanted nothing more than to dive forward, even sacrifice himself, but he knew D'jen's immediate reaction to anything unpredicted. He glanced at Madeleine, ready to protect her as a last resort.

"The boy's own guard wants him dead!" D'jen shook Julian, jiggling his trembling cheeks. "[English] You understand, boy? You're here because of your dear Sir-Francis Mayweather *and me.* All I had to do was leave a specific boat, in a specific spot, at a specific time, and show the world the blood of *one prince, princess and their little, poor, helpless baby,* splattered over Mursi land. Then, and only then, would I have the full backing of the Haranchis to grant me what even this dagger finally realized; I'm the rightful leader of the Omo tribes! Only I can unite us and only I can liberate us from the government!"

Out of the crowd, only Imamu stood unparalyzed. He steadied his scowl on the blade.

"[Surmic] Oh, little Imamu," D'jen said, flashing his golden molar. "All grown up now. How's your grandfather doing? Did he look something like this the last time you saw him?"

Julian's blood rippled between D'jen's fingers, smearing and coursing for all to see.

"D'jen," Akilu shouted. "Stop this! We can fix it—all of it. Just let him go."

"You're not calling the shots, boy. After all that you and the Kingdom have put me through, it's by time I got some vengeance. First with this psychotic brat, then by watching every last one of you Mursi burn as the Brit's thousand-pound bombs lay waste to your huts! And when all is charred and desolate, the Kingdom will actually pay me for this! I couldn't have asked for more!"

"You kill him," Akilu said, bathed in sweat. "And you're not walking away from here. You'll never be able to make that call. We won't let you!"

Despite the anxiety of those around him, D'jen sneered, his mind in a state of ataraxy, calm and untouched by the turmoil.

"Watch me."

He swiped.

Chapter XLI
To be Truly Evil, One Must Believe He's Not

Francis's figure loomed in the doorway of the king's chamber, with the roaring flames as a backdrop. His shadow cast far across the room, like a flashlight of darkness, consuming King Leopold and the assailant.

"[English] Who are you?" the king asked, squinting. "You're far too young to be Napoleon. Is that Sir-Francis; my boy's guard?"

Francis nodded at the mercenary, who retracted his gun by twirling then holstering it in a blink of an eye. He disappeared just as stealthily as he arrived, leaving behind only the king and Francis. Francis drew a short blade, sheathing it against the scabbard.

King Leopold dashed for the phone resting atop the nightstand, but Francis was younger, quicker, and sharper. The king toppled over the armchair, faltering and tripping towards the corner. Francis approached, one step after the other, taking his time as the fire trailed into the bedroom. King Leopold, sweating through his gritty wrinkled skin, snapped his gaze around.

No way out.

The flames grew into a firestorm, spreading to every curtain and rug, eventually igniting the fireplace. Francis kneeled, snatching the king by the batch of gray hairs clinging to the back of his head. The pull exposed his few remaining stained teeth.

"Francis, what is this? Any moment now—"

"No," Francis said, eyes momentarily closed. "This is a prepared moment. Nobody's coming."

"Then tell me what this is all about. I demand to know!"

Francis held the feeble ruler as if the raging fire would not consume them in the coming minutes. The wood paneling along the walls blackened and cracked as the heat ravaged through, exposing the century-old bricks.

Francis let go, thudding the king's head against the hardwood. He returned to the doorway and began kicking the structure. Stomp after stomp, it gave in, trapping the pair in the glowing room, painting them, and everything in sight, orange.

"Are you mad?" King Leopold asked. "We'll both parish!"

Francis returned his full attention, sporting an expressionless stare. With the surrounding blaze growing, a bystander would assume that the guard was immune.

"Did you know," Francis said. "My father once snuck me into the Grand National at Aintree. It was the first time I ever saw a horse race, because we never owned a telly." Francis gazed at the full moon through the soot covered window. Young again, he sat in the bleachers with Wallis. The king glanced between his back and the collapsed exit. "We had to leave before the race was over because security neared. So, I did what any other child would do; I hid."

The chandelier's mounting rods periodically snapped, sounding off like a series of gunshots every time one succumbed to the weakening ceiling. The 100kg, or 300lb, chandelier swung like a pendulum between the king and the guard, until it broke free, crushing Leopold's leg. As the grueling scream reverberated through the wreckage, Francis continued.

"But even in that crowded stadium, my father found me. I tried to blend in with another family, going all the way to appear like a typical boy my age."

The king's fragile femur broke through his leg's thin skin, making direct contact with the frayed electrical wires. However, it didn't electrocute him because the fire spliced the ceiling cables just in time.

"I cheered, pointed and smiled, but it was all an act. Even my fake family bought it, thinking for a moment that I was their son. But my father … he saw right through it, spotting me like a large, dark piss-stain on a fresh bed sheet."

"Get with it!" King Leopold groaned, finding his blood painting the soon-to-be charred slats.

Francis flattened one of the rippled rugs with his shoe.

"I'm a fair man, your highness."

"Fair? How's breaking into an old man's bedroom fair?! How's murdering my guards and destroying my castle, fair?!"

The asphyxiating smoke continued to pile from top down.

"You should be worried when your adversary knows everything about you, while you know nothing about him," Francis said. "I'm sharing things about myself as a courtesy."

"Oh, pipe down, lad! You're doing nothing but gloating. But you'll be sorry." The bed's canopy pillar collapsed, shaking the room. "Even if you get out of here, you'll be caught and strung up like yesterday's laundry."

Francis rolled his right sleeve up and pointed at his elbow.

"See that? That's the scar I got when I tried riding a bicycle without a parent around to teach me." Francis's scoff inadvertently included a snort. "I had to steal the bike from Archie—something he still hadn't pieced together. I swiped it right beneath his nose and that's when I was five. You really think I'm going to be 'caught' now, after 29 years of preparation?"

As the king's wound worsened and the air became intolerable, his face slacked with the reality settled in.

"See this?" Francis pointed at a quadruple set of scars, discoloring his left hand's knuckles. "I got these when I slammed my fist, over and over, into the flat's floor, after having just seen my father pass. You know why? Because we couldn't go to the hospital. Otherwise, my father would've been arrested."

Before King Leopold could respond, Francis continued.

"And this." A long scar right beside Francis's forearm, tarnishing his wrist to his elbow. "I got this gash when I fought Billy Clark for calling my step-mum a crack whore, only to get this one," he pointed to another scarred wound, "from her, when I later learned that Billy was right."

Leopold's attention paused when he realized the daunting depths of Francis's pain. The inferno devastated the once elegant Victorian décor, transforming the chamber into a gothic nightmare. The illusion of order and civility vanished into the ashes as the torched Roman clock chimed a haunting melody, marking 3:00 AM. Every fleeting second resonated through the room like a death knell, counting down the remaining moments before irreversible actions took place.

Francis rested in the majestic armchair, being the only piece of furniture untouched by the hellfire. He threw his head back, finding the ceiling ready to fold.

"Nobody felt bad for me." The crackling flames swirled around him like Satan himself. "And that caused me a lot of trouble making friends. That is until I found one … a girl." Francis forgot where he was for a moment. He forgot who he was talking to, finding himself in a therapist's office gripping a pillow. "After learning that we were one and the same, we took each other's virginities. But it wasn't as spectacular as others said it would be. It was almost like a chance to let our guard down. That's all. No games, no bravado, just our raw, naked selves, allowed to quit the act."

Francis lowered his face towards his fist, squishing up his cheek.

"She too, like my father, perished at the hands of an Augustus. Does any of this ring a bell, old man?"

Bloodied, groaning and frowning, King Leopold nodded.

"Yes, you're just like all the other bastard brats that poison this kingdom—blaming me for everything!"

Francis didn't crack an ounce of disappointment. He didn't let the adrenaline overtake him, nor did he sport any bit of schadenfreude. His brows knitted as he stood.

"You're right. I blamed you at first, ever since my mother's funeral, when my father told me about my bloodline. But as I aged, I realized people only blame others that they want something from, making them dependent. That's not why I'm here."

He walked over to the downed king, gasping for air. He placed his foot on his femur bone, bouncing it like a diving board. Through the geezer's shouts, still, no emotion.

"I could just wait for your abdication, but that's not enough and you know it. This is something I have to do. Because I only seek to restore order to the Kingdom. And this is how order is restored."

Francis reached into his pocket and pulled out a letter.

> *A supporter descended*
> *into the cellar and tapped*
> *the corner of a folded note*
> *against Francis's shoulder.*
> *"Here, Napoleon wanted*
> *you to have this."*

He unfolded the note and brought it close to King Leopold's face.

"Notice the handwriting? Of course not, because you never cared about Napoleon. That's why you were easily able to send him to the gallows."

Francis sat cross-legged beside the king.

"'*Dear Francis,*'" he read the worn letter out loud, word for word.

I tried, Francis thought. I really tried. Forgive me.

Upon reaching the end, he reread the axiomatic last line over and over and over. "'*I'll always love you.*'"

Tears formed in the cusps of Francis's eyelids. When each fell, they'd evaporate before reaching the floor. He turned, gently placing the letter over a log in the fireplace. The edges of the note broke their sharp angles, darkening while curling, until they glowed a menacing bright orange. With a lingering gaze, he witnessed his last cherished possession transform into a small heap of ash.

"King Leopold, we are the same, hungry for the same, driven by the same. Don't say you don't recognize me. I am your deeds, returning to steal back what you stole."

Debris rained from the crumbling ceiling, crashing down with thunderous force, threatening to bury the two beneath the wreckage within the minute. The king covered his face, but Francis stood tall through the carnage.

Before it was too late, he grabbed a blazing log from the fireplace.

"This needs to happen," he said.

"I'll never beg."

Francis approached the king. The torch neared his face, glistening a sheen of sweat over his wrinkled forehead. Scowling, Leopold glanced at his adversary, and for the first time, noticed Francis's charged irises.

"Y—you have my eyes …"

Silent and tacit, Francis stared back.

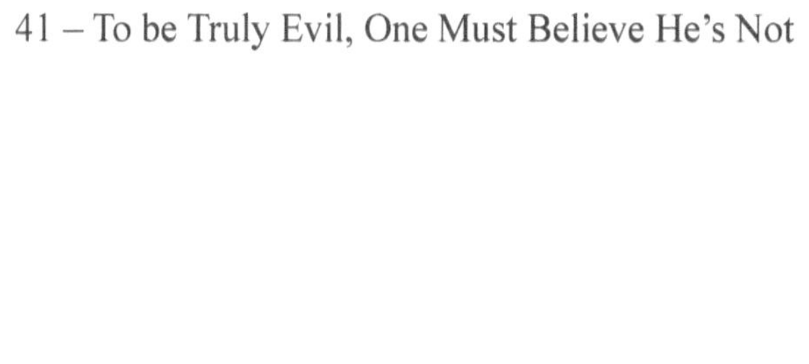

This page is intentionally left blank.

Moments later, Francis catapulted through the shattered tower window, heart pounding as he plummeted through the void with windmilling arms. He smashed through a nearby canopy, ricocheting off a stack of crates and slamming to a halt on the castle wall walkway.

Guards raced to his aid, their footsteps tapping along the stone path.

"Sir-Francis, are you alright?!"

Concern and fear filled their voices as Francis gasped, nodding performatively. He glanced up, finding the inferno roaring from the chamber's window imitating a flamethrower, engulfing the tower's top like a gigantic torch.

"He—he got away …" Francis said.

"What of the king?!"

Francis shook his head, forcing a tear out as he stamped his fist against the cement.

An explosion rocked the castle, sending shockwaves through the ground. The guards stumbled as Francis grabbed onto them for support.

"Come, now! The tower's unstable!"

Francis hooked his arms around their shoulders as they carried him away. His wet, blurry vision stole a final glance back at the tower, saddened only for leaving the letter behind.

Chapter XLII
Napoleon's Letter

Dear Francis,

*M*y time is near.

I can see my life setting before me like the calm upper half of the maroon sun dipping into the horizon. Although plenty have offered remedies, nobody can prevent the sun from setting. So, before the night consumes me, I need to leave these words behind for you.

If you're reading this, then it means you've made it into the castle—taking the path which I've abandoned. Here, you'll finally find the evidence of what I've been telling you. After you see it, your life will pivot, never again allowing you to return to normalcy.

You're a slave, Francis.

Just like everyone else.

Your Royal blood won't save you from this reality, nor set you free.

In fact, your blood will enslave you more, regardless of how ruthlessly you oppose it. Because if you took my path, yes, you'll find peace, love and family. But the idea of grandeur you're walking away from shall forever gnaw at you. It'll occupy a territory in your mind until your own sun sets. Know now that this buzzing is merely a mosquito without a home.

However, being in the castle, your blood won't let you stop until you reclaim what they've stolen from you. On your journey, there'll be a different torment. Not one of bolstering glory, no. You'll yearn for something that every soul craves.

Peace.

Without peace, there's only madness. And a madman always harms those closest to him.

I don't believe the madness which comes with the throne was worth it. The love I've found in you; in your mother … I wouldn't trade it for the world, let alone the throne. It's what freed me.

Father named me Napoleon, to take after Napoleon Bonaparte—a man who the Brits despised for his ruthlessness. Albeit, no Brit can ever deny his effectiveness. Father believed that carrying his name would make life an uphill battle for me. He always said that enduring hardships shapes character, hoping it would one day brand me as effective, like Bonaparte. And effective, I was.

I gave up everything for the innocent, and I don't regret it whatsoever. Father couldn't find the value of people, labeling anybody different from himself as expendable. That was either something he inherited or a symptom of the throne. But one thing is certain: the last person to taste freedom is he who strips it from others.

I didn't name you Francis to damn you with hardship. No. That's not what a father does. I named you Francis because France is the home of Bonaparte, and there's nothing I desire more than being home with you. Every time I hear your name, I'm home. Every time I write your name, I'm home. Every time I read your name, I'm home. And only in the warmth of a home does one find genuine freedom.

Now that you're inside the castle, I fear that freedom is something you'll never find. Your path from here on mandates you stripping souls from bodies. And as a madman, those bodies will include loved ones, young ones and, without a doubt, innocent ones—something I couldn't get myself to do.

But I'm not free of sin. Standing up for the thousands my father was willing to sacrifice forced me to abandon my brother. So, I can't be sure what sins your path will force upon Madeleine, but I'm demanding you to keep her safe. Otherwise, on top of being enslaved, you'll also turn into a mere mirage beyond the grasp of sanity.

Never interrupt your enemy when he's making a mistake, but who that enemy is, son, is knowledge I never wish to learn.

Know, Francis, regardless of your path, I'll always love you.

Sincerely,
Wallis Augustus

Chapter XLIII
Assault

D'jen swiped, slicing through a bit more than Julian's skin.

A distant, echoing crack sounded.

Streaming blood splashed over the generational dagger as it flung beside Julian's ear. The prince toppled to his side, rolling away, as if drunk, while clamping his neck. The red liquid smeared between his fingers, seeping beneath his nails, as he gasped. He stumbled into the foliage, using only one hand to soften the fall.

More claps resonated.

Bewildered, Akilu snapped around, seeking the source of the sound. He made sure to keep Madeleine in sight. Whereas for Imamu …

The generational dagger laid nearby the panting Julian. His blood rolled across its sharp edge, dripping before him, watering the land he despised so much. However, someone else's gore slid alongside his.

D'jen, eyes wide and mouth agape, collapsed like one of the Twin Towers, before falling flat on his face, pluming up the fallen leaves. An exit wound shaped the back of his head, exposing his brain through his shattered skull like an octopus's tentacles escaping a whirlpool.

"GET DOWN!" Akilu shouted.

—

A commando, eye glued to the scope, whispered, "Target neutralized."

"Which one?" the sergeant asked, camouflaged, like his men, with black face paint.

"D'jen."

"And the Royals?"

Focused on the point of interest, the commando adjusted the rifle's optics.

"Julian and Madeleine are in sight. No sign of Leopaula."

"Find her."

—

In an instant, the Karo scaled the trees and took cover behind downed logs. The Mursi scattered. Some fled back to the village, dropping their torches and starting a forest fire.

Imamu stayed in his place, fists tightened and chin lowered.

Prone, Julian hugged the earth as more bullets jetted overhead, puncturing the air and decorticating the trees. The generational dagger gleamed from the growing fire.

Imamu narrowed his eyes on it, too.

Julian reached for it.

Just as Akilu hurried to protect Madeleine, Imamu swiped the machete from his hip and soared through the air, throwing all his weight forward.

"THAT'S MY DAGGER!"

The machete sliced clean through Julian's extended arm, stopping at nothing. It established a wall between the elbow and digits when it stabbed the ground.

"[Surmic] Imamu, no!" Akilu shouted.

Julian's right hand fidgeted until the blood remaining in it soaked the soil beneath the wound.

Everybody witnessed the lone Mursi boy, after a lifetime of brutal oppression from the Kingdom, sever the blonde prince's arm, lift him by the collar and land blow upon blow. Julian couldn't contemplate defending himself before Imamu's fists of liberation lifted towards the black sky and thudded, over and over, against his nose, jaw and eyes—mostly his left one. Julian's face ricocheted back and forth between the pummels, morphing colors between every repetition.

Madeleine watched, frozen and taken aback, trying to process her husband's severed arm and D'jen's failed assassination attempt, with Imamu's justified rage.

Imamu's shouts thundered through the onslaught, reaching the ears of all. The unfiltered surge of vengeance purged through his veins, arteries and thoughts.

> *Yonas's goofy smile,*
> *beaten and bruised, as the*
> *haranchi held him up.*
>
> *The Mursi women and*
> *children pulled from their*
> *huts, screaming.*
>
> *The flames, cries,*
> *hunger—the haranchi*
> *laugh.*

*Madeleine's bleeding
brow.
Leopaula.*

Julian's blood painted Imamu's fist, more and more, every time he pulled it back. But between strikes, another crack tore through the forest, whizzing through the branches.

A sharp knock struck Imamu's thigh, pausing him. He reached into his satchel and found the butt end of a bullet sticking out of his phone as it sparked and smoke hissed around it. Before understanding, more shots fired, all striking Imamu's chest.

"Imamu!" Ike and Madeleine screamed.

Everybody ducked for cover as Imamu coughed up a wave of blood. With his grip still tight on Julian's collar, he struggled to stay standing. He glanced down, finding holes in his once smooth chest.

—

"[English] That's a miss," the commando said, reloading the rifle. "Just a bystander."

—

Through the grunts, Imamu latched onto the generational dagger's hilt.

"This—is—mine!"

Saliva dribbled through his clenched teeth. His blood, like sweat, dripped off his body and showered the disoriented prince. Legs giving in, he kneed the ground through the heavy breaths.

"Imamu," Madeleine called. "Grab his phone! We need his—"

Akilu grabbed Madeleine's nape and rammed her down. He threw himself over her like a bedsheet.

"[Surmic] Imamu," he said. "It's the Kingdom, they're here! Don't let them grab the Royals! They'll use this against us, instead of negotiating! Do not kill him!"

With the orange glow blazing Imamu's face, he nodded through the pain.

"[English] The phone—" Madeleine repeated before Akilu covered her mouth.

"Yes … Princess …" Imamu said, debilitated yet determined.

He supported himself with one hand and dug the other into Julian's pocket. Julian, with his lone hand, tried stopping him, but his strength lingered on the minimum. Imamu lethargically raised his arm, barely able to clench a fist. Despite being more of a slap, his punch ceased Julian's resistance. Once Imamu felt the phone's edge, Ike rushed to his aid.

"[Surmic] Come!" He wrapped his friend's arm over his shoulders. "We have to go!"

—

Akilu yanked Madeleine back, but she stomped on his foot with the apex of her heel. As he winced, Madeleine darted away. Akilu cursed before chasing after her.

She grabbed Julian's severed hand. Suddenly, Julian grabbed her leg, attempting to climb her.

"[English] Please!" Julian groaned. "Help me!"

His wound peppered with dirt and gravel, like a chewed gumball spit onto the shore. His forearm's bone protruded proudly from the few arteries slithering out, seeking to complete the organ, but grasped at nothingness.

Madeleine stepped back, never forgetting how he'd treated her.

"You just pointed a blade at me, Julian."

"P—please!"

Her body told her to run, but her heart, medical training and pity staked her in place. She slowly extended her hand.

—

"Princess is spotted," the commando said.

"Take the shot."

—

Akilu tackled Madeleine, leaving the bullet whizzing through her trailing hair. With a fireman's carry, he hurried her back so safety.

—

"Forget about her," Scarlett said. "I'm here to help. I'm all you need, Joules."

Julian, disheveled, bloodied and sweaty, crawled in a random direction, reaching for whatever vegetation surrounded him that wasn't on fire. His severed arm left behind a solid red smear wherever he went.

"Oh, baby, you're hurt," Scarlett said. She sported a pouty face, absent of the surrounding chaos.

"I'm not," he swallowed a dry throat, "going to die here! Get me out of here!"

Scarlett, dressed as a commando and tickling Leopaula, mockingly saluted. "Yes, sir! But you have to get to that hut, that strong clay one that you pissed on. That's where the brat's sim card will be. With it, you'll be able to call me, or Francis, and we'll get you back home."

Julian directed his attention through the flames.

"If you love me," Scarlett said. "You'll go there."

—

"Are you hit?" Akilu asked as Zola pulled Madeleine in.

"I'm fine, I'm fine! But I need—"

"No! You need to stay here!" All but lightning struck the floor when he pointed.

—

"Confirmation on the princess." The sergeant adjusted his binoculars.

"Negative," the marksman responded.

"Come again."

"I said, neg—"

"Repeat that, soldier. What was that? Speak up!" The sergeant pulled his binoculars away and frantically looked around, finding the tall, surrounding trees leaning, ready to snap and bury him. "What're you saying? *What is that?*"

The whispers subtly crept into the marksman's ears.

"Sargeant?" No response. "*Sargeant?*"

—

"[Surmic] Oh, God! Oh, God!" Ike said, pulling the perforated Imamu from the pandemonium.

"S—stop …" Imamu said. "Take me to her."

"No! I have to save Nala!"

Imamu anchored himself, escaping Ike's hold.

"Her t—torment," he sputtered as the blood filled his lungs. "We can't just—" Ike lifted him up, looking left and right. "We have to tell her the truth about—the truth about Leopaula!"

Chapter XLIV
The Breaths that Matter Most

"What is that?!" Zola backed away from the bloodied severed limb, with dirt and grime packed into the crevices.

Madeleine's restless hands fidgeted above the cooling, curling digits. She straightened the thumb, making sure she had full access to the print. A slight smile peered through her creased face.

"It's Julian's!"

Zola pulled Kamari away. "Why do ya have Julian's hand?!"

Ike burst into the hut, stumbling at the entrance and dropping Imamu. The satchel fell forward, sliding out its contents.

"Please help him!" Ike said, turning to leave, but Zola stopped him.

"[Surmic] What happened to him?!"

Ike slapped her hand away. "I have to save Nala!" He bashed into the wall, before faltering his way out.

As Imamu gasped and gargled, Madeleine turned him over, revealing his injuries trailing from the pool of blood beneath him.

"Imamu!" Zola dropped Kamari as she hurried over, but Madeleine pushed her away.

"[English] Imamu, Imamu, listen to me," Madeleine said. "You're going to be alright, just breathe, breathe. Focus on my voice."

She tore off her top and shredded it using her teeth. She tried applying pressure to the wound, but the more she wrapped and tied, the more she realized how severe his injuries were. With the vital organs hit, she witnessed them failing before her eyes. Her fingers flinched, withdrawing for a moment.

"Help him, girl!"

Madeleine froze, knowing that nothing could be done.

"*No ... No ...*" Madeleine shivered through her shaky breaths.

"Do something! Please!"

Although Kamari wailed from the corner, all Zola heard was Imamu's frail attempt to stay alive.

Madeleine tightened her jaw and fought through the doubts.

Apply pressure, she thought. *Check airway, breathing and circulation. No exit wounds, good. Position the patient to minimize—*

Imamu staved off Madeleine's efforts, grunting through the hiccups.

"Zola, hold his hands down!"

"Stop!" Imamu pushed the two off and scrambled towards his satchel's spilled contents.

He slammed Julian's phone down, smearing its screen red before cracking apart his damaged cell's panels and taking out the sim card. With a trembling hand, he clumsily inserted his sim into Julian's device and slapped it into Madeleine's palm.

"R—run. Call any—anybody and run. Nobody's coming to help you or your—your …"

"Do something, girl!" Zola didn't know what to do with her hands. "Save him!"

"Your daugh—"

They stared into each other's eyes. He shook his head, knowing the end was near. Her tears fell, one after the other, cleansing his wounds.

"I'm so sorry," Madeleine breathed.

Imamu hugged her, whichever way he could. He squeezed, gripping her smooth skin with his cracked hands.

"No," he mumbled. "I'm the one that's sorry."

With every word, more of the crimson stream flowed from his mouth. Zola dug her nails into her face, shielding herself from the sight of another lost son.

Madeleine didn't want to give up, but when she extended her hand, Imamu snatched and slammed it against his failing heart.

"Please," he said.

"Yes, anything!"

"Forgive me."

Madeleine pulled her hand back.

"No! All of this is my fault! I brought this madness here! My people—"

"No, not that … Leopaula!" The hut fell into a silence. "She's—she's not—"

"Leopaula? Leopaula's not what?!"

"She's not at Koka, nor," he glanced at Zola, "nor Kibish."

"Tell me! Where's my daughter?! Please!"

"Ju—"

"Tell me!"

He winced. "Julian—"

Madeleine pulled back. "*Julian?* Julian, what?"

Slipped between his teeth, the blood filled every corner of his mouth with a metallic ting. "*B—b—boat.*"

Droplets burst onto her abdomen, rolling towards her pelvis. His eyes tired as his head leaned towards Madeleine's slit-like belly button. "Julian … K—ki—" With every pronounced K, loads of blood clogged his throat.

"J—Julian knows."

His eyes drooped shut as he turned into Madeleine's quivering embrace.

He stopped talking. He stopped trying. A fading smile shaped his lips as the calmness of speaking the truth covered him like a fresh, falling bedsheet.

His chin fell as his breathing stopped.

Without delay, Madeleine set him down and started chest compressions.

Zola covered her face, but not her eyes.

With every one of Madeleine's pumps, blood purged from his wounds like orchestrated geysers. As one lung collapsed over the other, an imaginary cardiac monitor beeped, long and monotone, flatlining as the surrounding doctors stepped back with resigned shoulders.

Madeleine kept thrusting. "Stay with me!"

"Imamu!" Zola screamed.

Kamari cried as he struggled on his back like a turtle.

Startled, Madeleine leaped back as though a grenade had detonated in front of her. She thumped against the wall as she stared, empty and paralyzed, at the doting mother hugging her son's corpse.

The blood slathered between them, as Zola attempted to embrace what remained of her son's warmth. His eyes rolled open, but stayed in place like a bubble level. A serene coolness surrounded his pupils, showing the absence of the weight he'd been bearing.

"Imamu!" Zola wept. "Imamu!"

Her far-reaching wails pulled Amari's attention towards the hut, with the stumbling Julian not far behind.

Imamu's name echoed through the village, reaching all the way to the Omo River and its thousands of undervalued, misunderstood, ignored offshoots.

384

"Imamu!"

Chapter XLV
Never Share your Fingerprint with Anyone

Madeleine's hair frayed as she held a broken posture. Gunshots bellowed outside, reverberating across the ablaze village. Screams, cries and shouts entered every hut, but in the clay one, an imaginary silence lingered.

"Zola," Madeleine said through her shuddered breaths. "I'm so sorry—"

"Who did this?!"

"The commandos. The ones we thought Julian hallucinated. They're here. They killed D'jen and started firing."

Zola slammed her fist against her thigh, wanting to snap out of this nightmare. "Haranchi, haranchi, haranchi! Is there anybody left in the world that's worse than a haranchi?! Do they think our lives have no value?"

As Imamu's body stiffened, a chime sounded from Julian's phone.

Battery Level: 7%

The lock screen awaited the pin code … *or* *a fingerprint.*

"No, Zola. Your life is just as valuable as mine. And Imamu's death won't be in vain. I'll stop this now!"

Madeleine wiped the blood off the screen before placing Julian's severed hand's thumbprint over the sensor. Normally it would unlock instantly, but the phone knew something was off. The sensor swirled and scanned as Madeleine's heart thrashed around her ribcage.

The lock sign swiveled open; access granted.

"I'm in!"

Julian's hand thudded against the floor.

"Ya better call someone quick," Zola said. "Those commandos are getting close!"

Madeleine ignored the reality, and scanned through the once familiar phone, finding the icons shifted and some folders marked private. Taps later and the phone trilled, dialing Lordes.

No answer.

"Now what?" Zola asked, easing Imamu down.

"I—I don't—" Madeleine swallowed harshly.

With an opportunity this ripe, she couldn't pass it up. She tapped on the messaging app and began her discovery.

"Julian acted odd the last few months before we arrived. He kept his phone close and constantly checked it."

"So, what? How's that going to help us now?"

Madeleine momentarily lowered the phone. "I don't know, Zola! But it's finally a chance for me to learn why!"

Zola, covered with Imamu's blood, understood. She picked Kamari up and quieted him down, before grabbing one of the decorative spears off the wall.

"Ya do whatcha gotta, and I'll make sure nobody interrupts."

"Thank you," Madeleine said before getting back to snooping.

At the top of the list, messages between Julian and Scarlett took the spotlight, hovering over Francis's message chain. Line upon line, Madeleine found their conversations, going as far back as three months.

"Scarlett, Scarlett—who's Scarlett?" she asked, *yet she knew.* It could only mean one thing.

"Another woman?"

Madeleine nodded, a short, shameful nod. "I heard him say her name while he was talking to D'jen. But what's this?" She kept scrolling. "He's been texting her since we've arrived, and she's reading them, but she's not responding. Why?"

Amari burst into the hut, discovering his slain son bleeding out. "Imamu!"

Before he could reach him, a stray bullet whizzed through the window, disturbing the light billowing curtain, striking his shoulder. Amari clenched his side as he toppled forward, landing on Imamu's chest.

"Amari!" Zola screamed.

Just then, Julian barged in, face covered with dirt and blood. Gasping, he leaned against the entryway, leaving his open stump of an arm staining the door frame as it leaked like a limp garden hose. Upon spotting the generational dagger beside the rest of Imamu's spilled items, he dove. The moment his finger grazed the handle, Zola whacked his face with the butt of the spear, knocking him into the corner. The Lion Tamer's Skull tipped off the shelf, but before it hit the floor, Zola charged the spear towards Julian's bloodied neck.

"[Surmic] Zola, stop!" Amari grunted.

The tip of the spear stopped just shy of where D'jen partially sliced Julian's neck. The two locked eyes as Zola cemented her grip, blowing fumes from her nostrils—not realizing that she dropped Kamari again.

"Tell me why I shouldn't!"

Amari's sweat slipped over his forehead as he panted through the pain. "Because we need him alive!"

Julian snapped his eyes between Zola and the generational dagger, then at Madeleine.

"[English] Maddy! Give me the phone!" His hoarse voice, engulfed with irritation, caused her to flinch.

"Don't, girl!"

"Maddy, hand me the phone, so that we could finally get out of this hellhole!"

Madeleine moved back, measuring every step. "How're you still alive?"

"Because I refuse to die here! I'm going back home, far away from these heathens!"

"Back home?" Madeleine asked. "Where things were no different between us? Where—"

"Shut up! Just shut up and give me that phone. Now's not the time!"

Zola smirked through the tension. "Madeleine, this boy ain't got nothing but his words and he knows it." She kept the spear lodged against the most embossed tube in his neck. "He's just a cornered cat, with no option but to shriek. But it's just that, *a loud meow*. Do what you were doin, girl."

Madeleine nodded as the fear dissipated and her confidence soared. "Who's Scarlett?"

"What?"

"Who's ..." Madeleine said slowly, her tone full of knowing. "Scarlett?"

"You don't—you don't know what you're talking about—"

Madeleine glanced at his severed arm, close to the wound, then back at him. "You're fighting to survive, but not to go back home to your family." Julian tightened his lips, not saying a word. Madeleine tilted her head. "You're trying to go back to her ... You cheated on me with this Scarlett woman ..."

Julian clenched his eyes shut. "Just give me the phone."

"You're not denying it," Madeleine said before barking a silent chuckle. "Finally, some truth."

"You have no idea what you're saying, Maddy. Do the right thing and save us. All you have to do is hand me the phone—"

Madeleine turned back to the messages, reading them aloud.

> Julian: I thought about you while on the boat today. What I'd do to run my fingers through your hair once more. What I'd do to get you back. I hope you

understand it was a knee-jerk reaction and I'm sorry. I just couldn't risk having another child. Please forgive me.

Read Yesterday Morning

Julian: During football with the lads, I heard you, but I wish I could've seen you.

Read Yesterday Afternoon

Julian: I was on the verge of starving today, but I don't trust eating the food of these freaks. I know the one buffoon is trying to kill me, so what better way is there than poison? He only needs one of us for the ransom. Don't worry, love, I'll kill him first.

We're supposed to go to the "mines" today, but I know it's a ploy. That's when I'll do it. After that, I'll be able to use that prick's sim card, call Francis and return home, and finally see you again.

Read Earlier Today

"Julian," Madeleine said. "Who's this—this—Scarlett and why's she only reading your messages and not responding?"

— Meanwhile in the Detective's Office —

Beneath a dim dangling pendant light, the detective read the same messages off of Scarlett's phone, prompting the read-status.

"It's confirmed, detective," his aide said from behind an array of computer monitors. "These incoming messages are from Prince Julian's mobile."

The detective locked Scarlett's phone. "Then we have all we need."

—

The tears hurried out of Madeleine's eyes. "Julian, you cheated on me—on your family … and you've fallen in love."

"I loved you!"

Madeleine shook her head. "You never spoke to me like this."

Julian's sadness wasn't enough to be evident. "That's because you abandoned me for these people, Maddy! This is your fault!"

"You better quit squirming, boy, or else you'll be tastin' a whole lot of metal!" Zola struggled to hold the spear through Kamari's cries, her husband on the brink of death, and the mayhem raging outside.

"Who was she to you?" Madeleine asked. "I deserve to know!"

"Don't do this to yourself. What's done is done, *but we're not.* We can fix this—move past it. Just hand me the phone."

"You think there's still a future for us? After what I just learned—after what you did to me just hours ago? After pointing a blade at my face?! Julian, I don't know who you are. Eight years together, and I'm staring at a stranger."

The only thing between the spear and his neck was his thick scruff, which emboldened his depraved expression.

"Maddy, you know who I am. I'm the same person who fell in love with you during that event. The same person who threw away everything just to be with you. The one who hired Francis just because he was your brother—"

"*Francis* ..." Madeleine turned back towards the messages, opening the thread with Francis.

> Julian: Francis, SOS! I did something bad and need to get back. Send somebody—anybody. Hell, come yourself! Just get me out of here, now!
> *Read Yesterday Morning*

Madeleine rotated towards him. "You sent this right after we got to the village—"

"Maddy—"

"But, back then, the only thing on our minds was Leopaula, yet you didn't mention her ..." Like an arrow piercing towards its target, she narrowed her eyes. "*What'd you do?*"

Suddenly, the phone vibrated.

Incoming Call: Lordes Wright

Madeleine slapped the phone to her ear. "Lordes?!"

"Lady-Madeleine?! Is that really you?" His voice echoed.

"Lordes—yes! You have to help me!"

"I'm busy at the moment, my dear." After locking the entrance, he hid in the furthest stall of the visitor center's restroom, tucked between the toilet and the wall. "I couldn't answer earlier. I was fleeing."

"Fleeing? Fleeing from who?"

"Francis! He's done it—he's carried out his coup! He slayed the king!"

"Francis killed King Leopold?! Why?"

Zola, Amari and Julian shot their gaze over. Madeleine put the phone on speaker.

"First tell me, how're you still alive?!"

Madeleine didn't respond. She gripped the phone through her sweaty, shaking palms as the warfare outside raged. Bullets peppered the hut's walls, crumbling portions of the ceiling onto the floor.

"Lady-Madeleine," Lordes said. "Are you still there—"

"How can I trust you? I've been lied to by the Kingdom, by my brother, by Julian … How do I know you're not in on this, too?"

"Princess, we don't have time for this! Send a picture of yourself. It's the only way to foil Francis's plan; it's the only way to stay alive!"

"What do you mean?" Madeleine asked.

"Francis's commandos, they're there to kill you!"

"What?! Aren't they trying to save us?"

"Oh, sweet Madeleine. You're the only one innocent in all of this, caught in the crossfire."

"Tell me about Scarlett," Madeleine said.

"Scarlett? Why her, why now?"

"I'll be able to tell if I could trust you."

Lordes glanced around the stall, finding that he was still alone. He peeked out the window and found the center of focus was still around the burning castle, with Francis nowhere in sight.

"Scarlett was Francis's lover," Lordes said.

"*Was?*" Madeleine slowly lowered the phone as she turned towards Julian. "*You—you ...*"

"Julian killed her!" the phone sounded from beside her hip. "He killed her after Francis's plan didn't work."

"Ju ..." Madeleine's pupils fluttered in place as Julian struggled to avoid eye contact. "Julian ... have you lost your mind?! You cheated on me, then killed her?"

"Yes, Lady-Madeleine!" Lordes said. "That's exactly what happened!"

The phone chimed.

Battery Level: 5%

"No!" Julian barked, causing an additional slice along his neck. "She's right there, behind you!"

Nobody fell for it, especially Zola. Nobody, other than Julian, who stared at the hallucination, as real as anybody else in the hut.

"You have lost your mind …" Madeleine said.

"She's right there, I swear!" He pointed with his eyebrows, yet nobody even glanced.

Scarlett bit her lower lip as she grinned, resting her chin on her wrist as the other arm wrapped around her belly. "Busted," she said, shrugging as if it was all a joke. "But tell em more, baby. I love it when you talk about me."

Madeleine shook her head. "You're texting a dead woman, Julian …"

"Lady-Madeleine, she's the woman plastered all over the Kingdom. You must've seen her face all over Heathrow before your departure," Lordes said.

"I did."

"What's more astonishing is that you're both alive—"

Madeleine kept staring at Julian. "That's it. That's why we're here. It's not to get a change of scenery, nor to save our marriage; it's to save you …"

"That's right," Lordes confirmed, proving himself to Madeleine.

"Julian, by texting her, they're going to arrest you the moment you return home."

"No! Everybody here has no idea what they're talking about! Francis will save me—"

"Francis abandoned his family as a lad!" Madeleine slammed the wall. "He disappeared and never dropped by, even once. Francis is not loyal. Francis is behind all of this! You—you killed his woman—how could you still believe he'll help you?"

"Maddy … just give me the phone."

Madeleine unwillingly chuckled. "You're insane, don't you see? There's no leaving …"

"I'm getting out of here! Even if it means killing every last one of you!"

Zola shoved the spear closer. "A lotta meowing. That's all this is!"

"Lady-Madeleine, there's more you should know," Lordes said. "Allow me to tell you everything. I don't want my loyalty to Napoleon to be thwarted by Francis's thirst for vengeance."

"Napoleon?" Madeleine asked. "What does Napoleon have to do with any of this?"

"Lady-Madeleine …"

"What?"

Lordes glanced around, grimacing as the sweat broke through his skin.

"Tell me!"

Lordes looked into the dirty mirror, before nodding to himself with clenched eyes.

"Prince Napoleon is your father!"

Chapter XLVI
Anagnorisis

Battery Level: 3%

The shouts outside inched closer, led by Akilu ordering the Mursi to strategic locations. Shots fired from both sides, dispersing the faint whiff of gunpowder through the village's air, as Amari's hut remained the focal point. Neither flank relented, yet neither took ground. The Mursi would not allow another invasion, while the commandos bunkered behind their state-of-the-art killing machines. Meanwhile, the Karo were nowhere in sight.

In the hut, Madeleine held a stillness comparable to a monk. Beside her scabbed eyebrow twitching, she was a stone. She wanted to push pause but life fast-forwarded by. Blank in the face, her mind morphed into a nuclear blast zone. She feared that her head would explode if she didn't grab it in time.

"It's the truth!" Lordes said over the phone. "Napoleon, Julian's brother, he's your father! Everything said about him is a lie! He was framed!"

Beneath the spear, Julian blinked rapidly.

"Lordes, no," Madeleine weighed her words, "*Wallis* is my father."

"Lady-Madeleine, *Wallis* was Napoleon's alias that I gave him …"

Madeleine stopped. She glanced around the hut, feeling the force of time against her. Blood trickled over Amari's fingers as he clenched his wound. Kamari wailed on the floor beside his grandfather's skull. Dirt and pebbles filled Julian's severed arm wound, but it still gushed blood as Zola held him down. She set the spear, piercing him with her hawkish eyes, but threatening with more.

"I've met him," Amari muttered through the pain. "Prince Napoleon. It was long ago, but I remember he was like you. Looked like you. Talked like you. Cared like you."

Madeleine glanced down at Julian, *her husband,* who shuddered his head left to right. She noticed his cheekbones, the hint of brown in his hair, his nose and—

"No, no, no …"

His pulse.

Her eyes bulged as she shot him a questioning glare. Rich domes of sweat trailed the blood off her forehead and soaked her bra. It started with her tense muscles jittering, followed by a head shake that grew with every repetition.

"No, no, no, no, no," she said softly until her back thumped against the wall. "NO!" The room flinched.

Julian abandoned the thought and refocused on escaping. He wanted just a moment to convince Madeleine otherwise, but with the spear beneath his chin, he looked like a desperate salesman missing his quota.

"Maddy—"

"You're my uncle!"

"What?"

Madeleine, wide-eyed, fixated all her attention on stillness of The Lion Tamer's skull, taking massive breaths to prevent herself from fainting. "Yes, yes—it all makes sense now! This—this is why it was impossible for us to conceive—my body was rejecting the incest!" The odd rhythm of her pulse hammered her temples, prompting her to once again clamp her head. She looked at the spear's tip against Julian's neck. It bounced with the same frequency. "Our arrhythmia—it's genetic! We have similar blood! You're my uncle—you're my uncle!" Madeleine turned but had nowhere to run. "Dear God, no! You're my uncle!"

"Lady-Madeleine, time is short," Lordes said. "So, please, let me explain. Even if it's the last thing I do."

///

Nearly 40 years ago, the Kingdom faced an unprecedented financial crisis. It stemmed from many reasons, but it was too late for finger pointing. Crime skyrocketed, protests filled the streets more than traffic and riots became a daily occurrence. The Kingdom's council sought the most affordable resource to mend the economy. And lithium offered a glimmer of hope.

King Leopold bartered for the lowest price, eventually finding an attractive bid from Ethiopia. His council advised against it, citing human rights concerns. Despite recommendations for Bolivia or Argentina, the king stuck to Ethiopia.

Near Omo Valley, where you are, a small quarry housed enough lithium to band-aid the Kingdom's recession. The Ethiopian government was practically giving it away. The price was so low it was as if someone offered a fleet of cars for the cost of a bicycle. That's because they weren't interested in the money—they wanted something else.

The king appointed my father to investigate the goal of the Ethiopians. I was in my young twenties, and shadowing him, with the promise of filling his shoes one day. He learned that the Ethiopian government planned to transform the entire Omo Valley into a national park and convert portions of it into a hydroelectric dam. They wanted a revenue stream via energy and tourism. But that was easier said than done.

This valley wasn't just a valley. The fruitful swath of land housed the native Omo tribes, who the government branded as squatters; tax-free leeches preventing the country from raising its GDP. Back then, before social media, the Ethiopian government controlled the news. So, with no push back, they could force the tribes off the land, exiling them from their homes into the depths of the valley. Since then, the tribes became hostile towards any further hint of relocation.

The lithium quarry for sale was in the tribes' new home and the government faced the headache of dealing with the tribes yet again. Whatever they'd offer, the tribes refused. But when money is on the line, no regime backs down, and violence is usually the next step. However, the plight of the tribes came to light through their offspring. Some youth couldn't stand the difficulty of living in the valley, so they migrated into the city and spread the reality of their situation. Now armed with the public's sympathy, the government had its hands tied. Killing these squatters would prompt uprisings from their own citizens, along with international sanctions.

Therefore, they pivoted to a third party. A superpower. You see, if a force like the UK handled the tribes, the narrative would change. And when I say *handle,* I mean exterminate. That's what the Ethiopian government really wanted, hence their low cost for the lithium.

The Kingdom would spin the media, while nobody would expect the Ethiopians to stand up to such a dominant world-power. The government found a man willing to betray the tribes for profit. Someone named *D'jen.*

///

Amari grunted. *"That D'jen!* Of course he would."

Madeleine regarded Zola, who nodded back, confirming all Lordes said.

"Maddy," Julian said. "Lordes is a senile old man. He's envied Francis's position since Francis was promoted. If we die here, he'll finally get another chance at being a king's Royal Guard—the highest rank in the establishment. He's just playing mind games with you."

Madeleine studied Julian, his wound, his scattered hair, his broken nose and his black eye. But one thing blared the truth to her—his pulse.

"Lordes has been my Royal Guard since I entered the castle—"

"That's not the same, and you know it." Julian stared back as his pulse continued to jitter at the same tempo as hers.

Madeleine said nothing, turning back to the phone.

///

Lady-Madeleine, when Prince Napoleon found out about this, he demanded that King Leopold abandon the transaction. But the king cast him aside, chastising his son for not knowing the gravity of the economic struggle.

I still remember the scene.

> *"There are other ways to repair an economy! But slaughtering thousands of innocents, that's something we can't come back from—"*
>
> *"Quiet, boy!" King Leopold scorned. "This is politics! This is how it's done!"*

Soon after, Napoleon renegaded. He traveled on his own to Ethiopia to warn the tribes against the treacherous contract. However, the only person who spoke enough English was D'jen. Little did Napoleon know, he was warning the traitor.

After all parties signed the contracts, Napoleon found no other option but to inform the public. When King Leopold heard of his intentions, he condemned him as an insurrectionist, followed by the infamous death sentence.

That night, I helped Prince Napoleon flee with his expecting wife. I doctored new identification documents for him, as others smuggled him out of Windsor Castle. The two didn't seek asylum or commit suicide, as the tabloids suggested. No, they hid beneath their noses, blending in with the people of Slough.

In the following weeks, Francis was born. Napoleon suffered a treatable disease, yet being the Kingdom's most wanted man, he couldn't enter any hospital. He succumbed to his illness before you were born, asking me to look after you and Francis. You two are like my own children. This has nothing to do with jealousy of Francis's position. I'm honoring my dead friend's last wish.

I later learned that Napoleon had filled Francis in on everything, leaving him with the decision to either abandon all royalty, or fight to take it back.

As a teen, this decision plunged Francis into a darkness that none of us could comprehend. Not only was his right to the throne stripped from him, but it cost him an unimaginable upbringing, as well as losing both parents. He reached out to me after running away from Slough with Scarlett, his childhood darling.

///

"Maddy, this man is lying to you!" Julian clenched his jaw as he felt his life leaking out of his arm. "Francis never met Scarlett! Francis only heard of her a few days ago!"

"But you know all about her, right?" Madeleine's glare flickered with static, immune to the outside chaos drawing near. "So, I should believe you, right? *The cheater.*"

"I met her at a bar! She's a traveling business woman, I swear! Lordes is lying."

///

Scarlett grew up near your flat, Lady-Madeleine. A daughter to a single abusive father, she and Francis immediately clicked, instantly falling in love and aligning their goals to become one. Since Francis wanted to retake what was his, she became his staunchest ally, willing to do anything to help her dearest achieve his dreams.

I tried telling you everything before your marriage, but Francis made me believe the mission was more important than your father's wishes. He conned me, along with all of Napoleon's other supporters. I helped get him into the ranks of the guard, and everything unwound from there.

He verified all that Napoleon said by getting into the castle's documentation cellar while the world was distracted during your wedding. That same day, D'jen called in an attempt to revive the broken contract with Sir-Julian. Francis took the call and D'jen told him that the lithium quarries were, in fact, mines, far deeper and wider than what King Leopold and the Ethiopian government were negotiating over.

And this time, Napoleon wasn't around.

The tribes tried to resist but were overwhelmed—forced to mine the lithium themselves, while the rest migrated deeper into Omo Valley.

///

"Dis is what I was telling ya, girl!" Zola said.

Julian remembered too, but untrusting of Zola, he didn't let this alignment deter him. "Maddy, listen. Whatever our future holds, whether or not we stay together, we need to get out of here. And the only way that's going to happen is if you give me back my phone."

The phone chimed.

Battery Level: 2%

"Lordes," Madeleine broke eye contact, "go on."

///

Francis cut D'jen out of the deal just before the displacement took place, citing to us that although he needed him, he couldn't trust a man who'd betray his own people for personal gain.

While ironic, Francis wasn't undoing everything his father fought for without reason. That's because his plan would mandate stability after he seized power. Otherwise, the citizens would revolt over such an abrupt fissure in the hierarchy. Once crowned, he had to provide them with something. And with the recession still looming overhead, nothing would gain him the people's acceptance of a new ruler other than a sudden influx of money. And these days, lithium holds that potential.

We've all watched as the Americans did it for the oil in Iraq, so Francis found no qualm in doing the same in Ethiopia for lithium. Today, global order no longer permits invasions or expansions *unless prompted*. Hence, Francis's plan; assassinate every royal, heir and bloodline, with one in particular in Omo. In that scenario, nobody would stand in the way of him invading Omo after the assassination of Prince Julian in the valley. It was the simplest method to usurp all the lithium without requiring future negotiations.

The Ethiopian government would get what it wanted: Exterminated tribes.

The Kingdom would get what it wanted: Lithium.

And D'jen would get what he wanted: Revenge.

Win-win-win, for all, except the innocent tribes that Napoleon sacrificed everything for.

Francis studied the laws of the hierarchy before initiating his plan. He learned that if the entire Royal Family vanished, the parliament would conduct blood tests to determine the closest lineage to the late Royals, of which they'd crown a new king. And nobody would spearhead that list than the actual grandson of King Leopold.

///

"Girl," Amari panted. "Everything that man is saying lines up with what we know. I was with D'jen when Napoleon visited, but I didn't speak any English. And after D'jen just admitted that he killed my father, The Lion Tamer, everything falls in place."

Madeleine shook her head. "No. It doesn't explain why Francis would wait almost a decade to do all this. What stopped him from sending us here soon after becoming Julian's Royal Guard?"

"Exactly," Julian coughed as he avoided looking at his arm, "you scum might have a traitor like D'jen in your midst, but Francis is loyal! All of you are just so gullible that you can't see that."

///

You, Lady-Madeleine.

Out of all the Royals, Francis couldn't get himself to sacrifice you. Since running away, he consistently sought a way out to save you. He told me tales of your mother. He knew after leaving that she took out her drug induced rage on you, but that the orphanages of Slough were no better. That's why the moment he heard the news of you moving into the castle, he killed her.

///

Madeleine dropped the phone, head frozen in place.

That's what he mumbled at the spa, she thought.

Imamu's lifeless body stiffened in the room's corner. His corpse was ready for burial, reminding Madeleine that she never saw her mother after moving out of Slough. It finally made sense why the funeral was a closed casket.

"They told me it was a gas leak …"

///

She was the first in his line of assassinations, ending today with King Leopold himself. Francis's yearn for vengeance overtook his moral compass. With his meticulous planning, no one can stand in his way, except for you!

You see, the reason it took him years to carry out this coup was because he kept trying to wedge you away from the Royal Family. Because being married to Prince Julian made you royalty, which intersected you with Francis's plan.

This is why he spread all those rumors about your inability to conceive to the media. Then he amplified his efforts by pushing Julian towards alcoholism, and even infidelity. Although he stayed loyal at first, once Francis told Scarlett of Julian's preferences, there wasn't a chance in hell he could resist her.

While we prepared to label the tribespeople as animals, rapists, heathens—the typical slurs used to justify a genocide, Julian's murder of Scarlett threw a wrench into the mix. That kicked everything into overdrive, forcing Francis's hand to even sacrifice you. We coordinated through D'jen, but D'jen wanted assurance that we wouldn't double cross him again. He introduced the option of having the Mursi clan kill you, instead of the Karo, so that the Kingdom kills every last Mursi for denying him leadership.

Francis agreed and had me work with D'jen to alter the itinerary. Instead of meeting a guide, you instead found a specific *rowboat beside the Omo River*.

By now, I'm sure you know about the Mursi's kill-on-sight command for all trespassers. This is what Francis and D'jen counted on to have the three of you killed in Omo, hence my surprise that you're still alive.

///

Battery Level: 1%

Sounding off like a rapid series of thunderclaps, bullets struck the hut's walls. All dove for cover. Amari grunted as Zola kept Julian in place.

Madeleine pawed for the phone. "They're shooting at us!"

"Stay safe, dear! Some lad from the tribe called in to ransom you yesterday, allowing Francis to pinpoint your location. He deployed the commandos to make sure D'jen didn't fail! He already announced to the council that his men found you assassinated. All you need to do is send a picture of yourself to anybody, even Scarlett's phone, and—"

The phone chimed before vibrating.

"Lordes?!" Nothing. Madeleine checked the phone. The screen flashed SAMSUNG. More bullets penetrated through.

—

"—it'll ruin his plan!" Lordes checked his phone. The call dropped. He dialed her again, but it went straight to voicemail.

I have to contact the detective, Lordes thought.

He dialed the station when suddenly, the restroom doorknob rattled as someone fought against the lock. Lordes dropped the phone as he hurried to the furthest stall, fastened the latch and climbed onto the toilet seat. A few more aggressive rattles twisted the knob.

Suddenly, a bang.

The door slammed open, ricocheting off the wall.

Lordes covered his mouth, muting his shaky breaths.

Precise footsteps echoed over the water-stained tiles, pausing to pick up the phone and tap the red icon.

Lordes prayed with his eyes alone.

The steps stopped just beneath the stall's opening. Lordes strained his sights at the boots.

"Thank you for everything, truly."

Lordes held his breath as he noticed one of Francis's charged irises shining through the stall's slats. No weapon would save him now. The only sound from behind the fragile door was his sweat dripping onto the floor, then spreading through the mold-spotted grout lines.

"But I won't repeat my grandfather's mistake—"

"Francis, stop this! You've gone too far! You've turned me into the next Napoleon, forcing me to flee with the truth behind the king's sins—*your* sins!"

"Your efforts towards the Kingdom, my father and myself, will always be cherished …

But Lordes, I can't let you leave."

Chapter XLVII
The Danger of a Cornered Haranchi

Shots destroyed a corner of the hut, crumbling the structure even more. Rubble rained over Imamu's body as his eyes rested closed. Madeleine crouched, still holding the phone and screaming.

"Lordes!"

No answer. She dropped the device, landing it in the palm of Julian's blue hand. Julian didn't find the sardonic moment funny.

"[Surmic] Chief Amari," Akilu called from outside. "They've broken through! Brace yourself!"

Amari tried to respond, but saw double. His vision blurred with every blink as the shooting pain in his shoulder faded.

"Ammi!" Zola screamed, still bracing the spear against Julian's collar. "Stay with us!"

Madeleine clutched her head, absent of the surrounding moment. She frantically looked around, finding the once calm décor now riddled with blood, death and destruction. Kamari wobbled on his tummy, reaching for the corpse of his older brother, seeking any semblance of family.

This is real, Madeleine thought. This is what happens when haranchis enter an otherwise stable society. The Kingdom's embroidered order and civility … this is what it's built upon. And in the history books, they just lie and lie and lie, all to prop up the true nature of what we, haranchi, have done throughout the world.

"[English] This isn't the end," Julian said. "Maddy, we could still charge the phone in Imamu's hut—"

"That's if it's still standing! Don't you see? The commandos are destroying everything!"

"Then we'll charge it somewhere else! But first things first, tell her to pull this spear away from my neck!"

Madeleine shot a gaze at Zola. "Don't you dare—"

"I wasn't plannin' on it!" Zola tightened her grip, ignoring everything else. "Dis is a rabid dog. We cut em loose and he'll just bite."

"Hey! We still have a chance," Julian said. "You and I could still get out of this! Our problems … they're just that—problems. We could solve them. We can …"

"Are you deaf? Did you simply ignore everything Lordes said? Everybody knew of our incest, but us … This is what home is; nothing but lies, Julian! Lordes was the only one willing to break the norm!"

"Every word out of that geezer's mouth reeked of deceit. Don't tell me you honestly believe that we're related. Lordes has been in Francis's inner circle since we've been married. For all we know, he sent the commandos to kill us. We need to call Francis and speak to him directly. He saved our marriage by bringing us here, and he can get us out. He's the only one, Maddy."

When she compared his words to his visible pulse, his words toned to a mute. His heart beat was something he couldn't deny, twist or fake.

"Who do you think you're talking to?" Madeleine asked, tilting her stoic glare. "I know the chain of command. Francis is the only one with the authority to dispatch the commandos. You're just a liar, like all the other haranchi!"

"Maddy, please. We can still—"

"No! You cheated on me with this Scarlett, fell in love with her, then murdered her! How could you still think there's a future for us?"

Julian pinched his lips, ignoring the pain of his protruding bone.

Madeleine tightened her glare.

He turned away.

Madeleine stepped closer, locked on like a puma readying to strike.

"That's because there's more ..."

Madeleine's eyes widened. "As long as I don't figure out whatever this *other thing* is, then you believe there's still a chance for us." Madeleine's gaze darted around. "Whereas if I found out ..."

Imamu's corpse stiffened. The Lion Tamer's skull tipped onto its side, fractured by the falling debris. Cracks ran across every wall as fumes and shouts raced through the rifts.

"Your text to Francis ... Lordes ... he didn't say why you'd want to leave here so fast. He doesn't know ..." Madeleine stepped closer. "What'd you do?" Julian huffed and puffed towards the floor. Madeleine stepped into the puddle of blood, trickling out beneath his visible elbow joint. "What could be so bad that it tops everything we just learned?"

"Don't do this, Maddy; don't look back. We have our whole lives ahead of us."

"You think I could live on with something like this gnawing at me? Tell me what you did."

"Maddy—"

"I could dress that," she said, glancing at his wound, noting the rate of blood loss. "You could live—I could save you. But only if you tell me."

A pregnant pause hung in the air as the fighting drew near. He said nothing.

"You'd rather die …" She tasted the saltiness of her tears before jolting up and back, slowly shaking her head. "*No* ..." Her weak voice cracked like the ceiling, mouth gaping wider with every audible breath.

The bursts of outside gunfire flashed the inside of the hut. Pebbles packed Julian's wound. His exposed bone marrow, arteries and flesh resembled red worms wrestling over the dyed dirt. If he survived the blood loss, he was guaranteed an infection. But that wasn't enough to make him talk.

"Do one honest thing in your life and tell me!"

"HEY!" Julian's hoarse voice scraped through his constrained throat. "Do you want to live or not?! St—stop! Okay? Stop playing around and—and—"

"No, no, no, no, no," Madeleine rapidly repeated, trying to zone him out, as every one of his words imitated a sledgehammer, battering her heart.

Julian groaned and grunted, shooting an irritated glare at Zola. "Stop this!"

"[Surmic] Zola, don't. The princess is figuring it all out on her own," Amari said. "[English] It explains everything …"

Julian flinched a frown as everybody understood what he planned to go to the grave with. He was on his own, and carrying remorse won't save him. He cut the heavy anchor of guilt slung from his neck and evaluated his surroundings. As Kamari sobbed, Amari's eyes drooped. He lost his balance and toppled face first into the tunnel.

"You sure that's what you want, Maddy?" Julian asked. "You want me to fill you in and *tell you my big secret?* Are you sure you don't want to use your time saving these apes instead? Look at that old idiot over there. If you don't save him soon, he's going to die much before me."

The instant Zola glanced at Amari, Julian whacked the spear away and snatched the baby. A fiendish expression emanated from his eyes as he dug his fingertips into Kamari's head.

"I fucking swear to God—I'll twist his little fucking head off!"

Chapter XLVIII
Acceptable Casualties

"One more step and I swear to God!" Julian's spit reached the far end of the hut.

"*Please, please, please, don't—don't hurt him,*" Zola begged. Zola never begged. Yet she begged for mercy from her recent hostage. "PLEASE!"

Nobody moved. Nobody blinked. Nobody breathed. Save Kamari, innocently and ignorantly screaming for his life. Julian's bloodied stump smeared over the baby's torso, and with his other hand, he gripped over the infant's malleable skull like a vulture clawing its talons into a carcass.

Thorns snaked down Zola's throat, choking her every breath.

"Stop this!" Amari barked. "My other boys weren't enough?! What else do you sick haranchis want?!"

"What I want?" Julian panted, his grin widening as he realized the tide had turned in his favor. "I want my phone, I want that blade and I want to get the hell out of this hut!"

Madeleine stared, stiff and blank. Every blink, spaced. Every breath, shallow. "J—Julian, please. You know there's no getting out of here. Just put—put Kamari down. He didn't do anything."

"No! I've had enough of these games! I'm going to crawl through that tunnel, get to Imamu's hut and figure out a way to charge my phone. If anybody tries ANYTHING, this boy is the first to go! Do not tempt me!"

"*He's a child,*" Madeleine said, a crease etched between her brows. Her gaze darted between Kamari and Julian as her heart blackened by the glaring reality.

"Stop this!" Zola and Amari shouted in opposing tones.

Amari noticed Imamu's blood creeping towards him. He watched as the haranchi ripped his family apart once more.

Not this time, he thought, eyeing the spear nearby.

"Oh, you don't like this?" Julian experienced a sense of lightness, and not because of the loss of blood. "Perhaps I should've started from here, instead of playing this one's," he kicked Imamu's corpse with his heel, "little mind games."

"He's a child," Madeleine repeated, unable to believe her eyes. "You're actually willing to harm an innocent, defenseless child?!"

"No, Maddy! I'm not just willing—I'm threatening! So, quit trying to sway me. This boy's my ticket out of this shithole and you're the last person standing in my way! Now, do what I say, or else!"

"What kind of monster are you?" Amari grunted. "You're holding a newborn as a human shield! Where's your dignity, your humanity?!"

"Shut up, old man! Humanity requires being human, and that doesn't involve dying! Now hand me the blade!"

Madeleine stepped between the generational dagger and Julian, kicking the phone away. "No."

"Really, Maddy? You think I won't do it?" Julian squeezed so tightly that all but Kamari's head writhed through the wails.

"[Surmic] Stop!" Zola jerked forward, but Amari grabbed her. "Please let go of my baby!"

Madeleine eased her hands up. "[English] You and I know full well that those commandos will shoot us the moment we step outside. There's nothing to gain by hurting the boy. So, take me instead. Yeah? Nobody else needs to pay the price for what we've done to these people."

Julian calculated the option, but scoffed. "You've just made it outstandingly clear, Maddy; we're done. You think I'm that dumb that I can't see through your little ploy? You're going to run away the moment you get a chance. Now," he took massive breaths, prepared to do the undoable, "hand me that dagger!"

"You'd really do it …" Madeleine's trembling chin slowed to a stop. Her eyes grew. "That's because it wouldn't be the first time …"

"Scarlett was an accident!"

"Not Scarlett—just—just—shut up." Madeleine posted her palm up, blinking rapidly at the damp floor. She thought of the castle; the art, the decor, the bed, the servants, the media, the lights, the fame. It was all an illusion. The brutality before her—this is what the Kingdom's built upon. But one thing blurred the line between the two. A defining line. *Not Scarlett …*"

"Maddy, just give me the—"

"I will."

"*You will?*"

"Yes." Madeleine nodded. "I'll give you what you want. But first, let me hear you say it."

"Say what?"

She lifted her head, staring deep into his soul. "Tell me what you did."

Leopaula smiled as she curled in Madeleine's arms.

"Tell me …"

Her plump cheeks blushed.

Her rounded ears perked.

Her tiny toes curled.

A redness spider-webbed around Julian's eyes as Madeleine pieced it together. His pained swallow meant nothing to her. The final dots connected as no doubts remained.

Madeleine's bra rose and fell as she glanced around, spotting Imamu. She recalled his last words before taking deep, heavy breaths.

"You—you—you couldn't have … No, no, no, no, no." She held her forehead. The dizziness buckled her knees, but she clutched a shelf before collapsing.

Zola figured it out, too. "Oh girl, *I'm so sorry.*"

Amari's chest caved in upon understanding.

> *Leopaula laughed mid-tickle.*

Julian parted his lips, but said nothing.

> *Leopaula woke up, brightening the room as she smiled at her mother.*

Madeleine didn't blink, her gaze fixed on a random spot as the memories raced by.

> *Leopaula's two lower teeth poked through her gums as crystal-clear saliva balled against her lip.*

Tears welled as she looked at him, shaking her head.

Julian's mouth flinched as he weighed the pros and cons of telling her. "Maddy—"

"Tell me!" But she already knew. Everybody knew. "How could you …"

"It was the only way!"

Slowly Sinking

Madeleine stopped.

*Leopaula remained
asleep as Madeleine settled
her in the rowboat.*

Grip still tight, Julian waited.

Kamari cried no differently than when he was born.

Zola readied to pounce.

Amari grimaced, struggling to hold on.

"Okay."

"Yes?"

Madeleine nodded. She reached for the phone, paused, then picked it up. Julian tracked her as she placed the device on the floor between them. It was happening. He was going to go home.

"Thank you," he whispered.

Madeleine stepped back, studying his every move.

Zola lunged forward, but Madeleine snapped her arm out.

Julian kneeled.

His golden hair reflected the sunlight as their eyes connected for the very first time.

Dressed in her scrubs, Madeleine flashed a smile at the reporter-surrounded prince attending the event.

Although he faced the press, he gazed back at her. His mouth yapped for the cameras, but he kept staring at her, as if they were in a world of their own.

She blushed, looked down, then up, finding him still smiling.

The more they exchanged glances, the more their grins grew.

Bit by bit, he reached down. The grime flaked off his skin, dotting the black screen.

> *"Hello, there. I'm Julian." His voice was smooth and confident.*
>
> *Madeleine's cheeks bloomed pink. "Oh, is that right? I couldn't tell."*
>
> *"Maybe I should wear a name tag like yours." He glanced at her top. "Miss, eh, Madeleine Mayweather."*
>
> *"Maybe you should."*
>
> *Their conversation was stupid, but neither stopped smiling.*

Silence swallowed the hut with every movement stalked, every instant measured. Madeleine subtly reached to her side.

> *"I apologize if this is out of line, but I can't help but feel a connection between us," Julian said, dressed in a suit and tie. Each thread in place, every edge creased to perfection.*
>
> *Madeleine twirled her hair, unable to look away.*

*"Must be fate." They felt
each other's fingertips—
each other's heartbeat.*

"Must be fate."

Upon touching the smooth glass, he placed Kamari down.

Madeleine bolted before Zola, leaping over Kamari. The phone clattered against the floor as she ruthlessly shoved the generational dagger deep into Julian's gut. Driven with so much ferocity, she pinned him to the wall. His eyes widened, following every excruciating inch. Blink after blink, his unfocused gaze caught Madeleine's fallen expression.

She stole the blade back, trailing behind it a stream of blood blossoming from the wound and splashing over the phone. She shoved it in again, deeper this time, before removing and repeating.

Zola huddled over Kamari, shielding him from the brutality.

From the corner, Amari witnessed Madeleine's mercilessness engulf her judgment. He concurred.

Blood spatter decorated the walls, the child and the parents. The blows were so sudden that Julian couldn't react to his entrails scrambling with the bones and organs. She didn't let up for a single second even when he tried raising his hand, she kept going. The darker his filthy shirt soaked, the more she moved to a ripe new area.

Leaning against the far side of the hut, Scarlett felt the pain of every thrust, cringing along with Julian with each stab. He reached towards her for help, but she defeatedly fell to one knee, then flat on her face before all that remained of her was a replay of how he left her.

The blade didn't wear. It didn't lose its rigidity. It didn't tire. However, Madeleine did. And when that happened, Julian buckled. His head drooped over his eviscerated chest, resembling roadkill with shards of bones protruding out. His punctured lungs bubbled beneath the gore, like ketchup sputtering from an emptying bottle. He gurgled as the moment's weight silenced the hut.

Following a clank, the generational dagger rested slanted against the phone, reflecting Madeleine's blood-drenched, stoic expression.

Chapter XLIX
The Cost of Freedom

Zola held Kamari close, smearing her copious sweat against him. Although he nearly suffocated, Zola wouldn't dare let go. Never again. As the outside explosions rattled the hut, she glanced at Madeleine, who held a vacant gaze at the slain Julian.

"[Surmic] Amari, this is why she's here. Omo knew there was something wrong in her life—"

"Not now, Zola!" Amari fought to stand up. "The enemy is still outside! If we don't move now, nothing in any of our lives will matter!"

Shots pelted the hut, bursting off chunks of the wall. A blown fragment exposed Madeleine through the wreckage, with the commandos gaining a clear sight.

She stood dazed. "[English] This is all my fault—"

Amari snatched her down, leaving shots soaring overhead. He pulled her close to his family, huddling over them as his wounded arm dangled at his side. "Nobody blames you! But now's not the time—we need to fight back, otherwise the haranchi outside will kill us!"

The debris sprinkled over them like snowflakes.

"There's nothing we could do!" Madeleine cried. "They're far more equipped and prepared!"

"That doesn't matter! We, Mun, never give up! Not after the first displacement, not after the ethnic cleansing and certainly not now! We're going to defend our land, and we're going to protect you!"

As motivational as Amari's words sounded, when paired with his bullet wound and their besiegement, they were nothing but hot air.

"Hide her in the tunnel!" Zola screamed, as the only thing protecting them from the commandos' onslaught was a random collapsed wall.

"No! She's not some—" gravel and ash swirled like rain amid a hurricane, sprinkling their eyes, "she's not some rat—"

More of the ceiling crashed down, burying Imamu's body and crushing part of Julian's head. The mass balanced over the prince's blooded forehead, oozing out one of his eyeballs until it plunged out like a lost ping pong ball. Half of what remained resembled his royal persona, while the other revealed what hid beneath the surface—a grim, toxic splatter.

The imagery gripped Madeleine while Zola tried to quiet Kamari's screams. His piercing cry gave away their location, with the marksman adjusting his scope over the princess's forehead.

—

"I have Madeleine in sight," the marksman said, readying his shot.

The sergeant swatted beside his ear. "Take the—"

"Don't. Don't shoot. Let. Let them. Stay. Stay."

"Sir?"

"What is that—" The sergeant took off his headgear and began swatting at thin air, struggling to complete a sentence. "Soldier, I said take—"

"You're. You're lost. Lost. You. You can't see. See."

"Come again, sir. Sir?"

"Death. Death awaits. Awaits you. You. Run. Run now. Now. Or else. Else."

The sergeant grabbed his head and screamed at the top of his lungs, "Just kill them all!"

—

Amari yanked Madeleine closer. "This is resistance, girl! This is what it brings!" He gripped her hand, squeezing as she held her breath. "This is liberation! We'll accept nothing but freedom or death!"

An unpinned grenade clinked amid the angled destruction, landing square between Zola's feet. With bulging eyes, she froze between shielding Kamari or fleeing. Akilu dove after the ordinance as if a baseball, chucking it back to home plate before the buzzer. The explosion decorated the air like a firework, launching the shrapnel over the village.

Amari felt Madeleine's pulse. "They're here to silence the truth! Do not give in! Do not give up! This is the cost of freedom!"

"[Surmic] They're giving it their all!" Akilu called out.

Massive scorching trees snapped and croaked before slamming to the ground, shaking the earth.

"Resist!" Amari looked Madeleine in the eye. "Resist!"

They held each other close, smelling one another's sweat. With death's dread freely approaching, none of them were brave enough to let go.

The rifle fire, consistent as a clock, left no time to think. Madeleine clenched her fists and tightened her jaw, hoping to just wake up. "Let me make this stop! Let them take me!"

Zola covered her, wrapping her arm over Amari's.

Amari kept her head down. "Never! We won't back down! We won't surrender and we won't sacrifice you!"

Madeleine found him providing the cover of a father. The sound of the mayhem sauntered as she recalled her people ridiculing her, her husband lying to her, her brother plotting to kill her, yet in this village, these strangers were giving up everything for her.

"Thank you," Madeleine muttered. "Thank you, all. You're the best people I've ever met. I can't let another one of you die because of me!"

Madeleine broke free from Amari's hold, leaving him to only graze her calf.

"No, girl!"

Madeleine stood unguarded in the middle of the battlefield with her face grimacing towards the heavens.

—

An EMT tended to Francis's wounds as reporters surrounded the castle. They pointed their cameras as if they were rifles in a war zone. The police sirens blared along the mayhem, reaching a deafening crescendo. But through it all, Francis leaned against the ambulance with a calm smile spread across his face.

The medic tried applying ointment to his wounds, but soon realized that some … *weren't*. She glanced to find him already glaring back.

"They'll never believe you—a mere conspiracy theorist."

The nurse lowered her head, continuing her job with wide eyes, a shrunk mouth and fidgeting fingers.

Francis spotted the balcony hanging off the Royal Bedroom. He pushed the paramedic away, dangling the gauze roll as he got up.

—

Madeleine waited for the pain with a thrashing heart, but nothing happened.

She cracked one eye open, then the other.

The bullets stopped.

The fighting stopped.

The shouting stopped.

An uncertain calm crept in, blanketing the village. Some Mursi held their position, while others shrugged at one another. Akilu approached the haranchi side, rifle leading the way. The more he saw, the more his aggressive trek slowed.

He stopped, mouth agape. He eased his weapon down.

"[Surmic] What is it?!"

Akilu struggled for words. "They're all … they're all dead."

Every commando, without exception, lay face down. Akilu kneeled to check their pulse but found something protruding from their necks. He pulled one out. "Poisoned darts?"

Akilu glanced up, finding the Karo securing their blowguns.

"[Surmic] It's over," their leader said.

—

Sight planted on the French doors, Francis picked up his pace.

"I'm going to stand on that balcony one day."

"You know what," Scarlett said. "I believe you."

Their fingers intertwined.

"Sir-Francis," the detective held his hand up, stopping the freight train, "a word?"

The aide eyed the Royal Guard as if he'd caught a wasp in his web.

Francis juggled his gaze between the two and the castle. His exhale became audible.

"You're late," Francis said. "We've already caught the perpetrator behind the attack."

"Oh, is that right?" The detective raised his eyebrow.

"Yes," Francis said. "Sir-Lordes was behind this. He worked with Napoleon to tear down the Kingdom."

The detective dumbly widened his eyes. *"Napoleon?! Gee whiz, this goes far back, huh?"*

Francis glimpsed up, then at the pair, flinching a frown. "That's right. Maybe if you'd done your job, this could've been prevented, and His Majesty would still be around."

The detective bounced his head from shoulder to shoulder. "Maybe … but that's not why I'm here."

The detective shot a long, icy stare. Francis wanted nothing less than adding him to his list as his expression melted into a solemn, dour glare.

He pulled Julian's wedding band out of his pocket. "Remember this? This is why I'm here; I couldn't care less about whatever's ravaging the Royal Family or the castle right now."

Shit, Francis thought.

The detective smirked. "Overlapping your lies now, huh? That happens when one lives in deceit."

"Uhh," Francis snapped his gaze around, eager for any way to tie the two issues together. The ring glimmered from the blazing castle before him, waiting along with the detective and the aide. *"Sir-Lordes.* Yes."

The aide studied the detective, taking notes on his masterful body language.

"Yes?" The detective waited for more, watching Francis's sweat glow orange as it built over his forehead.

"Yes. He planted the ring at the crime scene. He murdered that woman." His nodding revealed the truth that his words didn't. "It was all Lordes. Everything."

"Then may I speak with Sir-Lordes?"

Francis found the breeze billowing the Royal Bedroom's curtain. It was so close.

"That might be a bit tough. My men stopped him in his attempt to escape. You'll find him in the visitor center's restroom—furthest stall. Now, if you'll excuse me."

Francis forced his way through.

"Sir," the aide pulled the detective's arm, "what're you doing? We have proof—let's arrest him, now!"

"Do you have a death wish, son?" The detective observed Francis's hurriedness and infatuation. "Look around, boy. Since when does a fleeing assailant hide out in the *furthest* stall? This is far greater than a simple murder case."

—

Mute, Madeleine finished dressing Amari's wound.

"Thanks," Zola said.

Madeleine, not saying a word, turned away, bumping past Ike approaching the fractured hut.

"[Surmic] Come in," Amari said, weakly.

"Where—" Ike lowered his head, "where is he?"

Amari tipped his head towards Imamu's chipped fingernails, peering from the rubble.

Ike kneeled over the wreckage, gripping his lifelong friend's hand. "*You idiot.*"

"Come," Amari mumbled to Zola. "Let's give him a minute."

Zola held Kamari with one arm and Amari with the other. With feet crunching the rubble, they gazed around. The once bustling village hidden in nature, now lied in ruin. Heavy smoke concealed the true scale of the devastation. Portions of the donga arena remained intact, yet littered with splintered wood and straw. Every well collapsed into and onto itself as the football field bore deep craters marring the ground between the goalie posts Julian demarcated.

As the forest fire dimmed to hissing embers, Zola leaned against an uncharred tree. The black smoke drifted away from the huts as the night sky blushed dark blue. Amari rested in her lap and looked over what he once used to govern. Akilu spoke with the Karo. Some Mursi cried over their loved ones while others cleaned up. A jitter from Zola nudged him. He rolled his eyes up, finding tears held back.

"21 years," he said. She didn't look down. "21 wonderful years with you, and I've never seen you shed a tear."

Her eyelids were cracking dams. "Nor will you."

Amari smirked. He regarded Madeleine, then Julian. "She has your insight." Zola silently stroked her husband's chest. "Your strength and your heart, too."

Zola chuckled. "Oh, son of the Lion Tamer, you're the only one who has my heart."

Zola's lap became warmer than a pillow mid nap as his eyes drifted shut. "I'm sorry, Zoo Zoo."

"*Zoo Zoo?* When's the last time you called me that? Besides, you have nothing to apologize for."

"I'm sorry for changing. I'm sorry for everything."

"Don't you dare apologize for trying to get your son back." Zola sniffled, refusing to lower her chin. She stared up, marveling at the rising sun piercing through the smoke and sparkling the dew overtop the debris. "We have bigger problems to worry about with Madeleine being here. Either way, we have to rebuild, otherwise Yonas won't have a home to return to. But let's just take it one day at a time. We need our rest."

Zola realized she hadn't talked this much with Amari since the displacement. She grinned, realizing she finally got her husband back. Her tightened cheeks pushed the tears out, dropping them onto his face.

He didn't react.

Her lip quivered.

He didn't react.

Her dam broke, but she refused to look down.

"Ammi?" Her sight became blurred and watery. She gently shook him, staring at the brightening sky. "We need to rest, right, Ammi? Tell me what you think."

More drops splashed over his cold cheeks as she shook more.

"I always loved hearing your thoughts."

With a hardened smile, Zola looked down. She slumped her shoulders before embracing her fallen husband and letting it all out.

—

A brigade of footsteps approached.

"A moment of your time, Chieftess?" the Karo leader asked, as Akilu's face slacked upon finding the lifeless Amari in her arms.

"Speak to him." She pointed to Akilu. "I want nothing to do with this madness you people call leadership."

Gripping Kamari, she stormed away, pushing through the crowd. The Karo leader faced Akilu. Akilu glanced back and forth.

"Chief Akilu, we're sorry for your loss, but time is not in our favor," the Karo leader said.

"*Chief?*" Akilu asked himself.

The Karo leader swallowed his pride. "We're principled enough to admit that we've been deceived by D'jen. So, we'd like to take this moment to make peace with the Mursi." He extended his hand overtop Amari's body. "Perhaps more."

Akilu stared at the hand, then at his predecessor, lost. "Our—" he choked, "our history has never been cordial. That said, we wouldn't be breathing if it weren't for you. You saved us, after everything."

Akilu kneeled, rubbing the dirt off of Amari's face as he stared at his friend and mentor. He kissed his head and patted his chest. "Thank you," he whispered.

He turned back to the Karo leader. "Perhaps it's time for the new generation to put these disputes behind us." He shook. "We'd be dishonored by turning you away. Our true enemy is out there, as for here, a de, wa de. A bhanano, wa bhanano. A ngokte, wa ngokte. [My home is your home. My land is your land. My fight is your fight.]"

The two sides shook, growing their grin with each bounce of their hands.

Akilu's equivalent from the Karo interrupted, diverting attention towards Madeleine. "The Kingdom will retaliate. So, let's take her to the embassy. Now."

"No," Akilu said. "We can't send her to the people who're trying to assassinate her. She's not a political pawn—she's a guest. And besides, there's no way a mother would leave her child behind."

—

Francis placed his fingertips against the French doors. With a soft nudge, they croaked and groaned as they swung over the tiled balcony. Nothing stood before him and it.

The detective and his aide watched from below.

Francis, ignoring the raging castle, took in the Kingdom's twinkling lights. He drew a large, chest-expanding breath, mixing the night air with throat scarring smoke. He gripped the railing and bowed, feeling a gale of vindication, yet lacking satisfaction.

"[English] Oh, Scarlett …" Tears scarred his sandpaper-like cheeks. He plumed a gust and surveyed the landscape. In the distance, he spotted the stone ridge of Cranbourne Park's barrier. He heard the faint music of his father's wedding. Scarlett's hair tickled his neck as the warmth of her palm seeped in. "I've made it. I've made it …"

Below, the detective scribbled in his notepad.

"We know he's lying," the aide said. "We have confirmation of the texts coming from Prince Julian's—"

"Boy, look around," the detective said, still writing. "This is an active crime scene. Which means overstepping right now will result in us ending up like Sir-Lordes. Someone loyal to Francis his entire life, yet slaughtered over a loo at his first attempt to redeem himself. What do you assume would happen to you and me?"

The detective clicked his pen and put his notepad away, glancing at Francis. Francis glared down. The detective tipped his hat and turned to leave.

"Let him be for now," the detective said to his aide. "We'll return after his little killing spree is out of his system. This isn't over."

Francis flinched when an accomplice tapped his shoulder.

"What?!"

The accomplice extended a phone out.

"Who is it?"

"Some chap named *Simon.*"

Francis turned back towards the lights. "I don't know any Simon—"

"But he knows you. So much so that he's congratulating you on your *coup* ..."

After a brief pause, Francis snatched the phone. "Who is this?!"

—

On the outskirts of the Omo River, Madeleine stared. The daylight raced across the savannah. The acacia trees appeared to be on fire as the water glistened and sparkled. Shadows stretched west, steadily drawing back east.

"The Karo agree," Akilu said, approaching. "We can't delay. We have to strike the mines before the haranchi receive news of what happened here. I could facilitate a way back home for you, or help you find asylum—"

"I'm coming," Madeleine said, attention glued to the river.

"Princess, it's going to be dangerous."

"No. There's no need for more bloodshed. Upon seeing me, the guards at the mines will stand down and I could order the release of the prisoners."

Akilu sat on the dirt beside her. He rested his elbows over his knees as he observed the new day awaken. "Then what? If you believe the haranchi will accept you ruining their mining operation, then you still don't know their true nature."

"I don't have all the answers, Akilu. But I need to help, so long as I'm here."

Zola approached, leaving the destruction behind her. "How long do ya tink that'll be?"

Lodged on the riverbank, a small, translucent object caught Madeleine's eye. She squinted before breaking away. "Please, just—just give me a moment."

Placing her feet on the lumpy river banks, the cool, damp earth chilled between her toes. Reaching down, she picked up Leopaula's binky.

She rotated it, grazed it, smelled it.

She pressed it against her forehead as the silent tears slipped down. Leopaula's warmth spread over her arms as her lips pinched above her trembling chin. Zola approached, placing her hand on her back. Following a weighted sigh, Madeleine opened her eyes, planted a kiss on the binky and tossed it into the calm current.

A gleeful bloop.

Madeleine gazed at the ever-flowing river in soundless contemplation. Sunlight shimmered off the surface as delicate leaves rustled in the wind. Birds tweeted, chirped, fluttered, flew. Tall, golden grass swayed in the breeze.

With each passing moment, the Omo River ebbed the binky away, vanishing it into the horizon.

Zola stared out with her. "Your Kingdom … it's not out to be what you was taught, huh?" Madeleine observed the water, mute. Zola parted her lips, but softly closed them again, letting her friend take in the moment.

The Omo River wobbled by, its surface undulating like a litter of children giggling beneath bedsheets. Its glisten slid and slewed over the pebbles and the boulders, leaving nothing dry.

Zola turned to leave. "Let me know whatcha plan ta—"

"I'd like to stay." Madeleine faced her, flexing a smile so wide that it practically reached her ears.

Chapter L
Slowly Sinking

— Three Days Earlier —

The creak of the rowboat crescendoed as the vessel slid over the calm river. Water gently sloshed against the curved hull, creating a faint ripple dissipating along the banks. The harsh summer breeze didn't irritate the batches of buzzing insects floating overhead. Flaps echoed as nearby birds took flight, avoiding the approaching outsiders. Noisy, disorderly and loud, the valley's nature played like a lullaby for the small family.

Through heavy eyelids, Madeleine kept checking on Leopaula, sleeping safely near the Karo symbol etched into the crest. Julian cracked a lazy smile as Madeleine struggled between resting and being a parent. He rubbed her back, telling her to relax.

Although sheens of sweat pasted the foreheads of the three, an aquatic coolness continued to draft through the vessel. Leaning acacia trees slid blotches of shade over the small family, all of which had their eyes closed.

The nostalgic aura plummeted Julian into a realm of suppressed memories. Good memories. Bright memories. However, a black droplet of blight splashed at the center of it all. It raced out, spreading thorn-laced vines through the serene pond which knotted and strangled any memory within reach. They squeezed, blossoming dark roses as Scarlett's erotic moan echoed.

Julian awoke in a panic, nails digging into his palms. The clear, cloudless sky stared back. Madeleine slept through his flinch. Her hair draped over her face, billowing over her nose whenever she took a breath. A skinny line of drool eluded her parted lips, getting absorbed by the boat's wood.

Julian decided to stay awake. Upon hearing Madeleine's light snores, a reel of their shared memories flashed through his mind. From King Leopold nearly having a heart attack when learning his son was interested in a peasant, to his act of rebellion, when Madeleine dared him to shave his head. He even remembered the time when the butlers stared dumbfounded at the mess the lovebirds made in the kitchen.

His shallow sigh dissipated into the air as he reminisced. The brightest moments of his marriage seemed like they never happened—a TV show, or a story someone once told him.

He crossed his arms behind his head, losing track of how far they traveled. Another blink and flashes burst of all the times he went out with Francis. Vivid replays looped in his mind, reminding him, over and over, night and day, day and night, that he was draining down a whirlpool. Strobe lights, fake smiles, booming bass, tattoos, punk hair, smoke, tattoos, animated laughs, selfies, piercings, tattoos, petals, vines, bit lip, wink, unclasped bra, kisses, tattoos, tattoos, tattoos.

Blood.

Clear sky.

With each flap of his eyelids, darkness, then light, light, then darkness, memories, then serenity, blink after blink. The warring factions fiercely battled over his heart.

Neither gave in.

Neither eased off.

Neither allowed him to breathe.

"Stop!"

Leopaula shuffled as he panted, gripping the edge.

Trying to prevent his lower lip from quivering, he bit down. Though he hid from the sunlight, his tears still flowed. He turned to Madeleine.

"I'm so sorry." Madeleine remained fast asleep. "I'll make things right, I promise."

He traced his thumb over her wounded eyebrow.

"I promise—"

Leopaula cooed.

Julian leaned over. It was the first time, in a long time, that Leopaula woke up without crying. Julian stood, careful not to rock the boat. He approached his daughter as she kicked in place through her blanket, smiling upon seeing him. But she wanted her mother.

He picked her up and re-swaddled her. The more he tried to rock her, the more she burrowed and clenched, looking for the breast. He kept pulling her away, but the more she fussed, the more his frown grew.

"Shh, you're alright." He rocked her, but she kept fretting. "Come on, you're going to wake her up." He rocked her a bit more aggressively. "It's okay, it's okay."

She kept moaning and reaching, as he winced and grimaced. His grip grew tighter as small, jittery movements overtook his fingers.

"Just—" Julian muttered. "Just—" He glanced at Madeleine. "Shut up!"

Madeleine shifted around. With worried lines across his forehead, he turned back to Leopaula, barely noticing Imamu fetching water on the riverbank.

As the boat rocked, Julian's gaze shot between the river and his daughter. He clenched her uncomfortably tight, glowering at her.

"It's your fault that we began fighting! You placed this wedge between us—forcing me to go out with Francis. You! You're the one that made me this way! You drove me out of the family and into Scarlett's arms! You made me kill her! You!"

Leopaula stopped. Her face turned red as her lip jutted out, trembling. A thunderstorm of worry brewed as her soft tummy heaved in and out. Her wide innocent eyes, brimming with hurt and confusion, flooded as she couldn't understand what she did wrong. She opened her mouth, cracking the glass before the loud shatter. Julian glanced at Madeleine, then the boat, seeking the binky.

Panicking, she slipped from his grip.

She thudded her head against the rim of the boat, scuffing it as the binky followed suit.

A splash.

Silence.

A stagnant, deafening silence.

Leopaula squirmed, fingers locked around the rattle toy, her mouth stretching in a silent, gurgling reflex.

Julian gasped as he reached down, slicing his arm along the oar holder. However, he stopped short of the water and stared as his daughter silently screamed. His blood rippled against the surface, hinting it red.

Other than the sloshing, muteness rang.

Time stood still.

Frozen in place, he widened his palms. Madeleine remained asleep. Imamu covered his mouth.

Julian sat, chest heaving.

He looked up at the clouds, feeling like that might've solved all his problems. But the sky lacked clarity this time. The animals solemnly stared. His hands shook as he tapped along the boat's edge for support.

The toy broke the surface, rattling as it buoyed.

Faint bubbles gyrated up.

With shuddered breaths, Julian peered into the
wakeless water.

453

His reflection mirrored back,

superimposing Leopaula,

454

Slowly Sinking into the darkness.

"Maddy! Wake up!"

"Wake up! Leopaula's gone!"

Thank you for reading *Slowly Sinking*, Dasher Canon's debut novel.
Share your thoughts on the fate of your favorite character by scanning
the QR code below and leaving a review—it helps tremendously.

[Amazon]

If you're willing to scramble your mind more, you could find some of
the surviving characters in *Therapissed*.

Stay tuned for Dasher Canon's upcoming title: *System Down,* an
homage to an entity of staggering proportions.

This novel is dedicated to A. Matar and his people:

Innovators beneath the crimson skies,

Survivors above the rubble,

Optimists throughout the livestreamed-genocide;

The last remaining humans among the rest of us.